Praise for Robin W. Pearson

In *The Stories We Carry*, Pearson gives us an unflinching look at a marriage and all its highs, lows, and loving compromises. It's also an ode to bookstores, the stories contained within them, and deep-seated dreams—both those we chase and those we release. Fans of inspirational fiction will love Pearson's latest engrossing read!

LAUREN K. DENTON, *USA Today* bestselling author of *Hurricane Season*

Robin W. Pearson has proven yet again that her pen is anointed. *The Stories We Carry* is a deeply moving novel about the burden of secrets, the ache of loss, and healing through a journey to God's truth. With rich storytelling and unforgettable characters, this story offered the gift of restoration. Readers won't soon forget the messages found between the pages.

RHONDA MCKNIGHT, Emma Award–winning author of *The Thing About Home*

In the small fictional town of Gilmore, North Carolina, novelist Robin W. Pearson brings to life an intriguing coterie of old friends, customers, and mysterious strangers, all drawn to protagonist Glory Pryor and the welcoming bookstore she lives above. As secrets from the past come to light, Glory and her circle must decide where the path to love and redemption lies—and whether they have the courage to follow it.

VALERIE FRASER LUESSE, Christy Award–winning author of *The Light on Horn Island*, on *The Stories We Carry*

In *The Stories We Carry*, Pearson illustrates the complexity of family dynamics with authenticity and grace. She paints a poignant picture of grief and regret as the characters grapple with learning when to let go and when to hang on tight. It's the type of book you close with a happy sigh and tears brimming in your eyes.

    AMANDA COX, author of *Between the Sound and Sea*

Crafted with exquisite details that make you long for more time in the lush Carolina mountains with the flawed, relatable characters and the charming bookstore they inhabit, *The Stories We Carry* is premier upmarket fiction at its best.

    JAYNA BREIGH, author of *The Hunted Heir*

Pearson paints a vivid and moving picture of the stories that shape us and what is required and gained in surrendering to love greater than our own. An emotional, thought-provoking story that speaks to the heart of every generation.

    CATHY GOHLKE, Christy Hall of Fame author of *This Promised Land*, on *The Stories We Carry*

A fascinating and insightful story. Beautifully written. . . . I felt immersed in the story from the first page. Robin W. Pearson's writing has that rare mix of depth, raw honesty, while still maintaining an undertone of humor and hopefulness.

    CINDY MORGAN, award-winning singer/songwriter and author of *The Year of Jubilee*, on *Dysfunction Junction*

Southern charm flows like molasses through barbed conversations in *Dysfunction Junction*. . . . Secrets and guilt wrestle their way to redemption in this quirky family tapestry. Robin W. Pearson's unique voice is complex and captivating.

TESSA AFSHAR, award-winning author of *The Queen's Cook*

Robin W. Pearson has a gift for capturing the complexity and nuances of family relationships. She brings a remarkable tenderness and compassion to the struggle we all face to know and be known in a family. Prepare yourself for a rich and satisfying read!

SARAH LOUDIN THOMAS, award-winning author of *These Blue Mountains*, on *Walking in Tall Weeds*

Pearson's excellent characters and plotting capture the complexity and beauty of family. . . . Pearson rises to another level with this excellent story.

PUBLISHERS WEEKLY starred review of *'Til I Want No More*

Robin W. Pearson's novels never fail to sing directly to my heart. . . . [Her] voice is strong and powerful. Listen up! You don't want to miss a note!

SUSIE FINKBEINER, author of *The All American*, on *Walking in Tall Weeds*

A heartfelt tale about faith and family, readers can walk toward the altar with Maxine Owens as she tends to her past wounds.

DEEP SOUTH MAGAZINE on *'Til I Want No More*

Robin W. Pearson's authentic faith and abundant talent shine through in this wholehearted novel. Bee and Evelyn will stir your heart and stay with you long after the last page of *A Long Time Comin'* is turned.

MARYBETH MAYHEW WHALEN, author of *Every Moment Since*

Pearson delivers a poignant debut that explores the faith of one African American family. The writing is strong, and the story is engaging, and readers will be pleased to discover a new voice in Southern inspirational fiction.

BOOKLIST on *A Long Time Comin'*

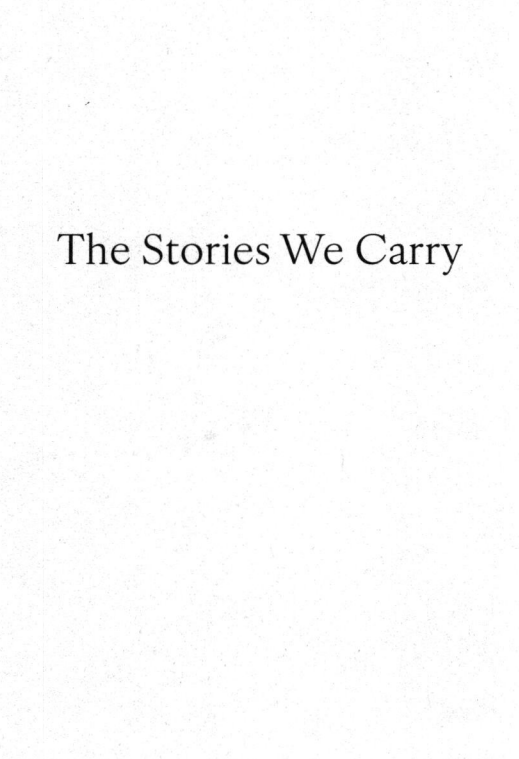

The Stories We Carry

The Stories We Carry

Robin W. Pearson

Tyndale House Publishers
Carol Stream, Illinois

Visit Tyndale online at tyndale.com.

Visit Robin W. Pearson's website at robinwpearson.com.

Tyndale and Tyndale's quill logo are registered trademarks of Tyndale House Ministries.

The Stories We Carry

Copyright © 2025 by Robin W. Pearson. All rights reserved.

Cover images are the property of their respective copyright holders from Shutterstock.com, and all rights reserved. Tudor house © Altin Osmanaj; window © Kurkul; vine © Chansom Pantip; flowering bush © Rungsan Nantaphum; books and cup © Maglara; steam © Galsand; rays © Oscar Gutzo.

Author photo taken by Bobbie Brown Photography, copyright © 2020. All rights reserved.

Cover design by Faceout Studio, Molly von Borstel.

Interior design by Cathy Miller

Edited by Kathryn S. Olson

Published in association with the literary agency of Books & Such Literary Management, 52 Mission Circle, Suite 122, PMB 170, Santa Rosa, CA 95409.

Scripture quotations in the epigraph, chapter 11, chapter 12, and chapter 28 are taken from the *Holy Bible*, New Living Translation, copyright © 1996, 2004, 2015 by Tyndale House Foundation. Used by permission of Tyndale House Publishers, Carol Stream, Illinois 60188. All rights reserved.

James 5:12 in chapter 8 and the Scripture quotations in chapter 13, chapter 24, and the author's note are taken from the New King James Version,® copyright © 1982 by Thomas Nelson. Used by permission. All rights reserved.

John 1:14 in chapter 8 and the Scripture quotations in the acknowledgments are taken from the *Holy Bible*, King James Version.

The URLs in this book were verified prior to publication. The publisher is not responsible for content in the links, links that have expired, or websites that have changed ownership after that time.

The Stories We Carry is a work of fiction. Where real people, events, establishments, organizations, or locales appear, they are used fictitiously. All other elements of the novel are drawn from the author's imagination.

For information about special discounts for bulk purchases, please contact Tyndale House Publishers at csresponse@tyndale.com, or call 1-855-277-9400.

Library of Congress Cataloging-in-Publication Data

A catalog record for this book is available from the Library of Congress.

ISBN 979-8-4005-0125-8 (SC)

Printed in the United States of America

31	30	29	28	27	26	25
7	6	5	4	3	2	1

To Eddie . . . tuck and roll

Come, let us return to the Lord.
He has torn us to pieces;
now he will heal us.
He has injured us;
now he will bandage our wounds.

HOSEA 6:1

Come and see a man who told me everything I ever did! Could he possibly be the Messiah?

JOHN 4:29

This small garden is half my world
I am nothing to it—when all is said,
I plant the thorn and kiss the rose,
But they will grow when I am dead.

ANNE SPENCER

PART ONE

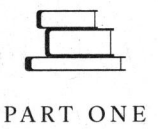

Dog-Eared Pages

1

IT WAS GLORY'S CHILDHOOD FRIEND who introduced her to *Roll of Thunder, Hear My Cry*, her all-time favorite book. She determined to become one of the Logans, bold and full of sass, for she surely loved as fiercely as they did. And she wanted to protect her family just as much—her big brother in particular. Her only brother and hero. The difference was they played for keeps, and Glory had lost big time.

Her bestie was also the first to redefine the word *drunk*, to give it a brand-new, sinister definition when she'd hissed it, her breath hot in Glory's ear and smelling nutty and cinnamony like the waffle cone they'd taken bites of. Instead of "She'd drunk a whole glass of Kool-Aid," Glory's friend made it a noun, and a proper noun at that, with a name and a familiar face: Glory's larger-than-life brother, Davis.

Ten years old at the time, just a year older than her favorite character, Glory had no idea what that word and its consequences looked like. Her church-going mama and daddy never would have allowed such a person or activity to abide in their home, let alone anything other than the kind of alcohol they dabbed on their daughter's skinned knees. But once her classmate had whispered its meaning, Glory had dropped both scoops of her prized ice cream . . . and their friendship. The girl had just enjoyed the telling a little too much, even to Glory's inexperienced mind. After all, a dog who brings a bone, carries a bone, something Mama had made clear, though the woman hadn't explained much else.

Now, six months shy of sixty-four years old, Glory knew that the man staggering across Springs Church Road was toting something other than bones toward the maple tree, chair, and blanket he considered home. He led her to wonder yet again what had become of her brother, because her ten-year-old self was right: her folks hadn't permitted anything but teetotalers in their holy and sanctified existence. Wondering and worrying were about as close as the middle-aged Glory would ever come to praying for Davis, or for herself or anyone else. Both were wasted efforts that took her to the same dead-end street; it was *working* that drove her to the answers she needed. Yet, she couldn't help but hope that, perhaps, her brother had managed to scratch out a living in some other small North Carolina town like Glory's, that he'd come back to himself and used that grin and winsome nature to help him turn things around. Hoping was all she'd had the courage to do; her guilt kept her from finding out if he'd ever become a hero to somebody else.

Ooh, there's Vernelle with the kids. Where've they been all this time since school let out? I'm glad to see his daddy ran a comb through that poor child's head. Mmm-mmm-mmm . . . they walk right by the barbershop every day; wouldn't take no time to pop in.

Realizing she'd been absentmindedly fiddling with the tattered edges of the page resting in her palm, she looked down and again read,

> *The shadows gave chase at our first step,*
> *as we hurried through the moon's evening light.*

*Our pulses throbbed and our hearts, they leapt
at the beauty only childhood perceives.*

*We didn't know to seek wisdom's former ways,
before the matter's end o'ertakes its beginnings.
We reveled in the now, lost then in youth's haze,
and those moments, they were better than these.*

No, there was no way her brother could be on this side of the dirt . . . or was there? Eyes almost shut against the tears that threatened, Glory peered through her lashes into the late afternoon sun. Her brain barely registered the man as he stumbled around the corner and disappeared behind By the Book, her home that doubled as her bookstore. Sitting there in her favorite position in her decades-old business, she set one label after another on her mental scale, offsetting its weight against her guilt, before dismissing it in favor of another more pernicious, heavier name to call herself. Something more fitting for what she had done, for all she had left undone. What those forthright characters from *Roll of Thunder* would never have done, though it was so like them to "revel in the now" and make the most of each moment.

Glory imagined her once-upon-a-time best friend flipping her ponytails over her shoulders, cupping her hand over somebody else's ear, and muttering, "Poacher. Thief." She wondered, *What other names would she call me if she knew? Liar . . . impostor?*

"Honeybun . . . Glory!"

Eli's voice, nearly swallowed up by the thousands of volumes on the surrounding shelves, elicited a sigh of gratitude from deep within her. She welcomed the distraction her husband tended to present, and she shed the self-condemning words like old skin, though her heart still felt tender and exposed. This painful habit of name-calling would reclaim her thoughts the next day and the one after that, the moment she took up her afternoon roost by her front window. Fretting had become her daily ritual the moment Eli had broached another scary word: *leave.*

"Baby girl, where are you?" His baritone ricocheted off the plastered walls of the back stairwell connecting their third-floor living quarters with the first two floors that comprised their store.

"I'm where I always am this time of day!" *You want to know where I am, Eli? I'm where I'm gon' stay.* Her thoughts always slipped into the vernacular from her childhood when she was deep in conversation with herself, another longtime habit of hers. She cocked a bejeweled ear to make sure her husband wasn't close enough to hear her and muttered, "Now, don't come down here talkin' more of your nonsense," before shaking her head. But Glory smiled a little because this game, *their* game, was more fun than the one she'd been engaged in when she was sitting by her lonesome. *That man.*

She tucked the poem back into the book she'd torn it from, but it no longer fit perfectly, and the feathery-light paper's corners extended past the others. Using the glossy squared tips of her fingernails, she pressed a braided red cord deep into the gutter until only the fringed end of her handcrafted bookmark protruded from between the pages, like a telltale splotch of blood. When Glory closed the precious book with a soft thump, it seemed to exhale, and she took an appreciative whiff of long-ago days. Her mouth puckered as she tapped along the gold-stitched diamonds crisscrossing the hardcover, as if she was about to blow a kiss to the author, and she tsked, "But I'm not playin' with you, Eli Pryor."

Setting her bracelets a-tinkling, Glory rested a silk-draped arm along the back of her chair and clasped the scarred, black, cloth-like cover to her chest. The scents of freshly brewed coffee and warm something-or-other—*Is that more snickerdoodles?*—wafted from the kitchen in back and commingled with the mustiness of the first edition that was dying at about the same pace she was. Winking at her faint reflection in the wavy, one-hundred-year-old windowpane, she vowed, "Mmm-hmmm, I see you there, and you're not going nowhere either, despite what Eli might say about it." Glory couldn't say whether it was her persnickety old self or the sprawling, historic Tudor that had sheltered her and her books from many a storm. Regardless, Glory Pryor meant every word. No way was she going to part with this place. It was who she was.

Resolved, Glory's vermillion-colored lips compressed as she smoothed the orange, gold, red, and blue fabric of her muumuu across her narrow, well-arranged lap and gazed at their "children," as she and Eli dubbed their inventory. When it first struck her years ago that these books would be her only babies and grandbabies and nephews and nieces, it had landed as a gut punch. The passage of time had nearly wrung the pain from this designation, and these days, she suffered only a quick yank of her heartstrings. No prolonged ache made the organ thud instead of beat in her bosom against the book she was now pressing to it, and it merely took a moment or two to resume its normal rhythm. Thank goodness she had Eli now, and he was good and plenty.

Glory listened to the faint thumping of her husband's steps in the back of the house, where he must have headed after coming downstairs. Eli was up to his usual antics, which accounted for the tempting smell of cookies. Their baker, Ophelia, would have a fit when she came back to work and found he'd been clippety-clopping all through her kitchen. Even though Glory considered the not-so-old troll both friend and family, the woman brooked no interference when it came to whipping up goodies; Ophelia took her work for the bookstore's café to heart. "You'd better leave your cousin's domain, or she'll have your head! If you know like I know, you'll join me by the window, my de-ah." She always said *dear* that way when it came to her precious Eli.

By this time of day, Glory found herself near or on this pale-yellow two-seater, its burgundy-and-green stripes worn to a soft sheen. She'd staked a claim on the overstuffed chair two decades earlier in the back of Downtown Cheapskate, a thrift store around the corner that carried the castoffs from the town's few well-to-do families. The moment she'd laid eyes on it, she'd known its unusual L-shaped back would fit just so, wedged into the corner of her bookstore's large front room.

For longer than Glory could remember, the sofa provided the ideal vantage point for her to peek through the triple-cased window without being seen by folks on the other side of the glass. Perched on its oversized, tufted cushions, she kept time by monitoring the birds or passersby, who- and whatever happened to be crossing Springs Church Road. She didn't have to look at her watch to know when Noemie was locking up Pearline's Jewels on her right or when that man with his bottle would be making his way from Hillman's in the middle of town with his free plate—*Let's see, today is Wednesday, so it must be barbecue and coleslaw*—to hunker down for the rest of the evening. "I should take him something sweet before we turn in for the night, whatever Eli is cooking up," she decided.

At last, Eli's footsteps clomped from the rear, his voice hitching a ride to each heel-toe. "I'm bringing you a cup of coffee. I need you to try it!"

Glory crooked a silver-streaked brow. "Now, you know better than that. I thought you were brewing some for yourself!" *First, he tried to take this store from me, and now my Earl Grey. This man must be losing his ever-lovin' mind!*

Eli sent a throaty chuckle ahead of him, as if it would extract a peace prior to his arrival.

Since her husband had started working with her full-time after he'd sold his marketing firm, Eli would squeeze in beside her some days, his coffee mug propped on a crossed knee that was grazing hers. If folks had a mind to mill through the aisles and rooms of By the Book at this hour, she'd leave her husband to hover over their guests, straightening shelves, dusting archways, and asking pointed questions to direct their search. All so she could wrap up business by six p.m. sharp and send them home with the perfect read. If pressed, she advised them to return Saturday when she and Eli closed later, at eight o'clock. On weekdays, they locked their heavy front door at the same time as the bank, along with the other stores and offices on either side of this old section of Springs Church.

If By the Book was empty and she had a moment to herself on a late afternoon such as this one, she lounged in her corner, half of her attending to a book and the other to the window. She liked being up front, especially since it was getting a might harder to hear the tinkling of the ancient bell triggered by the opening of the door in the entryway. Whoever ignored the Pryors' store hours, brandished on the plaque mounted on the brick wall, and depressed the antique brass latch on the weathered oak door deserved to be greeted right off. So, Glory positioned herself like an eagle in its roost, ready to swoop down and take care of business. Her business. Situated in one of the largest and quirkiest buildings still standing between the Ebenezer Baptist Church at the top of the street and the courthouse at its end, before it curved to the more commercial areas of Gilmore.

The floorboards creaked, informing Glory that her husband had at last crossed the threshold between the hall and the front room, where she sat. She wedged the book under her cushion and angled away from the window to give Eli and his suspicious brew her full attention. Her eyes widened when they landed on the cup clinking against the matching saucer in his large hand. "Good gracious—!"

"Darlin', I know, I know. But I need to ask your taste buds a question, seeing as how particular they are. If we're going to serve that coffee cake this weekend, we need to provide the right accompaniment." Eli's right hand extended the coffee to her; the other palm balanced two small plates barely big enough to hold the hefty squares of cake.

Reaching out both her hands to carefully accept his offering to the merry tune her bracelets played, Glory snorted, "Snickerdoodles after lunch and cake before dinner! What is this world of mine coming to? There was a time when I only snacked on cucumber slices and to*may*ta sprinkled with black pepper and salt. These hips of mine don't know what to do with you and Ophelia. And I take it Mama's favorite cup is the 'right accompaniment'?"

Over a half century ago, her mother had saved up a month's worth of coupons from the Winn-Dixie supermarket and picked out a porcelain, six-piece place setting—cups, saucers, dinner plates, and bowls—along with a chafing dish, all decorated with light-green vines and hints of blue. They'd sat on the top two shelves of her parents' chifforobe, and her mama would bring them out every Easter, Thanksgiving, and Christmas to grace their secondhand kitchen table. Delia insisted on washing them herself before wrapping them in brown paper and returning them to the safety of her bedroom.

One hot July afternoon, Glory had pulled up a chair to her parents' wardrobe and sneaked a cup from its tucked-away place. Her brother was out with friends, and she'd grown tired of entertaining herself. As she took a sip of her imaginary tea, her mama had caught her unawares with a tap on the shoulder, and the cup had slipped from the tips of Glory's fingers.

"Those idle hands . . . can't do wrong and get by," Mama had clucked, ever ready with an axiom and able to mix and match them skillfully. "What's done in the dark . . ." She'd hummed the rest, like the church mothers rocking in the front pews.

Glory had squinted into the dust motes dancing over her mama's shoulder and tried to decipher her meaning. Nothing much got by Delia or that God of hers, no matter the time of day. Despite Glory's protests and promises to reattach the handle with a blob of Elmer's rubber cement, Mama had dropped the precious cup in the trash bin in the kitchen, her eyes glistening and her mouth a straight line.

Glory had held on to the one remnant of those holiday dinners more tightly than she'd gripped that grocery store porcelain years ago. And here was her husband daring to serve her some coffee, of all things, in one of the few tangible memories she'd managed to salvage of her childhood. Her hands trembled a bit, and the steamy, light-brown liquid sloshed over the side of the cup into the saucer.

With a grace and agility that belied his size, Eli quickly set down the plates of cake on the deep window sash behind Glory and squeezed into the empty space to her left. He enveloped her svelte frame and steadied her hand with his warm one. "You alright? I can get you a different one."

"No, hon. I was just thinking Delia Gibson must be having a fit wherever she is, seeing me drink out of this," she laughed, wondering if her mama had ever shed tears over her daughter's brokenness or the cup's.

"'Wherever she is,'" Eli murmured, his eyes thoughtful as he repeated her phrase. "Can't bring yourself to say heaven, can you?"

"Or hell." Glory no longer counted herself among the praying persuasion; still, she was well aware of her options. "But what I can do is bring myself to try this coffee of yours, along with a bite of cake." She adjusted its position to avoid the chipped edge and took a small sip. "Huh. I will say it's not mud."

Her husband abruptly withdrew his arm.

Glory threw her head back and let out a laugh that was twice as wide and half as long as she was—and short-lived, once she saw his expression. She grasped his knee and waggled it back and forth, mindless of the coffee splashing into the saucer. "Baby, I'm just teasing you. You know I love myself some Earl Grey, but this coffee is giving it a run for the money." Still smiling, she slurped from the saucer first and then from the cup, unwilling to waste a drop of his loving effort though it didn't hold a candle to her tea. "What, is that hazelnut tickling my tongue?"

Eli looked as though he'd grown and harvested the beans himself. "I knew I could rely on those buds of yours. Yes, it's hazelnut. I think it'll taste good with the cake, and imagine how it'll smell in the shop. Books and brew."

"We're not serving beers, love, but I see your meaning." She hid her moue of distaste and set the cup gently on the deep windowsill, exchanging it for the second plate he'd brought her. That cake would ease the taste in her mouth, along with the memories that were more bitter than the coffee grounds.

"Eli, I'm surprised you're looking for ways to help the business." Glory took a bite and choked down her resentment.

He reached for his own cake, his knee bumping hers. "Why, because I'm trying to get you to retire? That doesn't mean I don't want to have some fun while it lasts, to ensure the success of the bookstore." Eli picked out a pecan with his fork.

"So we can command a better price if we sell it?" Glory's fork clanked to the plate, appetite dissipating.

"No-o-o-o. Because this is my child, too. And I'm only asking you to leave it for a while. *Later* we can sell it."

That word again. "But you didn't birth this baby; I did. It's the only family I have!"

Eli stopped chewing.

Glory huffed, regretting her words, and searched for a way to stem the flow from the wound she'd inflicted. She wrapped her fingers around his wrist, hoping her softened tone and gentle touch would dab at his sore spots. "What I meant was, it was the only family I had . . . until you came into my life."

"Came *back* into your life, you mean. We've been married almost five years now, Glory. Didn't it become our baby when we said our vows?" He slipped his free hand into hers.

Glory squeezed his fingers, studying the wisps of gray hair growing on his knuckles. "But I reared By the Book by myself for thirty of these past thirty-five. That's a lot of years of nursing and tending to and rocking this baby to sleep all on my own. And you're trying to make me let it go. What kind of mother would I be if I sold By the Book on your say-so? That would be the worst of times." She picked up his unfinished copy of *A Tale of Two Cities* he'd stowed on the windowsill and waggled it.

But her attempt at a joke seemed to fall short. "But what kind of wife will you be if you hold on to it? This store is killing me, Glory. You've got to make a choice: the fully grown baby or the baby's stepdaddy." Eli plopped the last forkful of cake into his mouth, obviously pleased with himself and his argument.

2

ELI AND GLORY HAD EXCHANGED VOWS on a sunny January day a few weeks before her fifty-ninth birthday. He'd nipped her on the ear and purred, "I fell for you way back in kindergarten, but it took fifty years for you to fall for me."

He'd pressed her so close to him, it raised more than a few eyebrows in their small, out-of-the-way area of the state. But many folks were extremely happy for the older woman who'd once called herself "Glory-ously single" when she'd suggested they read Agatha Christie's Miss Marple series during her women's book club. Little did they know it was resignation, not pride, that had inspired her declaration, and it was gratitude, not rebellion, that had motivated her to pull Eli even more tightly to her on their wedding day.

"Right there in front of God and everybody," Reverend McCluskey was heard to say, looking put out with his Bible in his lap. He had the best view of all the Pryors' carrying-on from the front row of white wooden folding chairs. The minister had no professional duties to perform since Glory had procured a local magistrate to do the honors, despite Eli's fervent request to ask a local preacher to marry them.

"Why? I'm as much a stranger to a man wearing a robe as I am to a man in a suit," Glory had responded curtly, as they'd nailed down their plans.

"But I have it on good authority there's another Man who knows you quite well, and I'd like Him to marry us." Eli pointed toward heaven.

"Well, you can ask Him to come. He can sit on either side." Glory ended the discussion with a kiss, then hunted down and secured the highest and most scenic spot in Gilmore, North Carolina.

Instead of exchanging vows at the altar of the Baptist church or that belonging to another denomination, Glory and Eli had erected a flower-covered arbor overlooking the other hamlets in the neighboring foothills, including Hickory Grove. They'd welcomed friends, guests from By the Book, and the remaining members of Eli's family—at least who he'd known about at the time. She'd welcomed one and all, even the man who'd sought shelter behind her home; he'd showered at a local gym and found a seat six rows back. Celebrating her marriage to the love of her life was worth setting a few tongues to wagging.

"Can you believe she's wearing . . . what did she call it? *Caramel?*"

"No, she said it was *cinnamon.*"

"I knew it was a color named for a food. But why not white, like other brides?"

"It's called *cayenne*. And it's because I'm not like other brides," Glory had retorted when she heard all the chatter. She had every right to wear white, but she relished the hullabaloo over her chiffon gown that floated in layers to brush the sparkly high heels strapped around her ankles; it served to bring more people to By the Book. They just had to take a gander at the wild woman who'd snagged the dashing widower and married him outside in January, of all things.

Sitting beside her husband that afternoon in front of the bookstore's wide window, Glory set their plates beside the coffee cups and reminded him of her words. "I'm the kind of wife who holds on to who and what I love. And that includes this store run by you-know-me. Why can't we travel more and leave By the Book in Ophelia's capable hands? She's run her own bakery storefront, and she hasn't started her food truck yet. I bet she can manage it, especially with her twins' help. Why must I sell the whole kit and kaboodle?" She caressed his cheek and kissed him, planting a glistening bright splotch at the corner of his mouth. "You wouldn't be jealous, now would you?"

He turned his head and caught her lips as she pulled back. "Of some brick, timber, and stone? Of course not. We talked about this for two years before we got married, so it shouldn't come as a surprise, Glory, our eventual move. Aside from developing an allergy to this musty old house and the pain in my knees from climbing three flights of stairs, I simply love my family more than these stacks of paper and this mound of brick. Don't you?"

Glory waved a hand as if shooing a fly. "Hush now, spouting all that nonsense. We in the literary world would call that hyperbole. You're just being dramatic. And this 'other family' you're talking about is still hypothetical, while my family members, the ones you're living with, are very real."

"What's real is the new path I want us to forge together, instead of simply walking side by side in our old ones."

The booklover in Glory couldn't help but admire his metaphor even as she turned a shoulder to him and stacked their abandoned dessert plates and saucers for him to carry. This freed her hands to take his cup and, more importantly, hers, to the kitchen. Her mama's treasure deserved her full attention, and if it was possible, she would've borne it with both hands. Slanted toward the window, she spied a hand turning a sign on the door of the day spa across the street to read *Sorry, We're Closed!* and pulling down the shade. *It's not even 5:30. His wife was feeling poorly over the weekend. I sure hope nothing's happened.*

While she hated to break her afternoon window-gazing routine, Glory thought it best to avoid further discussion of putting her place on the market. She strode toward the back of the store with lifted chin and long straight back, her vibrantly colored muumuu billowing around her ankles and her slides flapping against the soles of her feet. How could she talk about something that was out of the question?

Eli wasn't so quick to follow.

Glory plopped a thick wedge of cake onto a paper plate and sealed it with a double wrap of plastic. She kept a stack of disposables for the man she'd come to call Dude so he could easily throw everything away when he was done without having to bother with holding on to it for her sake. He had enough concerns without carrying hers, too.

He didn't always stay there, between By the Book and Pearline's Jewels. It depended on the weather and the season, how far his bottle took him, or the direction his mood blew. Glory often wondered who his people were and whether or not he stayed with them on the days when he could walk a straight line and his eyes were clear, whether Dude missed them or they missed him.

He was a good-looking man of some age she had yet to determine. Since her hair had turned almost completely silver in her forties, she knew better than to assign a year to the gray streaking through Dude's mustache and a beard that resembled barbed wire. All Glory knew about the lean and lanky fellow who'd stumbled into town a year or so before she married was that he had a sweet tooth and that like her, he loved to read—when he wasn't sleeping off the other thing she knew about him: his love for spirits, what he apparently carried with him in a brown bag, the kind her long-ago friend had whispered about and the right reverend probably preached on every Sunday. Just as Glory couldn't identify whatever he put to his lips, she never knew what to call him. So she named him Dude, without "the" and with a capital *D*, out of respect. From time to time, he even answered to it.

Glory tucked a thick paperback under her arm, barely able to press it to her side with her elbow, before she tapped across the terracotta tile floor to the heavy steel door in the back of their large, commercially outfitted kitchen. After disengaging the lock, she opened it wide enough to slip out to the rear porch. She stood there a minute, her backside against the door, soaking in the warm evening air and a few seconds of alone time. After nearly six decades of enjoying her own company, intertwining her days and nights with somebody else's was taking some getting used to—even if that somebody else was her precious Eli, who she'd waited for all her days without knowing it.

Whenever she sat alone by the front window or immersed herself in a favorite book, a part of her felt she was stealing time from him, especially since he'd retired—a smidge too early by her thinking. She'd never prevented him from joining her in managing a business she could run with her painted pinkie toe and her eyes covered with a silk handkerchief, but she hadn't asked him either. Not that she minded her husband's help, his keen insight. Eli came up with "reconfigurations" as he called them, ideas that she'd never considered, and they were much appreciated. Glory sighed. *But still.*

The small back porch peered into a small patch of grass and an alleyway. Behind the area, a shoulder-high fence ran from one end to the other of the row of buildings in this part of Gilmore, named after the family who'd owned the approximate seven hundred acres it was situated on. Many said the founders built the town between a rock and a hard place, with its view of the Blue Ridge Mountains.

The mayor had erected the fence as part of his beautification project a decade ago to hide the railroad tracks, a graveyard, the stone works, and broken-down, abandoned houses. Tree branches curled over sections of board, and people had hoed and dug and seeded and painted, personalizing their property, whether they rented or owned, lived or worked in it. During their courtship, Glory had enlisted Eli to build large planters to the right of the back door. On the left, under the gnarly, outstretched arms of a red maple tree, Dude had set up for the night.

When a mosquito landed on her hand she slapped it, making the plate she carried wobble dangerously. As she moved her foot to steady the dish, the door swung closed with a decisive *thunk*. She tugged on it, despite knowing it locked automatically from the inside. Immediately, she pictured her keys hanging on their hook. "Shoot!"

"Is that for me?"

"Mercy!" Glory's free hand tried to restrain her racing heart as she whirled toward the low voice behind her. The book fell to the pavement with a splat, but she caught the cake for the second time. As she squatted to scoop up her battered copy of *How Green Was My Valley*, she heard the creak and crinkle of movement and the scraping of approaching feet.

"Let me help you." One grizzled hand reached for the book, and the other extended a palm.

Glory took a second to notice clean, barely there fingernails before gazing up into limpid hazel eyes that looked like they'd seen more than they should have but held no grudges over the who, why, and how of what they'd witnessed. She smiled and accepted his dry, wrinkled palm. "Hey there, Dude. Thanks for the lift." She chuckled and pointed to the five-hundred-page book. "It took me some time, but it's a good one. Eli and I are going to watch the movie tonight and see how well it matches up. I'll let you know."

He nodded, and seemingly assured that Glory was firmly upright, he let go.

She gave him the plastic-sheathed cake and watched him return with his dessert and his reading material to the Adirondack-style chair the Pryors had provided him the previous summer based on expert advice and lots of research. Glory had concluded that it made sense that everybody had a birthday, so they should manufacture, and therefore recognize, Dude's. With a firmness that brooked no argument, she'd declared, "He's family."

"Oh, *more* family?" Eli had had the audacity to ask.

She'd laid an evil eye on him and continued threading purple ribbon through the three-inch-wide wooden slats on the back of the seat. It took some of Eli's gentle persuasion to convince her not to "Glory-fy" the gift the way she tended to and simply set it up by the fence.

"We don't want to scare the man off."

"He's a person, not a deer," she'd grumbled, but acceded to his removing and putting away the strip of satin before helping him tote the chair outside when they'd heard Dude was cooling off at the community pool. Neither of them said a word about their present, including the birthday boy when he ventured back a day or so later. He just sat down, receiving it with the equal measure of fanfare with which it had been offered.

I wonder if I'd make him uncomfortable if I walked ov—

Squeak! The door behind her swung back against the brick exterior of the house. Glory turned to see Eli framed in the light of the kitchen.

"Are you alright back here? You've been gone a minute." Eli rubbed the back of his neck and flicked a glance over her shoulder.

Glory figured she'd stolen enough time from him. It wasn't like they were some old married couple with more years spent together than apart. They were just old, and they could count their time as a legally bound twosome on one hand. *But still,* she sighed again. And with a last look at Dude, who was reclining in the dusky shadows of the quivering leaves of the maple tree, she left the fresh air behind.

3

GLORY USED HER SPOON to lift out the string and let the tea bag drip on the inside of her mug. Grateful to start another day with a steaming ten-ounce serving of black tea, she closed her eyes and lowered her face to let the steam tickle her chin.

"Still sniffin' chai?" Ophelia's voice sounded drier than the cloth she'd wrung out.

"Ha! My flavor's more effective than that." Glory staved off the sting of the baker's sarcasm with laughter, her eyes concealed behind closed lids lightly dusted with a gold shadow that matched the iridescent accents in her midnight-blue dress. Her way of attaching an "un-" to the day's "usual." She turned a deaf ear to Ophelia's persistent ministrations around the pitted concrete bar top in order to settle herself into the week ahead. The sharp-tongued other woman could always spot water and crumbs that, to most people, were invisible. Or nonexistent. *Always needing something to do.*

"How was your weekend?" Ophelia shook her cloth over the wastebasket. Seemingly satisfied with the patter of debris, she stood on tiptoe and started scrubbing another section. She and Eli were distant cousins, their family ties stretched so thin they could've married each other without raising an eyebrow. Yet they were close enough that, when he'd heard she needed extra income to support her food truck business, he automatically offered her and her son, Jason, and daughter, Mallory, positions at By the Book.

Glory hadn't needed to be convinced to hire them, not that Eli had asked. They'd needed another full-time host in the store after the last one had quit suddenly and inexplicably. Plus, by hiring Ophelia, By the Book could provide more than coffee, tea, cold drinks, and cookies and encourage people to make Glory's home their home and her books theirs, too.

At first, Glory feared that bringing on Ophelia and her new menu posed a danger to her precious merchandise. Eli's "reconfiguration" had addressed that problem by adding shelves of donated and old books around the café area to allow patrons to eat and read without damaging new products. What made Glory's hair stand on end were the comments that tagged along in Ophelia's sidecar, especially regarding her church-going habits—or lack thereof.

"Y'all make it to church?" Ophelia scrubbed at a spot in front of the covered glass dish holding wax versions of their rotating specials of kouign-amann, cheddar-and-chive biscuits, butter pecan scones, and pimiento cheese squares.

"Why are you always stirring that same pot, and it's barely seven o'clock? Put down the spoon, Ophelia. Sunday was the time for sermons, not this beautiful Tuesday morning. I'd appreciate it if you let me enjoy the start to my week." When Glory had opened By the Book, most proprietors recognized the Sabbath by either closing their doors altogether or opening them in early afternoon. She'd established Tuesday-through-Saturday work hours, allowing her a two-day "weekend" while showing respect for all the churchgoers. Though times and piety had changed, Glory never had.

The bookseller reared back her shoulders and raised her head to her full five foot nine inches, gathered her cup and saucer, and rounded the counter. Anchoring her foot under the bottom rail of a tall stool, she pulled it back to sit at the end where she'd left her pen atop her leather daily planner. An orange-and-yellow sun glued to its cover beamed at her, inviting her to commence her daily routine with the right mindset, beginning with sipping tea between bites of whatever pastry Ophelia had baked the day before while perusing her schedule for the week. To give the tea more time to steep and cool—much like her current temper—Glory unclipped the pink band around the planner and opened it. She hooked a glossy nail tip under a marked tab and flipped to the date, hoping that if she kept her head down, Ophelia would return to the kitchen, her usual spot at this time. This was her "me time," and she surely wished she could get to it. In silence.

"Where *is* my cousin this morning?" Swipe, swipe went the cloth.

"Exactly where I said I left him, sleeping on the wrong side of the bed. His side. Where he usually is at this time of day. You know Eli. There's something about Tuesdays when it comes to my husband."

"He's never been an early bird," Ophelia bristled, apparently to defend her family's honor.

"*Mayy-bee.*" The way Glory elongated the word conveyed that her concession didn't indicate approval. "But he moves like a turtle on our first official workday. You shouldn't expect to see him raring to go before half past nine, thirty minutes after I've unlocked the front door."

Glory knew Eli burrowed under the covers for more than an hour after she'd closed their bedroom door with as soft a click as she could manage. Long after her goodbye kiss had evaporated from his forehead, he'd drag himself to the sitting area in their bedroom to complete a puzzle, check his email, or do whatever he did there, then mosey downstairs to the kitchen for a cup of strong coffee and a bleary how-de-do with Ophelia. By the time she raised the green shade covering the door's egg-shaped glass, the spa across the street and Dollars to Donuts, the coffee shop down on the corner, had been serving guests for several hours.

While Eli's hustling days were long behind him, Glory usually sprang out of bed; on Tuesdays, after two days of unbroken "together time," she beat the worm to work. She meant to hoard those precious hours for a rainy day when she was feeling particularly overwhelmed by the needs of others, including the one who'd placed a ring on her finger. Glory was grateful their personalities and habits complemented each other, like two straight, perpendicular lines forming a right angle, what she discovered during their long talks before they got married.

Before Eli introduced the subject of leaving the store.

Sensing movement, she glanced up to find the baker facing her across the two feet of glazed concrete between them, her arms crossed over the bib of her striped, gray apron. Glory started counting down from twenty, knowing Ophelia wouldn't take that long to launch into a diatribe of her own making or one inspired by her cousin and "that wife of his." She spooned out her tea bag, let it drain, then set it in her saucer.... *Sixteen* ... *fifteen* ... *fourteen* ... *thirteen* ... *twel*—

"I asked about his whereabouts because it *is* the first Tuesday of August. Aren't we supposed to review the inventory and the menu for September? I need to do my shopping and start prep. October will be here before we know it, bringing the festival right behind it. You like to do things up for the two people who might wander into the store for the first time, and you'll be giving me more than eight weeks' worth of work. Not to mention, I have to outfit my truck. Every year, I tell you two we should stop waiting until it's nearing fall to plan. And every year, I find myself telling y'all—"

"'The very same thing.'" Glory's mellow contralto cut off Ophelia's higher, more strident notes, aiming to derail the redhead's train of thought. "Yes, I know all that. We'll get to the menu and the inventory. But I like to feel . . . " Her ideas flitted about like butterflies around her head, and her hands moved in similar fashion, trying to catch them. "Led? Mmm-hmm, that's the word: led. Books are creative. They inspire thoughts and ideas. And when it comes to that festival of theirs, I think that's how people should feel—led, inspired, changed. In fact"—she slapped her hands together, her bracelets clinking against each other—"that should be the theme!"

Ophelia was digging into the niche in the back corner where the wraparound counter didn't quite reach the wall. She retrieved the broom, then froze with it balanced against her shoulder, its rounded wood tip in line with her ear. "What should be the what, Glo?"

"The theme! For the festival!" This time, Glory ignored Ophelia's shortening of her name. She propped her chin in one hand and gazed out the window overlooking the café, past the clouds and the recently awakened sun that was struggling to gather the strength to pierce them.

"Why do you care? You refused from the get-go to involve yourself and your bookstore in the town festival. Have you changed your mind? And if you haven't, then why bother yourself with whether or not there's a theme?"

Glory rolled her eyes, the drumming of her fingers communicating her excitement, her only response to Ophelia's interrogation.

This would be the seventh year—a "jubilee" year, her mama had once taught her—for the annual, town-wide celebration of Gilmore's food, enterprises, produce, and crafts. Anything local and homegrown, from lemonade stands run by elementary students to handblown glass made by local artisans. Most of the stores along Springs Church Road held special sales and giveaways and decorated their windows and businesses. The three-day event culminated in a carnival held at the fairgrounds, a few untilled acres belonging to Willard Farm on the outskirts of town.

A few years after he'd erected the fence, the mayor had sought out the bookseller on his way home from church. Eli, actively engaged in courting Glory, led him upstairs where she was rearranging the stacks and pretending not to bask in her new beau's attention.

"We need By the Book for the festival. This place is a Gilmore mainstay. How would the young people describe it? Iconic. That's what it is."

She'd peered at him over her oversized maroon spectacles, thinking he could be selling snake oil. "You know I don't like attention, Mark. I'm just trying to run my little old place and live in peace." Gilmore's out-of-the-way nature had appealed to Glory when she'd moved there as a young woman. There was small chance of anyone finding her there since most of her family was either gone or dead.

"Little?" His ingratiating smile did as much to soften the edge of his skepticism as aftershave improved the smell of a pig. He threw wide an arm and turned in a half circle. "Old perhaps, but there's nothin' little about this three-story, five-thousand-square-foot house."

Is that envy or admiration? Glory hid a shudder at the way he took stock of her business, like a shrewd cowboy inspecting the withers of a horse he might buy. She sensed Eli felt the same when she saw him grimace, and she liked her suitor all the more.

The mayor smoothed his mustache. "Now, how would it look if every store on the street except the biggest and the busiest participated? What will folks say if your shade is drawn and your door locked? You already entice a ton of people to the town."

"Come on, Mark, 'a ton'? Methinks you exaggerate." She studied one title after another and separated them into piles.

"And methinks the lady protests too much," the mayor sneered. "That's a quote you should recognize."

"I should and I do. Most people get it wrong, the same way you did." Her arms loaded down with historical fiction, Glory stepped around the familiar, caring hands that reached for her and the other stacks of books. "No, Eli, I don't need your help, but thank you. What I do need are those days off Mark is suggesting I give up. He doesn't understand they're part of my weekend."

The mayor braced a fist on each hip, and his suit coat flapped behind him like a cape. "You're working right now!"

Eli, who'd been leaning against the stair railing, straightened up and took a step toward him. "Hold on a minute, Mr. Mayor."

"It's alright, de-ah. The mayor didn't mean anything by it." Glory waved off her would-be knight. Though chivalry looked cute as a button on him, she could do fine fighting her own battles. It was too soon for Eli to step into her brother's footsteps. "Mark's just excited."

She loaded the books on a nearby cart and began transporting them to another section of shelves. "I'm not usually working like this on Sundays. *Someone's* been distracting me."

Eli grinned at her as she passed him.

"I'm not saying it *isn't* a good idea, but I don't like the idea of a bunch of looky-loos out of something to do, descending on our little burg. Bringing their sticky hands into my store and touching everything after eating hot dogs and funnel cake and BBQ." She shuddered. "Leaving prints." The possibility that someone from Georgia or from college might recognize her also crossed her mind. After all, hadn't Eli sought her out?

Mark's patent leather loafers clapped on the ends of her wide-legged palazzo pants. "Think of the lost sales and potential new readers! If you're closed Sunday, you'll miss the biggest of our three-day festival. Based on our research, Friday, people are working; Saturday, they're running errands and coming over later; Sunday is for family time, even for those who don't go to church. Like you and Eli over there."

Any indecision on her part disappeared—*poof!*—with his thinly veiled condemnation. Here he was, fresh from the pew, conducting business. Glory rolled the two-tiered cart to the room on the second floor that peered over its pitched slate roof onto Springs Church Road and parked it between the shelves she'd already emptied. She had decided to mirror some of the first-floor sections, starting with modern classics. That way, anyone who couldn't make it upstairs wouldn't feel like they were missing anything. She reached for a book and feigned a deep interest in *The Nightingale*.

"Mark, maybe you should give us some time to think about this." Eli had followed the sparring twosome. His shoulder bumped hers when he stepped closer.

At first, Glory had balked at the word *us*. It was the first time that someone else had spoken for her since her parents had died, one following the other, after Glory graduated from college. The first time she'd allowed anyone to. Feeling a change coming on, in their relationship and in herself, she leaned into Eli. Turning to the mayor, she winked and pronounced, "You heard my man. Give *us* some time. We'll get back to you when By the Book is ready to join the party."

More than half a decade and a husband later, Glory considered finally joining the festival fun. As she pondered the pros and cons, both trepidatious and excited, her fingers continued to play an invisible piano on the cool concrete of the bar. "*Create. Inspire. Grow. Change.* Or something along those lines."

Ophelia's head rocked back like Glory had slapped her. "This festival is about entertaining some folks, gettin' them to spend some money in town and boost the economy a notch. Not changing their lives." She aimed the broom handle at Glory before resuming her sweeping. "That's what *church* is for, changing lives. You talk about Creation, read the Bible."

Glory's unrestrained laugh filled the octagonally shaped café area that had once been a formal dining room.

The other woman's mouth fell open.

"I don't mean to offend you, but if I find something funny, I'm gonna honor you by letting you know. My brother taught me that."

With a swish of her fiery, shoulder-length hair, Ophelia turned her back to Glory and sent her voice sailing over her shoulder. "Then I'll honor *you* by telling you the truth, Glory Pryor. You want to change your life? Open a Bible, not merely any old book. Leave your house and go to the Lord's house. Believe what He says. That's what my mama and daddy taught me, and what Eli's grandmama taught *him* once upon a time. I can't help my cousin grew up, married you, and forgot how he was raised." She sounded much older than she looked, but according to Eli, the thirty-four-year-old woman had always been an old soul. The way her marriage had begun and ended had also added some extra years to her that time hadn't.

Ophelia bent to brush the dirt into her dustpan then depressed the lever on the wastebasket with her foot. "And by the way, when Eli comes down, you tell him I said steer clear of my domain, or at least put things back where they belong when he's through. I'm going to the kitchen to finish up these croissants."

The polyester fabric of her brown pants swished as she made good on her pronouncement and pushed through the swinging door, tucking Glory's good humor and inspiration into her apron pocket for good measure. Deflated, the bookseller flopped against the iron scrollwork on her stool and tapped her pen on her planner, leaving black dots all over the calendar pages on which she'd blocked out the word FESTIVAL in red on the second week of November.

Dancing in bare fields
    where I once crawled and walked.
Laughing among the weeds
    where I'd mourned and balked
    at the bare furrows and earth
    which I'd planted and sown.
Now, joy and provision
    when once I'd known
    only sorrow.
Reaping hope for today,
    not merely wishing
    and sighing
    and crying.
Looking ahead to tomorrow.

Glory's fingers curled into a fist of their own volition, and her short nails nearly tore through the paper she'd ripped from the book, made tender with the passage of time. Time and lots of handling. She willed her hand to set free the page, and it drifted, slightly bruised but intact, to her lap, its left edge slightly tacky with glue. A tear splashed onto the crinkled words and others followed, scurrying down her face before she could catch them, nearly obscuring the next line of the poem: "... *naked vines* ..."

A far-off diesel engine rumbled and stopped, rumbled and stopped. As it chugged closer, Glory retreated deeper into the corner of the sofa out of the driver's line of sight and sucked in a tremulous breath to gather herself. Reading those lines about sorrow was one thing; expressing it for all the ever-loving world to see was quite another. Without seeing the blue cab or a clock, she murmured, "Johnson's Transport. Al is headed home." The white block letters receded on the rear rolltop door after the truck passed by the store and lumbered up the road, then turned left at the three-way intersection at the top of Springs Church.

Glory had nearly perfected hiding in plain sight over the past forty years, like a felon who'd sought and found shelter in the prison library he'd escaped from, who feared someone would hear his chains. She drew her legs to her chest, and linking her arms around them, she balanced her chin on her knees and harrumphed, "Or a chicken who works the assembly line at the Tyson's factory."

Those images helped Glory add another name to her ever-growing list: *Coward. Maybe I should incorporate it onto a banner for the festival and wear it around my neck.* The festival. She knew better than to consider it, this threat to her self-imposed, anonymous life as "only a bookseller"—yet another title, but one she'd worked hard to earn and even harder to hold on to.

By the Book was more than a business to Glory; it was her sanctuary. When she told Eli these novels were her babies, she'd meant it. Each title, every author was perfectly curated. Her former employee helped with her selections before skipping town, but now she sought input from her husband and Noemie Pearline, her friend and jeweler. Glory didn't always buy what was most popular or the most current; she listened to her heart and ordered what caught her eye and—when it came to her collection of cookbooks—appealed to her taste buds.

And like a child, her business had grown and matured over the years. After graduating from college, searching for fertile soil to put down the roots she'd yanked up herself, Glory had driven blindly from north Georgia and eventually planted herself in Gilmore. At the time, the buildings that lined both sides of two-mile-long Springs Church Road were going the way of most things in small towns—downhill. Slowly but surely, and for some, painfully. When she stumbled on the three-story Tudor revival built on a third-acre lot with its arched doorway, cross gables, front porch, and mullioned windows, she'd fallen for it. And the realtor—and future mayor, Mark Aston—had taken one look at her enthusiastic face and found a willing victim and new Gilmore taxpayer. Three months later, she'd moved in and was unloading her pieces of furniture and her mama's teacup, eager to live in virtual obscurity.

The townsfolk used to wonder why the single young woman had bought such a large house, and Glory heard many a rumor about her plans:

"She's opening a bed and breakfast."

"She's starting a children's home."

"She's tearing it down and building some fancy new store or modern home."

"I'm happy all by my lonesome," Glory staunchly avowed to anybody who would listen, then opened the doors to By the Book, her dream all along.

Back then, her stock took up only a single room, the large one in the back of the main floor that she considered her happy place. She'd kept the others empty until she could renovate and add more inventory. Today, her store encompassed the first two levels, and merchandise was starting to sneak to the third floor where she and Eli had commandeered three bedrooms and a tiny bathroom that had suited her fine until she married. When their two became one, they'd knocked down a wall and created an adjoining bathroom and a walk-in closet; they'd converted the bathroom into a space for a laundry. Eli designed a den of sorts out of the third bedroom, to retreat to his television shows when he was tired of tending to her books—and when he sensed Glory had tired of tending to him.

She uncurled her legs so she could take in what she had birthed, what she and Eli were growing together. Since she couldn't see everything beyond the shelves around her, she had to imagine the café on the left side of the house and the kitchen behind it; the hallway that led to the original gathering room where guests first entered the store and the intricately carved stairway curving up to the upper floors; the spaces on the right side that sprouted off from the grand entryway that were full of stands and displays and bookcases; the storeroom in back. But it wasn't difficult to envision it all; she could walk the floor plan in her sleep.

"Who forgets what their babies look like, even when they're all grown up?" she asked the empty room.

A dog yapped in answer, drawing her eyes back to the window. *Oscar. But if Mr. Graves is walking by, then it was . . .*

"Time to lock up, babycakes?"

"Yes indeed!" Glory counted the creaks on the stairs and knew she had three more to go before Eli reached the first-floor landing. It would take him another thirty seconds or so to wend his way through the maze of books to this room. She waved goodbye to the Yorkshire terrier who she was sure always smiled back at her, though Eli had said his bared teeth looked more like a growl than a grin. Then she tapped the glass to acknowledge Mr. Graves, who was gripping the leash as if his life depended on it. She knew it did. The dog wasn't going anywhere, but that man adored his pooch the way Glory loved her books.

Deciding to meet Eli halfway, she rose and stretched languorously. Forgetting how she'd wept over the page in her lap, it slipped to the floor and under the sofa. Glory went to retrieve it, but then she heard the last *creak* announcing her husband's imminent arrival.

"I'll get it tomorrow," she promised. At the door, she hesitated. Then hurrying out, she warned herself, *Now, Glory, you'd best not forget.*

4

THE CLAPPER DINGED against the copper sides of the bell, and the pane rattled with the closing of the front door. The sounds pierced Glory's subconscious, rousing her from a rare half doze at the counter. There was simply too much to see to, so much musing and planning to do; it was rare indeed when she allowed her mind, hands, and feet to rest. But she hadn't been sleeping very well lately—*A symptom of aging,* her primary care physician informed her when she bumped into him at the Publix grocery store. Glory had spent too much time with doctors as a teen and wasn't inclined to spend much more than those few minutes chatting between the jars of spaghetti sauce and boxes of tortellini.

Glory credited her husband with her interrupted nights. All his talk of selling and moving had stolen her peace, what little she had these days. To rid herself of the vestiges of drowsiness, she took one last slurp of the dregs of tea, now cold, and marked her spot in the catalog with one of the sticky notes she kept close by. Then she hopped down from the stool with an ease that testified to all her years of climbing three flights of stairs and urged her bottom half to wake after having perched too long on that stool.

"Oh, Mommy, look at that!"

The exclamation stirred Glory to full attention, and pleasure curved her lips, knowing what the little voice was oohing and aahing over—Alice, tumbling headfirst after the White Rabbit.

That morning, she'd placed an oversized pop-up book on the round entryway table, a book she displayed around this season of the year, when back-to-school sales led both adults and students to dream of books like sugarplums and consider the return to school. The house sat too far back and the front porch was too deep for the pages to lure passersby, but anyone who stepped into the store would spot the vignette right off and be tempted to venture farther inside. While she didn't get all the fuss over Lewis Carroll's tale, this illustrated version never failed to grab the attention of younger readers and their parents. A bookseller's dream combination.

"Mommy! Mommy, can I touch it?"

And those words were a bookseller's nightmare—Glory's, anyway. She willed her tingling legs and feet to move more quickly as she wound her way toward the entryway. *These long skirts . . .* She groaned as the calf-length hem of her rayon dress reached out for protruding metal edges and snagged on the corners of books. *These mamas today, the way they let their children have their way with everything. Too permissive for their own good or anybody else's!*

"Hey there. May I help you?" Glory called out as a warning, in case the woman folded to her child's request to touch. With one hand pressed to her chest, she emerged from between two book carousels, setting one to spinning as she brushed by it in her haste. "Whew! These bones of mine were trying to tell me to slow down. I should've listened!"

"Bennett, you know better. You're reaching before I ever answered.

Now, put it back." The younger woman didn't look at Glory as she slowly leafed through the large pages until she came to the scene with the Queen of Hearts and her cascading deck of cards. The pop-up stack of cards created a bridge from one scene to the next. Quietly, she mounted the book on the stand and steadied it.

Glory swallowed her *hmmmpf* and made a mental note to turn back to the falling Alice once these folks left. She bent at the waist to level the playing field between her and the child. "Well, hello there, young man. Do you like my book?"

He took a half step back and tucked his right arm between his mother's thighs, encircling her leg with his left.

"Ben-Ben." His mother threw an arm out to steady herself and hooked a finger around the joint of his thumb and slowly pulled it from his mouth. Then she eased his hand to his side while allowing him to maintain his death grip on her thigh.

Hmmm, he's a shy one. Seems a bit old for that thumb-sucking business. Glory took stock of the boy, determining him to be about six. As if to straighten a few books nearby, she edged away to pose as less of a threat to the child and to give the mom room to handle family business.

Sure enough, out of the corner of her eye, Glory saw her squat until her head was even with her son's, and with their temples touching, her mouth uttered words Glory couldn't hear. He punctuated her whispers with a nod or two in response to whatever she whispered. She pecked him on the nose, her eyes closing so briefly it was almost a blink, and straightened.

Glory feigned busyness until she heard a little cough. Rosy lips smiling, hands clasped, she spun to face them, setting her long skirts a-sway. "Ready?"

The woman nudged the little one toward the bookseller. "Bennett, don't you have something to say to Mrs. Pryor?"

Glory's eyes rested gently on him even as she chewed hard on the question. *How in the world is this stranger callin' me by my name like we've been introduced?*

"Uh, Mrs. P-Pryor, I'm sorry for touching the book. I just wanted to see." Bennett's voice could've kept his toes company in his scuffed blue sneakers.

"Then you should." Glory scooted around them, plucked *Alice's Adventures in Wonderland* from the gleaming mahogany pedestal table, and extended it to the child. She chuckled at his wide, light-brown eyes and slack jaw before laying her own eyes on the mother—who looked none too happy at Glory's gesture. "That is, if your mama doesn't mind."

"No, of course I don't." The woman fiddled with the gold pendant hanging from the chain around her neck. "Say thank you, Bennett."

"Thank you." Gratitude and wonder gave his voice *mmpf*, and his personality eked through.

Glory squinted at the simple cross between his mother's fingers and figured she was lying like the vintage Persian rug in Glory's bedroom. Everybody knew fidgeting was a telltale sign. But this stranger's veracity, or lack thereof, belonged to her alone. Her reading habits, on the other hand, were Glory's business.

"Good. You're welcome. I have a special seat in the back with your name on it, *Bennett*, and you can sit right down and enjoy this book that caught your fancy." Glory stretched her long, slender fingers toward him. "Want me to show you?"

Again, his eyes widened as he gazed at the gold, silver, and gem-studded bangles encircling her wrist as he clenched the oversized, colorful book against his chest.

"Mommy, you're coming with?" Glory kept her arm extended his way, assuming the sale; she believed that given time, Bennett would accept her invitation and his mother would inadvertently tour the store. Based on what she knew about six-year-olds, there was no way this curious fellow could resist the lure of the book or her sparkly jewelry. It was the same kind of temptation that sent Alice through the looking glass.

And Eve to the fruit, and then cast from the Garden, a voice reminded her. *Like I had to run to Gilmore.*

The boy's mother rotated the top half of her body a few degrees, pointing one shoulder toward the front door, while her feet remained planted. Mouth slightly open, her gaze flicked from the top of Bennett's head to Glory's face and back again. Brow furrowed, she nodded and murmured, "Oh, of course. Su-r-re." She reached for her son.

He'd already put his small hand in Glory's.

"There. Off we go." Pinching together the left side of her wide skirts, Glory led the way, trusting his mother to follow the two of them. "What do you like to read, Mr. Bennett?"

He giggled. His head swiveled from one side to the other, taking everything in.

"We read lots of biographies." The voice behind them kept in step as the three meandered toward the back right of the store. "Also, we're making our way through *The Children's Book of Virtues.*"

Glory tugged a little on the hand in hers to get his attention, hoping to give him the chance to join the conversation. "Oh, is that who you were named after—William J. Bennett, the author of that book your mommy mentioned?"

"My daddy's name was Ben—"

"Yes, like the author," his mother interjected.

Glory drew up to a guest who was perusing a carousel filled with used books and stopped. "Here for your bimonthly visit?"

"About that time." The man glanced down at the child. "I see someone playing peekaboo."

Glory scrunched up her nose at Bennett to elicit a giggle before returning her attention to the man. She made a show of raising her wrist bearing the watch. "You know what time it is, Mr. Baldwin?"

"That I do. I looked for you when I came in, but I had to find this all by myself." He shook the cookbook in his hand.

She bit her knuckles and winced. "Oof. You saw me dozing in the café?"

Mr. Baldwin flattened his palms together and leaned his cheek on them. "Out like a light."

At one time, before Glory considered her guest a friend, she'd had to stop herself from brushing the back of his wool slacks with the door when he sauntered around to the ticking of his own internal clock. Now, she didn't feel compelled to hurry him along. Sometimes they exchanged recipes or she gave him a to-go box of Ophelia's sweets, along with a treat for the dog he'd bought to fill his empty nest. More often than not, he wandered the store freely, as he had that day.

"Ahh . . . Leah Chase. You can't go wrong with her food." Glory shifted to include both the other woman and her child in the conversation. "Frederick here tends to walk in my store after five o'clock every . . . let's see . . . couple of weeks or so. He'll read a few magazines, page through new titles, and amble out the door a smidge before six. Isn't that right, Frederick?"

He shrugged. "There 'bouts."

Glory continued. "Usually, he sits in the café with an old book and eats something Ophelia made, and if he purchases anything, which he almost never does, it's a cookbook like that one he's threatening to buy today." She partially covered her mouth with her free hand and whispered *sotto voce*, "Or a copy of *Southern Living Magazine* because I caught him tearing a recipe out of it."

Fred's laugh formed a trio along with hers and Bennett's. "Hey, stop maligning me! You know I bought plenty of books for the school drive. And where would Dude be sitting if I hadn't recommended that chair for his birthday?"

"True, true."

"What drive?" Up until then, Bennett's mother had stood as a quiet arc on the outskirts of their circle.

"Oh, only a little thing. Our annual book sale," Glory explained.

"A little thing, she says. Well, I spell humility G-L-O-R-Y." Frederick shook his head. "Every spring, she holds a special sale and gives the proceeds to the schools in the community to help their libraries expand their catalogs. What books don't get sold, she donates. Win-win."

"I keep some of 'em, so win-win-win, and Eli does most of the work. He's not just my handsome front man."

"How is that husband of yours?" Frederick asked.

"Well rested. Like your puppy." Glory felt her hand jiggle, and in her periphery, she saw the woman whispering something to the child. While the grown folks were talking, Glory had noticed him scratching first his nose, then a knee and the back of his head, and dance from one foot to the other. "You know I don't like standing in one place too long, Frederick, so I'll let you get back to what you were doing. I'm off to show my new friend my favorite reading spot."

As they walked away, she waggled a finger goodbye and offered breezily, "Don't forget to check out the current issue of *Architectural Digest*. If you need me, I'll be back in a minute."

Once they reached the rear, Glory ushered her two newest visitors through a set of carved pocket doors. Inside the room, she had arranged three upholstered armchairs, a medium-sized coffee table with initials carved under it, and a long, lumpy sofa in the midst of floor-to-ceiling bookcases. Mallory, one of Ophelia's sixteen-year-old twins, had been tasked with keeping the cherrywood shelves, hip-high wainscoting, and the ebony baby grand piano glossy and dust free. Late-afternoon sun streamed through wide windows flanked by thick yellow curtains that puddled on the hardwood floor. Baskets of books marked "Not for Sale" were tucked into the back corners alongside three-foot-wide pillows big enough for Bennett to sprawl on. Glory raised her eyebrows at the boy. "I call this my happy place. Won't this be a fun spot for you to read?"

His eyes traced every inch before nodding slowly. He stayed put, his hand in Glory's, when his as-yet-unnamed mother moved up and placed an arm around his sturdy shoulders.

She couldn't blame the woman. Whether it was the rosy tint of his creamy cheeks, his tousled brown curls, or the roundness of his limbs and torso, Glory struggled to keep herself from picking him up and plopping him onto her lap with a copy of *The Velveteen Rabbit* and whiling away the afternoon. She reared back her shoulders with a sigh and unfurled her fingers from his. When Bennett inched across the thick, faded wool rug toward the flower-covered sofa, she urged him on with a grin.

"Thank you!" He hefted himself onto her own favorite corner and promptly opened the book.

Satisfied that he was otherwise occupied, Glory bestowed her attention on the other adult in the room. "Speaking of names . . . how do you know mine?" She pivoted for a face-to-face answer and had to suck in a breath. "I'm sorry. Are you okay?"

Abruptly, the stranger's expression changed. The eyebrows that had been aimed at each other like angry arrows retreated to their original positions and her pursed lips flattened. She seemed to swallow her emotions, and her fingers did the conga with her necklace. "I'm fine."

"If you say so." Glory acquiesced to the equivocation but resolved to steer clear of whatever the woman had going on. "I can leave y'all to it so I can check in with my other guest. Enjoy your time with my friend Alice." She made to return to the front of the store, with a tinkling of bracelets and a flash of color.

"Adelle."

The word stopped Glory in her tracks. She readjusted her neckline so that each shoulder was protected by the soft dark fabric. "Excuse me? I was talking about the book. *Alice's Adventures in Wonderland*?"

"My name, it's Adelle." In a second, she'd taken the few steps that brought her within arms' reach of Glory; her outstretched hand spanned the short distance remaining between them. "And I learned your name when I researched the store. I'm a freelance reporter."

"And then 'Miss Thing' tells me she's writing an article on the festival." Glory scrubbed her face with the cloth. "And wants to ask me questions about By the Book." She hung the rag on the rack beside the sink and splashed water on her face. Every time she rinsed with hot first, then cold, she could hear her mama instructing her teenaged self to clean her pores, then close them. Old habits, like old pains, died hard.

Eli poked his head around the gap in the bathroom door. "You know I can't hear you in here. All I can detect is the anger in your tone."

"I'm not angry, so my tone can't be angry." Voice cool and modulated, Glory dried her face with the hand towel and used it to dab at the dots of water on her pink cotton nightgown whose lacy trim brushed her ankles.

Eli stepped into the bathroom and took the towel. He patted her forehead before he looped it around her neck and used it to draw her close to him. "Well, your face is sayin' something different. There's a reason you took such an early bath. The sun is willing and able to carry on a conversation with us, and you're already in your nightgown." His voice was deep at her ear, like he was sharing a secret in a crowded room before his soft lips lingered on hers.

After briefly relaxing in his embrace, she yanked the towel from him and swatted his thigh, laughing. "You should've seen her face, Eli! All scrunched up like this"—she screwed up her mouth, narrowed her eyes, and drew in her brows—"looking all evil. Talk about angry! And then, she has the nerve to form her lips to talk to me about the festival."

Glory raised her voice to mimic the voice in her head. It sounded nothing like the woman she'd met. "*When do you have time to sit with me? I'd love to interview you, since By the Book is the cornerstone of Gilmore's finest event.* Adelle my foot. Ah-*don't* think so."

Eli, crouched over the laundry basket overflowing with sheets and pillowcases, pulled out a queen-size fitted sheet and shook it. "That was terrible, Glo'. You can do better than that. You *are* better than that."

"What kind of reporter can she be if she didn't know By the Book doesn't take part in the festival?" *Not yet, anyway.* "How can I be the cornerstone if I'm not a participant? And don't think I didn't hear that. I have to put up with Ophelia shortening my name, and her habit better not be contagious."

"Hint taken." Eli pressed the sheet to his body and flattened some of the wrinkles.

"Turns out her little boy—Bennett, what a cutie pie—is *four* years old, not six. Just a little big for his age. Or maybe he's not? What do I know about kindergartners? Those eyes of his . . . and he's already reading, Eli!"

"Yes, you told me." His eyes twinkled.

"Anyway. Ben-Ben—that's what *Adelle* called him—asked her about the book. When she went to see, I left the room without making any promises about an interview. She'd best speak to the mayor to learn about the festival."

Eli raised an eyebrow. "From what I understand, weren't you recently discussing that event you're supposedly not interested in? Going on about themes and creation and being led, if I heard correctly."

Glory resisted the urge to drop the towel over his smug expression. "I take it you've talked to your cousin."

"*Our* cousin, Ophelia, yes. If you and I ever get on the same page, we'll either have packed up or moved on by then. But you must know this type of article could contribute to the growth of Gilmore and the festival's success. The timing's heaven-sent."

"I wouldn't say that at all." Glory rejected references to things and places—and people—beyond her control. And she certainly wasn't getting into this nonsense about the move so close to bedtime. Chasing sleep was giving her enough trouble as it was. Picking up the opposite ends of the linen, she followed his lead and connected the ends of the sheet. "I hope you haven't spread those rumors to Ophelia. What did Mark Twain say about the exaggerated reports of his death?"

"I wouldn't call talking about a major change in our lives a rumor or an exaggeration, Glory. But no, I haven't mentioned them to her. Not until we've decided our next steps. As far as the festival goes, I would and I do say that. As a former marketing director and entrepreneur, I can tell you that nothing beats natural, organic publicity. It's not like Gilmore has a social media presence to speak of. People don't flock here by the tens of thousands for its annual party." He brought his folded ends to meet Glory's, then he halved the sheet again. "Which leads me to wonder how your new buddy heard about it."

Glory wanted to take umbrage with his words, but her husband was telling the truth, however simplified. Gilmore's residents threw a community 'party' basically for themselves and a few hundred residents of neighboring towns. It grew a tad each time but shouldn't warrant national attention. The local business owner inside her certainly wouldn't mind any trickle-down effect on her own business; the part of her that craved a more reclusive life retreated from the spotlight. Also . . .

"I don't trust my so-called new buddy, this Adelle Simonette." Glory finished her own thought, syncopating the syllables and emphasizing the *T*s. She dug in her drawer for her hairbrush to tend to her short, silver-tinged coiffure. Chopping off her hair was the best decision she'd ever made. Her eyes settled on Eli, who was withdrawing another sheet from the basket. *Okay, third best,* she amended, thinking also of the store. *Any man who volunteers to fold fitted sheets is a keeper.*

He met her gaze in the mirror. "You just met the woman. You don't know enough not to trust her."

"Exactly." Glory squinted in Eli's direction, not really seeing him or what he was doing. She was replaying the thirty minutes she'd spent with Adelle and Bennett. Stewing, according to her husband.

"All I know is, she has a four-year-old son who is absolutely scrumptious. I could just eat him. Once he got over his shyness, he carried on conversations like a little man, looking at you eye to eye when he spoke, barely blinking. I might have to get him a copy of *Alice's Adventures in Wonderland*, the way he tore into it."

Her husband carried his small armload to the tiny closet near the claw-foot tub and stacked the sheets on shelves according to color, as Glory had shown him. She'd explained that old habits didn't die because you married them to somebody else's, and he'd taken it to heart. "You don't like *Alice*—"

"But I get a sense about people. It comes from meeting and working with all sorts over the years. When someone walks into the store, I know who's planning to steal a book, tear a recipe out of *Bon Appétit* or *Southern Living*—like I caught Frederick doing—or do the puzzle in the newspaper. I can point out the nonreaders who only need somewhere to go on a rainy Saturday and the folks who'll buy anything I suggest. And I can tell you, that woman, that *Adelle* . . ."

Glory sorted through her jumbled thoughts as she lifted her plush purple robe from the hook on the door and slipped her arms into it. She raised the lapel to ward off the chill she felt once the shower's warmth had faded. It wasn't until she double tied the belt around her narrow waist that she could gather her feelings into an easier-to-sift-through, worrisome pile. *That darn festival! What does that woman know about me and my past? Why's she stickin' her nose in my business?*

Fed up, Glory's emotions finally spilled over. "That woman is up to no good, Eli. No. Good. Mark this day that you heard my words."

5

Adelle rose from Bennett's bed and drew the covers up to his chin. Before he could ask, she wedged the sheets and blankets between the mattress and the box spring until his head looked like the tip of a hot dog poking from a bun. She cupped his round face with her hands and planted a wet smack on his cheek, still damp from the bath. "There. Comfy?"

Giggling, pink where she'd kissed him, he worked his fingertips free to clutch the folded linen. His head went up and down several times.

"I'll take that as a 'yes, ma'am.'" She ran a finger gently down his nose, its shape reminding her so much of his daddy's. Something else to make her treasure the one and yearn for the other.

Bennett yawned.

"Good night," Adelle whispered and bumped his nose with her own, then waded through the fire trucks, police cars, and dinosaurs he'd left scattered on the floor from the bed to the door. Mercifully, the sole of her foot avoided the building blocks he'd used to construct the roads and bridges for his city. At one time she had enforced an "everything finds a place by bedtime" rule, but those long-ago habits and days went the way of the delicate white roses she'd tossed into her husband's grave. Gone and buried.

She regarded Bennett's blank bedroom walls and the taped-up boxes in his closet. *No need to decorate. We're only staying long enough for me to do what I came to do.* But Adelle wondered if resuming some routine would make the place feel more like home though they were far from anywhere that looked like it.

"Mommy?" Bennett's voice stayed her hand on the light switch that controlled the lamp.

"Yes, sweets?" Adelle tried to speak quietly, so as not to break the slumberous mood settling on the room, helped along by the heavy curtains she'd drawn over the closed shades. She prepared herself to perform an encore of "Amazing Grace."

"Do you think Daddy has met Geema yet?"

Such an out-of-the-blue question. She pressed her balled hand into her abdomen, anything to keep the sob from exploding up from her gut and out through the hole in her chest where her heart used to beat. Taking a second and only a second to compose herself, or otherwise he might notice, she responded as normally as she could manage. "Oh, wouldn't that be such an unbelievable reunion, Ben-Ben? It's hard to imagine Daddy's joy upon seeing his own mommy again."

Adelle returned to his bedside and knelt there, praying her hoarse voice sounded full of wonder, not woe. "I'm not sure about such matters, all the ins and outs of heaven and who will remember or recognize who or what. All I know is that we had a Jesus-loving husband and father, and since he left us both behind on this earth, he must be present with the Lord. That's as far as my understanding goes, Ben-Ben. As much as I can wrap my mind around. Will your daddy know his mother, father, and grandfather and my own father, as well as our other friends and family, or will his eyes be too full of our Savior to notice anybody else? Those are good questions we may get to ask God one day. Yet I have a feeling when we get there, we'll know everything we'll need to know."

She flicked the lamp switch to prevent her son from seeing her tears. A well-intentioned friend had once told her that people who loved greatly also mourned greatly. Those words provided meager comfort, less than a threadbare blanket in the Antarctic.

"Mrs. Pryor's dress was like an angel's, wasn't it, Mommy? I bet Geema's wearing one like it." Bennett's yawn took over his face, it was so big.

Another stomach punch. This time, it was anger Adelle swallowed, not sorrow. She could bear the weight of widowhood this time of night; the mantle of avenger was a heavier burden on her neck and her shoulders. Working to maintain a neutral tone, she uttered between clenched teeth, "I don't know, Bennett. Do you think anyone wears that shade of yellow in heaven?"

But Adelle realized that the child had fallen asleep the way the young and innocent do, suddenly and deeply, with his mouth open. Which was for the best, since Adelle didn't want to engage in any comparisons between that woman and God's saints and angels. *Talk about apples and okra! The slimy kind my daddy liked to eat. That's how unalike angels and Glory Pryor are.*

Back at the doorway, Adelle took a moment to pray for her son. She drew the door but left it partially open; the hallway light would softly bathe Bennett in its warm glow should he awake before morning. He'd been able to stay in his own bed for two nights straight, and she was shooting for a third.

Adelle padded toward the center of their rental house, pausing once to glance toward a noise coming from his bedroom. But the only thing following her were the impressions left by her bare feet on the loosely woven brown carpet fibers, and those were quickly fading.

Back in the small den, she considered dousing the light, curling up on the sofa, and pretending to watch an old show, but she hated to risk crying herself to sleep there, what she'd been doing way too often—here in Gilmore and back at home as well. *That* habit she'd maintained. Instead, she took a left turn for the kitchen in search of a suitable distraction: the popcorn maker, one of the first appliances she'd unpacked when they'd arrived in Gilmore last week from Cabot, Arkansas. Buttered popcorn had become a main staple for her since Bennett's dad had died.

Oh, my love. Adelle bit down on her knuckle to stifle her cry. Though she knew it was better to be with Jesus, that place wasn't here, with their boy and with her. And had her husband still been on the Earth, she and Bennett wouldn't be in this town and in this house, exacting an imperfect justice instead of leaving it to God—who, by her estimation, was taking much too long to work His will.

"Has it really been only thirteen months since you left us, Ben?" Adelle considered it progress that she no longer counted the hours and the days since her forty-year-old husband had succumbed to a bacterial infection that moved through his body like a high-speed locomotive. What had started out as sniffles and a runny nose had progressed to fever, coughing up blood, a hard-to-shake lethargy, and at the last, a midnight ambulance ride when she couldn't wake him. Ben had lasted eighteen hours in the hospital, never making it to the intensive care unit. *Toxic shock,* the doctor said. *Streptococcus pyogenes.*

"My family keeps losing, over and over. My father, Ben. I refuse to give up even more. I won't!" Adelle pounded her overworked hand on the laminate-topped island. She squeezed her eyes closed, but hot tears oozed out of the corners and made slow trails down her cheeks that carved a burning path to her soul. When Adelle opened her eyes, they overflowed, blinding her until she swiped them with the edge of her gray cardigan, the color of her favorite kind of days with her husband. Stormy days when the thunder and the rain drove the family of three inside to the couch to munch on popcorn and watch animated movies.

Snuggled up together on the sofa instead of crying by herself on it.

The sweater was her husband's, with the holes on the elbows and the ragged hem and an unraveling sleeve. Just as this was Ben's custom, she'd adopted it as her own: crunching on kernels for dinner because he was too busy working on a story or meeting a deadline or interviewing people. It was *his* career that Adelle had borrowed when she'd told Glory Pryor she was a reporter. Thank God the woman hadn't asked for more details, like who she wrote for or where the two of them hailed from.

Don't bring My name into this.

"Oh!" Adelle jumped a mile, knocking the large domed lid of the popcorn maker to the vinyl floor with a clatter. Sure it was her own guilty conscience she'd heard, she still glanced upward, her heart thudding. "Okay, Lord, I'm sorry. But I'm glad that Pryor woman didn't pester me for something more than who I was. I couldn't have manufactured the name of a paper or magazine. She's too sly not to check, and she's likely to do some digging. What was I doing, volunteering my last name and telling her I'm a reporter? Asking for an interview?"

"You've been through a lot, haven't you?" Not sure whether she was asking herself or the hard plastic cover, Adelle retrieved the lid where it had skidded by the range. When she saw the large crack branching off from an older split near the top, she burst into tears at this, the last straw on a day she'd wasted so much effort grasping for them.

Adelle snatched up the appliance, stalked across to the door, and yanked it open. Without stopping to consider what she was doing, she hefted open the green receptacle and chucked both parts, as well as the cord. They landed atop the heap of cardboard and plastic with muffled, satisfying thumps. Maybe somebody somewhere would make better use of the thing.

Returning inside, Adelle dimmed the lights and parked herself in the den. Aware that she couldn't do much without waking Bennett, she took a visual inventory of the kitchen, the hallway leading to the bedrooms on his side of the house, the opposite side where she slept, and the kitchen again. She spied a large box beside the fireplace and decided to dig into something more productive than the lone bag of potato chips in the mostly empty pantry. Using the scissors she'd left on the table, Adelle started to cut through the tape before noticing the broken seal.

The second she lifted the four flaps, it dawned on Adelle why she'd resisted tackling this box filled with books, pictures, frames, photo albums, hand-drawn and -painted artwork, and other memories. It had taken her until last spring to pack away these items from Ben's home office, and that was when she'd come across the diary, tucked between her husband's high school yearbooks. That was the night she'd made up her mind to come to Gilmore.

Friends and church family, after they realized they couldn't talk her out of her decision to move—however temporarily it might be—had convinced her to take these treasures with her for safekeeping. Adelle lightly traced her husband's profile with an index finger. "And here I thought breaking the cover to the popcorn maker was the last straw."

Adelle knelt over the box and riffled through her life. If only she could package her grief and her anger and set it aside the way she'd stuffed this container into a corner of the room. A photo of her in an off-the-shoulder white silk gown and her serious-looking new husband, mounted beside a copy of their wedding invitation.

Their first house with a *SOLD* plastered over a real-estate sign. Ben's framed college degree. His first published column in a local paper. A STAR award for one of his articles. Three small, fuzzy images of their little Bean, what they called their unborn baby until he became Bennett Jr.

Tears plopped onto the glass, heavy droplets onto leaves in a rainforest. Like clouds that were heavy and full, her eyes could not contain the outpouring of her sorrow. This storm had been building. She dug deeper into the carton, using both hands to search for evidence of her past, not only his or what they'd left together.

There! Adelle's self-portrait that Ben had insisted on hanging over their bed, a black-and-white rendering that she was secretly proud of. A small box containing a collection of rabbits that she'd been adding to over the years—one made of lava from their honeymoon trip to Italy. The leather-bound diary. A book of verses with a black-and-white picture tucked inside. *Daddy.*

A hand settled on her shoulder. The touch was too light to startle her, and it came too late for her to disguise her tears. The carpet that had swallowed her footprints had muffled her son's steps—or perhaps she'd expected him to show up all along. Adelle enfolded his tiny fingers with hers and drew him around in front of her.

"Hey there, Ben-Ben. What are you doing up?" Repeating her husband's name quieted her inner storm.

He stood there, legs akimbo and ankles bare in the navy Paw Patrol pajamas he'd outgrown a year ago. "I heard you crying."

Adelle tried to force a smile, but her lips crumpled at the edges. She ran a hand through his curls. "How could you hear me all the way out here if you're asleep all the way in there?"

Bennett shrugged and pointed at the pile. "Whatcha doing?"

She studied him for a second. "I'm looking at special books and photographs of Daddy and you and me."

"Is that what made you cry?" His observation was matter of fact, like he was asking if the rain had wet her hair.

Adelle sighed and nodded, hating that he'd become inured to her tears. Fresh ones threatened at the thought of her young son finding her sadness a run-of-the-mill event. Part of her wanted to poke the bear, to elicit a reaction of some kind. To not feel so alone in her grief. She caressed his soft babyish skin with her thumb. "Wanna sit with me for a little while? You may not remember what Daddy looked like when he was younger."

Bennett turned and without further urging, backed into her lap, the way she remembered him doing as a toddler. He looked up at her over his shoulder and patted her cheek gently. "I cried when I looked at these pictures yesterday, but that's okay, Mommy. Jesus cried, too, when He lost His friend, Laz-rush."

Her lips wobbled at his pronunciation as he wiggled into place and made himself comfortable in the hollow created by her criss-crossed legs, something he wouldn't be able to do in a few months' time if he continued growing at his current rate.

"My Sunday school teacher told me that when you love someone a lot, you miss them a lot, too."

So I've heard. That advice sounds better coming from you, she thought, her smile firming up briefly before collapsing altogether. All Adelle could do was rock him with her face buried in his crown, sobbing into his hair. Emptied, eyes so swollen she could barely see, she opened the album she'd been holding when Bennett had walked in and drew his attention to a photograph. "Do you know who that is?"

His round fingertip covered the faces of the gray-haired couple perched on a green-and-yellow riding lawnmower. "Bumpa and Geema."

Adelle had taken the snapshot of Ben's parents when they were working on their farm, located a few miles away from their family home in Cabot. They'd adopted her husband when they were nearing fifty and had died within months of each other when their grandson, Bennett, was barely two years old. Adelle thanked God they hadn't suffered through the unexpected loss of their only son.

"There's Penny." He tapped the corner of the rectangular printout, indicating a chestnut-colored horse standing in the background. "I hope she's getting her apples."

The elder Simonettes had left their home and land to Ben, and now his wife was left to figure out what to do with the property and the animals since his older sister had no interest in farming. Adelle had put everything in the capable hands of in-laws and neighbors for the time being, but she didn't know how long she could abdicate her responsibilities there. She promised herself grimly, *Long enough.*

Bennett flipped the page and pressed his nose against the plastic. "Who's that?"

Adelle grasped the book with both hands and brought it down so she could see. "Oh, that's Grandpa. You probably can't recognize him with the beanie." It had been a long time since they'd explored all this memorabilia, and it became particularly difficult once she'd locked it away. To her, all these faces and places represented all she'd lost. Tonight, cuddling Bennett, she started to recall all she'd gained from these experiences and people she carried inside, as she'd once carried her son.

He squinted at her, wrinkles crinkling the bridge of his nose. "What's a beanie? Like beanie weenies?"

Her laughter felt good to those rarely exercised muscles. "No, silly billy. Beanie weenies are baked beans and chopped hot dogs. That's what Mommy makes for you when I'm too busy to cook." Or too sad. Or too behind with shopping. Adelle patted her head. "A *beanie* is a hat."

"Oh. That's a funny name." Bennett reached for the corner of the page, ready to move on.

She flattened his fingers. "Wait a minute. Do you remember Grandpa? That was *my* daddy, like Bumpa was your dad's daddy."

The child shook his head slowly and settled against her. "Isn't Daddy with Grandpa now?"

"Yes, Grandpa is in heaven." Adelle rested her chin on his head. She had to clear her throat before she could speak, but no more tears threatened. "From what I was blessed to know about my father, he's one of the saints sitting on the front row beside your dad. He traveled a bumpy road in his earlier days, like most of us. But his faith and the life he chose later smoothed all that out in the years before he died. Grandpa was a good man who raised me all by himself."

"What happened to him?"

"He had a condition that made it hard to breathe."

"What about your mommy?"

She was one of the bumps in that road Daddy traveled, Adelle almost said. "I didn't know her the way I knew my father. She went away when I was very young, so he had to be both mom and dad for me." She unwrapped a ceramic rabbit smothered in packing tissue. "Do you know who made this?"

"Grandpa?"

She gingerly set it into his palm, watching him examine the intricately made ears and nose of the cream figure balancing on its rear legs and holding an orange carrot in its front paws. Adelle's rabbits used to sit on a high shelf in their kitchen in Cabot, in the bookcase she'd designed during their remodel. The collection was meant to be admired from afar, not enjoyed, not touched. She intended to protect it from the same little hands clutching the pottery at that moment. None of that mattered now.

"He did this? Wow!"

"Mmhmm, he did, when he was about my age."

"He was *that old*!?"

She tickled him and growled over his giggles, "Yes! He formed this from a mere lump of clay, little boy. And not only was he good at this, he was a creative genius." Adelle wrapped her arms around Bennett, and smushing her cheek against his, whispered, "A true artist."

Keeping him cocooned, Adelle scooted back to prop her back against the table and extended her legs in front of her. She finger-combed his hair. "People used to call your grandpa's house a junkyard, but he didn't care. He threw nothing away. He was an innovator, and he could find a use for what other folks considered beyond repair—probably because he said he wasted so much of his life before the Lord found him. Or rather, before he found the Lord." She leaned down so she could see Bennett's face. "Grandpa believed everything has a purpose—every life, each mistake, all the stuff we call 'accidents.' He was constantly telling me, *His eye is on the sparrow.*"

Bennett's hand was lying on the carpet. Adelle plucked the rabbit from his palm and turned it this way and that, studying it from every angle as if she'd never seen it before. It felt like she hadn't, not really. Not through the perspective of her father. "He'd write songs and sing them to me. Tell me stories before bed, mostly about what he'd made and seen in life. Daddy loved to travel once upon a time. Oh, you should've heard him!"

When Adelle peeked again at her son, she spied half-closed eyes and a mouth drooping to one side. All her talking must have prevented him from falling off that steep cliff of sleep. For a minute, she listened to his breaths slow and whistle through his nostrils, savored the rise and fall of his chest. Still holding him, she twisted to replace the rabbit in its tissue and opened another album . . . and read her husband's award-winning writing . . . and looked at more pictures . . . and smoothed her son's hair . . . until nearly two hours later, Adelle closed the last leatherette cover over the recumbent form of Bennett, who had succumbed to sleep an hour before.

Her face crusty and dry from the salty residue of spent tears, she set the book aside, covering faces of smiling friends and family smiling up at her. By wiggling her legs and toes, she got the blood flowing in them. Assured that she wouldn't fall once she was upright, she laid Bennett down and clambered to her feet. Steady, she tucked her hands into his armpits and grunting, threw him over her shoulder. As she lumbered down the hall, Adelle heard her husband laugh, warning her in the way he used to, *He's not a baby, Adelle. Wake him and make him walk. You'll regret spoiling that boy.*

But her only regret was not spoiling her husband during their twelve years together. Assuming they'd have decades to talk more and make more babies like the one she was carrying now.

Maybe you're wasting the gift of time God has given you with the child you already have, coming to Gilmore, running after the Pryors. Haven't you lost enough?

"No," she whispered and tucked the sheets around her son's sleeping form for the second time that night. She pushed his hand under the covers when it tried to find his mouth, like a tiny heat-seeking missile. "I didn't just lose it. It was yanked from me. But I will get it back."

Her mouth a straight line, Adelle again left his door ajar and the light on outside his room and headed back to the den. Gazing down at the memories peppering the floor, her eyes landed on the treasured rabbit her daddy had fashioned from a small lump of clay no one else valued. Less than a minute later, she was scrambling for the popcorn maker and its cord, half-in, half-out of the recycling bin. Back on her feet, the humid late-August air hugging her chest, the cicadas buzzed to their own rhythm that was louder than the blood pulsing in her ears. Eyeing the inky expanse above her that was broken by a few, far-off twinkling stars and the red blinking light of a passing airplane, she vowed, "I *will* get it back for you."

If someone asked her at that moment what "it" was, she wouldn't have been able to define it, but it sounded like the jingling of bracelets.

6

"Have you cleaned the windows yet?"

Jason stared at Glory, his face blank, his bottom teeth visible above his lip.

She resisted rolling her eyes. Wasn't she the adult who owned the store? He was a teenager and part-time employee. Glory gestured to get his attention and snapped her fingers, exasperated with him and with herself. "Jason, you did hear my question, didn't you?"

He blinked and at last removed a wireless white bud from his right ear. "Oh, yeah. I'm sorry, Mrs. P. I was listening to—"

"Something else other than me," Glory said dryly.

"Billie Holiday. Mallory turned me on to her. Wanna hear?" The aspiring musician held out his hand.

"No, but thank you." She took his chin by her index finger and thumb and tilted his head so she could inspect his left side. "Mmmhmm. Remember, when you're at work, you can't plug both ears. How are you supposed to hear me call, 'Jason, look out for the falling book!' or 'Jason, I've fallen, and I can't get up.' Or even more important, 'Jason, this guest needs you to find *A Gathering of Old Men*.'"

He dug into a front pocket of his oversized carpenter pants. After pulling out the case, he stuffed one earpiece into it and left the other in place. "I'm sorry."

"I know. But don't be sorry. Be better. *Do* better, darlin'." Glory patted him on the shoulder to ease the sting of her chastening. "Now, back to my original question: Have you washed the front windows yet? It's almost nine o'clock, and we'll be opening our door forthwith."

"Um . . ."

"Son, chop-chop." Glory clapped her hands.

"But it looks like it's going to rain."

She raised an eyebrow, her hands splayed palms up in front of her.

Sure enough, Jason's lips clamped shut. He rotated the bib of his hat until its visor hung toward the back of his neck, and with a sigh that ruffled the scraggly wisps of hair struggling for life over his top lip, he turned away.

For a few seconds, Glory watched Tommy, Chuckie, and the rest of the *Rugrats* characters undulate on the back of his T-shirt before stopping him. "The window cleaner and the newspaper are where I left them for you, on the counter in the café. In case you're looking for them."

He redirected his steps, headed toward the right, and disappeared down the hall.

Technically, as Ophelia's boy, Jason was her kin, but that familial connection meant Glory expected more from him instead of less. She'd have sent him on his way the day after he'd started working a few hours a week but for the blood running through her husband's veins and linking her to the teen. That, and she couldn't very well fire him and retain his dedicated mother and sister. By this point, Jason should be well aware of their morning routine, what it took to open the store. And if he wasn't, he should know to refer to the checklist she'd tacked to the kitchen wall. His mama could assist him on that score.

According to the list of opening tasks, cleaning the windows was one of Jason's Monday-Wednesday-Friday jobs, the first to-dos. Tackling the glass squares outside on Mondays set the tone for the week, helping the store recover from the weekend and preparing it for Tuesday, Glory's opening day. On Wednesdays, Jason did the glass inside. Glory took care of the front door Thursday and ignored the handprints on the rest of the windows in front until Friday. Then it was time to spiff up the exterior windows again, after visitors touched them on their way to and fro and birds and insects peppered the glass under the porch. On Fridays, Jason spot cleaned and helped prep By the Book for Saturday. It was tedious, yet important, work.

Glory pushed up her bell-shaped sleeve and adjusted the slim platinum watch on her wrist, a wedding gift from Eli that coordinated with the sterling silver and gold bangles on her other arm. 8:30. Barely enough time to arrange the chairs out front and to write the notes on the chalkboard, announcing Ophelia's special of the day. Glory also had to hang the advertisement for the upcoming book signing, a job she wouldn't entrust to Jason, who lacked the finesse to not only do it, but do it well. He had other work besides his opening chores, and his sister didn't come in until late afternoon.

"Ophelia!" Glory turned it into a one-word song that hearkened to "Layla," by Eric Clapton. Singing it sounded much better than yelling for her across the store, empty save for the staff this time of morning and Eli, sleeping upstairs. When her baker didn't answer, she sashayed to the rear, still humming the song, and pushed open the kitchen door. "Oh!"

A surprised Eli swung toward her.

Guilty, not surprised, she decided. *Like I caught you eating all of Ophelia's ham-and-cheddar scones.* Glory could've stuffed them in his open mouth.

"Eli, what are you doing in here?" She regretted the accusatory sound of the words she'd lobbed his way, but it couldn't be helped at this point. They'd sailed through the air. And from Ophelia's expression, they'd struck her dead center, where she stood partially shielded by her cousin.

She rolled out the dough on the floury stainless steel counter. "Can't a man be in his own kitchen?"

Glory wasn't in the mood to engage both Ophelia and her son in a span of minutes, so she ignored her. "Eli, isn't it a mite early for you to be downstairs? You haven't even kissed me good morning yet, and here you stand . . . in your own kitchen."

Ophelia set down her rolling pin, hard.

Eli patted the redhead on her shoulder, much as Glory had Jason, before ambling toward his wife. "I thought you'd be outside by now."

Glory cut an eye at Ophelia as he approached. She proffered her cheek instead of her mouth. "You're looking mighty dapper today, Mr. Pryor."

Eli studied his lower half, as if he needed to remind himself what he was wearing. When he faced Glory again, he appeared pleased as punch with his purple golf shirt tucked into gray trousers cinched under his paunch with a braided, black leather belt. He raised a loafered foot and pointed to his sock-free ankle. "Why, thank you, wife. Trying to keep up with the brains of this outfit."

Glory wasn't in the mood for any of his blandishments; those two looked up to something. "You're welcome, *husband*," she responded, her voice stiff. "Ophelia, when you didn't answer—and I see why, since you and Eli must have been too busy chattin' it up back here—I came in to tell you I'd be outside, setting up the chairs and the chalkboard. But since Eli is up and at 'em, he can watch things in the store."

Glory pivoted, her silky skirts swirling, and pushed open the door. She flicked a hand, making her sleeve slip down to her elbow. "Y'all go on back to whatever you were doing. I'm taking my brains and puttin' 'em to work." As she suspected, Glory heard Eli push through the door behind her, lickety-split, before she'd moved more than a few paces. They hadn't been married but a few years, but she'd come to know him well enough.

"Hold up there, baby." Eli wrapped an arm around her and drew her up short. "I can see your feathers are all ruffled, but there's nothing to be upset about."

She tried not to wrestle away from him, but she had things to do and wanted to be about them. "I'm not a chicken, Eli."

"What do you mean? Oh, the feathers! Hmmm, how about I liken you to a peacock then, because you strutted outta that kitchen like one, in that eye-catching dress you're wearing. Red is your color." He winked at her.

"Actually, it's burgundy, and a peacock's plumage is closer to jade." Perhaps if she wasn't the "brains of the outfit," his words would have achieved their desired effect, but his flirtation only served to rile Glory more. For the life of her, she couldn't see why the opposite sex thought compliments smoothed the way and made everything better. Such flattery only made men slippery and hard to pin down, like trying to hold vegetable oil in her hand.

"I've got things to be doing, Eli Pryor. Your cousin's son is probably counting the number of robins bopping on the grass out front, and the store is opening in less than"—she angled her wrist—"twenty-five minutes." She stuffed her hands in her pockets and waited for him to say whatever it was he needed to.

Eli pursed his lips. "How about we talk while we work?"

"We?" But she didn't wait for him to explain. If he'd said Glory had caught him sneaking an extra scoop of sugar for his morning coffee, she would've brushed it off. This was something else, this avoidance. And she didn't like it one bit. Neither did she appreciate his shoes practically catching on her heels, bare in her flip-flops, as she flapped her way to the front of the store. As much as she tried to ignore him, she couldn't, when he picked up one end of a chair she could—and usually did—lift on her own.

"Why are *we* doing a job I can manage by myself?" Glory glared at him as he backed out the door and duckwalked backwards to the spot where she arranged seating on Fridays. She smiled and nodded at Noemie Pearline, arriving at the jewelry store next to By the Book much later than normal, then spared the sky a glance. Voluminous, dark-gray clouds scudded across the northern horizon and indeed threatened rain as well as downtown shoppers. Grateful their front door and the windows Jason was cleaning were set deep beneath the overhang, she hoped for the best and returned for another chair.

"Because I wanted to talk without slowing you down." Eli spoke quietly, barely making himself heard over the jangling of the bell.

"Well, you are slowing me down." Glory picked up another seat and he held up the other end. This time, she scooted backwards out the door to place the chair catty-cornered to the first. "What is it?"

"If you slow down a minute, I can tell you." He huffed, obviously working to keep up with her brisk pace.

Glory sped up. She had a feeling she wouldn't want to hear what he had to say. "Eli—"

He caught her by the elbow and forced her to stand still. "We have an appointment today with a realtor." His announcement gathered steam and tumbled out of his mouth.

Her "What?" was more a reaction to what she'd clearly heard him say, though his words had landed all smushed together. Glory froze, bent over the small chalkboard.

Eli clamped his lips together.

She straightened so she could stare him down, her long legs nearly making them eye to eye. "Now, why would you go and do a thing like that? And is this what you were talking about with Ophelia when I caught you together in the kitchen?"

"Did you say 'caught'? Together? You didn't catch me at anything, Glory Pryor." Now, he was the one in a dander. "I was about to tell her about the appointment because I didn't want her to be surprised."

"You mean, the way your wife is feeling right now—surprised. Gobsmacked. Eli, we agreed we wouldn't tell anyone what we've been thinking about. *Thinking* about, not doing. And here you are making appointments and telling Ophelia. Yes, I caught you, doing the very thing we agreed you wouldn't do." Frustrated with him and with herself, Glory grabbed a fat piece of white chalk. She yanked the board by one of its sides, stomped out the front door, and set it down with a firmness that garnered Jason's attention.

"Don't worry about me," she snapped at the young man and wrote *Friday Feast* in large cursive and underneath that, *Ham-and-Cheddar Scones* in block letters.

Jason went back to spritzing window cleaner, mindless of the wind starting to pick up and casting the spray in every direction but at the glass.

Eli was by her side in a moment, wincing as he knelt. "Glory, we have to know what we're considering. Get a complete picture. If I left it up to you, you'd never set up a meeting, and we'd never see what we're working with. How are we supposed to plan a move if we don't talk to a realtor about this place?"

How indeed? When Eli had broached the idea of relocating before they got married, she'd nodded. At the time, anything had felt possible, even something as impossible and otherworldly as selling By the Book. Glory never thought she'd marry, and suddenly, she could see herself at the altar, holding a bouquet of lavender clematis and trailing honeysuckle vines. Marrying Eli was exactly what she wanted to do. The only thing she wanted to do. She would have agreed to buy waterfront property on the moon if it meant she would wear Eli's ring for the rest of her life.

Yet, Eli had wanted other things—not instead of her, but along with her. A widower of ten years at the time, he'd come to town to see the woman he once knew as Glory Gibson, his former elementary school classmate, on a lark; he was on his way to meet some of his business partners in Nashville, Tennessee. It had taken some hunting to find her, but once they'd rekindled their friendship and invested in a couple years of courtship, their reunion had led to their union. From the start, he'd been clear about his hopes and goals, though he'd stumbled through laying out his life's plans the night he proposed to her.

The two of them had squeezed into a set of swings at the park, located a stone's throw from the Baptist church that anchored one end of downtown Gilmore. Their arms were extended, their fingers intertwined, as they swayed slowly, back and forth, back and forth, to the chirp of the crickets and the occasional rumble of a passing car.

With her free hand, Glory fanned away mosquitos and the image of the newer mounds interspersed amid the crumbling headstones. "Interesting, isn't it—the juxtaposition of the children's playground with the church and its adjacent graveyard?"

"Glo-Glory," Eli choked out.

"What is it? Are you alright, de-ah?" She'd gripped his fingers and leaned forward in alarm, worried something terrible had happened that would transport him from the swing to the grave in one horrible, yet well-deserved, twist of fate.

"Um-hmm, yes. Glory . . . ." Eli had gulped, as if swallowing a glassful of water. "I love you. I know I always have, even if I forgot for a few decades and married somebody else."

Glory had started to laugh, but he shushed her with a brusque shake of his head, the moonlight behind him casting his face in shadow.

"I know you've made a life in the bookstore, but I think we have an even bigger life ahead. Together, if we're together. Um, Glory, we . . . *you* pour yourself into the store, and I want to help. And not only there but beyond it. To help you see there's more than those books. Because you're you, by being you. I want to show you there're people to love and who'd be blessed by your attention, something that has taken me most of my life to learn. People—*family*—who'd return that attention and love. What your books can't do. What my business didn't do."

For a moment, she'd tripped over the word *blessed*, one of those churchy terms her parents brandished like a huge flag over the work they did for the community. Rivers of sacrifice flowed her way, but somehow, they became rivulets when it came to her older brother, Davis, if not diverted altogether. He'd not been too blessed by the kind of attention his parents gave him while he was growing up.

Eli had tugged on her fingers, making her swing jiggle in his direction and away from her distant memories. "Glory, do I make sense? You're quiet."

"Well, you were talking, Eli, and I was listening. You shushed me, remember?" She used her feet to still her seat. "You make plenty of sense."

"Good, good." He slid off the wood slat suspended above the ground and stood in front of her, moving a bit stiffly after their hour in the swing.

In that moment, Glory knew what he was about to do—what she'd been hoping he'd do in her heart of hearts—and her breath caught. She didn't bother whisking away the insects that continued to assault her bare shoulders and arms and the tops of her feet her sundress didn't cover.

And sure enough, Eli grasped the chain that hooked her seat to the overhead steel beam and used it to help him sink inch by inch to one knee onto the hard-packed dirt. Suddenly, he seemed more sure of himself than he had a few moments before, when he was stumbling over his words; he returned to the confident version of himself who strode into her store, "looking for the first grader who stole my pencil case fifty-something years ago."

He covered their interlocked fingers with his own hand. "I told you how I wanted to find you and see if I was right: that you really were and are my first and one true love. The one that got away. It took some doing, but I finally did, even though it seemed like you had purposely moved underground, like a mole."

"Eli . . ." Glory's protest chugged to a halt and petered out, for she had indeed burrowed as deeply as she could without disappearing altogether. She operated her business with the help of the store manager, refrained from using social media, and rarely communicated with anyone from her hometown or college. His finding her had taken a lot of digging, something she hoped no one else would bother to do. With her parents dead and her brother good as dead to her, this man was the only person who still cared she existed.

Eli placed a quieting finger across her lips. He obviously had more pressing things on his mind besides Glory's undercover life.

She forced herself to still.

"We've also talked about my playboy lifestyle in the years between losing you and my first marriage, about the daughter I didn't know I'd fathered until a month ago. I promised myself that if I ever got the opportunity, I would be present for her in a way I never had the chance to be when I was younger, when I was married, after my wife died, and even now."

Glory caressed his rough, unshaven cheek with her knuckles. "But that's not your fault, Eli. You didn't know she existed until recently, and you have no idea who or where she is. *If* she is."

"It is my fault, Glory. I should've been more responsible at the time. My grandma taught me better. I made those choices, and if I'd been the man I should've been, it wouldn't have happened. And if it did, that young woman would've been able to trust me enough to tell me I had a child." Emotion choked his voice.

The man she'd come to know was so much better than the man he thought he used to be, and Glory hoped to show she accepted him as he was. How she ached to tell him to stop punishing himself, to forgive himself. If only she wouldn't sound hypocritical to her own ears.

That day on the swing set, Eli had cleared his throat and told her, "The situation has kept me from getting closer to you, and you from getting closer to me. But I don't think that promise has to supersede the one I want to make to you, Glory. To love you and cherish you all my days. To put you first. If you're prepared to promise me the same, to put me first—before anyone or anything else . . ."

Glory had nodded before he could finish his statement, believing that if it came to it, she'd follow Eli to Timbuktu or Tennessee, to live closer to the family who he believed so needed her motherly attention. The only thing that would keep her from him was the truth.

He'd slipped an emerald the size of her fingernail over her left knuckle, and it nestled into place like it had always belonged there.

Now, Glory shook off that memory and wrote *2 for $5* on the chalkboard. When she straightened, she twisted her wedding ring and stared at Eli, knowing she belonged in By the Book—with him—despite those wild ideas she'd pledged she'd consider.

"You're always talking about not having family. How Dude and these books were the only kinfolk you had until I came along." Eli continued his pursuit.

"Don't forget Ophelia and her twins. What about them?" She threw out the line and hoped he would take the bait.

"You've said yourself they're not my real cousins." Looking

chagrined, he lifted his chin at Jason in a belated greeting, who was starting at the other end of windows and bobbing his head to an indiscernible beat. "You're always teasing me about our dotted family line."

A horn blared and someone shouted, "Watch out there, now!"

Glory recognized Mr. Jackson's familiar manner of calling hello to Eli in the way that older men tended to do. Rolling her eyes, she swished back into the store, her shoes clapping against the bottoms of her feet, wishing she'd stuffed cotton in that bell over the door.

He'd moved aside to let her pass but quickly followed her. "Glory, I've learned more about my family, about *our* family—a daughter and possibly a grandchild. The rumors now have flesh and blood on them."

"Is that why you're worked up enough to call realtors? You've heard from your daughter?"

"I'm not worked up; I'm excited. Hopeful. I haven't heard from her; I don't even know her name or what she looks like. But now I know she's real. One of my old fraternity brothers confirmed that my former girlfriend was pregnant when I left town and that they'd heard she had a daughter. *My* daughter. Once I confirm the truth, I want us to be ready to go, free from the responsibilities here so we can stay away as long as we want. As long as it takes. It would kill me if I didn't do everything I could to right my wrongs."

"You're always so dramatic, Eli." To her ears, the words she often said sounded like a groan. She knew what it was like to have family somewhere and not be able to see them. The difference was, his was alive and well, and he was running after them; she was running from a memory.

"It's not drama, Glory. I dropped my life into your life—"

"I *welcomed* you into my life."

"Your life . . . my life. What about *our* life? Moving forward on a brand-new path that we carve together?"

"Brand new with a daughter that's forty years old, you mean," she ground out. Glory grabbed one of the two hip-high wheeled carts right inside the front door. On it, she'd stacked old periodicals beside a jar of pens, pencils, markers, and scissors under a sign taped to the rack that read *Take One/Use One*. It was hard for her to get rid of any type of literary material, and she invited potential guests to do a crossword, cut out a recipe, or simply sit a spell and enjoy the entire downtown area. Recycling was probably ingrained in her blood by her parents and folks from their generation who'd taught her to use old newspapers to clean glass. *Waste not, want not* wasn't a Bible verse, but her parents repeated it almost as often as *Do unto others*.

"Don't brush me off." Eli pressed his back against the door, allowing her to step unhindered toward the sidewalk.

Glory halted on the threshold but didn't look at him. "I'm not dismissing you. But this business about dying and killing, it's too much." She pushed the cart outside between the chairs she and her husband had already set up and quick-stepped inside to retrieve the second cart. It held rows of softcovers—familiar, backlisted titles to entice potential readers inside to look for new releases and later editions.

"What business?" Again, he flattened himself against the door.

Glory had to keep moving. That was how she'd survived all these years—by doing. She angled the cart to the right side, opposite the small seating area, so people wouldn't confuse the books they could scribble in with the ones they couldn't. Finished with all her opening tasks she checked on Jason, who'd wrapped up the window cleaning. *At last! That child, he would take an hour to prepare instant grits.*

After surveying her arrangements and the gathering clouds, Glory flipped the sign hanging on the door to *Open* and raised the shade covering the glass. Leaning around Eli, she cupped a hand around her mouth to issue a last command to her employee. "Run a moist cloth over the door because this wood is dusty from all the road work." She pointed toward the end of the street where a crew beat a steady rat-a-tat-a-tat-a-tat. By her calculations, they wouldn't be working much longer if Mother Nature had her way, but at least her door would get cleaned. "Remember: moist, not wet. Then see if your mama needs help in the kitchen."

"Would you stop and listen?" The pane rattled when Eli closed the door firmly; the clanging of the bell above him sounded as angry as he.

Glory finally stopped moving by the *Alice's Adventures in Wonderland* display in the entry and ran a hand through her hair, making her normally well-tended style stand on end. It wasn't that she was ignoring her husband; she had to keep the train chugging along until it had reached its end. *But you can't outrace the guilt, Glory. You know you're letting Eli down, too.* "Okay. I'm listening."

He huffed, this time with frustration. "You told me before we got married you were willing to go to the ends of the earth for us to be together."

"I wasn't lying; however, I didn't believe I'd have to. That you'd make me. Because *you* said you knew how important By the Book is to me. What about you? Were *you* lying?"

"I was telling the truth then, and I'm telling the truth now. It was decades before I learned I may have a child out there somewhere and a couple years more to accept I have a daughter, and I'm ready to hand out pink cigars, Glory. Forty-year-old pink cigars. I don't care that she was raised by another man because I intend to keep that promise I made before I ever saw you again. I laid that all on the table in the months leading up to my proposal, and you told me you understood.

"Yet, here we are still talking about this like you've never heard it before. You're running around, moving furniture, selling books, planning signings and events like not a thing's changed. Probably because nothing much has in your mind; this is how you intend to go on in perpetuity. But we have a grown baby and a grandbaby, and you talk more in one night about a stranger's boy named Bennett than you have about your own."

The front door rattled and opened, and Jason lurched through with the cleaner and a huge ball of crumpled newspaper. "It's starting to rain, Mrs. P., so I didn't bother with the door. Do you want me to bring in those displays?"

Seeing the muscles in Eli's jaw clench and unclench, she shook her head. "We'll see to it, Jason. Maybe we'll get by with a little sprinkle this time."

Thunder shook the Tudor, and the overhead lights blinked.

"On second thought, bring in the carts with the books. Leave the chairs and the chalkboard; we can wipe those down." She winced when lightning lit the sky. "You'd best hurry."

Glory waited until the young man had set down his armload and opened the door yet again before turning a weary gaze on Eli. "Now. What were we saying?"

He cupped her elbow and marched her deeper into the store, not stopping until they'd reached the tall pocket doors that enclosed Glory's happy place. There, it was unlikely they would be disturbed, but he lowered his voice. "That first time I saw you in this store and we had lunch and we talked for hours . . . At the end of the day, when I had to leave, I told you I was coming back. You believed me, didn't you?"

"Yes." Glory sounded as quiet as her husband, as stricken, despite the hopeful images his words conjured.

"I came back, stayed a while, and then I had to leave. But I told you I'd return once I sold my business. And that's exactly what I did, didn't I? Because the man standing before you is a changed man, and he keeps his word—which is part of the reason you love me. I know that. I cherish that. And it's important to me to keep my promise to you . . . and to them, too, despite the fact they've never heard it. But do you want to know what's really killing me?"

Glory nodded slowly, moved beyond speech by his passion.

Eli clasped both her hands in both of his against his chest, over his heart. "I know you love this store. All these books. Your customers."

Guests. She couldn't refrain from correcting him in her mind. *This is my home, and these people are more my guests than my customers. They're my family.*

Eli continued his list. "Dude. Mallory. Jason. Ophelia, who'll grow on you in time—more than likely because she's associated with this place here. Hmmpf, maybe that's why you love me as much as you say you do, because I agreed to move upstairs and so became a living, breathing part of this legacy of yours. But what kills me is that you're willing to give up everything. *Everything*, Glory. For this."

Her husband relaxed his grip to aim a finger toward the third floor, then forward toward the café area, the bookshelves, and at the room behind them. "And this. And that. And those. And here. You're willing to give up *us*, as long as it took for there to be an *us*, and your*self*. You're not By the Book, contrary to what you may think. I'm not really asking you to sell your home and exchange your dream for mine. I want us to live our dream, the one we make together. Your unwillingness to do that is what's killing me. But I'll fight like . . . like . . ." Eli seemed to search the room to see if the word he needed was hiding under the sofa or the piano.

"Let's just say I'll fight with everything in me to make sure your muleheadedness and your fear don't kill our marriage first. Because that's what I think it boils down to: fear. Fear of leaving what you can see, know, and trust. Fear of believing in something and someone that isn't you or what you built." Obviously done, he let go and took a step away from her, but then turned back to lean closer and kiss her cheek.

Glory grasped his fingertips at the last moment and halted his exodus.

Eli tugged at his hand to free it. "Yes, I'm calling the realtor to cancel the appointment. I'm sorry, you're right: I jumped the gun. I was excited, but I should have asked. Let me reassure you that I'd only planned to tell Ophelia we had a meeting at five thirty so she could keep an eye on things while we were occupied. I wouldn't have broken your trust."

She clung to him, forcing herself to step over her brother's shadow wedged between them. "No, Eli. Wait. We came up with our own vows five years ago, and neither one of us said anything about *'til the bookstore us do part*. But we did end them with *'til death do us part*. I didn't simply repeat what I'd heard in other weddings. I meant every last word.

"You're not the one who should apologize. I am. And I do . . . apologize, I mean." She wrapped her arms around his neck, and gratitude flooded through her when she felt her ribs squeezed in his tight embrace. Gratitude and trepidation. Glory tilted her face a little so she could look him in the eyes. "Give me until the festival. After that, we'll make all the plans we need."

Then she pulled him into her special room. There, they had the best view of the rain as it pelted the windows for the next hour. She wondered where Dude would find shelter.

7

Adelle did a do-si-do with Bennett on the sidewalk, leading him by the hand to her right side to insulate him from the traffic on Springs Church Road. She wouldn't risk losing him, too.

He stumbled. "Aw, man! You made me step on a crack."

She put her hand to her back and moaned.

Bennett crowed over her pretend pain. "How's your back, Mommy? Did I break it?"

Her tongue lolled out the right corner of her mouth. "I think I'll make it." To prove it, Adelle swung him high over the next break in the sidewalk.

The boy landed with a chortle. "Whoa-a-a-a!"

They'd both itched to escape their rental house. Friday morning's torrent marked the first of a weekend's worth of rain-soaked days, and she'd viewed the inclement weather as an opportunity to attack the remaining boxes the movers had stacked in the garage and in Bennett's closet. The only real break they took from unpacking was attending a nearby Sunday school and enjoying a hearty, Southern-style brunch after. Adelle determined to get things in order—the house, their life and schedule, and most importantly, her next steps.

Hence that Monday morning's excursion to historic downtown Gilmore. That was how she'd described it to Bennett when she'd helped him choose an outfit: his favorite cargo shorts with pockets for his cars, the red T-shirt with the faded blue trim, and his knee-high, yellow rain boots. She'd donned a less conspicuous pair of gray linen cropped pants, a pale pink blouse, and black canvas sandals. The more professional the better. When she'd checked herself in the mirror she'd murmured, "No striped caftans for me."

The sun and warmth had returned, but the humidity had retreated along with the storm. Adelle made the most of the day and parked their SUV by the church at the top of the street and walked the five wide, tree-lined blocks to By the Book. "This way, we can get the wiggles out and see what there is to see," she explained to Bennett. In Dollars to Donuts, the local coffee shop run out of a 1920s bungalow, she nursed a latte and he dribbled his hot chocolate on the table while they compared the kinds of bear claws—the ones people ate and the ones on the animals' paws. They talked about black holes versus donut holes as they walked through the secondhand store, and Adelle elucidated all the reasons he didn't need yet another red Radio Flyer wagon, particularly one with a flat front tire that cost as much as a new version.

"Besides, we brought yours with us when we came to Gilmore." Adelle swung their clasped hands forwards and backwards in a wide arc when they resumed their walk past old houses, up-to-date offices, and storefronts. "It's in the garage back at our rental house."

He poked out his lips. "I want another one."

Adelle, sapped from the debate and on the verge of chastising him, planted her feet in front of Rockin' Robin, a music store near the corner of the second block. When he kicked at an empty soda can, she gripped the baseball cap covering his head and turned his noggin toward the rows of records inside, visible through the clear double window of the brick building painted a stark shade of white. "Do you know what those are?"

Bennett twisted out of her hold and crossed his arms, apparently refusing to be mollified. "You said we're not supposed to point."

"Those are called records, and they're things. It's okay because I've taught you not to point at people. I also said you should mind your attitude, particularly when you're talking to me. Uncross those arms."

He sighed and obeyed, albeit slowly. "Yes, ma'am."

Adelle eyed him for a moment then extended some grace, what her husband had done as naturally as he breathed, and what she struggled to give—and accept. She balanced her hands on her knees to meet Bennett on his level and put her mouth next to his ear. "How about I take you for a ride in that wagon later, if the weather holds out? Let's pray the afternoon forecast is wrong and ask God to turn those white puffs I see on the horizon into fair-weather clouds."

He squinted at the sky. "You mean, cumulus clouds?"

"Yes, smarty-pants. I see all that reading is paying off." While she didn't believe in bribing a child to behave, she, too, was trying and failing to adjust to all the upheaval. Knowing what to leave behind and what to carry with her, what to leave buried and what to resurrect. It had to be harder for a four-year-old who had no idea what his mommy's plans were. If she had her way and the Lord had His, they'd be settled soon enough.

There you go again, that not-so-little voice chided. *Making your will God's will, instead of the other way around.*

Shrugging off the admonition, she puckered up and leaned in, and Bennett nodded and kissed her back. After deciding to forego the music store, he shuffled rather than bounced along beside her.

As they continued on their way, Adelle noticed an older man and his dog approaching from their left, on the side nearer the street. She edged right, closer to her son, to allow the pair more room to pass.

Bennett tugged on her arm and pointed with his free hand. "Mommy, that dog is smiling!"

He sure looks like he is! Adelle thought, pushing down his offending finger. "Shush, Ben-Ben. Remember, that's not polite." She nodded at the gentleman as an apology and in greeting.

"But I'm pointing at some*thing*, not some*one*," the child piped up. "I'm talking about the dog!"

"Bennett—"

"I think he smiles, too." Drawing beside Adelle, the man stopped and winked. "Would the little man like to say hello to Oscar?"

"Uh, well . . ." Adelle tended to keep herself to herself, as her daddy used to say, and she'd become even more reticent since her husband died. After all, Ben was the person she most liked to talk to. The stranger's friendliness, while not exactly off-putting, caught her off guard.

"Can I? Can I?" Bennett danced close to the dog.

Its tail wagged furiously, as if answering, "Yes, yes!"

Ignoring her natural inclination to correct her son's grammar, Adelle freed his hand but hovered while he took a knee beside Oscar. She rubbed her shoulder—it felt like Bennett had tried to yank her arm from its socket in his eagerness—but couldn't resist grinning back at both the dog and the child. Out of something else to say, she offered, "He's a cutie."

"My best friend. Oscar. All I have left since I lost my wife. She loved him, too." The man spoke quietly, sounding like he was making a personal observation rather than polite conversation with Adelle.

Not wanting to intrude on his private pain, she nodded. She understood. In the silence, Adelle retreated to her own thoughts, did her own kind of missing and mourning, what she hadn't planned or expected to do on their expedition to the downtown area, with the sun warming the middle of her back and glinting off the slowly disappearing puddles. But she'd come to learn that every day was a good day for weeping.

"My name is Charles, Charles Graves." The man extended the hand that wasn't wrapped around the red strap connected to Oscar.

"I'm Adelle. Nice to meet you, Mr. Graves. Oscar." Snapped out of her reverie, she squeezed his calloused palm in a brief hello. Her daddy had taught her well about respecting her elders. There was no way she'd call—*Is he seventy or eighty? Hard to tell*—by his given name.

"And who is this fine young man who looks like he wants to take my Yorkie home with him?" Mr. Graves's silky, silver mustache twitched. He tucked his hand into the pocket of his striped slacks.

"My son. Bennett." Adelle wasn't sure whether it was his sense of humor or his own grief that made her feel comfortable enough to share their names, what she typically wouldn't do so readily. The years behind her had taught her to look askance at the years ahead of her, as well as the people they brought with them. She scratched the nape of her neck under the loose French braid trailing across her shoulder. "Actually, I thought he was afraid of dogs. Your best friend must be very special."

The two watched Bennett stroke the dog's bluish-brown head and back and encourage it to sit by gently pushing down on its hindquarters. As kind as the older man seemed to be, passersby seemed to be similarly minded, for they silently edged around the small group blocking much of the sidewalk. Enthralled, Adelle couldn't find the wherewithal to hurry the child out of the way of the uncomplaining pedestrian traffic.

"Oh, nobody's afraid of Oscar. He makes friends everywhere he goes." Mr. Graves waved a hand in the direction the mother and son were traveling. "Glory down the way has special cookies baked for him. We look forward to those on the weekends, don't we, boy?"

Like sudden cloud cover on a clear day, his words cast a shadow over their pleasant exchange and broke the spell. Adelle's lips flattened, and so did the tone of her voice. "Well, we should get going. It was nice to meet you. Bennett, tell Mr. Graves *thank you*, and let him be on his way."

At first, the child continued to pet Oscar, whose ears turned like miniature satellite dishes, taking in the nine-inch-high world around him.

"Bennett." And that was all she said. All she had to say. Feeling slightly guilty that she'd rained on the child's sunny parade, she watched him spring to his feet.

"Thank you, Mr. Graves." He elongated each syllable.

After throwing a quizzical, yet respectful, look her way, the man nodded at Bennett and patted him comfortingly on his head. Mr. Graves, too, seemed to understand words unspoken, or at least accept them. A tug on the leash garnered the attention of his four-legged buddy, and man and dog were on their way without another word.

She and Bennett trooped along quietly, both their steps now dragging. Around them, cars and people passed each other on both sides of the two-lane road. Adelle tried to quell the swell of emotion that threatened to overwhelm her whenever she heard mention of Eli and Glory Pryor. What would she do when she faced them again?

"Why are you carrying Daddy's backpack, Mommy?"

Trust Mr. Eagle Eyes to notice. I almost made it to By the Book! "Just something I wanted to show Mrs. Pryor." Adelle had to force herself to say the name evenly, without an edge to the words.

"What is it?" He stretched for the bag's old-fashioned, burnished bronze buckle. The child couldn't go a day without asking a thousand questions. His curiosity seemed to multiply without his daddy to run interference.

"I need to . . . ask her help with something. You have the chops to be a reporter like your daddy!" She swung around out of his reach. "Let's hold up and wait for the light, Ben-Ben. We'll stay here until we can cross the intersection safely."

"Ooh, ooh! Can I read *Alice in Wonderland* again?" On the move once more, but with extra pep in his step, Bennett veered out of the direct path they were traveling across the street to jump into a large puddle with both feet, making the most out of his bright-yellow boots.

A woman headed in the opposite direction shot the mother-and-son duo a none-too-happy look and brushed off her wet pants.

Adelle flashed her an apologetic smile but was relieved she'd distracted him. "Be more careful, Bennett. As far as *Alice's Adventures in Wonderland*, I don't know. Mrs. Pryor might not let us in, *if* she's there. By the Book is closed today, based on the hours posted on her door. My plan is to see her as a visitor instead of as a customer."

Feeling like she was coming on like a nimbostratus cloud, full of continuous rain, she adopted a more hopeful outlook. "We'll see if Mrs. Pryor still has it displayed, but let's find out whether she sells something besides fiction, maybe check out her selection of biographies." These days, Adelle preferred truth in all aspects of her life.

He frowned, but then his eyes widened, and his countenance changed.

Adelle followed his eyes and spotted the huge circle of muddy water between the sidewalk and the street, nearly obscuring one of the areas marked for parallel parking. Before she could stop him, he yanked his hand from hers and dashed toward the space, just as a car whipped off the road to park in it. "Bennett!"

From out of nowhere, two sturdy hands snatched the child back and lifted him onto the concrete.

Father,
I'm thirsty. Can I get me a drink?
No, child, not from the kitchen sink.
Why pull up a chair and sip from there
when I know where there's water
flowing from an unhidden place?
It satisfies and cools, puddles and pools
and it won't leave a trace
of that thirst you first spoke of, my love.

Here. See. Walk with me to the base of yon tree.
Dip your cup in the inmost part.
There in the heart, daughter—

"Oh! Here you are. You said you'd be working in the other room with the young adult books. What's that you're reading?"

Her heart thumping against her rib cage, Glory casually refolded the page along an old crease and slipped it into the back of the book in her hand. She picked up her pen and fiddled with its cap to give her trembling fingers something to do. Immersed in thought, she'd not heard the wide oak treads announce his entrance. "Just thinking."

Eli's thick eyebrows conferred with each other. "Hmmm. I've heard of *Just Mercy* but not something entitled *Just Thinking*. Must be a one-page new release." He smoothed her hair from her forehead and pressed his lips to it. "I thought you were reorganizing the shelves."

She closed her eyes and enjoyed the weight of his hand, the

tenderness of his touch. Treasured the latitude and the forgiveness they conveyed. Glory hadn't intended to be disingenuous when she'd announced that she had to work on the stacks, but really, she needed to retreat to them, to be alone with her babies. If Eli had his way, she wouldn't be able to do that much longer, to lose herself in these areas in the quiet of the day, to trail her hands along the spines of her beloved friends and family. After ambling through the rooms, she'd found herself in one of the bell-shaped swivel chairs positioned at the end of a row, riffling through pages that were on the one hand comforting and familiar, and on the other painful and condemning.

Dropping her pen, Glory raised her hand and took his, squeezing it gratefully, and offered an excuse that was close kin to the truth. "I planned to reorganize, but once I got here, I started thinking about the festival . . . and all that comes with it."

"Ohhhh. The *festival*." Obviously, he inferred her meaning: the festival and his desire to move shortly after. He paused a beat before walking to the matching leather seat. "I came up to get your help, but I can see you need me more. Okay if I join you here for a second?"

She nodded, appreciating his respect for her alone time. Glory knew Eli was more the extrovert to her introvert, that companionship and conversations fed him like the sunlight and rain fed her favorite creamy-white gardenias in Gilmore's public gardens. Though the rewards were worth it, he required lots of attention.

"May I ask what you're thinking about exactly?" Eli's voice seemed to tiptoe through the dust motes dancing in the sunray over his shoulder.

"Sure, you can ask, but I don't think I'll tell you." Glory's arched brow dared him to ask again. She knew he recognized her need to reconnoiter after a day full of interaction and to-dos. And now, even more so, when he wanted to pull her away from all she held dear. Glory crossed a covered leg, her knees invisible under the silky material. It was Eli's favorite, this loose dress. He'd bought the muumuu on their Hawaiian-island honeymoon. Wearing it today was her own way of secretly telling him, *I love you, and I forgive you for breaking my heart.*

Eli took up the dare by leaning over and grabbing an exposed toe. He dragged a finger down the middle of her sole.

"Uncle!" she giggled. She had none to speak of, but she called out to the nameless, faceless man for mercy anyway.

"Shhhh! We have a guest downstairs," he whispered.

"A guest! But it's Monday."

He pressed a finger to his lips. "This is a special circumstance. Didn't you hear the commotion?"

"Then what are you doing up here? Wait—now I realize you mentioned a 'situation' before you got distracted." She peeked around the long row of shelves. They tried not to leave folks completely unattended, while still giving them some breathing room to explore the premises.

"Yes, the situation . . . what led me upstairs. She was asking questions I couldn't answer. But then I saw you looking all captivating and whatnot, and I forgot myself."

Glory sat up straight and slid her feet back into her shoes, all business now. Rising, she clipped the pen to her neckline and sidled past the shelves of classics toward the door leading to the landing. Each of the four rooms on the second floor held different genres: old and new classics and historical fiction; contemporary, literary fiction, and what the industry called "upmarket"—a blend of the two; novels geared toward young adults and teens; and a fancifully decorated room for children's books that had squishy chairs, plush rugs, a small stage, and puppets. The downstairs shelves held a mixture of genres and ages, some sections mirroring what readers could find on the second floor.

She stopped with one hand on the rail, ready to descend, and turned to Eli, so close behind her she could smell his minty breath. Expecting him to reel off some author's name or title he was less familiar with, she asked offhandedly, "What kinds of questions?"

"Something about a Bible."

Glory nearly tumbled down the stairs. "Bible? You know we don't carry Bibles, Eli. What exactly was the question? The closest thing to Bibles By the Book carries are the novels written by C. S. Lewis."

"Glory, honeybun, I know all that. You're constantly having to explain that we don't carry much besides fiction. The Bible isn't the situation. Surely you heard all the commotion a few minutes ago!"

Now he really had her attention. She pulled him into the closest room to their left. The butterflies Jason had hung for summer fluttered from the ceiling. "I didn't hear a sound coming from downstairs through these thick walls and the woodwork." *It must have been that poem.*

"Well, I was unpacking books in the stockroom, and I heard banging on the front door. I walked up front, and Ophelia was standing beside Dude—"

"*Dude!* This story is growing stranger and stranger by the telling of it. He's always ignored my invitations to come inside." Glory knew that was more than fine with Eli because he wasn't as comfortable with the relationship, such as it was.

"Yes. Dude. There he stands with his arms around some little boy who's crying. And his mother—the little boy's mother—is beside him, wild-eyed, wearing one sandal and totin' the other."

Glory pressed a hand to her chest. While she didn't know Dude from Adam, she would never suspect him of harming anyone other than himself with his daily poison. He wasn't her brother. And he wasn't her.

"You say Dude held a child. And the woman—"

Eli closed in and grasped the fingers twisting the fabric of her dress. "Baby, stop thinking the worst. From what I hear, the boy dashed toward the street to hop in some rainwater, and Dude grabbed him in time to keep him from gettin' run over."

"What! Where is Dude now? Where are . . . I mean, I can't believe you . . . I . . . Why did it take somebody asking about a Bible for you to come get me?" Glory made for the door.

He pulled her back inside, near the life-size dollhouse it had taken them weeks to construct. "Shhh, Glory. The woman with the child, she's who asked about a Bible. While I settled folks down, Dude took a shortcut home through the kitchen, and Ophelia helped the other two compose themselves with a drink and a snack in the café. That mama is a prickly one, let me tell you. I figured you wouldn't mind offering them our kouign-amanns or croissants, soften her up a bit."

Glory shook her head, wishing this man of hers would hurry it on.

"I was on my way to get you when the mama stopped me to ask about Bibles. When I explained that we specialize in fiction, she looked like she would have a cow. A big ol' jersey cow with white splotches, right there. I told her to eat something, and I'd find you. And here I am."

"And here you are, tickling my feet, chattin' me up like we're having a tea party. *Then* you tell me about this! Is there anything else, Eli Pryor?"

"Not as far as I know." Her husband shrugged and held out an arm to usher her out. "After you, Mrs. Pryor."

"Messing up my weekend," she fussed, gathering her dress and dashing to the stairs, the vibrant flora in the material shimmering. As she neared the café, she heard Ophelia cooing over what must be the child Eli had told her about. Glory had never heard the baker speak that gently in all the time she had worked at By the Book.

"I hear them coming now. An ant can't crawl down those stairs without us hearing it. Glory, Eli, about time!" the baker boomed.

Glory rounded the corner through the last display, and there, sitting in two of the stools at the counter, sat a mud-splattered, bloody-kneed, and tear-stained Adelle and Bennett, munching on Ophelia's pastries.

8

WHEN ADELLE SPOTTED MRS. PRYOR in her periphery, she had to choke down the delicate dough, now a rock in a throat gone dry. She tried to swivel imperceptibly toward the counter and pretend not to see the owner of By the Book, but she cocked an ear toward the woman as she approached them. Those gaudy bracelets of hers were more a giveaway than the telltale sounds of footsteps.

"Need more water?" The employee wearing the striped apron lifted the pitcher and filled Adelle's empty glass from her spot behind the counter.

Bennett drained his hard plastic cup and slapped it down on the concrete. "Mine, too?"

"May I have more please?" Adelle laid her hand on his arm and corrected him gently. She folded her napkin to cover the crumbs and wiped her mouth.

"Always on motherhood duty, even after all the excitement of this *situation*." The bookseller tsked and exchanged a glance with the gentleman who'd helped Adelle and Bennett when they'd entered the store, all in a tizzy.

Adelle had to move aside when the woman positioned herself between her and her son and stretched an arm along the back of his seat.

"And you, young man! Did you see a white rabbit and follow it, like Alice?"

Bennett's face lit up. "Oooh, ooh, can I—" He peeked around at his mother. "I mean, *may* I read the book again?"

Before Mrs. Pryor could respond, Adelle spun in her son's direction, and her outstretched legs made the older woman take a step back. "We talked about that outside, Bennett. Just because you ran out in front of the car doesn't change my mind about looking for biographies first. Also, if she's right about that book leading you into the street, that's the *last* thing I want you to read." Spying the couple sharing another side-eyed glance, she concluded, *He must be the lucky Mr. Pryor.*

"We don't carry much in the way of biographies, Mrs. Simonette, unless you're talking about biographical fiction like *Roots* by Alex Haley." The virtual stranger, smiling a little, hunched her shoulders and held up her palms, as if laying all her cards on the table.

The hair on the back of Adelle's neck tingled at this woman's feigned helplessness. "You don't carry *much in the way of truth* in this store, do you?"

Mrs. Pryor's wide eyes moved from one face to the other, as if searching for a life raft. "Excuse me?"

Adelle realized she'd overstepped when Bennett dropped his pastry and stared at her. She swallowed and brushed the wisps escaping her braid and tickling her face. "What I mean is, I told Mr. Pryor I was looking for a Bible, and you don't carry them. So, no biographies, no Bibles . . . ?"

"But we do have newspapers. Not that they tell you the truth either." The helpful employee swiped crumbs into her palm and brushed her hands together several times over a wastebasket. "Can

I get y'all anything else? I'm glad we had a few of these left from Saturday, which shocked me out of my shoes. But the Lord knew you'd be coming today."

"Too bad He didn't warn me," Mrs. Pryor grumbled.

Bennett tugged at his mother's sleeve. "May I have another queenie thing?"

The person behind the counter clopped in her thick-soled shoes toward the swinging door that guarded the kitchen from the café area. "A kouign-amann? Sure, I think there's one more left in—"

"Thank you, but no." Adelle stopped the woman in her tracks. "We should get on our way. If my little guy eats more bread and sweets, he'll never eat his dinner. Which I promise you, won't taste nearly as delicious as any of the food we've had here. I do appreciate it, Mrs. . . . ."

"*Ms.* I'm Ophelia, the baker and all-around-helper, but Ophelia will do."

Adelle stood and tucked her hands into Bennett's armpits and lifted him from the stool.

Looking disappointed yet resigned to his fate, the boy landed on the floor with a solid thump and took his mother's hand.

Mirroring the younger woman, perhaps subconsciously, Mrs. Pryor sidled to the man near her and linked her fingers with his, her eyes as narrow as her smile. "Well, before you go, I hope you consider walking with me around the store to gain a better feel for By the Book. Maybe there's another way we can help you."

To Adelle, her move toward her husband revealed her need for reinforcements, a request for backup. This sign of weakness and discomfort emboldened her. "I think I have a pretty good idea of what you're selling. What else can take the place of a Bible?"

"And I take it you're not a fan of fiction?" Mr. Pryor enfolded his wife's hand through the vee of his bent arm.

"Not much."

The bookseller's eyebrows furrowed. "May I ask why?"

Adelle's hip poked out when she shifted her weight to her left leg. She gazed into the distance as if the answer was printed on the covers of the books beyond the older couple. "I think authors use novels to work through things on the page they can't figure out for themselves."

"Ha!" Ophelia covered her mouth when all the heads swung her way. "Oops. It's kinda funny hearing someone say that in this store."

"I take it that goes for poetry, too?" Mrs. Pryor's voice was soft.

"Definitely," Adelle affirmed brusquely. "I mean, it depends on the subject matter. But you must admit, when it comes to writing fiction, it's all about plunking down the twists and turns of someone's imagination."

Mr. Pryor rubbed his jaw. "You don't encourage using your imagination?"

His question sounded curious, not condemning, and it made Adelle squirm. She didn't like how her back felt pressed against the wall and the heat of a spotlight on her face. "I have a four-year-old who's incredibly creative and . . . and . . . and fanciful and smart. But I want him to cling to truth. To know what truth is when he sees it and hears it."

She shrugged. "Anyway, we were on a walk through your cute town, and this accident happened. You can assume it rattled me, and I'm probably saying a lot more than I should and in a way I shouldn't. Again, thank you for your help. We won't take up any more of your day. You were closed for a reason."

When Adelle raised Bennett's hand, she saw him staring at her, quizzically—*He's judging me, and rightly so*—and she blinked away her guilt. Unable to bring herself to extend any gratitude to his wife, she nodded at the man at her side and then at Ophelia; it wasn't like Glory Pryor had done anything for them anyway. Adelle fought a sense of shame over her unusual behavior, but she felt so uncomfortable in the store. Since nothing that day had gone as planned, it would be better if she came back another time. Maybe they wouldn't have this audience.

"Don't forget your backpack." Ophelia briskly circled around the counter and recovered the battered Army-green bag propped on a stool. She extended it to Adelle, who slid the strap to the crook of her elbow.

The youngster shook the sack and cried, "That's right, Mommy. You said you brought Daddy's bag to show something to Mrs. Pryor!"

Her jaw dropped open, and Adelle knew that she'd been caught.

"Why don't we give your Ben-Ben more time to come to himself, poor baby. He can read his favorite book to Ophelia while we three chat. Would that be okay, Mrs. Simonette? Then you can explain why you hate fiction so much, and I'll see what you risked your lives to bring me on your walk through our cute town."

Is she laughing at me? How dare she call Bennett by my name for him! She doesn't know us like that. Adelle hid her rising temper by hunching her shoulder to scooch the strap of her backpack closer to her neck and out of sight of her son.

"Mommy? May I?" Bennett yanked on her shirt, his voice a stage whisper in the quiet room.

Adelle slowly eased her grip on him. Instead of ranting and raving as she was tempted to do, she forced her lips apart and spoke sensibly. "Sure, Bennett. But only long enough for me to tell Mr. and Mrs. Pryor a few things."

Glory worked to gather her wits about her in the time it took to retrieve the pop-up book from the entryway and return to the café.

And she made sure to take measured steps and not to hurry. For the life of her, she couldn't figure out what was going on with Adelle Simonette. The woman's son was absolutely adorable. So polite and bright. She bet he was a joy to any librarian. But his mother, she was another story altogether—one of those graphic novels with different fonts in bold and italics, and wild punctuation.

By the time Glory returned with her prized—and only—copy of *Alice's Adventures in Wonderland*, Ophelia must have overcome Adelle's objections to more treats, because both Bennett's small hands gripped a saucer full of the sticky layered pastry that her guests found so hard to spell and nearly impossible to resist. The young widow was nowhere in sight.

"Mind if we take this to your window seat?" Ophelia took the book.

Glory's eyes twinkled. "That's the perfect spot for some afternoon reading and people watching—as long as you turn the pages for him. Maybe Bennett will see Charles and Oscar. They should be headed back from the park soon."

"Oscar! Oscar!" The child hopped up and down.

She thought the child would drop his plate. "You already met them? Y'all do get around, don't you?"

"What's going on?"

Adelle's sudden reappearance made Eli jump, but Glory remained inscrutable as she straightened, her emotions a mystery even to herself. "Bennett was helping me calm down about his meeting Charlie and Oscar. I swear that dog grins at me every time he passes that winda, but Eli says he's daring me to count his teeth." She deepened her voice. "The better to bite you with, m'de-ah."

"Mommy says we shouldn't swear, *either by heaven or by earth or with any other oath.*" Eyes wide, Bennett solemnly recited the verse.

"*But let your 'Yes' be 'Yes,' and your 'No,' 'No,' lest you fall into judgment.*" Ophelia finished the quote and added, "The book of James.

Chapter five, verse twelve. It's nice to hear Scripture around here. Maybe you can recite more." She led them out.

Glory made a show of straightening the stools to mask her frustration. Though glad to see Ophelia go, she felt she was diving headfirst from the frying pan into the fire Adelle had lit. She squared her shoulders and faced them. "Well, let me take these things to the kitchen, and we can begin our official tour. Be right back, Eli."

After dropping the dishes in the large sink, she pasted on what she hoped was a pleasant expression and pushed through the door. She gestured to the shelves around the café area. "As you can see, this area is geared toward reading and eating, two of my favorite things, especially if I can do them together."

Her husband laughed. "You should see the grease prints!"

Glory slapped at his hands. "You know that's not so! I can't stand to harm a book. But unfortunately, not everybody shares my feelings on the subject. That's the reason I only put *well-loved* copies over here, things my guests can read without completely hurting my feelings."

She indicated a sign that cautioned, *Be gentle. Use a napkin, not the page.* "We also encourage them to bring their own books from home—hoping they'll buy one, too. I call them our guests, not customers. We treat folks like family."

"*Cuh, cuh!* Excuse me. Must have been a piece of croissant stuck in my throat." Adelle muffled her cough in the crook of her elbow.

"Mmm . . ." Glory murmured skeptically. "Need some water before we continue?"

The younger woman shook her head. "Please, go on."

"Well." Glancing around the store, wondering where to go on from there, *whether* to go on from there, Glory cut her eye at her husband. It was obvious that Adelle had other matters on her mind. She shuffled along beside Eli as the silence among the three mushroomed.

"How did you get started? What made you go into this business?"

They were standing in front of the front door when Glory heard the question behind her. Glory faced Adelle. "What made me open By the Book?"

"Yes, what were you doing that inspired you to open a bookstore of all things? Not a dress shop or a hair salon. Did you work in a library or—?"

"Why a dress shop?" Standing there with her arms crossed, Adelle put Glory in the mind of Bennett. "Can't women do other things? Aren't you a *reporter*?"

Adelle blinked. "Oh, about that."

The bookseller laughed, not unkindly. After all, she was in no position to throw a stone at someone else's plate-glass window. "Why did you tell me you were a reporter when that was your husband's job? Unless I have the wrong Ben Simonette. I just assumed, since Bennett said he was named after his dad."

Eli cleared his throat. "I'm sorry about your husband."

Adelle looked away from the couple and said nothing.

Glory shrugged at Eli and tried to communicate *What should we do now?* with her eyes.

He brushed off something only he could see from the table in the entry.

Deciding to press on and address the essence of Adelle's original question, Glory did some mental apple picking, selecting the parts of her life that she was comfortable with sharing and leaving the rest on the tree. She nodded at her husband and headed toward the opposite side of the store, hoping the other woman would follow. "Er-hmm, you told me you did a bit of research on the store before you came to Gilmore. Well, I'm pretty sure you didn't see anything about how I always loved to read as a child. Isn't that true, Eli?"

He chuckled. "Yes, yes. Even as a kindergartner, I can remember—"

"Forgive me, but I didn't come to wander down memory lane

with you, Mrs. Pryor." Adelle's quiet voice carried from the spot where she'd parked herself, beside the rack of used books where Glory had chatted with Frederick Baldwin the week before. She squeezed her eyes closed and spoke again after sucking in a deep breath. "What I mean is, I'm sorry. I really don't mean to be rude. I don't like acting this way. It's not me."

Glory sensed the woman's struggle and slowly drew closer, with Eli bringing up the rear.

When Adelle's eyes opened, they glistened with unshed tears. "No, I'm not a reporter. That was my husband. Not only did he love truth, he sought it, hunted for it. That's why he became a believer; that's the greatest truth Ben knew."

Glory didn't have to ask *Believer in what?* because she knew it was more like *Believer in whom?* Her mama and daddy worked twelve-hour shifts all week and prepared all day Saturday to spend the entire Sunday at church. Ironing clothes, pressing hair, cooking next day's dinner to respect the Sabbath, prepping Sunday school lessons. Again, it wasn't a *what* that stood out about her family's faith; it was a *who*. The truth was, neither she nor her brother were anywhere to be found in her parents' day-to-day worship of the God they believed in.

But it wasn't always that way. Monte and Delia had hurried to the altar when he was twenty-two and she was seventeen, with Davis arriving before her wedding ring had warmed Delia's finger six months. After Glory arrived three-and-a-half years later, the couple set their minds to training up both themselves and their children in the way they were supposed to go. No more partying, smoking, and drinking. Out with their old friends, in with the usher board; if the church doors were open, the family of four was sitting in a pew. Some of Glory's earliest memories involved playing tic-tac-toe with Davis on the church program and getting spanked for scuffing her white sandals chasing him in the parking lot.

Her mama never discussed their family's beginnings, but a curious Glory had come across her parents' marriage certificate and done the math. She knew better than to ask for an explanation. Glory did wonder if her mama would smile more at Davis if she told the whole truth about her past, if it would really set her free, like the preacher said. She'd asked her brother about his thoughts on the matter one Saturday morning when the sixteen-year-old had come in all sweaty from mowing the lawn—doing "man's work"—while she dusted doorsills and window blinds.

"Why are you worryin' yourself? She loves you plenty enough for us both." Davis's lips curled before he bent over the kitchen sink and rinsed the expression from his face.

"Boy, you better do that in the bathroom if you know what's good for you. Mama will have your hide."

He leisurely dried off with the good hand towel meant for company. "She'll have it anyway for something else. Might as well save me some steps. I'm goin' out, sis. Tell Mom and Dad—"

"What? That you're at Bible study?" At twelve, Glory had become used to Davis's Saturday-night routine.

"Close enough." He paused on the threshold. "Don't worry about Mom. You can't make her happy. Only God can do that."

"But she goes to church all the time!"

Davis had laughed. "I didn't say church, knucklehead. That's a building. They go there all the time to prove something. A pile of bricks doesn't make them happy. That church is a monument that attests to their faithfulness, how worthy they are of love or happiness even if they don't believe it."

At twelve years old, she could sense how smart her brother was though she couldn't understand all he said and didn't say. As she measured the height and depth of the shelves in By the Book, a wiser, sixty-four-year-old Glory considered the possibility she'd built her own monument. *What am I trying to prove by staying here? Would Eli think I'm worthy of forgiveness and love if he knew my whole story?*

A duet of laughter. Bennett's high, childish notes mixing with Ophelia's rich alto. All three adults looked in the direction of the window seat, located beyond the entry and in the room at the front of the store, hidden by the shelves and displays.

Glory shook off memories that had no place in her bookstore as much as her brother did. "Mrs. Simonette—"

"Adelle."

Glory inclined her head. "Adelle. Well, *Eli* and I are truly sorry for your loss. Your husband sounds like an upstanding fella, and please, don't give another thought to what you told me. Pure miscommunication." When she flicked her fingers as if clearing the air, she noticed how their visitor's eyes zeroed in on her jewelry. Glory stuffed her hands in her voluminous pockets and looked at her spouse. "Don't we all act as reporters at times, looking for answers, sharing what we learn?"

His silent agreement did not disappoint.

"In fact . . . *Adelle*, I think fiction reports a truth of its own," Glory continued.

"But fiction by definition isn't true. If anything, it's the opposite of fact. That's why we have the term *non*fiction."

"Well, I'm not sure exactly why we have that word, but fiction often shares real elements of the human condition." Glory tapped Eli's hand and resumed their trek toward the other side of the store. As she expected, it took merely a second before her sparring partner fell into step behind them.

"The need for love, the dynamics of family, the effects of hate . . ." Glory ran an index finger across the spines as she ambled down a row of shelves in the historical section. She half turned toward her audience.

"And lies." Adelle shoved her hands in her back pockets.

Glory felt the thrust of the two words aimed at her, and she parried with, "Sure, and also forgiveness and redemption. All themes you'll find in fiction. What do you think, Eli?"

His shoulder brushed his wife's as he moved by her to study the books arranged in alphabetical order by genre. "There's Christian fiction, right? I know I saw names I recognized from the catalog."

"They're mixed throughout—contemporary, women's, romance, YA," Glory murmured. *Eli, you know better than to venture down that rabbit hole.*

"An oxymoron if ever I heard one," Adelle scoffed, edging by the two of them in the narrow aisle.

Glory watched the backpack sway over Adelle's hips as she made her way through the stacks. "But why? Faith is another commonality among people. The need to believe in something."

"Or some*one*." Adelle paused and glanced back. "I bet your parents gave you that name for a reason."

"It's short for Gloria!" She wanted to shout, but she couldn't, not after all this talk about truth and lies.

Every year, her mama would sit on the end of her bed with their large, illustrated family Bible open on her lap and tell her, "Now, you know, we can't let this day go by without readin' from the book of John. It's the best way to celebrate your birthday, remindin' you where you come from."

Then Delia would read, *"And the Word was made flesh, and dwelt among us, and we beheld his glory, the glory as of the only begotten of the Father, full of grace and truth."*

When she was old enough, she and her mama would read the Scripture together, and it wasn't long before Glory said it from memory. After they finished the passage, Mama would list all the names she could've chosen but didn't because they wanted one that best reflected their faith and their prayers for their only girl child.

Glory clenched her teeth. *Their faith. It may have been full of glory, grace, and truth, but what about love? I wonder what the name Davis means.*

Eli draped an arm around his wife's shoulders and drew her close. "Because she's glorious."

Adelle closed her eyes as the couple embraced. Whoever Glory Pryor was, she obviously loved and was loved by her husband. Oh, how she missed Ben! Adelle pretended to study book covers as she continued to the next aisle.

"Adelle."

Hearing Glory's voice, she whisked away a tear and slapped her cheeks to add color. "Yes! I'm over here."

The two joined her near a door labeled the storeroom. The older woman raised herself on toes that were almost obscured by her dress to peer over Adelle's shoulder. "You still haven't shown us what's in the backpack."

She tilted away from the prying eyes. "We can talk about it another time. I think we already have lots to think about."

Eli linked his hands behind his back. "So you'll be around for a while? Do you think you'll be here for the festival?"

"The festival?" Adelle adjusted the straps.

"You know, the one you researched for your story. Not to beat a dead horse," Glory commented wryly.

"Honey." Eli's grin peeked through his frown.

Adelle had the grace to laugh, at the situation and at herself. "I do plan to be around. But from what I gathered, By the Book doesn't take part in Gilmore's event. The store didn't appear on a list of participating businesses."

The whir of the air conditioning system made more noise than anyone in their small circle until Eli managed, "Actually, we will this year. Right, Glory?"

Gone was the adoring look from the store owner's face. "That's right. This will be our first year." She held out her hands. "I'll take those if you're through with them."

Surely, there was a story there, from the look on Glory's stony face, and Adelle wondered how it would affect the plans she'd put in place. Hiding her curiosity under the guise of making polite conversation, she off-loaded the books she'd accumulated. "What's different about this year?"

The two cut their eyes at each other before Glory examined the spines. She slid one book onto a shelf and moved to a second. "It seemed the right time."

Adelle maintained the few feet of distance between them, but she was close enough to smell that this might be the long-awaited opening. This seemed to be an opening in their cozy, united front. "Oh?"

Glory slid *All Quiet on the Western Front* into place and left the section as if she hadn't heard the implied question.

Adelle hooked her thumbs in the backpack straps and addressed Eli. "Is there something wrong?"

He shook his head. "No, no. My wife takes her work seriously, that's all. Can't stand it when a book is out of place. Glory is pretty particular that way. Now, what were you asking?"

She watched the bookseller move farther and farther away from them. "You were talking about By the Book's joining in the festival this year. Maybe I can help, and you can help me. Since my husband died, we've been out of sorts, so I decided to explore the country with Bennett."

"What about his education?" Eli propped an arm on the top of a shelf.

Adelle shrugged. "I'm considering homeschooling. He's only four, so why not take our show on the road for a while? Maybe relocate." Actually, Ben had tried to talk her into educating their children at home long-term, not only their first few years of life.

"Anyway, we've been studying the fifty states"—*another truth*— "and as we headed through North Carolina, I saw Gilmore and heard about the festival. Maybe you can use our help with the planning, and while I'm lending a hand, you can help me learn to appreciate the value of what you do here, you know, selling lies to people. And hey, I'm an artist of sorts. Perhaps I can exhibit at the festival?" Adelle attributed the stab she felt to deferred pain from the accident earlier. It couldn't be a guilty conscience.

Eli straightened. "You know, Mrs. Simonette—"

"Adelle. Please. I asked you to call me Adelle."

"Adelle, you may have something there. My wife has a bee buzzing in her head, and I'm thinking it's going to take some work. You might be what she needs, what *we* need."

"Great!" Several somethings clattered to the floor behind her. Adelle wheeled around and confirmed her suspicion: books. Splattered like water droplets around Glory's feet.

"Eli, what are you going on about? Wait . . . don't tell me. More reconfigurations."

9

"So, there I am, with my precious books bouncing on my toes, books she'd had no intention of reading. And my husband is inviting this stranger to help me plan what I'm not sure I want to do!" Glory unwrapped the square of caramel, popped it into her mouth, and slid the wrapper in her pocket. As much as she wanted to lean on the glass, she refrained. Noemie Pearline was her friend, but she was nearly as persnickety about smudges as Glory was about dog-eared pages. One ankle crossed over the other, she propped her back against the wall by the door.

The Simonette woman had gathered her son and rushed out of the bookstore the minute after she accepted Eli's over-the-top suggestion. Out of words for her husband, Glory skipped her evening's people watching and found herself on her front step, under the swinging sign bearing the name of the bookstore. At first, she'd skirted her building in hopes of finding Dude and thanking him for saving Bennett. No one had mentioned the man in all the talk about truth versus fiction and the festival. When Glory hadn't laid eyes on him, she'd circled the block. Still no sign. Eventually, her steps had taken her next door.

Pearline's Jewels was the antithesis of By the Book. The owners, Noemie and her husband, Dale, had razed the old house that had once sat on the property and erected a modern building a few years after Glory set foot in Gilmore. Mirrored walls, light blues and silvers, metal, clean lines and glass, where the bookstore was mahogany and cherry woods, original stonework, pitched rooflines and chimneys, low ceilings, and natural light. Noemie dashed about in fitted pantsuits and knee-length skirts that fit her shorter, curvier figure instead of ankle-length, one-size-fits-all dresses and flowy pants. As Glory watched the jewelry store owner, engaged in her closing-up routine for the day, she took stock of what the two of them did have in common: their fascination with crystal chandeliers and their love for each other and their husbands.

And now, they shared similar suspicions about Adelle Simonette.

Noemie finished cleaning the watch she held and returned it to the empty spot in the display case. "Is she cute? You know how some men can act around a pretty young thing when they reach a certain age. Needing to shake their tail feathers and strut around a bit."

Glory shook her head at her friend, one of the few she had in town, and most certainly the closest. "Nah, Eli's not like that. He's always a fixer. It's in his nature. He can't restrain himself from leading the charge—and don't let it be a damsel in distress. It's Sir Eli to the rescue!" She pretended to wield a sword. "Nature or not, it burns my buns how he likes to go ahead of me and make decisions without discussing them first."

"Whew, child!" Noemie took the tray of watches from the display and climbed on a stool to set it in the topmost stack with the others. Upon closing the store, she had the onerous task of packing up the jewelry and moving it into the vault in back.

"*Whew* is right."

"So, *mi amiga*, what are you going to do?" Noemie had moved to North Carolina from Colombia in the late eighties. She frequently peppered her speech with both Spanish words and traditional Southern phrases.

"What else can I do but agree to Mrs. Simonette's 'help'? Right over a cliff she'll help me," Glory laughed, paraphrasing a favorite quote from the movie, *The Parent Trap*. "But there's something odd about her. I can't put my finger on it. It's more than her rapport with Eli—which would irritate me more if I were jealous or insecure. Maybe it's the secret grief the woman wears like a monk's cowl." *You're one to talk about secrecy and grief,* Glory chided herself.

Yet, it was something more. Something else. That first day, the stranger had strutted into her bookstore with such a determined, knowing air, like a bloodhound on the scent of a runaway. Today, flustered and hair flying, hobbling on one shoe, the woman looked ready to extract a gavel from her vintage backpack, bang it on the countertop, and pronounce "Guilty!" loud enough for all of Gilmore to hear. Adelle Simonette's silent appraisal and judgmental demeanor raised Glory's hackles.

Noemie kicked off her heels and yanked her white shirt, still starched and pristine, from her waistband. She loaded sparkling necklaces and bracelets onto the repurposed bakery cart.

Frowning, Glory offered, "I wish you'd let me lend a hand."

The five-foot-high vehicle stopped, and Noemie peered around the side; she was barely tall enough to see over it.

Glory held up a hand. "Yes, I know better than to offer." She raised her voice when her friend turned the corner at the back. "I've been known to allow people to pitch in at the bookstore . . . as long as they do what I say!"

Noemie returned directly, wheels squeaking. She used the key hanging around her neck to open the next display, and she transferred rings onto an emptied rack. "You didn't come over here to close up, Glory. That's my business. What you came to do was talk to me, seek my wise counsel. An altogether different kind of business."

"True. But one doesn't stop the other. Where is your helpmeet? Dale must have cut out early to go fishing." Glory craned her neck to see if she could spot his ancient blue Ford truck parked out front.

Noemie froze at the cart. "Helpmeet? That sounds straight out of the book of Genesis! Where'd that come from, Glory?"

Where had that come from? From somewhere bone-deep, a place that resounded of old hymns and looked like prissy church hats. It smelled like Old Spice, what Glory's daddy wore on Sunday mornings that didn't quite cover the motor oil and exhaust fumes from the garage where he worked all week. It tasted like the macaroni and cheese and candied yams served at Sunday School dinners, laid out on the paper-covered tables in the fellowship hall. While Glory had shared much about her life in Gilmore and her marriage to Eli, she'd spoken little about her past relationships—spiritual or otherwise.

"That wasn't you sitting in the back of my church Sunday, was it?" Noemie tapped her temple, appearing to think about it.

"Hush, Noemie. Or should I say, 'Naomi'?"

"Okay, *Glo-reee*. My name may have Hebraic roots, but it's no match for yours, which is the Bible through and through, from Genesis to Revelation! God in the flesh. Your last name is Hallelujah!" Noemie danced with the cart across the carpeted aisle behind the displays toward the doorway that led to the back.

Usually, Glory enjoyed hearing her friend Noemie's softly rolling *R*s that reflected her Colombian descent, but all this Bible talk got her goat.

Noemie reappeared, her face radiant. "There's smoke spewing out of your lobes, right over those beautiful earrings I sold you. *Dónde está tu alegría espiritual?* Where is your joy, *mi hermana?*"

Hermana, sister. Recognizing the word from hearing it so often, Glory swallowed the lump of anger that had risen in her throat. "You don't need to show me where my ears are, Noemie. My joy is next door, probably cooking dinner. Also, I did come here to get some, what did you call it?"

"Wise counsel. If that's not enough, I can offer you some fried fish when Dale gets home because you're right, he did indeed go fishing this morning. He can't take the boat out Saturday because we're having a sale, and it's all hands on deck in the store."

"I don't need fish; your stinky advice will be more than enough." Glory laughed then added seriously, "*You have been my friend. That in itself is a tremendous thing.* Or so said Charlotte the spider in so many words to her pal, Wilbur."

"*Charlotte's Web?* You're full of quotes today." Noemie spritzed the glass with cleaner and wiped it.

Glory itched for the bottle and a cloth, but she forced herself to remain still. "Probably because of my battle of words with Adelle Simonette. I felt like I was defending my whole way of thinking, not merely my profession. Books help me process life. They say what I want to say, what I can't say out loud. Sure, the authors may create fictional lives and settings, but the emotions they draw from are real—and so are the ones they evoke."

Noemie held up her palms. "Hey, you've convinced me."

Glory cleared her throat. "It's that other woman I couldn't convince, though she was deliberately being obstinate. My mama would've accused her of choosing ignorance. Adelle has to see how literature relates to our shared experiences."

"Like friendship, for one."

"Yes, like friendship. You missed a spot." Glory walked closer and pointed.

Noemie aimed the nozzle as if to spray her then started on another section. "Who are some of your favorite friends in books?"

Her repetitive circular motion on the glass seemed to hypnotize Glory. The only sound was the occasional squeak when the other woman scrubbed the counter clean. After a few minutes, Glory answered, "Frog and Toad."

"Why did I think you'd say Jo and Laurie, Huck and Tom, or Oliver and . . . ?" Noemie snapped her fingers. "What's his name."

Glory nodded furiously and drummed on her chin, thinking. "Yes, I know who you're talking about. The pickpocket in *Oliver Twist*. But I'm sorry, those are the characters that came to mind when you posed the question, especially when I think of us."

"Then I get to be Charlotte, and you're Wilbur." The jeweler stuck out her tongue and broke her own rule by leaning against her freshly cleaned glass.

Following the other woman's lead, Glory relaxed beside her. "Or Holmes and Watson."

"The Scarecrow and Dorothy. Pooh and Piglet." Noemie linked her fingers behind her neck, deep in thought. "You mentioned Jo and Laurie, but what about *hermanas*? Sisters can be friends, too."

"No, *you* mentioned those two from *Little Women*. I'd say Jo, Beth, Amy, and Miss Know-It-All take friendship to another level as sisters."

Noemie swatted at her. "Meg is not a know-it-all. She was doing her job as the oldest."

"Spoken like a true oldest."

Noemie's stare pinned Glory into place. "We never dig deep into your family. Remind me, where do you fall in the birth order? Were you and your siblings good friends?"

Glory's smile died on her face. A quick, painful death. "I'm the younger of two, and I adored my big brother. There was a great deal of hero worship on my part." She didn't flinch under Noemie's steady gaze, who'd heard different versions of these same lines over the years. "Until he started drinking, which I've told you about."

"Not much," Noemie prompted.

Glory buried her hands in her pockets so Noemie wouldn't see her clenched fingers. "My parents stayed on him. They expected a lot from the both of us, but Davis marched to his own beat."

"Must run in the family."

"Mmm . . . but not like Davis. He was so creative—the way he dressed, spoke, thought. Believed. He could've run the world with his brains and personality, but he decided to run them crazy instead." Glory pictured her brother with his laughing eyes, looking older than his years. He always stood head and shoulders—literally and figuratively—above other boys his age.

"His alcoholism didn't play well with the deacon and missionary boards at church, let alone my parents. Davis would sneak into the house, and I'd cover for him. They'd fuss whenever they caught him. Then he started staying out later and later, going away days at a time because he figured he could just delay the arguing, the lectures, and the punishment."

Growing warm under the chandelier—*or was it Noemie's interrogation?*—she counted her pink-tipped toenails as she spoke. "Then . . . one night there was a fire. I got hurt pretty badly, and my parents blamed his drinking." Glory raised her hemline a tad to reveal a hint of her scar tissue.

"They couldn't forgive him, so he left home. Which is a euphemism for 'they kicked him out and he had nowhere to go.' He disappeared. Eventually, I went off to college, and my parents died soon after I graduated. When we had the chance, when we were younger, we did the traditional brother-and-sister thing fairly well.

The problem was we didn't get to grow into friends because we didn't get the time together." Glory scrubbed at something sticky on the floor with her toe as her story trailed off.

The clock at the end of Springs Church gonged the half hour.

"Eli and Glory."

The melodious, soft voice on Glory's right was strong enough to lift her chin and reclaim her attention. "What?"

The jeweler raised one shoulder and blinked into the early evening light streaming through the front windows. "Married couples are buddies, too. The best kind."

Thankfulness made her want to hug her friend, but she settled for playing along. "Then I nominate you and Dale."

Noemie squeezed Glory's shoulder, showing her that she understood. "Since we've moved on to nonfiction, that brings up that Simonette woman. Perhaps you two can form a friendship. Why don't you take your bestie up on his idea about your festival planning? This quote thing might inspire people, like it did you and me."

Glory rested against the glass as she ruminated.

Noemie poked the bookseller's knuckle with a nail.

"Oops!" Glory snatched her hands away.

"Wait until I rub greasy prints on one of your precious novels."

Glory waggled a finger in warning before stuffing her hands into her pockets to keep them—and her books—out of danger. "You got me to thinking, Noemie. What if I designed famous quotes on large placards and posted them around town to advertise the festival? They would inspire people—"

"To buy books!"

"Sure. And jewelry . . . and apple fritters, massages, pottery . . ."

"But how does this relate to your new friend Adelle? If you truly want words that speak to a wide range of readers, you should gather them from more than the two people who sit at your dinner table each night. Or the two of us."

"Hmm, you have something there, but where would I get the quotes?" Glory went to press her fingertips to the glass again but reared back when she spied Noemie's raised hand. "You and Dale for one. Y'all would be a great help because you're readers."

"I've already helped! But I can't speak for Dale. Wait, we've been married for forty-three years, so of course, I can. Count us in. Who else could you ask?"

While Glory paced the store, her flip-flops slapping against the large tiles, Noemie walked to the front and picked up a rod with a rounded end like a shepherd's crook. She used it to grab an iron gate high above the windows. "What about Ophelia? She's a reader. You need folks from all along the age spectrum, too."

The bookseller went rigid. "Who do you have in mind?"

"Different ages. Younger and older. You have people in the middle. Middle-aged, that is. What young people do you know?" She lowered the bars.

Glory marched to the front left, opposite Noemie and reached for the bars. "Charles Graves—without Oscar—could represent the older demographic. This would draw him out of the house to converse with people other than his dog. Perhaps your neighbor, Frederick, could join us, in exchange for more recipes and free sweets."

Both Frederick Baldwin and the Pearlines lived in Hickory Grove. Noemie covered the door. "Talk to Jason and Mallory, Ophelia's twins. They could speak for the teens if they're willing."

"If Jason's mama can convince him to take out his earplug thingies long enough to contribute." Glory couldn't hide her doubt.

"You still need someone *younger*."

"I'm on to you, you know. You're not as sly as you think you are."

Noemie sauntered over to Glory and faced her friend head on.

"That Bennett you talked so much about. *So well spoken*, you said. *So smart. A four-year-old who reads like he's ten!* Sounds like he'd be perfect. But also, that means—"

"His mama. Adelle." Glory could've sworn she heard the sound of a guillotine falling into place. *Mommy says it's not right to swear,* a young voice reminded her. She grimaced.

"Who wanted to help anyway. Win-win." Noemie clapped silently.

10

ADELLE PUSHED ASIDE the plates and cups from their early dinner to make room for her drawing pad and pencils. She started to sketch, allowing her mind to reflect on the day's events. *So far, so good.*

She drew a house, a tree, then a rabbit—not the long-eared, well-dressed version from Bennett's new favorite story. Instead, the rabbit she'd had as a child came to life, looking ready to hop across the page. Next, she drew chrysanthemums among hydrangeas and tea roses mixed with dandelions, sunflowers growing along hillsides; Penny, the horse on her in-laws' farm; Ben's nose, his hand, his eyes. Bennett's profile. All the while, her hand busy with her colored pencils, she laid out her plans in her mind.

The day had started so auspiciously: First, a call from the leasing company with a promising lead on her home. The sun and a warm breeze chasing away the clouds that had clung to the sky for days. Waffles and bacon for breakfast. Walking down Springs Church Road with Bennett. Hot chocolate. Meeting Oscar and the sweet Mr. Graves. The yellow rain boots. Mud puddles. The accident.

"But that helped me gain entry to the bookstore to talk to Eli," she reassured herself. *Don't forget Glory,* she reminded herself, using amethyst to envelop a mountain in shadows, towering over a valley. She drew footprints leading through snow, then erased the beginnings of a winding country road, blew off the paper, and covered the faint pencil markings with tall trees with twisted branches. When Adelle flipped the page, she stared at the eleven-by-fourteen-sized sea of white. There was so much to do, even more to rectify, while protecting her son in the process. Making a way for them both. She asked herself, "What's next?"

"Are you ready to go, Mommy?" Bennett's call sought and found her.

"Yes!" Adelle closed her pad and set the case of pencils on top of it, then took their dinner plates to the sink. Adelle had promised Bennett she would take him and his Radio Flyer wagon on a loop around the neighborhood after he finished his green beans, comforting herself with the thought that technically, it wasn't a payoff since she hadn't made it conditional. It was a *when,* not an *if.*

"Who are you kidding?" Adelle asked the empty kitchen, rinsing away their meal's remains. "Not him and certainly not yourself."

"Who are you talking to? God?"

This time she didn't jump. Adelle was getting used to his popping out of nowhere, so she acknowledged him with a side-eye as she wiped her hands on the dish towel. She looped it over the handle of the dishwasher.

Bennett held high his red Converse sneakers by their strings. "I can't get them untied."

"What do you want me to do?" Adelle raised a brow and waited. She was trying to get him to make his needs known, not merely make announcements for her to take a stab at. That was the way he'd learn to humble himself and talk to God. To willingly, yet boldly share what was on his heart and trust Him to hear and respond.

"Could you untie them? They're all knotted up." He pulled at a lace with a missing aglet.

Yep, he's definitely nailed the 'expect an answer' part. She barely hid her smirk. "You're tightening the knot, Ben-Ben."

He frowned. "That's what I said."

Adelle reached for a sneaker and steered him toward the two seats at the table. She'd refused to bring more than two kitchen chairs. That way, she wouldn't be forced to think about who wasn't there every mealtime. Now the table was always full; no one was missing.

She patted the bottom of a seat. "Here, sit."

Bennett hefted himself into it.

Adelle scratched at the clump of string with her fingertip. It would've been much easier to pick at it if she hadn't gnawed away most of her nails, but she managed to loosen it. She exchanged shoes with him, taking the sneaker with the tighter knot and giving him the loosened one. "Okay, let's see what you can do. Sometimes the help comes just as you asked and believed, but you need to add some elbow grease. Right?"

He nodded and plucked at the shoestrings. Slowly he pulled, loosened, and tugged, until finally, he untangled the jumbled string. Bennett grinned widely and snatched the other shoe from her lap. "I can do it."

Adelle ruffled his curls. "Sometimes the Lord shows us He's willing and able and then equips us to do the work."

Bennett sighed and angled an eye at her but kept at the knot. "I did it all by myself!" He beat his chest like he was King Kong.

She high-fived him. "Good job. Thank You, God!"

"Thank You, God!" he echoed.

Adelle watched him slide his feet into his shoes. She couldn't resist one final direction. "You can prevent this problem altogether if you untie your shoes *before* you take them off, like I've told you countless times. God is always willing to hear us when we call and help us in all our troubles. But let's learn from our mistakes, son, and do better. Avoid the trouble whenever we can. Don't jump in every puddle."

He grinned and bobbed his head vigorously. "Don't jump in every puddle. Okay!"

Adelle watched his small fingers fumble with the string. She covered his hands with hers and made sure his deeply set eyes were locked with hers. "Bennett, like today. You ran in front of a car and could have gotten hurt . . . *seriously*. If it weren't for that nice man." She swallowed the lump that clogged her throat and pressed on. "If it weren't for—"

"Dude," Bennett interjected. "Mr. Pryor called him Dude. And that's the same name Mrs. Pryor yelled when they were upstairs. Before they came down and she let me read *Alice in Wonderland*."

"Yes. Dude. I'm glad you remembered his name. Let's draw him a card tonight and take it to him."

"Tomorrow?" His eyes lit up.

She sighed and nodded. Gratitude first, then back to the plan. "Bennett, God sent Dude to help us right when we needed it. That was grace and mercy at work. But I hope you learned that you must be careful. No more playing near the street or running away from Mommy. There's a time and a place to splash and play."

"Don't jump in every puddle. Like now, when we go for our walk?" He jumped to his feet.

Adelle hoped this lesson was sinking in. "Yes, like on our walk. But I'm serious."

His lips poked out like a fish, the face he made when he was ruminating on something. "You were pretty serious at the store."

She nodded.

"But Mommy, why did you tell Mrs. Pryor you were looking for a Bible when you were carrying one in Daddy's backpack? And what was the other book? It looked special. Did Mrs. Pryor give it to you?"

Adelle collapsed against the back of her chair. "What? How did you know what Mommy was carrying?"

He bounced from one foot to the other, obviously unaware of her consternation. "Because when you threw Daddy's backpack on the sofa, I looked in it. When we were walking you told me I could see later, and I thought that was later. Wasn't that later? Why were you fussing at Mrs. Pryor about helping you find a Bible, and you already have one? Is ours not good enough? Do we need more troof?"

Troof . . . truth. Adelle covered her mouth as her son hopped around the table.

Dude was nowhere to be found.

Glory peered down every side street and around every corner on her walk up Springs Church. Now that her feet were leading her toward her Tudor, she could picture Eli tapping his toe and glancing at his watch. She hadn't wanted him to think she was punishing him, but she wasn't quite ready to head home after Noemie had shooed her out, locked up for the night, and headed home to Hickory Grove to await Dale.

Out of places to search, Glory sank down on the steep steps of the church. Really, hers had been a half-hearted hunt; Dude's business was his own. And Glory had no idea what she would've said had she found him. Yet, she hated to think he felt accused or blamed for the incident with Bennett. "Shoot, you're a hero," Glory whispered. "A name I can't add to my own list."

These wide concrete steps were the closest she'd come to the church in a good while. Spent from the day, her unprotected feet achy from the walk, Glory rested and stared up at the sun's last hurrah. Burnished orange streaks stretched across the sky, setting afire the splotches of dark gray clouds that promised more rain to come. She almost applauded its slow descent behind the tall steeple. Though she hadn't planned to ever put a foot inside Ebenezer, this imposing redbrick building had served as one of the main reasons she'd been drawn to this historic community. There was something about a town whose anchor was a cross . . . Glory couldn't put a name to it.

Yet, she could assign memories, mostly of Davis.

Her brother skipped Sunday school more than he attended, and his absentee record grew exponentially once he had a driver's license he could flash at the ABC store. He used his winsome ways to pull the wool over the eyes of the folks behind the counter of the Georgia package stores, especially since he was always big for his age, like some of his relatives. But Davis's smooth talking and good looks had little sway with Monte and Delia Gibson.

She pictured him slipping in the window of his bedroom, what Mama and Daddy had caught him doing more than once. He'd climbed into his twin bed, wedged his back against the wall, and pulled the covers up to his chin. Davis was so long and thick limbed, he had to curl up like a baby to keep his large feet on the mattress, his knees drawn toward his chest.

"Tell Mama I'm sick, li'l sister. You know they'll trust you. You're the angel in the family, the smart one," he cajoled.

Everybody knew who the smart one was in the family, and it wasn't Glory. She was the obedient, hardworking, youngest Gibson who kept her head down and stayed in the background. Everybody—from the principal who documented his tardies to the lunch ladies who sneaked Davis an extra carton of milk—knew her brother was a genius. His parents were well aware of that fact, which made life so much harder because he was wasting all his "God-given talent and abilities that could be used for the furtherance of the Kingdom."

At twelve years old, Glory was proud to know it, and thanks to her former best friend, she also was on to the reason for the Listerine on Davis's breath. That sharp smell smacked her across the nose most Sunday mornings.

"Nuh-uh. I ain't sayin' no such thing. Why are you just gettin' home? If they'd seen you, Daddy would-a snatched your hair out by the roots."

"Come on, baby girl. You don't want to hear all their carryin' on this beautiful Sunday mornin' if they suspect how busy my Saturday night was." Davis yawned and rubbed his eyes.

"They know better than to believe me, sayin' you're sick and sleepin' in. You weren't feelin' poorly last night before we went to bed. I heard you've been going to the pool hall!"

"Well, I'm sick and tired now. You best believe that. Please turn out that light," he groaned, his head burrowing deep into the pillow. "Do me a favor and take my troubles to the cross and leave my body here. The Lord knows where to find me." He'd burrowed under the blanket, knowing full well that his adoring sister would cover for him that Sunday morning and for many mornings following—until Davis was too "sick" to do much of anything other than sleep in, and their folks had finally had enough.

Briefly, with an eye toward the top of the steeple cloaked in a darkness that would soon cover the ground, Glory considered asking their God where Davis was, since her brother was so confident He cared enough to know his whereabouts. Then she shook her head and stood, her bones creaking and rattling into place. She'd rested long enough on that step—too long—and her backside was sore. If she didn't take herself back to the house lickety-split, her sheriff would hop on his horse and initiate his own one-man posse to match the search party she'd launched for Dude, who was most likely settled for the night.

Plodding rather than striding on her return, Glory glanced at the buildings she passed. Some were dark, seemingly resting as she had, until proprietors returned in the morning to wake them. Others, private homes, had lights and life in the windows of the houses, and she peeped at the silhouettes of busy people having dinner, watching television, and carrying on the business of living.

She shuddered and picked up the pace past Baker's Memorial and Crematorium, an imposing, two-story colonial a couple doors down from Gilmore's much cozier public library. The funeral home was strangely bright, and she pictured it with the Christmas lights they draped along the balcony above the double front doors.

"I guess people are dying more than they're reading. And going home is worth celebrating." Glory cast a last glance over her shoulder at the light above the crematorium door that beckoned to her, eliciting images of her brother once again and the haunting words of a poem:

Come, family—
you far-off sons,
mamas, and daughters,
the least and the lost.
You are the ones
I've been searching for,
yearning for,
no matter the cost.
Whither thou art,
thither and yon,
flung far and wide,
or longtime gone . . .
come.

Gather round.
I'll leave the light on.

Tears fell at the pace she trod, slowly and steadily; she brushed away the last of them as she reached the brick pavers leading to By the Book. She steadied herself with a hand on the mailbox post as a warm breeze hinting of rain plastered her skirts to her calves. Finally, tired of serving as a buffet for the mosquitos and gnats and ready to face Eli, longing to be embraced by him, she hurried round the house to enter through the kitchen door in back. On the way, she gave herself a stern talking to.

"Now, Glory, don't bother Dude. Don't look in his direction. Give the man some privacy. That's his home, at least for the night." Still, much as she couldn't help but glance over her shoulder at the funeral parlor, her eyes cut toward the chair in the shadowy spot under the maple. The *empty* chair under the maple. Deflated, she took her key and turned the lock.

The bright light greeted her. And so did the sight of Eli, slowly rotating a spoon in a large saucepan. "Hey, there."

"Hey, yourself." He smiled and wiped his knuckles and palm on his apron, permanently stained by saucy red splashes and greasy splotches.

The familiarity of the movement made her smile this time. Feeling like a far-flung wife, she shuffled over—all her weary legs could manage—and encircled his waist with her arms. Pressing against his back, she peeked over his shoulder. "Yum, shrimp gravy. Need me to stir the grits?"

He twisted and kissed her cheek. "No, I've got it. You have a good talk with Noemie?"

"I did. We came up with a fantastic idea for the festival that you'll love, and I can't wait to tell you about it. Noemie is great at problem solving. Almost as good as you." Glory knew he'd probably used his phone to track her progress from Pearline's to the church and back and even double-checked her whereabouts with Noemie. Grateful, she planted a wet smack on his neck and stepped away to wash her hands.

"Glad to hear it. Maybe she can help with another problem." Eli lifted the lid on a smaller pot bubbling away on a rear eye.

Glory's stomach clinched. His casual tone didn't fool her. Her hands were dry, yet she continued wringing the hand towel as she tried to decipher this troubling situation he'd alluded to. *The festival? Adelle or Bennett? This daughter of his? Somebody else asking for a Bible?*

Thirty interminable seconds passed while her husband tapped the spoon against the rim of the pot. Then he set it down and faced her. "We've been robbed, Glory."

PART TWO

Clinging Vines

11

"What did Margaret Mitchell write in *Gone with the Wind*? Today's another day!" Ophelia set a plate in front of Eli and Glory and slapped her hands together. "I'm substituting apple fritters for this week's special, so I need you to taste 'em and tell me if they need more cinnamon. Quick now, because I'm preparing the dough and chopping more apples."

Glory wanted to tell the baker that the word Scarlett O'Hara had used was *tomorrow*, not *today*, but she chose not to pop her overly inflated balloon. In fact, what Ophelia said seemed more fitting. Today was just another day in the life of a bookseller and in the life of a wife.

Eli took a bite and gave a thumbs up. "I wouldn't change a thing. Glory?"

She patted her tummy to satisfy his cousin's need for a compliment, not a recommendation. "Thank you. I'm sure it's delicious as always."

"Great. Gotta get crackin'." Ophelia hastened from the stockroom.

"I still can't believe you're not upset." With a shake of his head, Eli polished off his fritter.

Glory nibbled the pastry, counting the calories she'd accumulated since her husband and his family had come into her life. "Your shrimp gravy comforted me in my loss."

Seven days had passed since Eli had discovered that a vintage copy of *The Great Gatsby* had gone missing from a display. He'd been locking up after Ophelia had finished kitchen prep and all the ruckus caused by the Simonettes, and he'd noticed the place where the book was supposed to be. But it wasn't.

Glory watched him peel back the long strip of clear tape on the box in front of him. "Are those the rest of the books we're expecting for the upcoming signing?"

"I can't believe you're this calm about the theft. It's valuable."

"You're not telling me something I don't know, husband. But life goes on."

"And insurance goes up."

"True. If we file." She crumpled up the tape and reviewed the packing list inside her box. "Twenty-two copies here plus what you opened, which means we're all set."

Several times a month, By the Book welcomed writers and readers to special events—talks; workshops; signings; demonstrations; giveaways; or collections for hospitals, schools, and the community center. Glory was preparing to celebrate an author's latest children's story about a talking piano.

Studiously avoiding her husband's eyes, she scanned the book jacket. "Listen to this endorsement: *On a scale of one to ten* . . . Get it, Eli? Scale, piano? Do you think Jason might remove his earbuds to join us that weekend?"

"Glory."

His grim tone informed her *I'm on to you.* She met his gaze.

"Honey, I must admit I've never read *The Great Gatsby*, though if you tell anybody, I'll deny it. So, que será, será."

Eli balanced the brilliant-yellow picture book in each hand as if weighing her response. "What do you mean, *what will be, will be*? We're talking about a few thousand dollars, not the lyrics to that Doris Day song. What you had was a rare copy, and we don't know how long it's been missing. My first thought was that someone took it that day, but we were the only ones in the store."

"Does your *we* include Ophelia, Jason, and Mrs. Simonette?" Glory angled her head.

"And Mallory, Bennett, and Dude?" He mirrored her movement.

"No, none of them. Which is why I determined it must have been gone a while, unbeknownst to us."

"How do you know its worth? That thing has sat in storage since I bought it, well before we got married." Glory had splurged on the vintage copy of *The Great Gatsby* at an estate sale the year after By the Book opened. Acknowledging her own distaste for the classic story led her to lock it away in a chest in her closet, just as she'd locked away her guilt-edged memories of her brother. Setting out Fitzgerald's popular story for the world to see—one that remarkably, the former English major could never bring herself to read—had taken effort, but she considered it progress.

"It's ironic that you finally displayed it, only for someone to steal it almost immediately." Eli lifted the new books from their cardboard home and arranged them in four piles on the table in the center of the room.

"I've never liked that book, partially because most people love it so, but also because it worships a lifestyle—greed, lack of self-control, self-destruction—that hits too close to home for me when I consider how Davis threw away his life. But I feel something akin to relief."

"Are you worried at all about your insurance premium?"

"Freedom comes with a cost."

"I hear the shrug in your voice, but don't dismiss it out of hand. I'll talk to our guy. You haven't had a claim since we married, and that's worth something."

"Eli, my hope is that it's on the wrong shelf somewhere. Our guests pick up something in one place and put it down somewhere else, ignoring the caddies placed throughout the store."

"But if I'm not mistaken, you had *For display only. Do not touch.* beside the book."

Glory shrugged and reviewed her to-do list. "If I put too much thought into this, I'll get worked up, to think somebody walked out with one of my books! Honestly, I'd rather talk about the festival."

His eyes lit up.

Glory held up a finger. "And I don't mean what happens afterwards, because that's where your mind leaps—our leaving Gilmore. I'm talking about our Famous Quotes Group that's meeting tonight."

"One step at a time," he responded, the wattage in his eyes dimming. "Who's coming?"

"Frederick, Noemie and Dale, Jason and Ophelia. You did remind her, didn't you? And she doesn't have to bake a thing. My waistline can't stand it."

"At least you have one," he chuckled, adjusting his belt, "although I'm the only person who could find it in those beautiful tents you wear." He loaded the books on the cart behind him.

Glory's eyes widened, but she hid the hurt by digging in the upper cabinets for some doodads to decorate the room for the reading. Her husband knew why she preferred to wear these so-called tents, however "beautiful" they were. Suddenly, strong arms spun her around. Plastic thorns poked her fingers that tightened around a bunch of artificial roses. "Oh!"

"Baby, I'm sorry. I love everything about you, what you wear . . .

and what you don't. Forgive me. Please." He pressed his lips to the valley between her shoulder blades.

Icy and stiff at first, Glory slowly thawed to his touch. Resistance melting, she let him draw her even closer, and her tears wet his collar. Culpable, crocodilian tears. If she could only ask for and accept the forgiveness that she offered him. She swallowed as a children's book flashed across her mind. *Lyle, Lyle, Crocodile.*

Eli leaned back and used his thumb to dry the skin under her eyes. "What is it? I'm old and tough. I can take it."

She briefly rested her forehead on his chin and extricated herself from his embrace. "I was going to ask for—for . . . your help arranging chairs for the meeting. I hate to ask for help with jobs I can do by myself, but we can get it done faster and better together. As Mama used to say, *Many hands make light work.*"

Mama also used to tell me a lyin' tongue never finds rest.

"*That's* what you couldn't spit out?" The lines on his forehead deepened and his arms relaxed their hold.

"You could delegate this to Mallory and Jason, but if it's what you want . . ." Eli began dismantling all the cardboard packaging. "I'll take these to recycling, but first, you were telling me about tonight's guest list."

She wondered at his ability to pivot, at how easily she could flourish a few flags and sound a bell to distract him and redirect the conversation. Glory set the flowers under the book stacks and grasped the cart's handle. "Did I mention Charles Graves is coming, and *without* his dog? And knowing you as I do, you invited your Adelle Simonette and my newfound little friend, Bennett. If so, that will make eleven of us all totaled."

That evening, Adelle aimed to put her ancient Subaru in one of the parallel spaces directly in front of By the Book and leave no room for error. Hands shaking, she adjusted the rearview mirror to spy on Bennett who was altogether too quiet for a four-year-old dynamo. Just as she'd suspected: his head was leaning toward his left shoulder, drool leaking onto the seat belt.

She drummed her head against her seat. "Ugh. These folks who don't have young kids! They don't have to worry about dinnertimes and bedtimes." Adelle flicked on her left signal and turned onto Springs Church Road. She slowed to the regulated thirty-five miles an hour, which gave her plenty of opportunity to admire Gilmore, a quaint town God laid gently at the foot of the mountains. As much as she tried to resist, she was beginning to feel more comfortable here.

Here was an eclectic mixture of old and new styles—modern remodels fighting for purchase among all the traditional and historic, the yellow-and-blue paint on Ye Olde Ice Cream paling next to the neon sign for cigarettes mounted on the roof of the 1930s bungalow. A man in a suit tugging on the locked door of the glass-fronted post office and couples strolling hand in hand toward the movie theater that offered two-dollar classics. And of course, By the Book. About the only thing *not* to like about this burg, but the very thing that brought her here. Yet, slowly, even that place was growing on her, like lichen on a fallen log. Hadn't Dude saved her son's life?

"Always a drama queen," Adelle chided herself, thinking of the sheet of poster board propped on the floor next to Bennett. They'd folded it in half to make an oversized card and covered it with a large, red, lopsided heart. He'd spelled out *T-H-A-N-C-K Y-O-U* in large block letters above the symbol for love. She'd resisted having Bennett redo it and hoped the Good Samaritan considered the misspelling added character—along with the torn corner and smear of ketchup from hitching a ride in their car for a week.

Adelle navigated the parking, switched off the ignition, and dropped the keys into her purse. She peeked at the bookstore and noted how the lights inside shooed away the shadows on its porch. It was Dude she had to credit—or shake a fist at—for their return to the scene of the crime. Dude and of course, Eli, who'd shared that the one-named man had returned to his spot behind their house.

When Adelle had answered the landline the other day, Eli's voice had taken her aback. She'd had the telephone installed for Bennett's sake, in case of emergency. "Oh, hi. Mr. Pryor. How'd you get this number?"

"Eli, please. You and Ophelia exchanged information when you stopped by with the card for Dude. She said she'd let you know when she saw him next, and . . . well, Dude is home, for want of a better word. It's what Glory says, so I guess that's what it is." The chuckle that followed his words sounded like he attached it as an afterthought.

"Oh. Th-thank you." Adelle squeezed closed her eyes to the picture of Eli and Glory. That couple, whether they were separate or together, twisted her tongue into knots.

"Also, if Monday evening is a good time, we're organizing a festival think tank. That is, if you're still interested in helping out." Eli juggled his phone.

"I'll see." Adelle considered it as she sat in her yard, supervising Bennett's pell-mell tricycle ride in front of the house. She moved her foot to circumvent a small black ant's expedition over rocks and blades of grass.

Eli shifted on the other end of the line.

"Yes, sure, that will work, Mr., er, Eli. What time? Of course, Bennett is my plus-one."

He laughed. "He'd better be. Glory won't let you through the door without him on your arm. See you at half past six Monday evening, if that works for you. It shouldn't take more'n an hour. We don't open

Monday, but we're accommodating the Pearlines who will be closing up the jewelry store."

She'd wanted to snap, *No, that doesn't work for us. We don't eat until six o'clock, like most people!* but assured him, "I'll make it work." *Who's going to accommodate this widowed mother?*

Sitting in the car, listening to her son's breathing deepen as he transitioned from dozing to sleeping deeply, Adelle wondered if that was what she was doing, making it work, when it came to these plans of hers. Unbidden, Proverbs 26:27-28 popped into her mind: *If you set a trap for others, you will get caught in it yourself. If you roll a boulder down on others, it will crush you instead. A lying tongue hates its victims, and flattering words cause ruin.*

There was so much she hadn't considered, including her own feelings. Her own beliefs. Her own son.

"Mrs. Simonette—Adelle, Bennett, you're here! Early." Glory threw wide the door and ushered in the mother and son. "We're in back, still getting everything ready."

Adelle nudged the child across the threshold. "He had to go potty, and everywhere else on the street is closing up."

The woman's words hinted at an apology, but her tone said otherwise, and so did the upward tilt of her chin. "Obstinate" was how Glory would describe her to Eli later. But she forced her poppy-colored lips to smile and suffer Adelle's head-to-toe examination. She extended her black dress that had thin white-and-gold pinstripes running from shoulder to hem and curtsied. "You like? I thought I'd wear something special for the occasion."

Adelle had the decency to flush at being called out for staring. "Yes, you look lovely. I'm feeling underdressed."

"Not at all. Come in," Glory said, thinking, *That's what you get* as she closed the door. At one time, a look tended to make Glory feel uncomfortable in her own skin; it felt heavy and hard to bear, cumbersome, like breaking out of prison with her ankles and feet bound. When she was in college, folks never knew what to do with themselves when they saw her scarred legs, supposedly the sign of healing from the fire. Doctors said they were trophies. Badges of honor. The mark of survival. Her mama called them a testimony and praised the Lord for them. Glory viewed the thick and leathery, shiny, red marks for what they were: evidence of her guilt. They'd faded with time's passage, but no amount of slathering on fade creams or salves could mask or assuage the pain of knowing what had happened.

So her clothes had to do the trick.

When Glory grew tired of explaining and redirecting and ignoring, and pantyhose and tights were no longer in fashion, she tried leggings. But they felt constrictive, much as the prying eyes and the whispers confined her. Ultimately, she took to wearing long dresses and wide pants as a means of protecting herself from the curious or worse, piteous stares. The loose material moved with her. The silks, rayons, and polyesters, they were forgiving and comforting. Folks admired and questioned and wondered, but her muumuus and gowns transformed her, like Clark Kent's telephone booth of days past. When the would-be newspaper reporter stepped inside one, he emerged a superhero. A good guy. The one who actually saved instead of merely pretending to.

That was why Glory could roam through this ragtag group of sidekicks—and that Adelle Simonette—and prattle on about the power of story, looking into the eyes of folks who considered her an eccentric bookseller, friend, taskmaster, and wife.

"Let me show young Mr. Simonette where the facilities are while you head to the café. Ophelia arrived early, too. The others should be here in a few minutes." She turned up the heat of her grin when she laid eyes on Bennett, and fighting the urge to swoop him up in a big hug, she stretched her hand toward him.

Adelle shifted him closer to her side.

"What are facilities?" He scrunched up his face at the bookseller.

"I'm glad you asked. It's a super-duper fancy word for bathroom." Glory's words must have reassured the little boy because he let her lead him. She winked at Eli as he passed them on his way toward the front.

"Adelle!"

Glory shook her head, bristling at the excitement in her husband's voice. *He'd better not hug that woman. Noemie's right: she is right cute in those holey denims of hers.*

The tension in Adelle's shoulders eased when Eli clasped her hand between both of his. She felt so out of place in her jeans and T-shirt and Bennett in shorts and sneakers when that woman opened the door wearing an evening gown and fancy slides with feathers across the toes. Still, she had to admit the older man appeared rather dapper in his lightweight linen sports coat and chinos.

"Hi, Eli. Thanks for inviting us. I may not look like it, but I come bearing lots of ideas."

He guided her deeper into the store, through the hallway that led toward the café. "I'm glad to hear it, and you look fine. And about your ideas, I should explain that Glory and Noemie—"

"Noemie?" Adelle fell into step beside him.

"Pearline. I guess you could say she's Glory's best friend. She and her husband opened the jeweler's not too long after By the Book turned its first page."

Adelle lassoed the words *guess you could say* and let his joke go free. "Is she not really her best friend?"

Eli cocked an eye her way. "You are quite the reporter, aren't you, with an ear for details. I was only using a figure of speech, extra words to fatten up my sentence. They're good friends alright, those two. Noemie and Glory are thick as thieves."

What an appropriate description. She only nodded and said nothing more.

"As I was saying, those two have already cooked up a plan for the festival, and I think it's a solid one. They need some help fleshing it out and coming up with quotes. Which is why we invited y'all here tonight." Eli threw out a palm and invited her to go ahead of him into the small area they'd converted into a café, empty of people but filled with the scent of something warm and savory and a smattering of small round tables and chairs.

When he disappeared into the kitchen, Adelle stared at the large sheets of paper and jars of pens, pencils, and colored markers set up on each table and thought she was the last person for this book-related job, whatever it entailed. And well they knew it, after the last discussion they'd had. Half of her couldn't wait to hear the specifics, while her other half dreaded it. All of her wanted Glory to bring her son back from that bathroom forthwith.

"*Hola!*"

Adelle whirled toward the voice belonging to who could only be Noemie: a diminutive, yet commanding, woman dressed in a well-fitting, forest-green pantsuit and pale-pink shirt. Her flipped-up collar framed the large diamonds sparkling in her earlobes. Adelle cringed inwardly, wishing she'd read the memo about the dress code.

"H-hello?" Adelle hated the uncertainty in her voice as she picked at a crusty spot on her jeans. *And where is my boy?* In another minute she would hop onto one of these chairs and scream his name.

"I'm Noemie Pearline." The jeweler strode forward in heels that added four inches to her height, her hand reaching for Adelle, dark eyes piercing.

She accepted the handshake and stole a quick glance at the large antique gold clock on the wall. "Adelle Simonette."

"Yes, I know who you are." She flashed two rows of white teeth that matched the brilliance of her eyes.

Mmm-hmm. Somebody's been talking. Adelle smiled back. "Either you're a little early, too, or everyone else is late."

"Where's this little Bennett I've heard so much about?" Noemie's head swiveled back and forth, her thick, shoulder-length auburn hair swaying.

"I've been wondering that myself." Adelle peered past the woman.

"The question is, where's Dale?" Ophelia's question entered the room before she did. She appeared bearing a tray. "Jalapeño-and-pepper-jack popovers, everybody! Hey there, Adelle. It's good to see you again. You might better take one to sustain you with this crowd."

Noemie opened her mouth and pushed on the baker's shoulder. "Are you saying she'll need fortifications? But we're all family here!"

Ophelia said nothing but turned toward Glory, entering with Bennett in tow and the customer named Frederick bringing up the rear.

"I heard that, Ophelia." The bookseller elbowed her gently.

"I meant for you to," her employee responded in a singsong. "Help yourselves, ladies and gentlemen. I'll get my cousin to bring out iced tea and cups."

Adelle bent low next to Bennett, "Did you wash your hands?"

His chest heaved, and he droned, "Yes, ma'am."

"Then come sit next to me." She felt overwhelmed and desperately sought a corner to cower in. The farthest table and chairs would have to do, so Adelle gripped his hand for dear life and proceeded in that direction. A slightly familiar, soft tenor stopped her.

"Mrs. Simonette, is it?"

Rotating toward the newest greeter, she pressed a hand to her chest and grinned sincerely.

"Mr. Graves!" Bennett abandoned his mother's hand.

"Hello there, young man. I wasn't sure if you'd recognize me without my little friend."

The child circled the older gentleman's legs as if the dog was hiding behind him.

Adelle shook her head at her son but was glad Mr. Graves's laugh broke through the sadness that drifted around him like morning mist above the grass. She could see him; yet it veiled his true self. This was only the second time she'd conversed with this person, but she recognized him as a kindred spirit, having shared a similar loss.

"Hello, Mr. Graves. It's so good to see you again, even without Oscar. Right, Bennett?" She willingly exchanged her need to comfort herself by fading into the background for a need to comfort the older man and draw him out of his shell.

The boy kicked at a nonexistent ball with his toe and mumbled, "Right."

Charles Graves chuckled again, then coughed. The unusual sound may have dislodged something in his throat. He bent and cupped the side of his mouth, helping Bennett hear him in the jumble of words and sounds rising in the compact space, like a bathtub filling with water. "Don't worry. We'll soon talk Mrs. Pryor into letting me bring my friend. Maybe even by the next time."

Adelle's stomach dropped. *Next time?*

"Dale! *Finalmente!*" Noemie moved away from Frederick toward her newly arrived husband. "It took that long to close the shop?"

Glory flew on feather-covered shoes from the room, her dress billowing. "I'll lock the front door. Can't have anything else going missing or someone thinkin' we're open."

Adelle risked a glance at Bennett as Glory sailed out, but he appeared not to have heard.

Eli pushed open the swing door and held it. Two teens with the same upturned noses, square chins, and dark, curly hair entered, clutching two sweaty glass pitchers filled with water and iced tea. Eli dipped back into the kitchen, only to reappear with a tray of plastic cups and napkins. Frederick unburdened him and set the load next to the popovers and drinks on the concrete countertop.

Bennett dashed away from his distracted mother and clambered onto a stool. He accepted a napkin from Frederick and stuffed his mouth.

Adelle gritted her teeth, frustrated. None of this was what she'd come here for—to Gilmore or to the bookstore. She hadn't planned to chat about her reading habits, build rapport with virtual strangers, talk about the chew toys dogs liked—*bless Mr. Graves's heart*—or nosh on baked goods, however yummy they were. It was time to regroup.

She gently touched the elderly man's arm and stemmed his flow of conversation. "Pardon, but I think I'll get Bennett home. He's probably feeling overwhelmed by all these new people, and it's awfully late in the day. We didn't have time to do more than eat a ham-and-cheese roll-up and some saltines before we left the house, which you can tell by the way he's scarfing down those popovers. Maybe you and I can meet for coffee and hot chocolate and talk one-on-one—or rather, *two*-on-one, about how we're dealing with the death of our spouses. I could use a little wisdom for managing life on my own."

"Death?" He rubbed the back of his head. "My wife isn't dead."

Adelle's stomach twisted painfully for the thousandth time that evening. "But . . ."

Eli, who'd been standing with his back half turned to Adelle's left, stepped closer. "Charles, you should try a popover. Mmm-mmm-mmm."

Ophelia put her foot in 'em, let me tell you. And ask her about the peanut butter treats she made. She's considering them for her food truck, and after tonight, we'll keep them in a jar on the counter for dog owners like you and Frederick. No more random dog treats for Oscar."

The older man moved away, his shoulders slumped, as if a puppeteer had relaxed his strings.

Eli leaned in. "I didn't mean to eavesdrop, Adelle, but Charles's wife isn't dead. She suffered a stroke a few years ago and developed vascular dementia. She's in the late stages."

She touched her fingers to her lip. "The first time we met, he said he lost her."

Eli took a deep breath. "In all the important ways, he has. They've lost each other after sixty-two years of marriage. She's in a care facility now and probably doesn't have much longer for this world. Perhaps soon he'll have to bear the title of widower, but not today, dear. Not yet."

Chin trembling, Adelle envisioned her life raft floating away, with Charles Graves sitting in the middle of it, the one person she felt connected to in this room full of strangers. In the whole town, if she was being frank. *Thank You, Lord, for my son. Bennett!* She wheeled to get him, but there he was, snuggling up with Glory Pryor.

As though someone called her name, Glory zeroed in on Adelle. The older woman's brown eyes seemed to ask a question Adelle couldn't understand before she leaned over and murmured something in Bennett's ear. When his thumb headed for his mouth, Glory gently redirected his fingers and held on to them.

After much whispering and head shaking, Bennett nodded and straightened his shoulders. He stepped a little in front of Glory, clapped his hands, and yelled, "May I have your attention! It's time for the Famous Quotes Group to begin!" Then he ducked behind Glory's skirts.

12

"Y'ALL WERE WORTH SKIPPING my afternoon sidewalk gazing. Thank you for making time for Eli and me." Glory leaned her cheek against her clasped hands and smiled at the people seated at the varied mix of wood-, stone-, and glass-topped tables scattered about the room—Eli and Frederick; Adelle, Bennett, and Charles; Jason, Mallory, and Ophelia; Dale and Noemie.

"In *A Tree Grows in Brooklyn*, Francie Nolan described the world as hers for the reading, and I know how she feels. The right book at the right time can become a good friend or even a family member. Francie had 'one for every mood.' Just like I have tubes of lipstick."

Dale smirked at Noemie, and Mallory giggled, but Adelle frowned.

Glory pushed on. "That's why I asked all y'all to join me at By the Book today. I'm hoping the Famous Quotes Group—that's you, if you were wondering what Bennett was shouting about—will share parts of books and stories that inspire you or speak to you in some way, that explain why a particular book is a good friend and fits your mood. Write it down on that sheet of paper in front of you." She pointed at their tables.

Eli stood. "If you're like yours truly who struggles to recall details, feel free to wander about the store looking for your favorite books to use as reference guides."

Noemie leaned toward Dale and whispered loudly, "If you buy those same books and take them home, that's okay, too."

When her friend's words garnered a chuckle from everyone, Glory thought, *Maybe Mrs. Simonette does have a sense of humor.*

A gleaming silver skull danced in the air, catching Glory's attention. Her eyes followed the other four rings, including the one encircling the teen's thumb. "Yes, Jason?"

"Why can't we use our phones to find famous quotes? That's easier."

His mother jabbed a finger on the table. "Easier doesn't mean better."

Glory applauded her softly. "Finally, something you and I agree on, Ophelia! Yes, Jason, you could google titles and compile a whole list. But it wouldn't reveal what's important to *you* personally, what stands out to you. Maybe it's the lyrical nature of—"

"So, I can choose music instead?" Jason's face lit up.

Glory hesitated. "I reckon so. I'd never considered that."

Mallory raised her hand. "What if we haven't read the same books? I don't listen to what my brother listens to. How do we understand what we don't know?"

"And what does any of this have to do with the festival?" Ophelia propped her chin on the knuckles of her left hand.

The questions don't fall far from the tree, I see. Trust Ophelia and her children to have plenty to say. Glory pushed on. "In a book group, people read the same thing and get together to discuss it over pimiento cheese and almond crackers. This isn't like that. We're talking about quotes or scenes only. Themes. What people connect to regardless of the story. We'll discuss them before we share them, or in Jason's case, play them."

Jason jiggled to a rhythm only he could hear.

"Along those lines, what if you're not a reader . . . of fiction, I mean? I have a sense I won't have much to contribute to this effort. Which is supposed to be about the festival. At least, that's what I was told?" Adelle sat back in her chair.

"Well, if y'all would let me explain." Running a hand through her silver strands, from her forehead to her nape, she wished she had one of those fans her mama and daddy used in church once upon a time. Glory still remembered the picture of the funeral home on the back of it.

Noemie slipped out of her blazer and draped it over her chair. "*Disculpe.* May I? Most of you have been to the fairgrounds in November. People come from all over—children like Bennett, grandparents, young people like Jason and Mallory, and mothers like you, Adelle. They're hoping to find candy apples or antiques or barbecue and art, homemade jewelry, or a good time. In the end they'll share a similar experience, even if they don't have the same, um . . ." She churned her hands together.

"Expectations?" Dale supplied.

"Yes, yes—expectations! Now, this year, By the Book is joining the party." Noemie jiggled her shoulders, and her lips parted in a wide grin. "And this is how Glory and Eli will contribute to the festival, gathering literary quotes to get people to thinking—"

"About their *books*," Adelle scoffed.

Noemie's vigorous nodding made her thick curls caress her shoulders. "But most importantly about life. About love and family and friendship and community. Even shopping! Everything our festival and life here in Gilmore centers around. Don't we have a common story? I suggested she gather a representation—men and women, little people, old people, and in-between people—to gather thoughts from all walks of life. You're those people."

Frederick didn't bother with requesting permission to speak. "I'm a little confused. Exactly what will you do with these quotes and lyrics or whatever it is we're coming up with? I brought some ideas with me, but I'm not sure if it's what you're looking for." He reached for the leather satchel propped against his leg.

Eli used the back of his chair to push to his feet. "Hold up there, Fred. We'll get to what you have in a minute. As we started to explain, once we compile a list of the most provocative or most meaningful ideas, we'll print them and then post them around town a couple weeks before the festival. I told Glory this would generate excitement in the community, get people to talkin'."

Glory squirmed a bit. That suggestion hadn't sat well with her, but once Eli got a seed planted in his head, there was no uprooting it. She worried over how far word would travel.

"I checked with the printer, and he'll need a few weeks to get it down right. Colorful, big cards."

"What he means is *muy caro*." Noemie rubbed two fingers together and winked at Glory.

"That's neither here nor there. What's important is the schedule. It's August, which means we only have a month to meet before we'd need to send these to the printer."

Another hand rose, this time more tentatively. Charles said quietly, "Perhaps, as an accommodation, we could ask a *non*reader to act as secretary or designer and assist the group in fleshing out our thoughts."

Adelle mouthed *Thank you* to Charles from across the room.

Noemie shook her head slightly at Glory and pressed a fingertip to her lips.

The bookstore owner wanted to ask Charles Graves what it was about the woman that elicited such protectiveness and chivalry on the part of the menfolk. While she didn't like it much, this show of sympathy for Adelle, she had to admit to herself that she appreciated the olive branch he'd extended. She forced a smile and remarked, "Those are all good thoughts. Any more questions?"

The nine others glanced at one another until Frederick piped up. "How long and how often? I can smell something good, and it's making me hungry. It's time to take my stomach back to the house."

Everyone laughed.

Glory signaled to Eli, who threaded his way through the tables toward the kitchen. "I'm glad you asked that, Frederick. I know we asked y'all to come out at an awkward hour—right after work for some and at dinnertime for others. To prevent this from being a hardship, Eli and I prepared something more than these delicious popovers of Ophelia's."

"It was mostly Eli," her husband shouted.

"Hush! *We* thought it would be special to have our inaugural discussion over dinner. That is, if you can stay."

Most of the group trooped into the kitchen where a feast awaited—at least in the single mother's eyes. Covered platters filled with mashed potatoes, smothered chicken, roasted carrots, biscuits, and—if the oven light was telling the truth—dessert. Once Frederick returned from making a call, they prayed and squeezed in around the Pryors' private six-square-foot table after lining up at the island to spoon food onto their plates.

But as hungry as Adelle was for food and fellowship, it killed her to pick up one of those heavy earthenware dishes and serve herself some of the creamiest potatoes to ever grace her tongue. Sure, she was grateful the woman had actually accounted for people like her and Bennett who hadn't eaten before the meeting, but extending the meeting without asking was mighty presumptuous. Either way, she stewed, the meal looked delicious and came right on time. So much better than the hot dogs she'd planned to boil once they were ensconced in their own kitchen.

Two might be company, but that was certainly a meager number to cook for. Fourteen months ago, Adelle prepped meals inspired by Ben's likes and dislikes. Chicken salad with grapes and walnuts instead of tuna salad on saltines. No cream cheese unless she served it in possum pie. Barbecue with vinegar sauce, but no slaw. Adelle couldn't say what her own favorite foods were anymore. While cooking for a four-year-old wasn't complicated, it taxed her emotionally. These days she scrounged for food like the birds in the fields, eating here and there, picking off Bennett's leftovers; she'd lost a dress size since Ben died.

"Everything alright, Adelle?" Glory's question floated across the opposite side of the table.

Debating within herself the reasons Glory would single her out, Adelle bumped the child who was basically sitting in her lap in the tight quarters. "It's all delicious, isn't it, Bennett? Thank you for hosting us, Eli . . . Glory."

Her son nodded, engrossed in gnawing on his remaining strips of meat.

Glory set down the pitcher of tea. Before Adelle could refuse, she plopped another gravy-covered piece of chicken onto the boy's plate. She fingered one of Bennett's curls when he dug into it.

"I know we're busy eatin', but can y'all talk around your chicken bone and share your ideas?" Dale was born and raised in what was called the Queen City—Charlotte, North Carolina, about two hours away. He'd settled in the area after graduating from Western Carolina University.

At first, the only answer to his question was the clink and clatter of utensils striking plates.

Frederick finished chewing and wiped his mouth. He unhooked the latch on the bag he'd brought with him into the kitchen and withdrew a book. "I read this years ago and it stayed with me for some time. It's called *The Deep End of the Ocean*."

"Wait. That's an old movie with the actor who plays in the Marvel movies?" Jason asked.

"Michelle Pfeiffer," Mallory supplied. "You saw it with my friends during my sleepover. Isn't it based on a true story?"

"We're not talking about movies." Glory's voice was terse as she refilled the ice bucket.

Frederick opened the thick novel and removed one of the green sticky notes. "I don't think it's a true story. Here's one quote that struck me: *Home is not a place, but a feeling of belonging.*"

"I'd agree with that. Your home is more about how you feel inside and the people around you instead of your address, and I believe that's a good theme for the festival. Wouldn't you agree? We want visitors to feel at home here in Gilmore, the way we feel around this table."

Adelle could've been eating stones, her stomach felt so heavy. She set down her fork.

"Here are a couple more that run along the same lines." Frederick stuck his finger in the book, opened to another section, and peeled off a green square. He pressed it to the table beside his plate and read: *We are all connected, and our actions ripple through the lives of others.* And one more . . . *Family is not just blood, but the people who choose to be there for us.*" He closed the book. "Good stuff."

Cringing inwardly, Adelle risked a glance around the kitchen, and her eyes landed on her hosts. Glory looked about as comfortable as she did.

Dale hit the side of his head. "Isn't that story about a family losing their son? The kicker is that—"

"Are you okay? You're about to hit the floor!" Ophelia jumped up and caught the platter of biscuits that was leaning precariously from Glory's hand.

At her side, Eli pressed a napkin into her hand and guided her to her seat.

She dabbed her glistening forehead. "I'm fine, fine."

Ophelia reached for the water pitcher in the middle of the table and refilled Glory's glass. "Are you sure? Drink this."

Noemie hovered at her friend's side. "You're so busy tending to us, you haven't touched your own food."

"I'm sure that's it. Mama would say I have 'the sugar,' and that it's because of all the extras I've been eating." Glory tilted her head in their baker's direction.

Bennett balanced on his knees in his chair and whispered loudly in his mother's ear, "Sugar? She ate too many cookies?"

Adelle patted his leg to settle him. "I'll tell you about it later, Bennett."

Dale snickered. "*Sugar* is another name for diabetes, a medical condition that affects how people process what they eat and drink. Some people call it that."

"And by *some people*, our friend over here means folks in our generation. My aunt lost her legs to complications from the disease, and it's no laughing matter," Frederick chided.

"But as far as I know, my wife isn't a diabetic. Glory, enjoy your meal. We can handle our own drinks." Eli tapped the rim of her plate. "Now, what were you saying, Dale?"

"May I, while my husband chews on it?" Laughing, Noemie reached around her husband, whose mouth was stuffed. "Hmmm. I'm not sure which character it was, but I remember reading something about trials . . . Here we are. *Life is a series of ups and downs, but it is in the downs where we find our true strength.*"

"If that ain't lifted straight from the Scriptures!" Ophelia cried out.

"It is awfully close," Adelle agreed.

Glory quoted quietly, "*That's why I take pleasure in my weaknesses, and in the insults, hardships, persecutions, and troubles that I suffer for Christ. For when I am weak, then I am strong.*"

Adelle stared at the bookseller. "You know that passage?"

"I don't sell Bibles, but I know what's in them. I had to memorize that verse from Second Corinthians for the Easter pageant when I was in the fourth grade."

Ophelia shook the ice in her glass. "God is our Creator, and everything originates from Him. I'm not surprised you'd find that in the book since there's nothing new under the sun. That's also in the Bible."

Eli shook his head at his cousin. "I didn't read *The Deep End of the Ocean*, but I did see the movie. That would be a hard thing to forgive, losing a child that way."

"The book addresses the themes of brokenness and forgiveness, and also hope—not to give anything away to anybody here who hasn't read it. She points out that our hardest struggles happen in our heart. That calls to mind that Scripture from Ephesians that warns us that we don't fight in the physical realm, against flesh and blood, but in the spiritual." Dale scooped up the last of his potatoes and gravy with a biscuit.

Noemie crossed her utensils over her empty plate. "Adelle, I heard about your fiction versus nonfiction debate. As a believer, I can tell you I see so many faith threads in novels, outside of Christian fiction or biblical fiction. The authors may not have intended to weave them through their novels, but God can use anything and anyone. It's like the book says, all of us are connected somehow."

"*The book* meaning the Bible?" Adelle asked absently, keeping one eye on Glory.

"Haha, no. *The Deep End of the Ocean*, this work of fiction.

Frederick read it a moment ago." Noemie wiped her mouth and turned her attention from Adelle to Glory. "My friend, I recommended it to you. Did you ever get around to reading it?"

"No." Glory pinched the word the way she did a chunk of her bread.

Adelle tried to gauge the woman's expression. While she didn't know much about Glory Pryor, she definitely seemed bothered by something. *Maybe you're projecting your own discomfort with this subject,* she thought.

"Well, you should," Noemie insisted. "And I agree with Dale. It's an old book that people may not recognize, but there are good quotes that might be useful because it's about the love of family and belonging. I don't like the language all the time, I will say, but it describes what we share here, and what you find in your community—your family, town, your friends. Love and loyalty and brokenness. Think about how you include Dude in your family. I'm sure you're helping him in ways you didn't expect and aren't aware of."

Loyalty. Bile burned the back of Adelle's throat and soured her stomach. She fought the urge to grab Bennett and dash from the Pryors' kitchen. *How can the two of them sit there and participate in a discussion on those two gifts like they know anything about them, and laugh and go on like it's nothing?*

Glory suddenly pounded her fist on the table, tears streaming. "Noemie, the last thing I want to do is talk about somebody else's missing son, fictional or no. That's a book I can write myself! Mama and Daddy never found their son, my brother. Never! Despite the loving and loyal community."

Eli covered her fingers. "Baby . . ."

Glory snatched her hand away.

A crestfallen Noemie patted Eli's arm. "No, she's right, she's right. *Lo siento, mi amiga.* We should've known better. There's a reason I didn't suggest the book to you in the first place, and in the moment I forgot."

Adelle gazed round the table at all the people who knew the backstory Glory hadn't bothered to share with the newcomers. *What have I gotten myself into?*

"Mwah. Mwah." Glory kissed her friend on each of her cheeks. "Talk tomorrow?"

Noemie winked. "Sure as shootin'."

"Ha! You're sounding more and more homegrown every day. If you don't watch yourself, we won't be able to tell where Colombia ends and North Carolina begins." Glory waved goodbye to the couple and locked the door behind them. She rested her forehead against the wood.

"Tired?"

Without turning, Glory nodded in answer to Eli's question but gratefully accepted the arms he wrapped around her middle.

"What can I do?" His soft words tickled the hairs on her nape.

"You can remind me why I thought these meetings were a good idea."

He spun her in his direction and held her close, pinning her arms to her side.

It was just as well. She hadn't the wherewithal to raise them the few inches to return the embrace, though questions buzzed about her brain with an energy lacking in her limbs. She counted his heartbeat until she reached one hundred twenty before raising another subject along the same lines that pestered her. "You know how we've talked about being old and needing something new?"

When she felt Eli's chin bump against her crown, she assumed he'd answered with a *yes* and trudged forward. "Is that part of why you're dying to sell By the Book? To move to some new, exotic clime? Marriage—check, check. Owned a business—check, check. Had a child—check. Retired—check."

Eli pulled back and tilted her face. "This had better be that lemon meringue pie talkin' because I know you're not serious. You're so full to bursting, all that tartness is overflowing from that lovely mouth of yours." He kissed her. "Yep, sweet and sour."

Glory laid her hands on his chest to create room to think. "I'm serious, Eli."

"I can tell, love. From what I've heard, my old girlfriend lived in Myrtle Beach. I don't know if I'd call it *exotic*, but I for one could stand a break from inhaling and exhaling all this book glue and these fancy words. *Clime.*" He shook his head.

She delicately pummeled his chest with her fists. "Well, beach sand and boardwalks sound exotic to me, after living in the shadows of these mountains most of my adult life. It's six hours away and about twenty degrees hotter and more humid."

"Maybe. You're still feeling some kind of way about our plans to leave this place."

No amount of teeth-clenching could keep Glory's deepest thoughts from squeaking through them. "*Our* plans? *I'm* not plannin' on goin' *no*where."

13

"Glory."

She brushed at her cheek.

"Glory."

Groaning, she snuggled deeper under the blanket.

"Honeybun."

Glory shivered when she felt a cool rush of air on her exposed shoulder. Blinking slowly, she tried to focus in the dark room and reach for the covers. "What's today?" she asked hoarsely.

"It's Sunday," Eli whispered.

She promptly rolled to her left side away from him.

He shook her. "Glory, wake up."

Sighing, she raised herself to an elbow and glared at his shadowy figure. "Eli Pryor. Why are you waking me in the middle of the night?"

"It's not the middle of the night. It's very early in the morning. I want to take you somewhere, and we need to leave as soon as possible. You might want to put on a sweater." He paused. "Glory, are you awake? Did you hear me?"

She rested her head on the pillow for another second before holding out her hand and letting him gently pull her upright and to her feet. Less than thirty minutes later, Glory was ensconced in the passenger seat of Eli's Lincoln Aviator, sipping Earl Grey from an insulated thermos. So far, she'd counted two women walking their dogs, a lone jogger, and a man sitting on the curb of Springs Church Road. Though she pressed her nose to the cool glass, a bleary Glory couldn't tell if it was Dude as they passed him at forty-five miles per hour.

"You neglected to tell me where we're going." At this time on a Sunday, she was supposed to be stretched out in her bed for at least four more hours.

"After the week we had and the group meeting tomorrow night, I thought we could use a short getaway."

"You have a point; a getaway sounds nice. But there was no way to get away later in the day? We woke up the birds!"

"Uh-uh." Eli pressed the button to open the lid to his cup.

Glory's nose wrinkled at the smell that drifted through the car. *Coffee.* "At least you got my tea right. Otherwise, I wouldn't be able to forgive you for dragging me out of bed on the only day I get to sleep in."

He chuckled and patted her thigh. "Nice pants."

Following his advice, she'd slid on a pair of blue palazzos with a matching striped tunic. "Thank you. But I'm serious. I may be more of a morning person than you are typically, but I save my cheeriness for weekdays, when I've gone to bed before midnight the night before. My Sundays are for chattin' with you over a plate of grits and bacon, reading the paper, and maybe enjoying an afternoon snooze on the sofa. They're not for driving out of town on barely lit streets while the rest of the county sleeps in—like I'm supposed to be doing."

He spared her a glance. "As you've said a few times. But they're also for adventure. Stop all the worriation. I don't hear you complaining when you're shelving books on a Sunday afternoon. You might be home in time to write your letters while you listen to the choir."

She started, his words catching her in the middle of a yawn.

Eli signaled a right turn and took the exit onto the highway. "Yes, I've spied you bopping to the choir that sings down at Ebenezer. You must enjoy listening to it; otherwise, you'd write in the den on the third floor, at the back of the house. That's why the directors mounted speakers outside and have that congregation raising the roof: so they can minister to all the folks like us who forsake the pew."

Glory angled her body against the door. With five years under their belt, they knew each other's ins and outs. Better than some couples married five times as long. Still, she didn't have to like it. And he didn't have to know that one of her reasons for sitting on their front porch was gaining a better vantage point of the sidewalk and anybody strolling by. A part of her held out hope that Davis might find her one day, and Sunday mornings seemed as good a time as any. Possibly better.

She watched Eli sip from his mug. "What about you? You're the one who uses Sundays and Mondays to pretend you're truly retired. You'll regret this come Tuesday morning when I'm shaking the alarm over your head to wake you."

Her husband had taken it to heart, starting a second act as a full-time bookseller. Traveling, fishing with Dale, and watching Glory piddle around the store filled up much of his off-hours despite her efforts to steer him toward a hobby to keep his idle mind off planning their move.

Eli stretched across the console to take her hand. "Stop complaining. There's a big world out here for you to see, and you don't know where we're going. Why's it so hard for you to leave the store's confines?"

Because inmates don't get to leave the prison when they're serving a life sentence. *I can't let Davis come back and find me gone, even if it's only the memory of him.* Glory listened to the tires eat up the tarmac as they crossed a bridge and determined to make the most of their together time. She squeezed his hand. "Okay, I'll trust you."

"That's what you said five years ago." The light from a streetlamp cast a shadow over his face, but it didn't conceal his smile.

She yanked the hair on the back of his wrist.

A few minutes later they pulled off the main road at a sign marked *Scenic Overlook* and wound up what was little more than a gravel path barely wide enough for one-way traffic. After driving about a half mile, he parked between two other vehicles. "We should hurry to find a good spot." Eli alighted from the car and slammed the door.

In a huff, she followed him in the half-light around to the trunk and waited as he removed two chairs and a blanket and leaned them against the vehicle. When he draped an insulated bag over her shoulder, she decided enough was enough.

"Eli, I'm about to act like a five-year-old and kick and scream until you tell me what's going on."

"I see that 'I trust you' thing lasted all of thirty minutes. Since you can't wait until we get there for the surprise, I'll tell you this much: we're going for a little walk. What do you think?"

"I think that sounds like a hike in the dark, with snakes and spiders I won't be able to see. And I thought our meeting with Ophelia over her infernal menu planning scared me!" The baked goods his cousin provided were an excellent value-add, to borrow her husband's marketing term, but they also complicated Glory's life. Now this from Eli.

"I call it a big walk, and you call it a little hike. As long as we don't call the whole thing off." Eli sounded pleased with himself.

Glory shook her head. "Still working on that stand-up routine,

I see. What I can't see is me traipsing over hill and dale at this hour, especially in these wide-leg pants—unless our policy covers my tumbling down the mountainside. I'm afraid I do think we should call the whole thing off."

"That's why I have these." Eli shone a light on a rectangular cardboard package.

She squinted at it. "Hair scrunchies?"

"Consider them pant scrunchies. You'll look like a genie when you walk. Besides, I'm not talking about a hike, big or small. Only a stroll with the medium-size hill as the backdrop. And in case you can't see me, I'm holding up three fingers."

"Do you know how long it's been since you were a boy scout?" Glory sighed.

"Ahh, I can tell you're wavering. You won't regret leaving the house, I promise. Aren't you afraid of turning into a hermit?" He picked up a chair with each hand and set out.

"But I'm not wearing hair ties on my pants," Glory grumped, unable to come up with another reason to get her out of going. They'd made no other plans for this relatively cool, early Sunday morning, so saying anything else would make her sound peevish, difficult, or lazy. *Or more peevish, more difficult, and lazier.*

"Come. We don't want to come this far and miss it." Eli's voice floated over his shoulder.

She adjusted the strap and trudged behind him. "Could you specify what 'it' is?"

"The sunrise over a picnic breakfast!"

"Oh . . . wow. The sunrise?" She perked up, immediately ashamed that she'd put up such a fuss. Grateful she'd heeded his advice to put on pants and thick-soled shoes, Glory crunched behind Eli. Already, the swiftly approaching day was creeping along the edges of the well-worn path that cut through the woods. A morning breeze wisping through the trees towering over them made limbs sway and fallen leaves dance and scuttle across the ground.

"Be careful you don't twist your ankle on a pine cone," Eli warned. "I'm too old and out of shape to carry you back to the car."

She quickened her pace, her long legs matching him stride for stride. Within minutes, they broke through the tree cover and found a space among the others who were similarly inspired this Sunday morning. Eli arranged their collapsible chairs side by side and unburdened her of the food carrier that had bumped against her hip during their trek.

"After you." He turned up a palm. When she sat, he spread the blanket over her lap.

Glory had worked up a light sweat and didn't really need the added layer, but his thoughtfulness warmed her heart. After he dropped beside her, she scooted closer to him and laid half the cover over his legs. "I'm aware I'm not the easiest person to surprise. I steered my own ship for nigh on sixty years, Mr. Pryor, so I'm working on it. Lots to get used to."

He tipped his forehead against hers. "You're worth the effort."

"I should hope so." Her words were hushed, having sensed a change in the atmosphere. She linked arms with her husband, preparing herself for what was coming.

The light wind swept down the hillside and began to dispatch the mist hugging the shadowy pines, alders, and birch and shielding them from view. The trees stretched above the low brush toward the patchwork of light-blue, gray, and purple skies above them. Suddenly, a fiery orange ball burst over the distant ridges and burned through the haze of clouds, awakening sleeping birds who raised a chorus of tweets, whistles, trills. A few fluttered, startled from their nests, when the sun's onstage appearance sparked scattered applause from the audience seated on the hillside.

"Aaahh. It's incredible." Glory's voice trembled. Overcome by the resplendent birth of a new day, she didn't bother blinking back her tears, letting them flow unchecked. Her arm tensed against Eli's, holding him tightly. "Thank you."

He patted the fingertips clutching him. "You're welcome."

Glory wasn't sure who she was actually thanking but said nothing further to disturb the moment. The raucous cries of the wildlife around them had that part covered. She leaned back in her seat as tinges of pink and yellow crept across a sky that gradually brightened until the whole area was bathed in light, save for a clump of far-off clouds on the edge of the horizon. Following Eli's lead, she pushed off the blanket and welcomed the warmth of the sun's smile on her face. She couldn't help but smile back.

The two of them kept their seats as others eventually packed up. As Eli unzipped the bag he'd packed, Glory cheerily acknowledged strangers who took exaggerated sniffs of the Pryors' breakfast as they hauled themselves back down the hillside or trooped farther along their hike. Appreciatively, she peeled back the silver-foil-wrapped sausage-and-cheese biscuit Eli had prepared for their picnic.

"You love well, darlin'. How early did you get up to do this?"

"Early enough." He feigned a yawn then took a bite of his sandwich. "But losing a little sleep and expending a little sweat to wrangle you out of the house was worth it." Eli indicated the sky, which was now fully awake.

They chewed in silence as the area emptied. A few people stood by the railing protecting them from the drop-off, aiming cameras at the tree line. Though shadows had started to gather, they didn't eclipse the freshness of the morning.

Eli folded up his napkin and mustard packet inside his foil and stuck it inside the bag. "A few minutes ago, you said, *Thank you.* I assumed you were talking to me, but you weren't. Am I right?"

Trust you to stir the embers. No need to rekindle the fire. Glory brushed a flake of biscuit off her bosom. "I was merely expressing my gratitude for the moment. Wasn't it amazing? Can you believe I've never witnessed this? Mama and Daddy attended sunrise service Easter mornings, but they let Davis and me sleep in. They probably considered it their once-a-year date. After he left, they stopped going." She slowly chewed her last bit of breakfast, hating to finish. And hating to continue the discussion.

He crossed his arms behind his head and stretched out his hairy legs. "You're deflecting, Glory. It's okay, you know. I felt it, too. That . . . that wonder. The awe of beholding something so much greater than yourself. It's similar to the way I feel when I stand on the shore and gaze at the waves. Today, though . . . Today felt different somehow. *More.*"

Following the direction of his eyes, Glory stared at the expanse of variegated green hues extending for miles beyond their rocky outcropping. It was broken only by pops of red, yellow, and brown—leaves that were readying their autumn wardrobe and dead branches and trees that had snapped at their base. She frowned at the clump of dark clouds chugging toward them from the west. Their steady march made Glory fear the abrupt end of her rare excursion.

So focused on an internal perspective, Eli seemed unaware of their impending threat. "When you look at a book, you know those words don't appear out of nowhere and get bound and stitched together. There's a writer, an author. Experiencing this sunrise, same thing. It emphasized the power, the unmatched *magnificence* of creation. Of the Creator. An Author."

Eli's whispered comment was barely discernible enough for his wife to hear. Yet, his message came through loud and clear. Like her, Eli had been raised with a Bible in his hand and a hymn on his tongue.

At that moment, thunder rumbled, and a far-off jagged streak lit the storm clouds the sun hadn't completely chased away. A teenager and her friends scampered to grab their blankets. Another man snapped a picture before his hiking partner yanked him from the overlook and toward the path.

Glory sighed. "Well, Eli, I suppose the Lord giveth, and the Lord taketh away."

The patter of rain on the roof roused Adelle, who'd hovered over sleep most of the night. She flopped to her back and threw an arm over her face before flipping the pillow to the cooler side. Turning her back to the hazy glow sneaking through the window blinds, she grumbled, "Why did I think moving to the middle of the bed would change anything?" *Lord, please give me an unbroken hour of rest.*

Just as she started to drift, heavy thunder rattled the windowpanes. What seemed like seconds later, Adelle heard the doorknob thunk against the wall and footsteps pad quickly to the bed. When she felt the mattress sink slightly, she rolled to her left side, snuggled Bennett against her middle, and drew the covers over them both without opening her eyes. She didn't bother extracting his thumb she was sure he'd stuck in his mouth. They'd both suffered through their share of storms and needed whatever comfort they could find.

Her lids felt sticky when she opened them to bright sunlight, and she wondered how much longer she'd slept since her son had curled up beside her. *Since you dragged him into bed, don't you mean, Adelle?* "Maybe I need a dog. A big one," she murmured into Bennett's hair. "I definitely sleep better with someone beside me."

With Ben beside her.

Adelle eased her arm from under the child without dislodging him and crept around the bed. Deciding to forego brushing her teeth to avoid unnecessary noise, she eased from the room and shut the door with a soft click.

A peek at the clock over the electric range announced it was 9:30. She bit her lip. "Do I wake him so he can eat breakfast and dress for church, or do I let him sleep in? WWBD?" *What would Ben do?*

It wasn't that her husband had replaced Jesus in her mind; she hadn't mounted Ben on a pedestal to pray to him or expect him to respond. She thought of him first because he had always been the decision-maker, the wise, quick thinker who heard the question and answered it immediately. Adelle was the flip side of their coin; she held up a finger to test the velocity of the wind and agonized over its direction. Losing Ben had been the impetus for coming to Gilmore; she wouldn't have implemented this plan to reclaim what was hers by right if he hadn't up and died. But now, it was her responsibility to carry through without his stabilizing, daily presence.

"Can I do it?" Adelle spooned grounds in the filter and fit it in the coffee maker.

Should you do it?

The spoon clattered to the counter and dark granules rolled everywhere. She grabbed the dishcloth from the sink and raked the grounds into her palm. Adelle wondered over the source of those doubtful words. *Should* had never entered her mind; that was a given.

While the coffee brewed, she went to the family room for her Bible and journal. Shaking, she fumbled her materials, and everything hit the floor—pages splayed and pens scattered. Adelle fell to her knees to pick up the jumble, glad the carpet had muffled the noise. She shoved the pens in the pocket of her robe and straightened the thin, crinkled pages before she closed the Bible and rested her chin on it.

As a child, Adelle's daddy had taught her to treat it as more than the Good Book; she was to consider God's Word a treasure to keep safe and hide in her heart.

"But how am I supposed to get it in there? Won't it hurt?" She'd flattened her hands against her tiny chest.

He'd set his baby girl on his lap. "Not always. However, it might sometimes, precious one, I'm not gonna lie. Just not in the way you might think. You remember how we play hide-and-seek?"

She nodded. "That's my favorite!"

"When we play that game with your friends, and I'm the seeker, you don't want me to find you. You look for the best hiding place and stay as quiet as possible so you're the last to be found."

Adelle poked out her lips. "But you always find me first."

"That's because you run behind the same tree every time!" Her father tickled her feet that were swinging back and forth under his legs. When she settled down, he continued, "Now, when it comes to hiding God's Word in your heart"—He tapped the Bible—"that means you read it and study it all the time because you want to understand it. You run to it first, like I run to that tree, and I run to you.

"In order to get to know God and His Word, you must spend time with Him, loving Him as your Father. And after all that time in His presence, His Word wiggles its way down deep inside you. Not only in your mind, but into your heart. Nobody can take it away from you even though they witness it by the way you think, talk, and act. You tuck it inside you in your favorite place, but you want to seek Him and find Him."

"But why did you say that could hurt? Reading is fun, and I like to hear you tell me Bible stories." She scrunched up her face, puzzling it out. Hiding God's Word sounded like it should be a good thing.

Her father inhaled deeply. "Let me see how to explain it."

Adelle waited, noting how he cocked his head to the side, like when he molded his clay animals or wrote things down in his diaries.

That meant he was working on something important and wanted to get it right. She tried to keep still.

"Sometimes, the lessons in here are hard to understand or believe. We might think they don't apply to us. But everything within these pages has meaning and application—um, that means usefulness—to our lives, baby girl. It's like when I have to spank you or send you to your room or take something away that you enjoy. I'm teaching you about consequences and telling the truth or correcting you when you do wrong. Jesus paid the price for our sin, but we have to deal with the consequences of our choices, even Daddy. It's hard, but it's okay.

"God has to do that sometimes, and we hide that in our heart, too, so we can see how much He loves us and wants the best for us. We have to work at seeking and understanding. Believing and trusting Him when it hurts and we don't want to. Does that make sense?"

The young Adelle had nodded that day, still confused. This morning, the older Adelle understood a little more, though God's ways were far beyond her most of the time. "I'm hiding these scriptures in my heart just like you taught me, Daddy, and I'm teaching Bennett to do it, too. But it pains me sometimes."

Nestling the Bible in the crook of her arm, Adelle stood and walked to the kitchen table to wait for the coffee to finish. She took the pens from her pocket and opened her leather journal. Some of the pages had gotten crimped when she dropped them, so she unfolded the corners.

One wrinkled sheet was hanging out of the pocket in the back. Adelle slowly extracted the Scripture she'd torn from her father's journal and read over and over to ensure she'd never forget it. She couldn't say this passage from Isaiah 59 was hidden anywhere; rather it had seared both her heart and her mind. And it hurt. She read it out loud: *"Therefore justice is far from us, Nor does righteousness overtake us; We look for light, but there is darkness! For brightness, but we walk in blackness! We grope for the wall like the blind, And we grope as if we had no eyes; We stumble at noonday as at twilight; We are as dead men in desolate places. We all growl like bears, And moan sadly like doves; We look for justice, but there is none; For salvation, but it is far from us."*

Her lips flattened. At one time, justice had seemed far from her, but now she could almost touch it. *There's no should about it. I'm going to do what I came here to do. Starting with returning to that Famous Quotes Group come tomorrow night.*

14

"Must be a kink somewhere." Glory yanked at the hose. Water gushed from the nozzle. She snatched the weeds at the edge of the bed and aimed the stream at the fragile green sprouts that had greeted her that afternoon. "I should take a photo and show it to Frederick. If it weren't for him and his gardening tips, I would never have grown something back here."

Satisfied that she'd soaked the new spinach, she directed the stream to the row of carrots. This was her first year of planting more than spices on the shelf in her kitchen, and she'd fretted over planting these vegetables, particularly this late in the year. It had taken much encouragement and expert help to convince her to venture outside the house and expand her interests beyond books. She let the water flow on the next row, careful not to wet her skirt, and gazed up at a flock of starlings swooping through the silvery sky. "Eli's right: If I'm not careful, I'll become a hermit. Davis wouldn't want me to pay that heavy a penance."

Glory glanced over her shoulder at the chair bumping against the fence. Still empty, save for a few red-tinged leaves the maple had shed. She had to admit that part of her desire to start a garden back here was to engage Dude in more conversations, to get to know him better and possibly lure him into helping with it. Perhaps if he had more positive outlets, he'd invest in something other than the bottle.

The back door opened, and Eli poked his graying head around it. "Hey there, beautiful. Folks have arrived. How's it looking over there? I'm surprised you need to water them, what with the rain we've had."

Glory had shooed her husband away when he'd offered a hand with the seeds. As a result, he tended to keep his distance. She pointed at the new growth. "That was Sunday. But look, we have cabbage! And over there, the spinach. I'll pluck the rest of these cucumbers, but we'll harvest green onions and garlic before you know it." Glory admired her handiwork.

"*We*, she says. Maybe you can give me a tour tomorrow and I'll finally get to see it up close and personal. But in the meantime . . ." Eli leveled a thumb in the direction of the room behind him.

Her exterior smile belied her interior frown because she knew he meant the Famous Quotes Group and not the kitchen. "Okey dokey, I'll be right in. Give me a minute to clean up."

Eli wedged a foot in the door and leaned farther onto the stoop.

"Good gracious, I said I was coming! Yesterday, you accused me of never leaving the store, and now you're trying to rush me back in. I can't please you, de-ah." Glory raised her hem and stepped over the puddle formed by the water dripping from the raised beds.

"I'll give you five minutes before I send Adelle out here to get you."

When she pretended to spray him, he snorted and ducked inside.

Glory turned off the water at the bib and took her time curling the hose around her arm, pushing the boundaries of her five-minute reprieve. Skirting the rivulets trailing down the paved area, she made her way to the back door that Eli had kept open with a brick they used for that purpose. Picturing the evening that awaited her, she groused, "Whoever came up with this idea must have been out of their mind."

She smacked her forehead. "Oh, that's right. I did."

Adelle plopped down a plastic bowl next to the plate of cherry tomatoes and cucumbers she'd seasoned with salt and pepper. She opened a large box of Goldfish crackers and filled the empty container. Her food joined platters of cheese and salami, grapes, and what looked like brie oozing from pastry.

Ophelia entered the café area, bearing a dish of sausage balls.

"I thought we were keeping it simple tonight. Since we're starting at seven, we were supposed to eat dinner before we came and share light snacks. Someone didn't get the memo," Adelle chided the baker, indicating the appetizer and the brie.

"You know we can't send this baby home after serving him only a handful of crackers shaped like fish. That would be lame, and this host doesn't do lame." Ophelia touched her chest, her smile large enough to include Adelle and Bennett, nearly hidden behind his mother.

"Now, little man, you've seen me enough by now that I won't brook any shyness on your part. Why, I bandaged your boo-boos and read to you on our first date! Want a sausage ball?"

Adelle peeked at her son.

He edged around her legs. "Thank you, Mrs. Brown." He accepted the plate and a napkin. "If you're Mr. Pryor's cousin, why aren't you a Mrs. Pryor, too?"

Ophelia shook her head briskly at Adelle to prevent her from shushing her child. "Good question. Because I got married a long time ago to someone who isn't a Pryor. And that wasn't my last name anyhow because Mr. Pryor and I are cousins way, way, way down the line." She stretched her arm and indicated a distance far from her body. "His grandmama's half brother was my uncle's second cousin once removed, or something like that."

Adelle squinted at her but couldn't quite do the math.

Bennett took a bite. "Where is your husband? Is he coming tonight?"

Adelle noticed the baker's eyes harden a bit and she jumped into the conversation. "Bennett, let Mrs. Brown put down her platter and be about her business. Oh, look, there's Mr. Graves! Why don't you go ask him about Oscar."

The boy popped the rest of the sausage ball into his mouth and scampered over to greet his favorite dog owner, leaving his shyness behind along with his empty plate.

Adelle touched the other woman on her arm. "I'm sorry, Ophelia. He didn't mean to be rude. Bennett's naturally curious and didn't know not to ask."

Ophelia brushed off the apology as she squeezed the platter between the cucumbers and the brie on the concrete bar top. "Did I say he shouldn't have asked? My Mr. Brown is long gone. Not in the same way as your husband maybe, but about as permanently. Left me to raise Mallory and Jason on my own, without even a how-de-do. But God is good anyhow, and I'm not gonna worry about it."

Adelle was getting used to the woman's forthright manner that aged her about twenty years. Ophelia's words didn't sting the way they would have a month ago. *I suppose she's bandaging my boo-boos, too.*

"Anyway, fill your plate. We'll have a full house soon. Oh, looky there. It's as I said: the gang's all here." Ophelia waved hello to Noemie and Dale, entering the café as Eli exited the kitchen with Frederick at his side. "Let me go find my children and put them to work."

Braced for Glory's appearance, Adelle worked to maintain an impassive expression while keeping watch over her son. Unable to resist the aroma, she forked three sausage balls onto her plate, along with some cucumbers and tomatoes and a hunk of baked brie. Mouth full with the first food she'd eaten since that morning's apple, she leafed through the books in the racks, nodding her head to the soft jazz emanating from unseen speakers. As she let down her guard inch by inch, out popped the weasel.

"Hello, Adelle. Good to see you. I wasn't sure you were going to brave our little group again." Glory proffered her cheek to Eli.

Those two must be attached by an invisible rubber band. Adelle forced the food down her throat. "Hi, Glory. Of course. Nothing could have kept me from tonight."

"Honey, ready to get started? Folks will need to get home, especially our little folks." He gave Adelle a one-armed hug.

She sensed his wife bristling as she accepted it, albeit stiffly. Adelle relaxed when he stepped aside to make way for Jason and Mallory, hopping from table to table, arranging pads of paper and jars of writing implements. She expelled a shaky breath between the tiny *O* her mouth formed as the two strolled away, hand in hand. The king and queen in their castle.

"Anybody ready to kick things off with a quote?" Standing at the front of the room, Glory twisted her wedding band round her finger, hoping no one noticed the wet splotches at her hemline from rushing her garden cleanup. Spying Bennett perched on Eli's knee made her stop short of wringing her hands. Something about that boy's mama set her teeth on edge, but he eased her frazzled nerves.

"Y'all have the floor." Relieved to cede the limelight, Glory sat beside her husband and the four-year-old and waited for everyone to find their places. Under cover of chairs scraping on the wood floor, she whispered to him, "Do something. Say . . . anything."

Eli plopped the child onto Glory's lap and reached under his seat for the half-full crystal bowl marked *Famous Quotes*. He stirred around the slips of paper, unfolded one, and read, "*The Screwtape Letters* by C. S. Lewis. Hmm, let's see." Eli shrugged when he flipped it to the reverse side. "Nothing but that. Perhaps the customer thought the entire book was a famous quote."

"I'd agree with that!" Frederick's enthusiasm was apparent. "My son and I read it together recently, and he was amazed at how relevant it is."

Of all books, Glory cried inwardly, listening to the conversation around her. She saw Adelle checking out the racks of used books. "What do you have over there?"

"I spotted *The Screwtape Letters* on the shelf earlier." She removed the book and carried it to the seat she'd found at Ophelia's table. She turned page after page.

Frederick loosened his tie and draped his suit coat over his leg. "There was this part that described the safest road to Hell. Simple things like playing cards that distract man from what is good. The 'gentle slope.'"

Dale slapped his thigh. "My mama could've written that section herself! Come Sunday, we couldn't think about a game of Go Fish or else she'd lay down a sermon longer than the one we'd heard at church. She called cards the devil's game."

Noemie snorted. "I wonder what she'd think if she could see

you playing solitaire for hours on end now that the kids are gone. Shuffling those cards over and over."

"And the way I see folks do it on their phones at the nursing home. Probably because it's easier to play a game than to watch their loved ones slip away."

From Charles's faraway stare, Glory could tell how painful his visits to his wife must be. She tried to comfort him. "Take what Lewis said to heart, Charles: look on the past with a grateful eye and with love on the here and now."

Glory thought she spied a wistful expression on Adelle's face, but it disappeared almost immediately when Jason walked to the bar and filled a plate.

"*Look on the past with grateful eyes* . . . Is that a quote you can use to advertise? I haven't read the book, but it makes sense to me." The teen munched on a slice of cheese on his way back to his seat.

Ophelia raised a hand. "I agree with you. That's a good word right there. And thank you for steering us back on track and reminding us why we're here—to plan for the big to-do in November. We're not supposed to be having a book discussion group. While *some* of us continued our weekend fun, the *rest* of us were already hard at work. This morning, I drove the food truck to the community college, and then I came back here lickety-split to ready the dough for opening tomorrow. And let's not forget making these sausage balls."

Frederick laughed when Ophelia took a breath. "*The Screwtape Letters* is right: women do talk more when they're tired."

"Well, Mr. Lewis never met my Glory," Eli retorted.

"And he never met my husband either," Glory rebutted quickly. "I don't think anything ever quiets you; I don't care how tired you are."

"Glory—"

"But that's what makes you such a good couple. Your differences complement each other." Noemie's reassurance bridged the troubled waters between her friends and diffused the tension. "The same is true for Dale and me. When we got married, we didn't completely lose ourselves in each other—and you two had so much more 'self' after living on your own so long. But your individuality strengthens your union."

"My 'self' didn't strengthen my union," Ophelia grumbled, swirling the liquid in her glass. She smiled when Adelle patted her back.

Glory wondered at the camaraderie between the women. She loved the baker as a member of Eli's family, but they had yet to establish a similar rapport.

"Lewis talks about that in his book, too, regarding our spirit life. Something about our self-will . . ." Frederick snapped his fingers.

"I think I have it here," Adelle volunteered. "*When He talks of their losing their selves, He only means abandoning the clamour of self-will; once they have done that, He really gives them back all their personality, and boasts (I am afraid, sincerely) that when they are wholly His they will be more themselves than ever.*"

Glory's eyes narrowed as she listened to the younger woman read.

Frederick pointed a finger at Adelle. "Yes, that's it! God gave us specific gifts and personalities, but we can't do much good on our own. None of us but all of Him. When I design furniture, it's with certain woods and materials in mind. I think my chairs are great, but what good are they in my factory or in a showroom? They're not artwork. They become beautiful and useful once the customer is sittin' in one at the kitchen table or on his back porch. I must let go of what I planned for it in order for that chair to come into itself, if you will, and serve a purpose."

Glory shook her head. "That analogy works as far as you being the creator or designer, Frederick, but how does it apply if I'm the chair? I don't think it's the same thing. And I'm sorry, it's a great quote from *The Screwtape Letters*, but . . ."

"But what?" Ophelia asked. "You don't believe it? And by the way Frederick, I love your example!"

"Of course you would, Ophelia. You're working for your cousin who expects me to give up myself and all my life's work, but I don't understand it. Maybe I want to be a kitchen chair, but you designed me to rock back and forth in the bedroom. What does abandoning my self-will mean exactly? How does giving up who I am—becoming less of me—make me entirely more than who I am?" Glory's wide sleeve flapped over Bennett's head when she threw out an arm toward the shelves and carousels around them.

Eli's mouth worked but uttered no words.

Glory reached around the youngster and rubbed her husband's knee to soften her accusation. "My folks weren't interested in me becoming more like the God Screwtape was afraid of, what with all their shouldn'ts and couldn'ts. They wanted me to look and act like them. They tossed my brother out on his rump because he wouldn't accede to their will, which they pretended was God's. That's the only 'abandoning' I was party to."

"You didn't get along with your mom and dad?" Mallory scooted closer to her own mother.

The bookseller sniffed. "I don't know who in my generation ever considered 'gettin' along' with their parents. You, Frederick?"

His laugh was wry. "Well, I was raised by my grandfather, then my aunt and uncle. But I'd have to say I've never used those words when it comes to my relationship with them. Obeyed, definitely . . ."

"Amen!" Eli could've been perched on a church pew.

"Ran from." Dale rubbed his lower back.

Glory winced and nodded slowly.

"Cried over." Adelle hugged her son.

A few *mmmhmmms* chorused in agreement.

"Buried." Frederick's low tone could've pronounced a benediction.

Glory waved a hand, her eyes closed. She felt Bennett shift on her lap. When she peeked at him, he was gazing up at her, unblinking.

"But 'got along with'? No. I'll have to yield to my wife on that point." Eli squeezed her hand.

No one made a sound for a minute, save for Jason's crunching.

Finally, Noemie suggested wearily, "Eli, perhaps you should reach into the bowl again."

15

ELI UNFOLDED A STRIP OF PAPER. "Well, would you look at that! A quote from *Roll of Thunder, Hear My Cry*. And this handwriting looks suspiciously familiar."

Noemie and Dale chuckled.

Eli motioned for Mallory and murmured something to her behind his hand.

Adelle checked out the faces in the room. Again, it seemed they were enjoying a punchline to a joke she hadn't heard. Feeling isolated and friendless, she wished she could lure her child her way. "Why is that suspicious?"

Glory poked her husband's arm. "Because that's my favorite book in the world, that's why. I've always loved the Logan family. Loving, faithful, determined."

"And don't forget saucy and stubborn. Headstrong." Eli crumpled the paper.

Well, that's fitting. Like follows like. Adelle smirked. She knew it had taken some gumption for Glory to start her bookstore at a young age and keep it running successfully all this time. Especially since it was built on such a rickety foundation.

"I had to read the book for myself because you've talked about it so much over the past five years. People say a picture says a lot, but according to Mildred D. Taylor, nothing is sharper than words," Eli attested.

"Wait a minute, husband. What she said was, *One word can sometimes be sharper than a thousand swords.*" Glory moved the child into his own seat. She uncapped a marker and laid it on the sheet of paper in front of him. "What do you think that means, Bennett?"

"Words can cut you and make you bleed?" He scribbled lines and circles on the page.

"That's a great answer, Mr. Simonette!" Mr. Graves called out from his place at Frederick's table. He rose and hobbled off toward the hall leading to the restrooms, murmuring, "This generation, weaker and wiser."

Adelle considered switching places with Mallory's empty seat next to Ophelia but remained where she was. Without giving much thought, she said, "That quote sounds right up your alley by the way you've lived your life, Glory."

"What do you mean by that?" Noemie appeared ready to wield a weapon of a different kind to defend her friend.

"Probably because my wife makes a living off words. She is a professional wordsmith," Eli cut in.

"Hmmpf," Noemie huffed, sitting back in her seat. She crossed a leg over her knee and let her precariously balanced high-heeled shoe swing from her toes.

Dale rubbed her forearm.

Glory grinned Adelle's way. "No more than you, Mrs. Simonette the reporter."

Touché. Adelle dipped her head toward the bookseller and decided to let the matter drop.

Ophelia spoke up. "It puts me in the mind of the Hebrews passage that likens the Word to a sharp, two-edged sword. Proverbs and James also talk about the power of the tongue. I'm always telling my two to 'speak life!'" She looked around. "Where did my daughter disappear to anyway?"

"I sent her on an errand for me. Here she comes. Thank you, Mallory." Eli reached out for the copy of *Roll of Thunder, Hear My Cry* that she'd brought with her.

"They all seem to be for me, these quotes," Glory tsked. "Wasn't part of our reason for inviting Adelle to convince her how much we can learn from fiction? Y'all all seem to be using this as an opportunity to pound me over the head with Scripture."

"Maybe we should add Bibles to our inventory," Eli murmured.

Glory cocked an eye his way.

"You told me that fiction communicates truth about the human experience. We Bible-thumpers can't help that the truth y'all bring up with these quotes originated from the Word." Adelle shrugged. "That's the kind of information we should share on these posters."

"This isn't about Bible thumping or proselytizing. We're advertising for the festival. Maybe you should take your ideas to the church down the street so they can print them in the program," Glory grumbled.

Adelle glared at her. "Maybe you should take your*self* to the church down the street." Bennett looked up with alarm, causing her to regret the anger in her tone.

"Sticks and stones, sticks and stones," Mr. Graves chided, shuffling back into the room. He exhaled loudly when he plopped into his seat.

"Seriously," Jason mumbled to his twin. "This is starting to feel like the WWE."

"More like *Word* Wrestling. Without the entertainment," Ophelia whispered in response.

Adelle listened to the three beside her comment on her behavior and flushed in shame. Bennett should send his mommy to time-out for showing out in front of everybody. Her daddy had taught her better.

Frederick rattled the pens and markers in the jar. "My Aunt Julia used to tell me that words couldn't hurt me, but I beg to differ. In my life, I can see how they can cut you to the quick!"

"Yes, yes. Wield them well." Ophelia jabbed a finger on the table with each syllable.

"Like the sword," Noemie emphasized.

Glory tapped the hardcover. "You know, Uncle Hammer said something powerful when he warned Stacey against listening to what other people had to say."

"Why don't you read it?" Eli handed her the book.

She stared at her husband a good second or two before accepting his invitation. After a brief search, she read, *Then if you want something and it's a good thing and you got it in the right way, you better hang on to it and don't let nobody talk you out of it. You care what a lot of useless people say 'bout you you'll never get anywhere, 'cause there's a lotta folks don't want you to make it.*"

Glory's sleeves ballooned in colorful waves around her slender wrist when she wrapped an arm along the back of Bennett's seat. "Don't listen to naysayers, little one. Miss Glory wouldn't have this store if I'd heeded the advice of folks who didn't know how to dream."

The child nodded and returned to drawing.

"Is that how you built By the Book, on your own dreams? *In the right way*, like Uncle Hammer said?" Adelle's stomach clenched and her voice shook—from outrage, not fear—even as she braved the questioning looks from Frederick, the teenagers, Ophelia, Noemie and Dale, and Mr. Graves. The other couple across the room seemed engaged in some silent exchange and only had eyes for each other over the top of Bennett, busy with his picture.

Ophelia craned forward. "You two seem awfully cozy over there, Eli. What's this all about? Every day I come to work I hear hints of this and that. Anybody else sense this undercurrent running between them that they're keeping from the rest of us?"

"Why don't you tell them, husband? Tell your cousin and everybody else what dream I'm working so hard to hold on to." Glory sashayed to the bar and poured herself an icy glass of the amber liquid.

"Glory." His tone sounded a warning.

She sipped in answer.

Bennett edged to his right when Eli leaned forward on the table and rested his weight on his elbows. "We're scouting out the real estate market. Testing the waters."

"What kind of waters? Are you thinking about buying a vacation home? I hear the farther you travel up the mountain, the higher the price," Frederick offered.

Glory raised a brow at Eli. "Go on."

He cleared his throat. "Not a vacation home. A home home."

Ophelia jumped to her feet then took her seat at the behest of her children. "You mean *moving*? I take it to mean you'd live somewhere else in Gilmore and dedicate this building solely to the store. Doesn't make much sense financially, but I can see putting a little distance between you and work."

It was obvious that Eli expected his wife to throw him a life raft, but she left him to flail alone. "We are thinking of . . . taking a leave of absence from By the Book. But it's only a topic of discussion at this point."

Adelle's heart picked up speed in her chest, and she wondered, *Did anybody else hear the way that woman just repeated 'we' under her breath?* Her ears remained tuned in to Eli, but she kept Glory in her line of sight.

"I knew it. I knew something was going on." Ophelia bit down on her bottom lip.

Noemie sat up straight. "Glory, is this true? You're thinking of closing the bookstore?"

Aren't you her best friend? Shouldn't you know this already? Is there anyone who knows everything about Glory Pryor? Adelle asked silently. *If my memory serves me correctly, Mildred D. Taylor would have something to say about Glory not acting like a true friend.* So intent was she on studying Glory, she almost missed Bennett scrambling down out of his chair. He was nearly upon her when she spun to swoop him up.

Frederick leaned back in his chair and stretched his long legs into the aisle between the tables. After hitching up his suit pants at the waist, he crossed one arm over his stomach and stroked the low, silvery stubble on his cheeks with the other hand. "My wife read this book with McKinley when she was homeschooling him. The family had to pull together to save their land and to forgive. They endured some hard times, and I imagine it was hard not to let the bitterness eat them alive, having to let go of what they loved, what they'd worked their whole lives to hold on to.

"The folks in *Roll of Thunder* weren't furniture designers, but I get their pain," Frederick continued. "We had this tree in our yard once, an old oak tree. And one day, Etta noticed some type of foam coming out of it—leastways, that's what we called it. We contacted a specialist, 'cause y'all know how I feel about wood, my love-hate relationship with it. Well, the tree man came out and inspected that oak, and he told us it was infected with this bacterial disease called slime flux. Yes, Charles, it's as terrible as it sounds."

Frederick shook his head along with Ophelia sitting at the next table, her mouth scrunched up to her nose. "He tried to treat the problem with soapy water, but there was not much anybody could do.

Those bugs ate the tree from the inside out. Now, to look at it, you wouldn't-a known what was going on inside. But we had to spend a lot of money we didn't have at the time to cut it down because it was rotten. And one good storm . . ." He clapped his large hands together.

Bennett jerked upright in his mama's lap.

"Oh!" Mallory cried and laughed nervously with the others.

"I wouldn't call that a cost but a wise investment, taking down that tree," Mr. Graves said quietly.

"Yes, indeed, Charles. We couldn't have afforded *not* to. That oak would've come down eventually, probably taking our house—and our family, more importantly—right with it. That's what unforgiveness does, and holding on to the wrong thing. They'll eat a person from the inside out, right under the unsuspecting noses of your loved ones. Believe me, I know."

Adelle hadn't realized she'd been holding her breath until she slowly let it out between barely parted teeth. He'd told his story without barely raising his voice, all the while reclining in his chair. But what he had to say—punctuated by the slapping together of his hands—had grabbed everyone's attention and held on.

Glory drained her glass and walked back to her table. Everyone quieted as she picked up the book again and turned several pages. "There's this part . . . yes, here, this conversation between Cassie and her daddy, David. *I asked him once why he had to go away, why the land was so important. He took my hand and said in his quiet way: 'Look out there, Cassie girl. All that belongs to you. You ain't never had to live on nobody's place but your own and long as I live and the family survives, you'll have to. That's important. You may not understand that now, but one day you will. Then you'll see.'"*

She closed the book around her fingers. "When I read this, I made a promise that I would never give away what's precious to me, what was given to me. That's how I've always felt about By the Book. Ever since my talks with Eli on the subject got more and more serious, I asked myself, 'How am I supposed to give away this place?' At least in the beginning. Now—"

"Nobody gave you anything when it came to this store!" Eli's typical, gentlemanly manner of speaking thundered instead, filling up every inch of space in the café the books and the people didn't fill.

Bennett scooched against her and Adelle squeezed him to her chest. Oh, that she could ask Glory, *So, who is it who gave you the bookstore?* Would the woman's answer be fiction or nonfiction? Could she tell the difference after all these years of lying to herself?

But Eli had questions and opinions of his own. "You *worked* to build this business. And you work every day and then some to grow it and maintain it. Nobody's asking you to give it away. Sell it? Maybe. And that's a maybe because right now, we're only planning to leave it for a time. But not give it to anybody. Get a return somehow from all your years of labor and sit down and rest a little while, like they used to sing on Sunday mornings." By the time Eli finished talking, his tone had quietened, his words seasoned by affection instead of frustration.

Glory clasped her husband's shoulder. "De-ah, you interrupted me. I said that I asked myself that question in the beginning. *Now*, I need to ask something else: How can I give away the love that's been given to me? It's more precious than these books or the land the Logans fought to keep. *You're* my family. If leaving this store is what it takes for my family to survive, then . . ." She wiped beneath her eyes.

Eli covered her hand with his, presenting a united front to the stunned group.

Adelle clasped her hands tightly around Bennett's middle to still their trembling and hide her shaking from the others.

"Are you okay, Mommy? You cold?"

She leaned closer and put her mouth next to his ear. "I'm fine, baby. Are you comfortable? It's kinda chilly in here with the air conditioner blasting."

But she wasn't fine. Adelle was riled up. That woman was sitting over there moaning and groaning about having to give up all that had been given to her. *How about all you stole? All you took, not worked for. All you took from me. From us.*

"You can go on upstairs. I'll clear up. Really, I insist." To avoid making eye contact with Eli, Glory stored the last of the jars of pens, markers, and pencils behind the bar. She could sense his hesitation.

He loaded the unused disposable plates and cups in one arm and retrieved the last stack of napkins. "I'll put away these things and head up. Don't stay up late trying to accomplish too much. I'll set my alarm to wake up earlier tomorrow than usual and finish what's left." He strode toward the kitchen with his load.

"I see you were as ready to go as much as I was ready to see you go," she told the empty spot where her husband had stood.

The other members of the Famous Quotes Group had issued one hasty apology after another and quickly scurried from the café with their empty dishes, leaving Glory and Eli to restore order while simultaneously preparing the store for Tuesday morning. The group probably needed to process all that had transpired that evening. Exhausted at last with the effort of transforming her grimace to a smile, Glory had decided to pardon her husband.

She didn't have the heart for it—either cleaning that night or opening the next day. Really, opening up to him was what Glory lacked the fortitude to do, rehashing the evening and reviewing what was said and what went unsaid that evening. She preferred to bandy about the conversations in her mind, in true introverted fashion. *But where?*

"The porch. I'm going to the porch," Glory resolved and turned a blind eye to the trash that screamed for collection and the tables that cried out for rearranging. She clicked off the lights and trusted Eli to follow through on his offer. "You did say you were a man of your word."

"Ahhh." She felt her anxieties melt away the second she slid out of her mules. Deep down, she feared Eli had acquiesced a little too quickly; it had been way too easy for them to head in two different directions—he to the front stairs and she toward the front door. Yet, she missed her evening's window watching and the time alone. There wasn't much to see this time of night, but she'd content herself with counting the fireflies flitting about their patch of yard.

Glory plopped down onto the porch's top step to revel in the hint of fall that tagged along with the breeze. Locking her arms around her knees, she rocked back and forth under cover of the darkness that was deepening by degrees as one light after another flickered out along Springs Church. She tried to imagine how life would look elsewhere, specifically, near her husband's still-lost daughter. The sound of the waves versus the rumble of trucks. Air thick enough to slice instead of crisp, clear autumn evenings. Fresh-caught shrimp and bream rather than freshly picked apples and peaches. Grandbabies replacing book babies. Unbidden, another poem crept into her mind:

> *I will not pass this way again,*
> *by way of sorrow, torment, and fear.*
> *There's life in the knowing, let my heart apprehend,*
> *that joy now takes residence here.*
> > *Once I was searching and seeking*
> > *through torrent and blast,*

*Yet, peace is now speaking
of new hope, holding fast.
The studying of war . . . All that is past.
Forever and a day draweth near.*

Could it be that peace is around the corner? That the waves I feared would overwhelm my own dreams will wash away this pain of the past as they recede? Glory's thoughts hummed to a familiar tune that grew louder until she realized that her subconscious had detected whistling coming from the left. Sharp, pure, and high-pitched, the musician could have performed the theme song for *The Andy Griffith Show* she'd watched as a child.

Hmmm, what is that? I should know it . . . Wait, I do know it. That's "Overjoyed," our song by Stevie Wonder! Accompanying the music was the off-tempo rhythmic sound of jangling and clopping that put Glory in the mind of cowboys in the Wild West. She edged a little deeper within the porch's shadow and craned her neck to spy out the walker. Within seconds, a lanky form clanked into view—a man, with his hands in his pockets, wearing a loose-fitting jacket and a baseball cap. As he passed under the light of the streetlamp in front of By the Book, Glory realized it was their backyard neighbor: *Dude.* Of course.

Before she could wonder at the why of her next movements, she dashed down the steps toward the retreating shadow that stretched out behind him. So eager to catch up she left her shoes, forgotten by her front door.

16

Though she ran lightly in her bare feet, Dude spun her way at the corner as he was about to launch into the chorus of the Stevie Wonder song. Glory drew up, breathless, sixty-four-year-old body parts aching from the unusual burst of activity.

"Hey there," she panted.

His mustache and beard parted in a faint smile. "Hello. Out late?"

Glory wondered at his calm. If someone had run up behind her in the dark, she'd definitely have more to say, to scream in fact. She gulped and tried to match his offhand demeanor. "Yes, well, kinda. We just wrapped a meeting, and I saw—I mean, I heard you—walk by. Where'd you learn to whistle like that?"

"In my band."

In my band. Those three words told her more about the man in that one moment than she'd learned in the six years she'd known him. "We played it at our wedding. Eli and I. I mean, the tenor saxophonist played the song during our reception." Glory could hear herself—winded, strained, nonsensical, excited.

"I know. Jojo is a friend of mine. I came to listen to him play sax."

Again, the smile. Easy, and it reached his eyes, barely visible beneath the brim of his cap.

"Is that why you came to my wedding?"

He nodded. "Good stuff."

And here she'd thought he'd come out of gratitude for being included, because he liked her, since she saw him as a person—any number of reasons that revealed how entitled and prideful she was. *He came for himself. He didn't come for Eli and me.*

He lifted his cap, smoothed his hair, and settled it again on his head. "How was the movie?"

"Movie?"

"I finished *How Green Was My Valley*. Was it as good as the book?"

"Oh . . . right!" Glory couldn't explain the pleasure filling her. "Where are you headed? Nosey question I know."

"Home."

Glory tried to follow the direction of his finger which could have aimed to the North, South, East, or West; she was loathe to ask specifics, though her curiosity nearly ate her alive. "If you have a minute, would you like to come inside for a cup of coffee? I can share my thoughts on the movie."

Dude's hand in his hip pocket was holding back his worn striped jacket, revealing ragged tears on the hem of his shirt and holes on the thighs of his jeans. He turned toward the end of the street, where the courthouse reigned supreme with a bright light shining on its steps and the United States and North Carolina state flags rippling in the wind.

The state of his clothes could mean he's extremely wealthy or very poor. Neither tells me anything about his character, who he really is. As she waited for him to respond, she surreptitiously checked for the brown paper bag that held his liquid diet but didn't spot it.

His hazel eyes met Glory's gaze and held it steadily, as if taking measure of her before he decided. After a beat, he said, "As long as you change that coffee into tea."

"Are you out of your ever-lovin' mind?" Eli set down his cup with such firmness, coffee splashed on his shirt.

"If that were tea, it wouldn't stain," she murmured, watching him swipe at the spot on his cuff. Her husband knew better than to bring that strong-smelling brew near her anyway.

Whenever they ate together in the kitchen, they always sat catty-cornered from each other, which made the large table seem like an intimate table for two. This morning, Glory wished she'd put her place mat on the other side from him. Or better yet, on the counter in the café, where she usually welcomed Tuesday mornings.

Today, however, Eli had beat her downstairs. When she'd pushed through the swinging door into the kitchen, still wearing her robe, he was sweeping up the remains of her late-night conclave with Dude, dressed for the day in black gabardine shorts and a starched, gray-and-white button-down shirt.

"I'm starting to think I made a mistake telling you." Glory riffled through the drawer, taking her time searching for the large fork she needed. For some reason, she'd thought he'd find it remarkable, not horrifying, when she explained how Dude had shared tea and leftover sausage balls with her at the kitchen table.

"You made the mistake last night when you chased a stranger down the street and invited him into our home." Eli held his head and stared at his empty plate.

"Which won't be our home much longer, if you have your way. Would you feel better if I'd said we ambled through the bookstore rather than sat in the kitchen? Eli, we leave our front door unlocked so people we don't know can freely enter and exit our house practically every day, and I carry on conversations with them, unchaperoned. Whether you're here or not." Glory laid three strips of bacon in the hot cast-iron pan.

"Between the hours of nine and five, not after midnight. When your husband is sleeping upstairs and you're wandering around here by yourself in this big house."

This five-thousand-square-foot house, she remembered the mayor saying. Glory flipped over the pieces.

"Do you have any idea what could have happened to you?"

Glory slowly pivoted to face him. "Why, Eli? Because you think he doesn't have an address? Is that what makes him dangerous?"

Eli winced. "Come on, Glory. Surely you know me better than that. I posed the question because you have no idea who this man is. You can count the number of slices of cake or pie and bowls of ice cream you've taken him." He held up a hand that silenced her. "And yes, books. But having a bead on his reading habits doesn't mean that much in the grand scheme of things."

"Would it matter if he had a four-year-old child? Could I invite him over for tea then and encourage him to stay a while?" Glory returned her attention to the bacon, her temper as hot as the blue flames under the skillet. *And you'd better not shush me again,* she fumed.

"How'd I know you'd manage to bring up Adelle in this conversation?" He stalked to the sink and ran cold water over his sleeve.

"Who said anything about Mrs. Simonette? I merely *posed* a simple question, as you did." She tightened her belt. If she didn't hurry, she wouldn't have time to eat and change before their first customers arrived. Glory was grateful Ophelia had to take her children to the high school's open house that morning and was coming in later.

"Huh." Looking put out, Eli rubbed a little soap on the spot and rinsed it.

"I'm grown, Eli, and I was taking care of myself before—"

"I came along, I know." He slammed the cabinet door after replacing the detergent.

This time when he completed that sentence, he sounded angry to Glory instead of weary, and she wondered which was better and which was worse. She dropped two slices of American cheese into the grits bubbling on the range and replaced the lid. "Well, it's the truth. You're trying to make me afraid of Dude, but I won't let you."

"Not so. What I want to do is shake some sense into you."

"Eli!"

"Of course I wouldn't, Glory, but somebody else might. Dude might, for all we know. You think you know him because he's been hanging around your backyard for a few years. But he's been hanging around in a lot of yards and under bridges and behind bars."

"Homelessness doesn't equal criminality, Eli. It's a terrible circumstance, not a character trait."

He pressed a paper towel to his shirt and shook his head. "I meant the kind of bars that serve alcohol, Glory, not the ones that folks get locked behind. Dude is somebody's son, and he could be somebody's brother, father, or uncle. Someone's friend. A talented harmonica player and whistler. But he's an enigma to you. An unknown. A person who might very well have your rare copy of *The Great Gatsby* in his pocket. That's what I'm saying."

In the silence that ensued, Glory lowered the heat and pressed the slices to the hot pan to make sure the fat and the lean cooked properly. Then she lifted out each piece and set them on a paper towel to drain beside the kielbasa she'd already cooked for Eli. By the time she finished, she had cooled off a bit and felt able to reason with the man she'd married. "Do you have more accusations and insults to lay at the man's feet, or are you ready to listen, husband?"

"I got ready the day I said *I do* to you . . . wife." His voice was tense enough to support a high-wire act.

Glory cracked three eggs in the bacon drippings, sprinkled them with salt and pepper, then broke the yolk with her spatula; Eli couldn't stand them runny. "I'm not sure why I ran after him. Maybe it was hearing the familiar song—our song, by the way."

"'Overjoyed?' Stevie?"

"Yes!" Heartened by his response, she peeked over her shoulder at him. *Mistake.*

He was frowning, affronted. "Why our song?"

"Because it was *our* wedding. It would've been weird if the saxophonist had played something else." Feeling as hot and salty as her grits, Glory flipped the eggs and let them get brown and crispy before scooping them out of the pan onto their plates. She stirred the contents of the pot one more time and decreased the heat to simmer.

Delia Gibson was never far from her, the bitter and the sweet. After watching her humbly serve her father every day, Glory typically considered it a joy to make Eli's breakfast when she had the opportunity. This morning, she considered it something else altogether.

With her mother in mind, she took a deep breath as she cooked. "Don't you want to know why he was whistling our song?" The second hand on the kitchen clock traveled around its face one revolution before she heard the scrape of the chair on the tile.

Eli joined her by the range. "Yes, I'd love to know why."

She bumped him with her hip. "Because he played in a blues band with Jojo—our saxophone guy, in case you don't remember—when they both lived in Louisiana. Dude heard he'd moved up this way and that we'd hired him, so he came to the wedding to hear him. After I invited him, of course."

"Of course." Eli opened the cabinet to the right of her and

retrieved two stoneware plates. "What instrument did our neighbor play, besides his lips as he related his life story?"

"Haha, the joke's on you, funny man. He played the mouth organ, otherwise known as the harmonica, and the piano. I think Dude would enjoy that event we're hosting. The author is going to play a few instruments for the children. I'm sure Adelle would love to see him. Dude did save Bennett's life."

"I wonder where he was coming from at that time of night. Drinking behind somebody else's place?" Eli spooned the grits over the eggs and divvied up the proteins on each of their plates.

Glory stuck out her tongue. "He has an apartment. Yes"—she chuckled when he froze and glanced at her over his shoulder—"yes, he does. Somewhere not very far. He's a bit . . . eccentric—but so am I—and he rather likes camping outside. Dude stays in town when he isn't able to drive safely, so he's eccentric but responsible."

Eli bore their food to the table and set their plates in their usual spots. "And frugal, considering he resides in our backyard most of the time."

"Well, I'd say it's one of the cooler places to stay, based on the two cool cats who live here. It's also safe and clean—"

"And free. And you bring him good books and good food to go with his good liqueur. Is that right?"

"Sounds about right. But this accomplished musician is in the process of recovery. When he hasn't been playing with a group right over the line in Tennessee, he's been attending AA meetings, not that it's any of our business." Glory followed him to the table.

Once she was seated, he spooned a bite of his breakfast and chewed slowly. "This is because of your brother, isn't it? You think by helping Dude you're helping Davis."

His eyes lit up, lightning in a storm cloud. "That's why you named him Dude, isn't it? *D* for Davis, to honor your brother. It hadn't crossed my mind until this very moment!"

Glory had married this man to love and cherish all the remaining days of their lives; she hadn't hired him for hourly therapeutic care. She swirled the grits on her plate, then chopped up her eggs with the edge of her fork.

"Honeybun, what do you think? Does that make sense?"

"Yes, on some levels. I don't know about the name thing—maybe I should take another psychology class to connect those dots—but I, I see your point." Glory balanced her fork like a seesaw between the tips of her fingers.

"I was never able to really help my brother. Not in the way it counted. I aided and abetted his drinking problem because I thought it kept the peace. Sneaking him in the house, sneaking him *out* of the house. Jumping in the middle of more arguments than I care to think about. But he was amazing. So smart and so kind. Davis built toys for me because we didn't have an extra pot to pee in, despite all my parents' hard work. They were putting so much money away for our education, you see. They wanted their children to be the first to go to college."

Having lost her appetite, Glory propped her fork against her plate. "It was my fault they kicked him out, Eli. Of course, the house had burned down to the ground, so there wasn't anything to kick him out of. But I was the one who got the college degree, when he got nothing. He'll never know he was more a help to me in the end . . ." Her words petered out.

Eli reached across the table and linked their fingers. "It's okay, darlin'. It wasn't your job to save him."

It wasn't his to save me either. He did it anyway. Glory gripped Eli the way she would a life preserver in choppy seas of unknown depth. The coffee maker beeped, alerting them it was switching off. The sound also signaled that it was time for her to get herself together. She gave his hand one last squeeze, released it, and allowed a watery smile.

"So, finally we have the identity of this mystery man. What's Dude's real name—Carl, Robert, Eddie . . . ? How's the old slogan go—*inquiring minds want to know.*"

Glory gasped and covered her mouth. "I forgot to ask!"

17

"Mommy, how am I gonna have a birthday party without my friends? Will they know where to find me here in Gilmore?"

Adelle realized he didn't know that *here* for them wasn't Gilmore but Zirconia, North Carolina. They'd awakened early that Thursday morning, and immediately, her child had clamored to go to By the Book to see his new "friends," Eli and Glory Pryor. Adelle had decided a distraction was in order, so she'd driven them to a U-pick farm called Sky Top Orchard, in the Blue Ridge Mountains.

She caressed the back of his neck. "Well, I think it might be a bit difficult for them to travel to Gilmore with such short notice, Ben-Ben. Your birthday is right around the corner, and I think most of them will have started school."

His face fell so far Adelle thought he might trip over it on the hard-packed ground. "But I'm gonna be five! And Daddy told me I could have a big party when I turned five years old. He said that was a big one. Doesn't that mean it's important?"

I'd call his death pretty major, and he missed your fourth birthday, too. The realization sprang to mind before she could prepare herself for it. *Uh-oh, here come the tears again. Not today, Adelle! Don't start crying over the apples.* Adelle dropped to a knee in the grass. She told herself if they could make it to the playground just over the rise . . .

"Bennett, I know you miss your friends. I miss them, too. And my friends. And the farm, and Penny." Immediately, she regretted taking that route.

Her son's bottom lip trembled, and the puddles forming in his eyes rivaled his mother's.

"Oh, baby. It's okay to cry. If you want, we can sit right here in the grass and bawl together. Like you told me a while back, Jesus got sad, too, and when you love someone as much as we still love Daddy, it's natural to miss him. Perhaps I should hire other people to weep and wail with us." She hugged him to her, inhaling the strawberry scent of his shampoo on his freshly washed hair, knowing he didn't understand what she was talking about.

"Or first," she suggested, her lips moving against his neck, ". . . first we could go to the barn and see the animals. Some should be roaming freely, too. We might feel a little bit like we brought home with us, once we see bunnies and chickens and perhaps feed the goats."

She pulled away a little so she could see his face and swiped the tears his thick eyelashes were working overtime to hold on to. "Would you like to go to the playground before we cry, or head there after?"

One hardy tear struggled through and dribbled down his flushed cheek. He mumbled, "After."

Adelle's lips caught his tear in a kiss before it dripped to the ground, quickly followed by her own. "Me, too."

Abandoning a plan, Adelle let the wind blow them in the direction they should take at the farm. First, they invested about forty-five minutes meandering through the pastures. Bennett took his time naming each goat, duck, and chicken before sidestepping along the fencing until her good sense took over her grief and she made him climb down. Right when he remembered his tears over missing his friends and his father, she challenged him to a race. "Ready, set, go to the playground!"

They made a dash for the swing sets, enjoying them until he tired of pumping his legs back and forth and Adelle refused to push him. Then she led him to the caravan of half barrels the farm had painted to look like bees buzzing behind the tractor pulling them. When the train stopped, she let him loose in the sandbox.

Adelle hung back from the various groups of adults watching their own children dig through the dirt for buried treasure. She coveted what felt like seconds, precious time when her son was safely entertained and she could immerse herself in her own thoughts instead of his. Refusing to waste it on idle conversation with people she would never see again, she closed her eyes and thanked God for the gentle massage of the breeze on her face, the feel of its fingers ruffling her hair.

"Adelle? *Eres tú?*"

Alarmed, her first thought was *God?* But it couldn't be. Though His ways were beyond her, surely He wouldn't speak in Spanish if He had something to say to her. Adelle opened one eye. *No!* Once she opened the second, she confirmed that yes, it was indeed Noemie Pearline wearing a stylish orange plaid shirt tucked into khaki shorts cuffed at the thigh and feet in creamy low-top, canvas Converse sneakers. Gaping at Glory's best friend, Adelle felt grungy in a shapeless graphic tee hanging over faded denims and ancient running shoes.

Eyes wide like her outstretched arms, Noemie cried, "It is you! I told myself, *No es posible* . . . Adelle, out here at the Sky Top Orchard?

But *sí, sí*, it must be possible, *porque aquí estás*! Here you are!" In her excitement, Noemie's words traveled back and forth, virtually from one continent to the other.

Adelle sighed, mourning the untimely death of her "me time." Yet, it couldn't be helped: Noemie was no figment of her imagination. Figuring the woman meant to embrace her, she stepped toward her and leaned in.

"Oh? Oh. Okay, that's what we're doing? Lovely!" Noemie said with some surprise.

A mortified Adelle couldn't do anything but carry through with her hug of greeting, and the two women embraced awkwardly . . . and quickly.

"Yes, 'tis I, Adelle of the Famous Quotes Group." She attempted to make light of their uncomfortable moment with a dramatic introduction.

The jeweler scanned the play area and waved. "Oh, there's Bennett." She returned her attention to Adelle. "So, you must be getting settled in Gilmore because you've enlarged your territory and found our gem. How are you enjoying the orchard?"

Adelle's smile widened slightly and more sincerely when she recognized the phrase from the prayer of Jabez. "I'm having a good time. *We're* having a good time. It was good to get out of the house on such a beautiful day. This is more for the respite than the apples. Much sweeter."

Back in Cabot, their family had found themselves hunkered down in their storm shelter one August, listening to tornadic-level gusts and hailstones pummeling their property. Thanks to God, they'd emerged to minimal property damage relative to what their neighbors had endured. She recognized this seventy-seven-degree day with light winds under light-blue, cloudless skies as nothing short of a gift from God. This mountain was territory she could handle.

Noemie nodded as if she understood there was much Adelle hadn't said. "*La gracia de Dios.* The grace of God. All settled in then?"

"Getting there. As long as my little guy is good, I'm good, too." Adelle could tell that Noemie wanted to dig deeper, but she kept her comment surface level. "I wouldn't have expected to see you here midday Thursday. Who's minding the store?"

Cries from the area of the sandbox snagged the attention of both women. They watched a mother throw her screaming toddler over her shoulder, his mouth covered with dirt, and stride from the playground.

Noemie chuckled. "Dale can manage things without me, what with his new assistant. I'm here with my grandchildren. They're over there."

Adelle followed her finger and spotted a girl of about five being pushed on the swing by a taller boy of eight or nine. "Ahh, they're beautiful."

"They're my hearts, those two. My first and only grandchildren, but God willing, more to come. My daughter had to travel this week for work, so I offered to care for them today and tomorrow."

"So, you've hired someone to help in the store?" Adelle tucked her hands in her back pockets.

After Noemie's quick check on her grandchildren, she wiggled her eyebrows at Adelle. "You could say that. We're training our older son to manage Pearline's. You know, passing on the baton to the next generation. However, no fishing for my Dale until the weekend, poor baby."

For the first time, Adelle noticed her genuine warmth, and the tension in her shoulders eased. Noemie's sunny personality was usually clouded by her best friend's chilly demeanor.

"Have you picked apples yet?"

Adelle didn't process what she said at first, but after a minute, the question registered. "Apples? Uh, no, not yet. If someone was viewing Bennett and me from a drone, they'd see we've taken a rather willy-nilly approach to our visit here. He was sad about celebrating his birthday without his friends, and we both started feeling sorry for ourselves and missing Ben. I call it an emotional snowball."

Adelle scrutinized the grass, the child who was still squalling, the robin pecking the ground, the splotch on the side of her shoe. "We might buy some apple donuts, eat our sandwiches in the picnic pavilion, and head home afterwards."

"What? You can't be serious!"

The exclamation caused Adelle to finally lift her head.

Noemie's mouth opened wide. "Leave Sky Top without picking apples? You can't live around here without creating your own apple-picking story." She clasped a soft hand around Adelle's forearm. "We'll go together."

"Is that what I'm doing, living around here?" Adelle muttered under her breath as Noemie took a couple steps forward.

She whistled shrilly, commandeering the attention of everybody in the play area, including Bennett, who stopped pouring sand over his feet. Noemie's two grandchildren scampered up, and she wrapped her arms around their shoulders and explained what they were doing next.

"Yes, Grandmother," they chorused, their large brown orbs staring at Adelle curiously.

Realizing that it was a done deal, Adelle waved her son over.

Despite making eye contact, the child finished emptying his pail onto his legs and wiggled his toes, obviously loving the feel of the sand running between them.

Hiding her annoyance behind what she hoped was a pleasant expression, Adelle gave up on mentally willing him to move and yelled, "Bennett!"

He glanced up and brushed the sand around his feet.

Noemie whistled again, and Bennett squinted their way. "Come, come. Let's go. Mommy and I are leaving."

To Adelle's chagrin, he instantly kicked the bucket out of his way and hopped over the other children crouching in the box. His legs churned up dust as he ran over and asked, "Where're we going, Mommy?"

I'm taking you and your hardheaded bottom home. That's where you're going, Adelle wanted to say, flames licking her jawline. Instead, she steered him by the shoulder to catch up with Noemie and her grandchildren.

Noemie sat her two at the end of the picnic table across from Bennett and unzipped her large, insulated bag. "So, what do you think of the Famous Quotes Group?"

Adelle doled out their sandwiches—peanut butter and chocolate hazelnut spread for him and ham and Swiss for her. She dropped several varieties of bagged chips on the table; it was second nature to pack extra for her finicky son. "It's . . . interesting."

The older woman laughed. "That's one way to put it, I suppose. When Glory introduced this idea that first night, she likened herself to Francie in *A Tree Grows in Brooklyn*. I read it with Glory—"

Of course, you did. Adelle hid her smirk by pretending to drop her napkin.

"—and that book spoke to my heart. The author went to college here in North Carolina, like my Dale."

"At Chapel Hill." The words just popped out of her mouth.

"Oh, you're familiar with it, Miss Nonfiction Reader?"

Adelle shifted uncomfortably in her seat under Noemie's

questioning gaze. *You've always gotta show what you know,* Ben used to tease. She gulped down the bite and explained, "You mentioned it was basically autobiographical, so I have heard of it."

After a pause, Noemie meted out their lunches. "Yes, Betty Smith was older when she published this first book of hers, and it was a major success. We opened our jewelry store later in life after our children were in school, when many people are retiring, so her story encouraged me. It's never too late—that's what I learned!"

Adelle checked on Bennett before unwrapping her sandwich. He was talking animatedly with the others. In a studied, casual tone, she asked, "Glory and Eli know all about that, too, don't they?"

"What do you mean?" Noemie opened the lid on her plastic container, revealing a hearty mixture of red and green lettuce, cucumbers, red onions, and tomatoes.

"They married at, what, sixty years old? Talk about never too late." Adelle took a bite.

"You're right. They're an inspiration."

Adelle ruffled through the bags of chips and chose the barbecue. "That's definitely one way of looking at it."

Noemie poured dressing over her salad. "The author of *A Tree Grows in Brooklyn* says to read to your children daily until they can read themselves, and then *they* need to read every day, everything they can get their hands on. I guess it's also never too early! Actually, that would be a good post for the festival: *It's never too early and it's never too late.* Don't you think Glory will get a kick knowing she's inspired us?"

Adelle raised her eyebrows as if considering it.

The older woman smiled at Bennett. "Young man, based on what I witnessed, I bet your mommy agrees with that idea of reading early even if she hasn't read *A Tree Grows in Brooklyn.*"

"Uh-uh," Bennett mumbled around his chewing.

"*Uh-uh?* Uh-uh what?" Noemie prompted the child.

"I think he means I *do* agree. What's not to agree with? Bennett, wipe your mouth," Adelle told him sharply. Feeling the eyes from across the table, she focused on attending to her son and waited out the silence that grew by the second.

"Well, let's keep that idea in mind, *It's never too early and it's getting late*, or whatever it was I said." Noemie leaned across the table to swat at a fly hovering over their food.

Adelle chuckled. "*It's never too early and it's never too late.*"

"Right, right." Noemie crunched more salad and swallowed. "Dale and I were talking about *A Tree Grows in Brooklyn* on the way home, and if I remember correctly, Francie didn't much like old people because she was afraid of turning into one. I wonder what Charles would have to say about that."

"He might not appreciate being called old." Adelle opened her chips, hoping she'd stay out of trouble by keeping her mouth full. Unable to help herself, she said, "I imagine he'd say that, as hard or as lonely as aging might be, life is beautiful. Keep living, even if there doesn't seem to be much to live for. But I don't think that's something you want to put on a poster."

A delicate yellow butterfly landed on the edge of the table. Everyone stilled and watched its wings slowly open and close. Bennett stuck out his finger and it fluttered away. Adelle followed the rolls of the hills in the distance and felt for Mr. Graves because she understood his sadness and prayed that like her, he looked forward to that time when there would be no more sadness or tears. When such things would fly away.

Noemie cocked her head toward her grandchildren, engaged in tug-of-war over a straw, breaking up the quiet of the peaceful scene. "These two . . ."

Adelle chuckled at the brother and sister, admiring their

grandmother's ability to let them duke it out for themselves. How would Bennett get these early life lessons in navigating relationships without a sibling to rub against?

"*Mi hija*—my daughter—can't understand why her father and I are preparing to pass on the baton to her brother when it comes to the business. Not that it'll happen anytime soon. I think she's afraid that without waking up and going to Pearline's every day, her parents will lack purpose and give up. She's so driven—always going, going, going. She pushes and pulls, like her little ones down there. But Dale and I feel a pull toward something different and new. Don't all of us mature, old*er* people reach a point when we feel as if we've seen it all, done it all?"

She continued, not waiting for Adelle to agree. "We're not cynical. It's more like we're satisfied; it's a feeling of *enough*. We have children and grandchildren; we've run a successful business, and we're done with all the rigamarole. But we're not giving up and buying the uh, uh . . . what's the saying?"

"Farm. Buying the farm," Adelle supplied.

"*Sí! La granja*. We're not ready to buy the farm and give up living. We're only asking, *Qué sigue?* What's next?"

Immediately, Adelle visualized gold and silver bangles and muumuus. "Do you think that's why they want to sell the bookstore? They're asking *Qué sigue?*"

Noemie's face shuttered and she flashed a noncommittal half smile. "You'll have to talk to Glory and Eli when we see them again. They can tell you better than I."

Adelle sensed she was circling the wagons to protect her friend. She admired Noemie's loyalty, but it put her on the outside. Searching her own heart, she asked herself, *What's next for me, Lord?*

Noemie rose to collect the remains from their lunch. "Mind

sharing what you're ruminating on upstairs, Adelle?" She tapped her temple.

"Oh, nothing." Her words proved as forthcoming as her next steps.

Bennett wiggled closer to his mother. "Are you thinking about Daddy, Mommy? Whenever you get quiet, it's because you're sad about him."

His voice was hushed, as if he meant his question to be for her ears only. The problem was, there were several more pairs of ears around them. Adelle wrestled with an answer fit for public consumption.

Bennett bounced on the bench. "I know! Maybe if you tell Miss Glory she'll help you get your store like hers. You're always dreaming of books, Daddy said, and talking about—"

"Ben-Ben, hush. Sounds like you were too much into grown folks' business." Adelle wished she could cover his mouth.

"Nah, nah, let the boy talk. It's obvious he loves his *mamá* and wants to see her happy. Also, it's good for a child to see his parents dreaming and praying. *Mi papá* always wanted his own business, and now look at Dale and me. Our children have watched us weep and pray over them all their lives, even as adults, and I believe it moves them to do the same."

Adelle chewed on her bottom lip. Whenever the two of them made their escape from this place, Adelle was going to tell this boy a thing or two about sharing their private business. And she'd explain that under no circumstances was he to call that bookseller by anything other than "Mrs. Pryor."

"Mommy? Miss Pearline was talking to you." Bennett rested his hand on her shoulder.

"I'm sorry. I didn't mean to put you on the spot. I just wanted to get to know you better. But if it's too personal . . ." Noemie's white-tipped nails were splayed against the base of her throat.

Wryly, she confessed, "I guess the jig is up. Do you remember the part in *A Tree Grows in Brooklyn* where Francie shares her dreams of buying all the books she ever wanted? Well, I did, too. More than would fill all the shelves in Glory's happy place."

Noemie rested her chin on a fist and her lips curved slightly, looking not at all surprised. "Sounds like you and Glory have lots in common. Running your own bookstore . . ."

Adelle choked back the memories, the bitterness.

"Yeah, yeah, just like Miss Glory!" Bennett affirmed.

Adelle nodded, hating to peel back that tiny bit of the onion. Yet, her son's upturned face urged her to keep going. "Little Man here already shared the whispers between my husband and me, how we dreamed of owning our own version of By the Book. Then he died."

"Your dreams didn't. It may not look the way you planned, but you can still own one. Remember, it's never too late." Noemie's answer was matter of fact.

Adelle looped an arm around Bennett and drew him onto her lap. On this point, she and Noemie were of the same mind.

"What do you think about this one?" Noemie plucked a Golden Gala apple and held it for Adelle to judge.

Adelle couldn't keep the nonchalance from seasoning her words. "Like I said, I'm not as particular as you are. As far as I'm concerned, if you don't see a worm waving hello, put it in the basket with the rest." The rest, meaning the five other apples her partner had given the go-ahead to, compared to the pounds of apples the children had run ahead and gathered from the trees and the ground. Noemie had such a persnickety approach to apple picking, Adelle was surprised the woman didn't rinse the fruit with a bottle of water before she put it in the basket.

"Oh, no, no. It must be *perfecta*." She whipped out a napkin and polished it.

Adelle doubled over and tears of a much happier kind ran down her cheeks. When she straightened and regarded Noemie's puzzlement, she laughed again.

"You must be tired of me." Noemie dropped the apple in her basket and moved to another tree. "I'm happy I'm not stealing your joy. Dale refuses to come with me anymore, but I tell him, this is the same way I treat my diamonds, my gold—everything. You can't love my eye in the store and hate the way it works everywhere else. I take me with me."

"*Perfecta*. I take me with me." Adelle snapped her fingers several times. "Everywhere I go, I keep popping up, too, Noemie."

The other woman raised her hand.

Adelle high-fived her.

Without conferring, they skipped several trees to catch up with the children. They worked in tandem for a while, with Adelle selecting apples from the higher branches and passing them to Noemie to inspect. Bees whirred by, attracted to the fruit rotting on the ground.

"What really brought you to our fair city, Adelle?" Noemie twirled an apple in the sunlight.

"My car." Adelle winked, brushing at what she hoped was a fly. "And family. Bennett." She'd started with the biggest circle and successively narrowed it until she named the bull's-eye. Everything she did was for Bennett.

Really?

She spun to look at Noemie, but Adelle already knew the other woman hadn't said a word. She recognized the voice, if she was honest.

"Do you have family here?" Noemie circled the tree and peered through twisted limbs.

"I have my son, for sure, and he has me. Today that didn't feel like enough." Adelle kept one eye on the three little ones cavorting through the grass and another on hidden gems others had missed. All of her remained on guard to avoid any verbal missteps.

"I'm sorry." Noemie stopped searching and devoted all her attention to Adelle.

"Thanks—"

"No, I mean it. I'm so sorry about your Ben. I don't know your personal, God-designed pain, but I understand the sorrow from irreplaceable loss. *Mi papá murió.*" Noemie's eyes closed for a long second and then opened. Tears sharpened her gaze. "My father died after I moved to the United States, leaving *mi mamá* alone in Colombia. She never recovered from it."

Adelle whimpered and stumbled a little from yet another wound. "I'm—"

"No . . . please. If I may?"

The three words glued Adelle to the spot.

"Mama never recovered because she had no *esperanza*, no hope. No Christ. But you and I, we grieve with that hope, with the knowing. There's no way to replace Ben, but God can replace your sorrow, friend. And you will see him again. Live with that hope. With Christ."

Bennett hopped up to Adelle, followed by his new friends. "Mommy! Mommy! Guess what? I have friends now. Can they come to my party?" He tugged at her hand and squinted up into her face. "Is it time to cry again?"

Noemie stroked his head. "Those are your baskets over there? Gather them and come back to us, and we'll get some apple donuts for dessert."

Her grandson grabbed his sister and they both jumped up and down, chorusing, "Donuts! Donuts!"

"Your *abuelita* has made a new friend, too, so we should celebrate. Now, go!" She shooed them off and spun to face Adelle, her palms up.

"Is it okay if I hug you, for real this time? You can say no, but it's not about me. It's for you. I promise it'll be quick."

Adelle stared at her. Then she nodded and blinked rapidly, steeling herself for the touch.

Noemie grasped her by the arms and pulled her close, enfolding Adelle in her embrace.

Once there, Adelle sobbed on her new friend's shoulder, loud cries that made other people give them wide berth. She didn't move when she heard the children's feet pummel the ground and felt Bennett's arms circle her waist.

Noemie whispered, "When you feel like it, you can tell me the real reason you came to town."

The drive home felt like twelve hours to Adelle. She must have glanced back at Bennett twenty times, and he was steadily maneuvering his Hot Wheels car around his seat belt and across the leather cushion on either side of him. About two miles from home, she angled the rearview mirror so he could see her eyes. "Bennett?"

"Vroommmmm . . . Yes, ma'am?"

"Did you have a good time today at the apple farm?"

Bennett grew very still and nodded slowly.

"I'm glad. The donuts were *mwah*!" She kissed her fingertips to lighten the moment. "We're going to look up some recipes to use all the fruit we picked."

"They're falling on the floor!" He regarded the large, overflowing basket full of apples. "I hope we make donuts."

Adelle signaled a right turn and used it as an opportunity to slightly redirect the conversation. "Speaking of the Pryors, I'd rather you call them by their last names, as Mommy taught you. That's how we show respect for our elders who aren't our family members."

Bennett's head leaned to one side. "But Miss Glory said it was okay. She asked me to call her that because we're friends."

She turned her frown into a smile when she stole a peek at his reflection. "I understand what she's trying to say. Glory . . . *Mrs. Pryor* . . . likes you. What's not to like? When you're friends with someone around your age, you tend to use their first names, like you did with your new friends. But when they're a lot older than you, it's better to use their last name, out of respect. Just like I call Mr. Graves 'Mr. Graves' when I address him—not 'Charles'—even though we're friends, too. And the way you said Miss Pearline. Does that make sense?"

This time, his expression informed her she'd connected with him, and she took that as motivation to keep going. "I'm sorry if Mommy seems sad."

"That's okay. I get sad, too. Pastor Littlejohn said that makes us like Jesus. He's a man of sorrows, he says."

His simple, plainspoken explanation made Adelle's eyes well. "Yeah, I guess so," she agreed, her voice thick. "Ahem, Bennett?"

"Vroom . . . vroooomm . . . ouch! Yes, ma'am?" He untangled the car from his hair.

She stifled a chuckle as she drove onto their street. "Sometimes, we're going to have important you-and-me conversations, or you're going to overhear me talking to somebody else—or simply to myself— and . . . and I need you to keep those private conversations to yourself. Put them in a file in your mind marked *For Bennett's Ears Only*. Okay?

If there's something you want to share, ask me first. It's probably fine, but make sure and check with Mommy."

Adelle navigated between the jumble of toys and yard equipment stacked on both sides of the garage and parked her Outback. After she switched off the car and unbuckled, she spun to gaze into her son's large, heavily lashed eyes head-on. "I don't know when you'll see Mr. and Mrs. Pryor again. I'm thinking you won't get back there anytime soon." *Now, how do I get there without him?*

His lips poked out. "No more books?"

"We have plenty here, and there's also the library and other places to get books besides their store. That gives us new places to visit. Right?" Adelle didn't feel as excited as she sounded, but she had to play the part.

"But—"

"Bennett, there's a time and a place to question. This isn't either of those." She opened her door.

"But Mommy. What about Dude's card? It's still back here on the floor, and it's getting crunched by the apples. When are we going to give it to him?"

18

THE BOOKSTORE WAS HOPPING that Saturday morning.

From the second-floor landing, Glory watched Ophelia greet three new guests as they entered, toting bags from another local shop. They looked to be out-of-towners—people stopping through on their way to or from the mountains. Eyeing their shorts with all the extra pockets and hooks and their dusty, ankle-high boots, she noted to herself, "Remind Jason to buff these floors before he leaves tonight."

Glory absently twirled the large gold loop in her left ear as she watched the strangers strolling through the shop. She loved guessing what guests were searching for. "Let's see, she's hunting for a best-selling, book club pick . . . I think he'll only buy a bookmark and pretend he didn't come for the café . . . Oh, they're back! . . . Maybe without their mama, they'll look at YA instead of the historical fiction . . . Aww, straight to the children's section for their grandbabies."

Before Glory could finish her game, Mallory's voice tracked her down on the landing, declaring, "If she can't find it or hasn't heard of it, it doesn't exist. Let me find the owner."

Realizing she was being called to action, Glory hurried downstairs, careful to lift the end of her dress to avoid taking a spill. At the bottom, she adjusted the large frames that nearly covered her face. Glory didn't really need them, at least not the way most people needed glasses. She used her specs to ensure people saw less of her, not to enable her to see more of them. Assured they were secure on the bridge of her nose, she glided over to introduce herself to the couple standing with the teenaged host. *Ahh, the hikers.*

"Mallory, could you help those young ladies over there? Thank you." She turned to the dust-covered duo in front of her. "Hello there, I'm Glory Pryor. Welcome to By the Book. How may I help?"

And so it began.

About an hour later, she was bagging up *The Call of the Wild* and *Into Thin Air* for the twosome fresh from their mountain excursion. While they busied themselves oohing and aahing over the store, she predicted in a for-her-own-ears-only volume, "They'll stick these books on the shelf before the middle of next week and forget all about them until next year this time."

"What did you say?" the female hiker asked.

Glory dropped a bookmark in the bag. "Please accept this handmade gift as a thank you. Have you read Jack London before? No? So good. You'll also enjoy Jon Krakauer's narrative. That's this one." She dipped into the bag for *Into Thin Air*. It was obvious their activity had spurred a sense of adventure they wanted to perpetuate through their reading, for the moment. Still, she appreciated their business. "Please come visit us again when you're back this way."

"Oh, we will. The fresh air, the people, the mountains, the sky. Not to mention this place," the woman enthused. "I love it all! We'll definitely 'buy the book' again."

Glory smiled. "Happy reading!"

Her husband smirked. "I'm sure you're tired of hearing that one."

"Never, not as long as you're spending money in my store. When it comes to my books, I don't play around."

"Ooh, look, a raffle! What does *Famous Quotes* mean? Do we have to guess?" His wife lifted the medium-sized bowl partially obscured by the rack of paper bags on the corner of the desk.

Glory's husband, smelling of sandalwood and vanilla, suddenly appeared at her elbow. "Hello there. I'm Eli Pryor, this beautiful bookseller's assistant. Wow, that sounds like quite the title, doesn't it? Maybe *I* should write a book." His wink was conspicuous enough that it was obviously meant to engage them all.

"You have plenty enough to say," Glory teased.

"That I do. Actually, what Glory was about to explain is that we're asking our guests to help us with a project," Eli continued.

"Oh, is that what I was about to do?" Glory murmured.

"Yes, ma'am," he answered before returning his attention to their guests. "We're gathering book quotes as we prepare for the town festival coming in November and our store's upcoming thirty-fifth anniversary. If you'll share your favorites, you might see them plastered around town in a month or so. Also, include your email address and sign up for our newsletter, and we'll let you know which ones we choose so you can show off to all your friends."

What newsletter? Glory tried not to gawk at her marketing guru in action as he handed them pens and precut strips. She listened as the two guests debated which authors and books to use.

"Feel free to select more than one, and don't worry about getting the quotes perfect. If you include the title, we'll figure it out. It's more about the meaning, not the wording," Eli encouraged.

Thirty minutes later, the two wrapped up their project and left the store, swinging a small cardboard container along with the bag emblazoned with the By the Book logo. Eli had convinced them to stop by the café for one of Ophelia's specials.

Glory grabbed his arm and shook it so hard, his entire body moved. "What in the world, Eli! How can I afford you? You're too good at this. And what's this about a newsletter?"

"Simply using my powers for good, my love." He stroked her back.

She leaned into him. When they were together, they seemed to have a mutual, yet unspoken need to be within touching distance of each other. Eli may have wanted to make up for all the time lost; Glory was sowing seeds for the time to come. "Well, I appreciate it. If last Monday was any indication, we need outside help. Those meetings make for good discussions, but they're mighty drawn out. And so far, we've only come up with one real idea. Mine!"

The bell chimed above the door and a guest walked in chattering loudly on her phone.

"Do you know what else we'll need before long?" Eli asked. "Another assistant or host, whatever you're calling a part-time worker." He indicated the different groups milling about the store, visible from their spot near the front door where Glory had positioned the desk and the cash register. "I hate we lost our experienced help a few weeks ago, because Ophelia, you, and I won't be able to keep up with the increased traffic."

Glory gathered the books that earlier guests had considered but left stacked on the desk. "Oh, we'll be fine. Most folks are coming in now because of the signing later. It'll lighten up."

Eli signaled for Mallory to keep her eyes on operations and fell into step with his wife. "Maybe, but it's sure to get busier the closer we get to November. And imagine the people who'll troop through the store during the festival. Plus, the holidays will follow soon after."

"I hadn't thought of that." Glory stopped in the middle of an aisle and let a father and his three children pass.

"Come back for the reading later! There'll be music and storytelling for people of all ages, but especially for one, two, and three."

Eli indicated the two little girls leafing through picture books and the baby boy held aloft in the man's arms.

Witnessing his interaction with the family, Glory held her breath, hoping against hope that Eli had reconsidered staying in Gilmore once the festival was over. After all, he mentioned a newsletter. *What would be the point of starting one if he hasn't changed his mind?*

Eli returned to her side. Sky-blue shirt sleeves neatly folded back three times as was his custom and his index fingers hooked through his belt loops, he surveyed the store with a bemused expression. "For the life of me, I can't see how this is going to work, Glory. All the packing to do, the selling off of inventory. Mallory's still relatively new and isn't up to the job, not even if her brother pitches in when he's not busy with other work. And we can't forget that Ophelia's insisting they cut their hours by half when high school resumes. I figure a newsletter will help us get the word out about our closing, and maybe we'll get a buyer that way. Or maintain online orders in the future. Who knows? But no amount of reconfigurations will turn the five helpers we have into the six or seven we need."

And just as quickly, he cut the string to her hope-filled balloon and sent it sailing high into the sky beyond her reach. As far as her husband was concerned, the move wasn't a discussion point; it was a given.

"Then, what do you suggest?" Glory scooped up more randomly placed books and stacked her armful on a cart. There'd be more time to reshelve them later, to miss them later. She blinked away bitter, stinging tears. *How can I give up my dream to chase his?* An interminable silence forced her to look up.

"We're going to need some support around here. How about we write *We're Hiring* next to the list of specials on that chalkboard?"

For the third time that week—"Three too many," she remarked under her breath—Adelle parked in downtown Gilmore. Unbuckling, she dropped her keys in her purse, checked the traffic, and emerged with the small bag of apples they'd brought for Dude. She helped Bennett alight from the other side onto the sidewalk.

"Don't forget the card, Mommy!" His high-pitched voice trilled the reminder like the notes to a song. When he dragged it from the floor in back, it sent a small, die-cast truck sailing from their car. It came to rest behind the Outback's rear tire.

"How about I keep up with your toy, and you carry the card since I have the apples. We can look out for each other." She stuffed the car into her pocket.

As they walked toward where they'd last seen Dude, Adelle made a mental list of all she'd rather do besides return to By the Book: clean the men's bathroom at the gas station, cut the grass with her toenail clipper, gulp six tablespoons of castor oil, climb Grandfather Mountain in her bare feet. Yet, she determined to show the man the appreciation he deserved for his selfless act. When Dude saved Bennett's life, he effectively saved hers.

"Where do you think he'll hang this? Should we have bought him a gift card to a restaurant and taped it to the inside?" Questions like these had pestered Adelle at two in the morning when she lay alone.

Tongue in the corner of his mouth, he was obviously concentrating on not stepping on their homemade creation or dropping it into the storm drain.

"Let me see that." Adelle took the card and his hand and helped him onto the sidewalk at the corner.

The sun had greeted them this morning, but rain had followed on its coattails right after lunch. It had petered out on the drive over. Still, the afternoon was a dreary one, and the still-full clouds threatened to burst. Too humid to wear a raincoat, too cumbersome to carry an umbrella, Adelle and Bennett braved the heavy droplets that plopped onto their foreheads from roofs or awnings hanging over the walkway. She cringed, remembering the immediate "Definitely not!" she'd shouted when he'd requested to wear his yellow rain boots.

On the walkway leading to the front steps of the bookstore, Adelle hesitated and stared at the porch. If the people milling around inside were any sign, the chairs, chalkboard, and the cart full of books provided a warm welcome to most; to her, they served as a warning, and not only for her pocketbook. *Guard your heart with all diligence!*

Bennett tugged on her arm. "You said we had to hurry to beat the storm. Why aren't we going in?"

Because I'm not up for chatting it up with 'Miss Glory' so soon, plan or no plan. Aloud, she answered, "I'm trying to figure out the best way to eat this elephant."

He squinted up at her and swiped at a raindrop that landed squarely between his eyes. "Huh?"

Adelle resolved to get herself together. "Let's go around back. Dude isn't likely to be inside."

"Why do you call him Dude? Isn't he *Mr. Dude*, like you call Mr. Graves *Mr. Graves*?" Bennett dragged his feet through a shallow puddle, sloshing his mother's feet with rainwater.

"Watch it, Ben-Ben." She guided him around the next watery circle collecting on the concrete. "You know, that's an excellent question. Maybe I would, but I don't know what else to call him. I don't know his age or whether Dude is his first or last or in-between name. This is a special circumstance, I guess. But you should probably call him Mr. Dude . . . maybe." It sounded ridiculous to her own ears, but she stuck to her guns the way parents tended to do.

"Okay."

"Let's be careful," she whispered, not knowing why they had to be careful or why they were whispering. The wide driveway separating By the Book and Pearline's was empty and well kempt, with a patchwork of black-eyed Susans sprouting in the closely cropped grass growing between the two buildings. The clouds made good on their threat and the fine mist became a drizzle and then a steadier rain by the time they traveled from the street to the fenced area behind By the Book.

Adelle frowned at the empty chair sitting under the thick, overhanging branches.

"Where's Mr. Dude?" Pressing against her, Bennett tilted the large sheet of cardboard in her hand horizontally and sought shelter under it.

The man had more sense than she had, traipsing out in an impending storm. He must have taken cover somewhere, and they should follow suit. "Let's leave the card." *Where?*

"But it'll get wet. And what about the apples?" His obvious disappointment turned into a whine.

The red heart they'd colored had bled on the soggy paper that was tearing apart in her hands. "It's already wet, Bennett, and we're getting wetter by the second. Let's go since we missed Dude. I guess we'll have to make him another, and the apples will keep."

Fighting the urge to drop the card and skedaddle, she set down the bag and used both hands to crush it. Adelle hurried her son toward the large bins to the left of the back door, ignoring his resistance, to discard the trash they'd once considered a gift.

"But Mommy!"

Feeling him slip, she turned to catch him, which made her drop the messy wad. Red fruit tumbled from the bag and rolled everywhere. "Are you okay?"

He nodded, but tears mixed with the raindrops on his cheeks.

"Oh, Bennett . . ." Adelle knelt, ignoring the pebbles poking her knees. She slicked his hair back, her stained hands left pinkish smudges on his face. Imagining she looked as bedraggled as he did, she kissed his forehead and guided him away from the fence toward the driveway. "I think I have a towel in the car."

The back door opened to the Pryors' Tudor. "Adelle? Bennett? What in heaven are y'all doing back here?"

"Miss Glory!" Bennett ran toward the light shining onto the stoop and threw himself at the woman bathed by it.

The bookseller caught him with the arm that wasn't holding the door and stared at Adelle.

By now, she was fairly certain her own tears were mingling with the steady rain, and she prayed they were undetectable. "Hey. We were trying to leave our thank-you card and apples for Dude."

Glory's eyes traveled from the trash on the ground, to the child wrapped around her middle, and back to Adelle. Then she seemed to take measure of the skies above them and the rain that was gathering speed.

Adelle didn't know what Glory was about to say because at that moment, she saw the ever-present Eli appear behind his wife.

He beckoned. "I thought I heard voices. What are you doing out there, getting soaked? Come in, come in!"

She hesitated until Bennett's over-his-shoulder appeal slowly drew her. After retrieving the apples and the balled-up card, she slogged on leaden feet to the back door. Adelle nodded hello at Glory as she slid past the couple into the bright kitchen.

19

ADELLE EDGED AWAY from the hot kettle.

Ophelia poured steaming water into her visitor's cup. "Can I get you anything else, Adelle?"

She shook her head. Her spoon clinked against the porcelain when she pushed the leaves deeper in the water.

"Okay then. I'm going back to oversee things out there. Jason is a fish out of water without someone to oversee his work, and Mallory is helping with the event. When Glory finishes up with the readin' they'll be back." Ophelia's rubber-soled clogs *shooshed* briskly from the kitchen.

Adelle gingerly lifted her cup and inhaled the warmth of the tea as it steeped. Despite the summer weather outside, her body was a wintry day inside; she couldn't shake the chill from her stint in the rain. Eli had worked to make her and Bennett comfortable the minute he ushered them inside—calling for towels, offering them seats at their table, heating up the kettle—but Glory's icy reception hadn't helped matters.

The bookseller had swept from the kitchen and back to the store floor to welcome her visiting author, leaving Adelle by herself. Glory had hurried back to ask for Eli's help with the audio-visual equipment. "I can't tell my right from my left when it comes to all this technological mumbo jumbo," she'd apologized, propelling him by his shoulders from the room.

Glory had returned alone thirty minutes later, right before the event's four o'clock start. She'd sashayed over to the table where Bennett sat beside Adelle, sipping his iced chai that Ophelia had taken a break to prepare for him. "May I borrow your son? I think he'd get a kick out of the piano playing and the reading. And there's a ton of kids! I could use a little helper." She'd chucked the child's cheek with her knuckle.

When Bennett had asked permission with his wide brown eyes, all Adelle could do was flatten the hair standing on end and smooth the wrinkles in the shirt still drying on his body. Before she could suggest the woman use Mallory's assistance, off he'd dashed without a yay or nay, his hand safely ensconced in Glory's.

"Say 'thank you' to Mrs. Pryor!" Adelle called before the door swished once, twice behind them. She'd hunkered there until Ophelia had popped in again and insisted on refreshing her tea.

Now, she waited alone for her son, counting the minutes until they returned to the place that wasn't quite home—but neither was Cabot, not without Ben. Though her husband's scent still clung to his sweaters and shirts and the car's interior, it had faded from his pillow. Deep down, she had a feeling it was more his memory she sensed. *But thoughts of my dead husband are a warmer welcome than the one I received from Glory today.*

"Okay, enough. I need to get out of here." Adelle slapped the table, rattling the cup on the saucer. She searched her bag for pins and stuck them in her hair to make herself more presentable and left the kitchen, slipping out unnoticed by Ophelia's son, who was ringing up a customer in the café.

Adelle proceeded up the hallway that led to the home's great hall. It was bordered by shelves and displays, and shoppers—*Guests, Glory calls them*—moved through rooms sprouting from the entryway. At loose ends, she ambled toward the display that had first caught Bennett's attention.

The front door flew open. A frazzled-looking woman stepped in and shook her umbrella onto the porch. She hooked its crook over her arm and braced the door to allow an older woman, her back curved by an unseen burden, to hobble in supported by a cane. Behind the elderly figure's halting *tap-TAP, tap-TAP* trailed a teenaged girl, her eyes glazed and impatient, and lanky hair dripping rainwater down her face and neck. She jerked a boy of Bennett's age inside, his wet shirt clinging to his chest. They stepped off the mat stitched with multicolored book spines that spelled *WELCOME* and shook themselves dry, and the mother hastened around the group in her wedge-heeled sandals and damp pink tennis dress and peeked in the first rooms she came to.

Adelle quickened her pace to touch the woman's shoulder. "Excuse me. I suspect you're looking for the reading and signing. It's in back right before you get to the storeroom. If you want to take these two, I'll show your mother back."

The woman expelled a sigh wider than she was and drawled through cracked rose lipstick, "She's my mother-in-law, but that would be *he-yuwge*. Thank you so *mu-uch*. Y'all, come on. Motheh Smith, this nice lady is going to help *yew*." She motioned the children forward without a backwards glance. They trotted to catch up to her.

Adelle smiled and hunched a little to place her mouth closer to the woman's ear. She offered her arm as the woman's second cane. "Hey there. I'm Adelle, Mrs. Smith. We can take our time and enjoy the walk. Is this your first visit to By the Book?"

"Oh, sweetheart, no need to shout. I can hear you fine." Mrs. Smith's voice was firm and strong despite her frail appearance. "I tried to tell that daughter-in-law my son brought into my life where the meetin' was, but she never listens to me. Unlike Glory. She's always got an ear for what I have to say, probably because she never leaves this place. That woman is a blessin' to this community and us old ladies with the book groups and such. Her store feeds my spirit."

Adelle stumbled.

Mrs. Smith paused. "Are you alright, baby? I know my rickety legs don't work better'n yours."

Adelle reared back her shoulders and patted her companion's hand. She took a step forward. "Oh, yes, ma'am, I'm alright. Mrs. Pryor would be encouraged by hearing that. Okay, here we are." She barely parted the heavy pocket doors to allow the guest's narrow shoulders through to her daughter-in-law, positioned right at the room's threshold.

"There's Bennett, safe and sound, next to Saint Glory," Adelle muttered, peeking at the two near the piano. He had an elbow propped on her thigh, listening to the author play. *Everybody seems to love her. Maybe she's not who I think she is.* She set her mouth. *Or maybe her gowns are only sheep's clothing.*

Confused, Adelle returned to the main hallway. Apparently, most people had either entered the store for the express purpose of attending the reading or had discovered the event once they were inside. The few milling about found ready assistants in Mallory, Jason, or Ophelia, serving in the café. Feeling like the person in the Robert Frost poem, "The Road Not Taken," Adelle chose the less-traveled path that led to the Tudor's front room, where she'd been told Glory spent her afternoons.

The striped oversized chair whispered her name at first, and she tried to turn a deaf ear to its call. She spent a few minutes strolling around the room, hands in her pockets, fingers spinning the wheels of Bennett's truck. Soon, however, Adelle found herself scooting back into the chair, set in the corner where the view of Springs Church and the rolling hills beyond—*Glory's view*—shouted too loudly to ignore them. Peering through the rain-streaked glass, she tucked her feet under her and absently pushed the toy along the ridge of the upholstery.

The quiet swish of tires on the pavement and occasional, far-off jangle of the bell lulled her. If she closed her eyes, she could pretend her husband was in the kitchen, pouring them something to drink, and Bennett was busy with a puzzle in his room. When she heard the floor creak she swung toward the sound expectantly, half lost in her memories, sending the die-cast car flying.

Eli's face creased with a smile. "There you are! I've been searching for you."

"Mr. Pryor!" Fully in the here and now, Adelle sat straight. Immediately, she started smoothing flyaway strands, feeling physically and emotionally in shambles.

He slid his hands in his pockets as he approached her. "Are we back to that—*Mr. Pryor?*"

She wiped under her eyes. "Oh, no, no. I forgot where I was and you caught me off guard."

Eli's happy eyebrows knit with concern and his eyes lit with understanding. "Something tells me you're a coffee drinker like yours truly. How about I bring you a cup?"

Adelle felt a nod coming, but she refused to go from *caught off guard* to *letting her guard down*. "How about I follow you to the kitchen? We'll have to make it quick because I'm sure Bennett will come looking for me any minute." Adelle held herself still as Eli studied her face.

His chuckle was low and conciliatory. "Okay, but I wouldn't count on seeing him anytime soon. Your little musician is learning how to play the oboe as we speak. Oh, and you lost something."

Eli knelt on one knee and stretched an arm under the sofa. He came up with a typewritten page and the tiny replica of a Dodge Ram truck. "I'll hold on to this because it must belong to my wife. However, this belongs to you." He dropped the four-wheeled collectible into her upturned palm.

They returned to the kitchen in a congenial silence. Adelle waved at Ophelia, wiping the counter in the café, and pushed through into the kitchen. She examined the well-appointed room with its tall, cherry cabinets that touched the ceiling, pale-yellow walls, and pearly white marble countertop. Stainless steel appliances looked freshly polished and fingerprint free, proof that no one who played with Tonka trucks frequented this area. The space was large enough to fit an island under three Tiffany-style pendant lights, where Ophelia must do most of her prep work, and a square table that sat eight comfortably—and based on the other night, eleven uncomfortably. It was apparent that Glory loved this house enough to make sure each inch was tastefully decorated, yet cozy, and stamped with personality and practicality.

Eli poked his head into various cabinets around the kitchen, retrieving what he needed to make coffee for the two of them. He poured beans into a grinder and hit the button, filling the kitchen with its whir. He peeked at her over his shoulder and asked, "So you're fit for company now?"

"Only if it's yours," she quipped, surprising herself that she meant it. His effort to make light of his concern, as well as his toothy grin, warmed her as much as the drink would.

He filled the stovetop percolator with water and grounds and lit the gas. Then he sauntered over, sharp as a tack in his crisp blue button-down shirt. Bare ankles peeked out from under cream-colored slacks.

What would Ben have looked like in twenty years? She strove not to feel self-conscious in her muddy gray shorts and orange T-shirt that had seen better days. Her canvas sneakers were still drying by the back door, so she hid the borrowed slippers and her bare toes under the table. There was nothing she could do about her hair which could have used a conditioner, a detangler, and a brush.

Eli plopped down in the seat Bennett had abandoned earlier in his haste to get to Glory and the author event. "I'm very sorry you went to all that trouble to see Dude. When I told you he was back, I should have explained that I didn't know for how long. He goes with the wind, to borrow words from Margaret Mitchell."

"I believe that the correct word is *gone*. Wrong verb tense but an apt description for him." *Still with the jokes, Adelle?* She rolled her eyes internally and tucked a curl behind her ear.

"Don't tell my wife I messed up that quote. What'd you think, by the way?"

Her eyes questioned him.

"You know, the Famous Quotes Group. I hope you'll come back next week. Any ideas?" When he stood, Eli grunted and massaged his knee.

Adelle appreciated the whiff of his cologne when he limped over to the corner cabinet. Little boys tended to smell like sweat, ice cream, and potato chips. "I'll have to check our schedule, see if we can make it. I have a feeling we'll have no lack of ideas. Sorting through them will prove the challenge, deciding which to use."

"Fair."

"You're generous to host such a large group and think *book stuff* on your evening off. How do you like mixing your work and home life? Do you struggle with things like establishing boundaries or preserving your privacy?"

Eli froze with one hand on a cabinet door, his back to her.

"Did I say something wrong?"

He spun slowly, holding a small sugar bowl. "No, I'd say that's pretty insightful."

"I hope I haven't offended you."

"Not at all. I was serious about your insight. Please take it as the compliment it was intended to be." Their eyes held for a moment before he returned to his preparation. "It took some getting used to, living above the bookstore, feeling like I'm *on* the minute I step downstairs. Hearing people walking around my *house* when I want to shout, 'Go home and read your own books!' But it's Glory's life, which means it's my life. And it's a beautiful life."

Adelle nodded, her heart thudding painfully. "Speaking of working in a bookstore . . . Ben and I used to talk about owning one."

"You've never hinted at wanting to be a bookseller. What—planning on selling Bibles and commentaries and concordances? Maybe a biography or two? Nothing wrong with that. A worthy aspiration, if you ask me."

She shook her head. "Nope. Good ol' lying-to-you fiction."

He leaned against the cabinet and crossed his arms. "Well, well, well."

"I'm surprised you hadn't heard. I talked to Noemie about it."

"Pearline?"

"As if there's another one," she snickered. "We ran into each other at Sky Top apple farm and Bennett revealed my secret aspiration during our conversation." Adelle thought about the hug Noemie had given her. Until that moment in the orchard, she hadn't known she needed one.

Eli set the French vanilla creamer and the sugar cubes on the table. "That's quite a revelation."

She traced the rim of the teacup she'd left on the table before exploring the bookstore. "What do you mean?"

The old-fashioned coffee maker finished gurgling, indicating it had completed its brewing cycle, but Eli didn't move. He held her gaze, his face deadpan.

Adelle had the grace to blush. "Oh. Right."

"You basically ripped my wife's life's work to shreds, and now you say you've dreamed of owning your own bookstore. I believe Maya Angelou said something in *I Know Why the Caged Bird Sings* about the pain of carrying around untold stories. Do you have a story waiting to be told?" As if Eli could tell she needed space, he broke eye contact and strolled to the other side of the room. He shifted around cups, picking up and setting aside several until he withdrew two.

Adelle took the gift of that time to consider what story she could tell. Much like Eli, she selected and discarded one after another.

"You know, I won't kill you if I'm not entertained by whatever you decide to share." He slowly filled both mugs with a fragrant brew.

Adelle listened to his laugh. It was light but somehow deep and rich at the same time, like the coffee he poured. Ben had a good sense of humor, too, and he knew how to include people in the joke without making them the butt of one. She agitated the last bit of tea and studied the leaves at the bottom as if they'd reveal life's deepest secrets.

"I used to be pleasant to be around—at least, my husband thought so. When Ben was alive, I used to sit and listen to him laugh because just hearing him made me laugh, too. We would curl up on the sofa on rainy days and read to each other or simply read our books at the same time. I'd share parts that made me cry or mad or that were so well written I couldn't keep them to myself. He told me about his articles and described all the people he interviewed. We talked about scriptures that bolstered our hearts or convicted us."

Adelle stuck her finger in her cup and twirled it in the liquid, partly unaware of what she was doing. "We put our heads together and whispered our hopes and dreams to each other. Bookstores, newspaper columns, trips to Europe, more babies . . . We were going to take expensive vacations after we had all the children we wanted to have—and that was a lot—despite the fact it took forever to get pregnant the first time. But it was wonderful to simply enjoy Bennett, to let him be the baby all by himself for as long as God said. Then I had a miscarriage, and I was having trouble getting pregnant again, and then . . . and then Ben was gone. Taking all my laughter, my happiness, my hopes, and my stories and his columnist career with him. And of course, our bookstore."

Adelle stopped spinning her cup, and after a second or two, the brownish eddy inside it stilled. She wiped her finger on a napkin and didn't notice Eli closing the distance between them. Yet, when she felt the weight on her shoulder, she almost put her forehead on his knuckles and cried. But this wasn't the time, and it wasn't the place. And he definitely wasn't Ben.

"Mommy!"

She heard him before she saw Bennett burst through the swinging door, and Eli stepped away, leaving Adelle's shoulder bereft. Swiveling in her seat, she threw her arms wide to receive the four-foot-sized hug that launched itself at her. "Oopf!"

Her son clamped her damp cheeks with his sticky hands. "It was the best! You should've been there. He played the piano and everything! Can I learn to play the piano? Mrs. Pryor said I could take lessons here if I wanted to. Did you know *author* is a verb, too? Mr. Pickens *authored* three books—about a piano and a banjo and a harp. He's a musician. I got to play the C scale on a windwood called a boboe."

"I bet he means an oboe. It's a woodwind instrument." Eli's eyes twinkled.

"And all the kids clapped when I finished. Then the author—"

Adelle covered his flushed face with kisses to gently shush him. "Excuse me, little man. But who are you?"

Ben had made up a game. Based on his work as a reporter, it taught their son the who, what, where, why, and how of the world around him. Adelle found it also served to slow down the child when he was traveling at two miles a minute. Times like this one. She was surprised it had come to her at this moment.

He chortled. "I'm Bennett. What are you?"

"I'm a mommy. Where are you?"

"In By the Book, the best place in the world. How are you?"

The best place in the world. His answer stopped Adelle in her tracks. *My why is because it's time to go and the when is right now,* she thought to herself. She set him on his feet and rose right as Glory pushed into the kitchen.

"But how are you? You didn't answer, Mommy." Bennett pouted.

Adelle acknowledged the woman's presence with a slight incline of her head. "I'm fine, Bennett. Tired and wrinkly and kind of stinky, but fine. Say thank you to the Pryors, and let's be on our way." She edged Bennett to the back door.

The child planted himself in front of her in a rare show of rebellion. "No! Mrs. Pryor said we were having dinner with them after I helped clean up. Everybody's gone now, and we came to tell you. You and me never have good food anymore at our house. Just beanie weenies and frozen French fries."

"Bennett Simonette, absolutely not! I won't have anyone who talks to his mother like that sitting at my dinner table. No, sirree. How do you think that makes your mother feel hearing such words coming from your mouth?" Glory sounded taken aback.

Adelle gaped, robbed of words by the bookseller's outspoken defense.

Glory walked to a recalcitrant Bennett. She tilted his chin upward and smoothed his eyebrows with a fingertip. "When I was little, we had even less to eat than beans and franks sometimes. Mama would set a nice table, and our stomachs would get to growling, thinking about ham or fried chicken with a side of mashed potatoes. But when we sat down, there'd only be a bowl of greens and a square of cornbread or a plate of neck bones and white rice. And when I say neck *bones* I mean it! Who else in this room knows how much meat is on one of those?"

"Mmmhmm. Amen," Eli hummed in agreement.

"My parents worked hard for every bone and every bean, and let me even *think* to say a mumbling word of complaint about what they put on the table . . . !" Glory closed her eyes and pressed her lips together, as if the image was too horrible to envision or share. "Let's just say, I wouldn't. And neither should you, Bennett. Now apologize to your mother for sassing her."

The child cast down his eyes.

Never would Adelle have imagined feeling something akin to gratitude for Glory, let alone admiration; both emotions fought for preeminence. In the end, thankfulness won out, and she searched her mind for an appropriate response.

"Trying to find the right words? They're easier than you think," Eli encouraged.

"Oh, I—" But Adelle realized he'd directed his ironically timed question to the boy.

"I'm sorry," he finally whispered.

"I forgive you," Adelle responded automatically.

"Humpf, that wasn't loud enough for me," Glory grumbled under her breath, but she patted the child on his shoulder and walked to the range. She turned on the heat under the kettle and examined the area. "Eli, who's all this coffee for?"

Keeping watch on the two catching up and a miserable-looking Bennett who hadn't moved an inch, Adelle exchanged the borrowed slippers for her own shoes. She felt like Mr. Rogers from the PBS show of her childhood.

Suddenly, Glory hissed, *"What?!"*

Eli explained to Adelle, "Seeing how good you were with our guests earlier, I suggested we should offer you the part-time position in the store. We were about to post it."

She finished tying her laces and tucked in her shirt. "What guests? Oh, Mrs. Smith! That was no trouble. I was only making sure she got to the reading while her family secured seats. They were running behind."

"Yes, they were!" Glory exclaimed. "Interrupted the author in the middle of his playing and made him lose his place, with the way those kids came in, stepping on everybody. And their mama prances in like we were all waiting for her to show up."

The teakettle whistled, and Glory flicked the knob.

Adelle could tell Glory was still steaming as she stalked to retrieve the first cup in view. "I hope volunteering to walk Mrs. Smith to your happy place didn't cause trouble."

Sliding on a glove, Glory lifted the kettle and poured water into her empty cup. "It was *you* Leona Smith was raving about? I thought she meant our former employee, which confused me because she seemed not to recognize her. That makes sense now. Her daughter-in-law is a piece of work, both her and those children. But I suppose thanks are in order."

"No, no. I did what anybody would do—anybody who knew where the event was being held. She's a sweetie, that Mrs. Smith, and she thinks the world of you." Adelle glanced at Bennett and back at the older woman. "It's you I should thank, Glory. What you said earlier to my little guy. We're both at sea without Ben, but he needed to be taken down a notch. I have to admit you're good with him."

Glory smiled a little as she dropped a tea bag into her hot water. "*I have to admit?* That sounds like you don't want to."

"I don't. It's hard to acknowledge I don't know everything when it comes to my son." *My son instead of our son. That's getting easier to say.* Distracted, Adelle said, "It's hard to believe you don't have children of your own."

Glory's pupils constricted and darkened. She swallowed hard and without a word, she marched from the kitchen, leaving her tea to cool on the counter.

20

"You know she didn't mean anything by what she said. It's not something she thinks about, your . . ." Eli's mouth opened and clamped shut.

"What, my *childlessness*? Is that the word you're trying not to say?" Glory wanted to move her feet, but they were trapped under the heavy arm crisscrossing her ankles.

"That's not the word I was going for." Eli fiddled with her toes.

The two of them were sitting in the cozy, dimly lit den sculpted from the extra bedroom on the third floor. They'd pushed a wide, deep-blue velvet sofa into a niche against the wall between a corner cabinet and an end table, both piled with everything except books—a box filled with stationery and pens; a compact stereo system; a set of photographs taken during their childhood, at the wedding, in the store, and on their honeymoon; an unopened jigsaw puzzle and board games; clay animal figurines; lamps; Delia's teacup that Glory had rescued from the kitchen; and a dying philodendron Noemie had given her. An armchair, a leather recliner, and a wide square ottoman completed the seating area which faced their one television Eli had mounted.

While the room lacked rhyme and reason, Glory loved it more than her happy place. They retreated to it on the weekends—she to her thoughts, journals, and coloring books, and he to documentaries, sports programs, and old movies. Separate but together. Recently, they'd started a British crime drama, and that Saturday night, it claimed one-fourth of their attention. Three-fourths was devoted to their debate over hiring Adelle for a part-time job Glory had yet to concede they needed.

"Then what was the word you were going for? We've both suffered in our own way, and I don't mean to add to hers. But I thought it was an incredibly thoughtless thing for her to say."

He gently stroked the top of her foot. "Even though she didn't say it?"

She tensed up. "It's what you said I can't believe! Extending that offer to work here? There's no way that would work—although it would fulfill her lifelong dream. Can you believe Adelle dropped that bomb about a bookstore? She's kept that tucked in her pocket all these weeks, with all her talk about truth and lies and only reading Bibles. I told you she was hiding something."

"I wouldn't say she was hiding anything. We only recently met the woman, so of course, we don't know all her hopes and dreams. We're five years into a marriage and sixty years into knowing each other. Have you entrusted me with all of yours?"

"Oh, husband . . ." Glory buried her face in her hand, silently acceding his point. It took everything in her not to run from the room and scream somewhere. "Ophelia, Mallory, Jason, your yet-to-be-found daughter. Now Adelle and Bennett. You can't save everybody and his mama. Was I one of your projects, too?"

"Come on, you know better than that. Finding you saved my life, not the other way around. And when it comes to everybody else, I help where I can." His hand worked its way to her ankle. "How about we give it some thought over the next couple days and see what happens?"

"As long as I don't see her escorting any other guests around my store come Tuesday. First, I run into my old employee, who had the nerve to show her face today after leaving us in the lurch. Then I hear about Adelle, wandering around our home. What was she doing? You should worry about her, not Dude."

"Glory. She wasn't wandering, unless that's how you want to describe all our guests when they visit the store. Isn't that what you said? More than likely Adelle missed her son and wanted to check on him."

"Y'all are quite chummy, you and Adelle." Glory averted her eyes to study the framed oil painting of trees and their changing autumn leaves she'd hung over the sofa.

"And I hoped y'all were getting along better. Maybe you're not friends, but I could see you were developing a mutual respect. Noemie seems to like her." Eli's hand stopped moving.

Silence sat between them for a moment.

Glory ran her fingers through her short hair and scratched her scalp. "Let's not kick off our weekend arguing, especially over Adelle Simonette. You know how exhausted I get after hosting Saturday events, how it usually takes me the next two days to recover. The store is my mission, and I pour myself out for my guests. And today was no different, Eli. If anything, I'm feeling even more exhausted."

With some effort, Eli threw a leg around hers, wedged it under the cushions, and faced her. He pressed his thumbs into the soles of her feet. "What is it about the Simonettes? You have such an animus toward the mother, yet you adore the son. How is it possible for both emotions to spout from the same fountain?"

"Eli," she groaned, pressing the heels of her hands into her closed eyes. "Why have you accepted this high calling to protect her?" For a few seconds, the only sound in their den was an English detective ordering a pint for her mates.

Finally, he answered. "I'm honest enough with myself to admit I don't know. I suppose it's many things, Glory. First of all, she's a widow, raising a little boy on her own. Her husband died—what, a year ago?—and she's reeling. My first wife and I didn't have the same kind of relationship she had with Ben, and I was still a mess. Maybe because I didn't have a child to lean on."

Glory opened her eyes to listen to him. Her head felt too heavy to keep upright, so she propped it on her knuckles.

"Secondly, she's living in a new town, far away from all her family and friends. I was raised by a single mom, too, surrounded by meddling aunts and uncles and cousins, and that was hard enough. And thirdly . . . well, thirdly, she seems like a nice person. Smart, outspoken. Easy to talk to."

"Says you," Glory grumbled.

"Says me and Noemie, after their apple-picking trip. But you and I agree her son is a firecracker. It would've been nice to know her husband. They're a nice family."

She took a deep breath. "And she makes you think of your own daughter and grandchild."

"And yes, she makes me think of my own daughter and grandchild. Which is a fourth thing. As much as Dude reminds you of your brother, Davis." He shifted her dress above her knees to knead her bare calves.

As usual, Glory had to fight the urge to hide her scar tissue. Far from relaxed, she filled her lungs with air and let it out on a slow count of ten.

He paused and squinted at the television. "I've never met my daughter, but if she was in need and alone, I hope someone would take her into their hearts, if not into their home."

Glory shifted her legs to the floor, away from his hands. "Have you taken her into your heart, Eli? Is that what you want us to do, take her into our home and give her a job at By the Book? Better yet, perhaps we should turn this room into her weekend getaway."

He bent and scooped up her feet and placed them back on the cushion, then repositioned himself to stretch out beside her. Strong arms enfolded her. "I don't know how I feel about them other than a sense of responsibility. What about you? Can you answer my question about why you feel such animosity and suspicion toward her and such love for her son?"

At first, she resisted him, physically and emotionally. Having this discussion made her feel itchy inside. Finally, she laid her head against his and whispered, "To borrow your words, I'm honest enough to admit that I can't."

Eli's belly shook against her as he chuckled quietly.

Tired though she was, Glory couldn't help but chuckle along with him, and she scooted closer. "I don't know about you, but I have no idea what's going on. Do you want to play Scrabble instead?"

Eli switched off the television with the remote. "Actually, I have something to show you." He stretched out his arm and fumbled around on the table. A box tumbled to the floor.

She covered her mouth at the explosion of burgundy tiles. "I guess we're not playing Scrabble."

"We'll play rock, paper, scissors to see who picks them up. Now, where is it?" He adjusted his position. "I brought it so you could read it to me."

"You know the rules. No books allowed in this room. Not my day planner nor a magazine." That was part of the reason she adored this space. Nothing that resembled work crossed the threshold. Glory shut her eyes and listened to the rattling of things moving around on the table.

"Don't worry, it's not a book. Well, only a page from one."

"What are you talking about, Eli Pryor?" Opening one eye, she located the blanket that had pooled on the floor and scooched deeper under it. She didn't move when she heard the crackling of paper.

"Gotcha! Listen . . ."

"Dancing in bare fields
   where I once crawled and walked.
Laughing among the weeds
   where I'd mourned and balked . . ."

Glory pushed herself away from him and landed flat on the floor, sending Scrabble tiles sailing to the four corners of the room. She sat there, her arms braced behind her, uncaring that her legs were exposed to her thigh. "Where did you get that?"

Eli gaped at her. "What's wrong with you?"

"Where did you find that, Eli?" Glory snatched the sheet, gasping when it ripped.

Her husband pushed himself upright on the sofa.

"Eli, I asked you—"

Eyes narrowed, he slid the torn paper from her hands and matched it to the corner that was pinched between his two fingers. He read again, barely loud enough for her to hear,

"Dancing in bare fields
   where I once crawled and walked.
Laughing among the weeds
   where I'd mourned and balked
   at the bare furrows and earth
   which I'd planted and sown . . ."

Glory pulled her dress down to cover her legs and crouched on her knees with her head bowed.

> *"Now, joy and provision*
>   *when once I'd known*
>   *only sorrow.*
> *Reaping hope for today,*
>   *not merely wishing*
>   *and sighing*
>   *and crying.*
> *Looking ahead to tomorrow."*

When he tried to turn it over to read the words on the back of the page, Glory covered his hands with hers. "Please don't."

"Why? You have to explain why you're behaving like this." He grabbed hold of her wrists and pulled her up to sit beside him. "Who wrote this?"

Glory's shoulders sank as she stared at the familiar typewritten words he clutched. She wondered if they still bore the stains of her tears. She whispered, "You broke the rule."

"What?" Sounding uncharacteristically impatient, he repeated, "What rule, Glory?"

She managed a humorless, half smile. "About allowing work-related material in this room. May I?"

Eli followed her gaze. He nodded and gave her the page.

Allowing the torn corner to drift to the floor, Glory scanned the poem and considered all that had sprouted from it, unbeknownst to Eli. Like the climbing hydrangea that grew well in the shade, her secret had produced fruit in the dark. She murmured the next lines she had committed to heart, easy to do since they'd sprung from it. "Though untended, my once naked vines flourished."

Questions contorted Eli's handsome face. "You know this poem by heart?"

"I should, my love. I wrote it."

PART THREE

This Side of the Dirt

21

GLORY BRUSHED DUST OFF the artificial topiary set in the corner of the room on a stack of out-of-print books, most of which she'd found at a library sale. Such housework wasn't on her to-do list, but right now, she'd do anything not to look at Eli. If she faced him head-on, she'd find herself telling him the whole story, and that she couldn't do. Not tonight, if ever.

"You found that page under the sofa in the front room. I remember when it slipped under there, and I told myself not to forget to come back for it. I guess I did. Forget, I mean. I'm usually known for my memory, but with all my worrying these days, I'm slipping."

"I don't understand, Glory. You said you ripped this from your own book of poetry, and that you wrote it in college? How did I not know about it? What's the name?" His confusion floated across the room to her from his spot on the sofa.

Every question he posed signaled his growing doubt and weakening trust. Any other time Eli would've made his way to her, over hill and dale. *How can I fix this?* she asked herself. *Didn't your mama teach you that only the truth can set you free?*

"*My Former Days.*" She rubbed a plastic leaf between her fingers until it shone.

"What did you say?"

Glory turned, continuing to fiddle with a limb she had snapped off the decorative piece. "That's the name of my book—*My Former Days: A Childhood Elegy* by C. Logan. Cassie Logan, the character from *Roll of Thunder, Hear My Cry.* I always wanted to be her when I was a child, and when I got published, I finally got my wish by claiming her name for my own."

Eli seemed to ingest the information the way she used to eat the liver and onions her mama served—in one big chunk that was hard to swallow. "But . . . I mean . . . So, you wrote this poem—"

"A whole book of them, yes." Glory spoke quietly.

"—Got *them* published. And you made enough money to buy your house in Gilmore."

"*Our* house." She silently pleaded with him to correct himself, but he didn't.

"You're still getting paid for the book, checks you deposit in some bank account I know nothing about. Is that about right?"

"About right, but not all right." Glory willed him to tear his attention away from the poem she'd given back to him the minute she began sharing her story.

"Then good gracious, woman, tell me all!" Eli leapt to his feet, his wife suddenly in the bull's-eye. "Have you ever trusted me, or do you think I'm a gold digger out for your money? You must, since you hid this information all this time. You can't know me at all." He bowed his head.

She tripped over her dress in her haste to get to him. "Eli, Eli. No."

His profile was stone. Implacable and immovable. "No? Yes, Glory. *Yes.* Don't tell me no, as if I'm one of those people in your books, and you get to interpret their actions and feelings. I'm hurt.

I'm devastated. I said you don't know me, but I don't know who *you* are."

"I'd like to tell you, Eli, if you'll listen." *At least, I'd like to tell you some*, she amended.

He flicked a hand in her direction before stuffing them both in his pockets.

While Glory could tell it was a far cry from eagerness, she took it to indicate his willingness, and that had to be good enough. She remained at his left side, hovering near his shoulder, close enough for her breath to touch him even if she couldn't.

"You know about the fire. It destroyed everything we owned, and it nearly took my life. When I used to look at my legs, I wished it had. One of the few things it didn't take was a journal. Davis's journal. I was holding it when my brother pulled me from the house, and I never let go of it during my stay in the hospital."

"Even though Davis left you, after starting the fire in the first place."

Glory squeezed shut her eyes; the lies nearly seared her lips shut as well. When she dared to peek at him, he had turned in her direction by a small degree. This incremental opening of a previously closed door motivated her to keep talking. To use her words as a wedge. Like Scheherazade in *The Thousand and One Nights*, telling this story might yet give life to herself and her marriage.

"It was that journal that pulled me through. Over the years, as I healed and grew stronger, those thoughts inside that book blended with mine, and I transformed them into poetry. I continued to work on those poems—never intending to make them public, mind you. Eventually, I graduated from high school, and I earned a scholarship and went away to college. My parents were so proud . . ."

She'd told Eli this part. He knew that she was the only one in her family to attend anything beyond high school, a blessing and a burden because she couldn't fail; if she did, everyone else did, too—her parents, her grandparents, her aunts and uncles. Her brother. When Glory went to college, she took everybody with her. Yet, it was the weight of her guilt that nearly broke her; their hopes and dreams she could bear.

"Then your parents died." Like a sundial, Eli slowly turned her way.

Glory felt the warmth of him moving in her direction, but she didn't touch him. "Not even six months after I walked across that stage to get my diploma mama had a heart attack, and I believe Daddy died from a broken heart right after. They weren't meant to be in the world without each other. The fire had taken so much from them, and their despair over pushing Davis away took even more. I think they both only wanted to live long enough to see one of their children realize their own dream. Delia and Monte never considered this world their home. They believed heaven was better."

"Isn't it?" He seemed far away from her. "I think your parents were on to something."

"Eli—"

With an abrupt shake of his head, he shut down her protest. "But what about the book, Glory? It's interesting how you've told me most of this in bits and pieces during our relationship, leading me along the path like Hansel and Gretel, but you've never told me word one about the book. *Your book.* Where, when, and how does that come in?"

It was her turn to put some distance between them. She shuffled to the table at the end of the sofa and straightened the mess Eli had made. *Searching for truth will do that.*

Her husband grasped her upper arm. "Glory, what about the book?"

"What about it?" she snapped, shaking him off. "You're making a big deal out of something that isn't."

She swallowed. The right to be angry was solely his; she owned no part of it. She angled the photographs. "Somehow, I left my journal behind in class, the one I was using to rework all those . . . thoughts. One of my professors saw it and read them and felt they had promise. During the year after I graduated, she helped me edit and prepare my work for submission, and they were accepted and published."

"And became a bestseller. Remarkable. Why not use your own name?"

Because I couldn't. She laughed wryly then vocalized her thought. "Because I couldn't. I was—I am—still hurting—and those were private. I feared how people would respond. How Davis would respond."

"Why Davis? He was long gone by then."

"But he'd never given me permission to read what he'd written, let alone share it, to make his thoughts my own. I couldn't expose him or me." Glory surprised herself with the confession; she trudged on feeling a bit less burdened. "By writing under the pseudonym C. Logan, I became Cassie for a time, that bold, courageous, whole go-getter I always wanted to be. When I needed to be. At the same time, I could keep living as Glory Gibson, daughter of Delia and Monte Gibson." Glory knelt and picked up the four wooden trays from the Scrabble game.

"And you've never heard from him."

Since Eli's tone was more a statement than a question, Glory didn't respond.

"After starting that fire, I'd expect not. If anything, he owed you this house to replace the one he took from your family."

This time, he'd gone too far. She had to speak for her brother. "Don't—"

"Where did I fit in?" Eli stood in front of the lamp, casting a shadow over the floor.

As she emptied the letter tiles into the velvety bag she wrestled over what to defend—Davis or her marriage. The need in her husband's eyes made her decision. "I became Glory Pryor because I wanted to be."

Eli bent a knee beside her and scooped up squares. "What about the money, or is that okay to ask, Miss *Logan*?"

"It turns out that colleges and high schools love poetry, and for some reason, churches do, too. Must be all that talk about the wilderness. So, when those checks come in, I deposit them, donate them, invest them." Glory crawled to the edge of the rug and collected the *E*, *R*, and *S* she'd spotted. She held out the sack for her husband, and they collected wooden squares in silence.

When the last was dropped into the bag, Eli helped her up. "You don't spend it on travel, that's for sure. I can barely get you to leave this house."

She pressed a hand to his chest. "Because my home is here with you. I know some married couples believe in keeping secret nest eggs from each other. They consider them 'escape plans' in case things go south. That's not me, Eli. We lived separately most of our lives, but no more."

Glory placed a hand on each side of his face and hoped he could see beyond her nose and cheeks and lips. She wanted to show him her heart. "I have a debt to pay that has nothing to do with money. It's not about that. Never has been, baby. One day, I hope to make you understand."

At first, Eli seemed to look everywhere but at her face until at last, his eyes locked with hers. He sighed and gathered her close. "One day . . . but not today."

"Not today, but know I love you so much." It was more a promise than a profession. She stood on tiptoe and touched her mouth to his earlobe.

Eli stood to his full six foot two and lifted her from her feet. "I love you more."

Glory locked her arms around his neck, reared her head back, and blew out a breath, relieved that they had come through on the other side of this. When he set her back down, she saw his expression. "What's wrong?"

"That was only one page, one poem, 'Bare Vines.' Where's the rest of the book? Based on our conversations with authors, the publisher sends you the first edition as well as other copies. You must have one somewhere, and it's missing some pages."

"Wh-Why does it matter?"

"Because I plan to stay up all night, reading *My Former Days: A Childhood Elegy*. There's obviously so much I don't know about you, and I want to learn. I'm going to hold your hand."

Glory relaxed her grip though he didn't. After a minute, she tapped his shoulders twice and his arms fell to his sides. She crossed the room to the corner shelf and slowly lifted the dying plant to stare at the book that rested beneath it after bringing it back upstairs.

"You've been keeping it in this room all these years?"

Eyes closed, as close to praying as she'd come in years, Glory took the book from where she'd hidden it in plain sight and she returned to her husband. "I suppose I broke the rule, too."

22

WHEN GLORY WOKE, she ran her hand over the left half of the bed. It was empty and cold. She opened her eyes and rolled toward Eli's side. The cover was smooth, and two pillows were stacked neatly from the day before. No circular depression or wrinkle to indicate he'd ever laid his head there for an hour or a minute.

He'd never come to bed.

She flopped to her back and stared at the ceiling, her ear cocked for signs of life. On a typical Sunday, she awoke first and waited for him to stir. Glory couldn't rest with the birds twittering in the oak tree behind the fence; Eli was a more determined sleeper, who didn't move until he'd had his eight hours. Last week's predawn adventure had been well worth the change in their routine. Today's unusual start filled her with foreboding.

Glory flipped back the blanket and swung her legs over the edge of the bed. She stuffed her feet into slippers and tiptoed to their attached bathroom, trying to avoid disturbing Eli who had to be sleeping in their third-floor den. *My Former Days* was barely a hundred pages, so he must have elected to sleep on the couch rather than beside its author. She'd let him snooze a bit, but once she roused him, she'd steer him to their bed.

More than an hour later, dressed in a loose-fitting, yellow poplin maxi dress, Glory opened the door to her room and listened. Nothing but the occasional ticking as water trickled through the pipes behind the plaster walls. She checked her watch: *9:42.* Glory eased across the hall, avoiding the noisiest floorboards, and slowly opened the door a crack.

She expected his head to pop up over the arm of the sofa at the faint squeak of the hinges, but nothing happened, even when she called, "Eli?" Glory abandoned her efforts to be quiet as panic crept in and made itself comfortable, and she said more firmly, "Eli."

What if he died in his sleep? The shock of my book, combined with those extra pounds he's carrying, his busy schedule, and his age. They all proved too much, and he had a heart attack in his sleep. What if . . . what if God took him to punish me for all my lies and secrets, for ignoring Him all these years? Mama said what's done in the dark will come to light. Glory stood in the door, afraid to walk into the room and see his prone form, his arm tucked under his head the way he laid on his pillow.

There was nothing left to do but force herself to move. Every second took hours as the door swung wide. Sure—and yet unsure—of what she'd find, she closed her eyes and stepped deeper into the room, rounded the chair, opening them to . . . nothing but pillows. And that blasted book of poetry.

God had still taken her husband, just not in the way she'd feared.

Relieved and frustrated, Glory snatched up *My Former Days* from the cushion and ripped out pages in bunches. She imagined sitting beside Charles Graves in the next meeting of their Famous Quotes Group, mourning for a spouse who wasn't dead but who was dead to her. Glory flung the book and fell to her knees with a guttural cry. Then she beat the floor with her fists until they hurt. Over and over, she cried, "Eli! Eli, where are you?"

Chest heaving, she stalked from the room and down the stairs. She searched all the rooms on the second floor, including the bathroom. Satisfied she'd inspected every nook and cranny, she hurried to the main floor, her ballerina slippers tapping on the wooden treads. At the bottom, she listened, then called, "Eli! Are you down here?"

Only silence answered her. The anger that burgeoned upon finding her book on the sofa imploded. Her shoulders sagged, and her bottom lip trembled. Glory dragged herself from room to room before walking to the last place she expected to find him: her happy place. She wasn't surprised to find it empty, save for the furnishings and the dust motes suspended over the baby grand piano.

After exhausting the right side of By the Book, she ventured left. The only thing warming her L-shaped sofa were the sun's rays beaming through the triple-sized window. Before backing out of the octagonally shaped front room, she watched late worshippers, a couple who lived within walking distance, hurry down the street toward Ebenezer.

Glory slogged to the café, empty like the rest of the house, and finally to the kitchen. She hadn't started here because she'd maintained the tiniest hope that Eli wanted to surprise her with breakfast in bed. Perhaps, at that very moment, he was sticking a rose in a slender vase and preparing to bring it upstairs. Never mind the fact that they didn't own such a vase, and she hated roses because they conjured memories of her parents' casket sprays.

Glory pushed the swinging door. The range, island, cabinets, refrigerator . . . but no flowers or pancakes. And no Eli. She fell into her seat at the table and sobbed into her clasped arms, all her anger and frustration dissipated. Solitude felt oh so different than being alone. For a long time, she'd chosen the one. Now, it seemed, she'd been left with the other.

At last, spent, Glory filled the kettle and flicked on the burner. After selecting a pack of Earl Grey from the cupboard, she tapped it against her palm, the sound echoing in the kitchen. She started making plans as she upended the cup draining in the rack and set it on the saucer, then dropped in the tea bag. How in the world had she not noticed how big the house was? How empty? Maybe she would still sell it or move to a smaller place nearby and walk to work the way people did in the movies. A whistle pierced the quiet, interrupting the tumult of her thoughts.

The porch. Take your tea to the porch and sit with Him awhile.

"Who—what?" Nearly dropping her cup, she spun, sure she'd heard someone speak to her, but the same desolate space greeted her. Where had that invitation come from? She poured the hot water with shaking hands, sloshing some into the saucer and on the counter. When she picked them up, the porcelain rattled against each other. Glory considered her seat, catty-cornered from Eli's, then checked the time on the oversized, antique gold wall clock: ten forty-seven. The choir should be standing any minute.

Feeling as if the decision had been made for her, Glory left the kitchen and marched toward the vestibule. Setting down her cup on the round table to free her hands, she grabbed one of the chairs they stored there and opened the front door, jumping when the bell dinged in the otherwise silent area. Once she caught her breath, she placed the chair on the far left of the porch, where a leafy crepe myrtle on the other side shielded her from view. Glory went back inside the house for her tea and returned to her seat. *Just in time.*

"You're right, Eli. I do love listening to the choir," she admitted, knowing he was nowhere near to hear her.

The Lord hath promised good to me,
His word my hope secures;
He will my shield and portion be
As long as life endures.

"Amazing Grace." She remembered holding one side of the brick-red hymnal and her brother the other, trying not to giggle because the organist's eyes rolled back in her head when she sang the high notes. Mama would point at Davis and her and threaten them from the choir loft. Glory smiled to herself as she sipped, murmuring over her cup, "I loved those days. If only I'd held on to them, held on to my brother somehow."

Hold on to God, child. He still promises good to you.

Clink! "See, Eli? You always tease me for taking my tea like a little old lady, with the cup in one hand and the saucer in the other. But that longtime habit kept me from scalding myself!" Glory rested the drink on the wide brick column for safekeeping and considered the good in her life . . .

Her friends—Noemie and Dale, Charles, even Frederick. They'd brought companionship and laughter when she was on her own and had encouraged her when both she and the store were struggling to find a place in the community.

The store, her mainstay. Her home. All the guests who'd trooped through its doors and the stories they purchased as well as the ones they carried with them and left behind.

Her family. Bennett . . . the little boy with the remarkable eyes who felt like the grandson she'd never had, the grandchildren Eli wanted to open her heart to. Mama and Daddy, willing to sacrifice everything for her, including her brother. Davis, who taught her how to trade "bigger" nickels for "smaller" dimes with the younger kids at church, who skipped his class to punch out the boy who was bullying her, who designed animals out of aluminum foil and clay. Whose suffering, addiction, and thoughts transformed her life and paved the way for her future. Who took the fall so she wouldn't have to.

Eli, her Eli. He strolled back into her life one day and took hold of her heart. The one who wanted to strip away her strongest connection to her past and her pain, By the Book. Not only was he a good thing; he was the best thing.

What about the One who gave you those experiences, those things, and those people?

Glory closed her eyes to the question and to the voice. When she opened them, the choir had launched into another song, encouraging people to behold God's works, praising Him for being with them in the fire, as a shelter, and through the storm. *The fire.* Had He been with her even then?

Yes.

At fourteen, she was the good girl: she studied hard to earn good grades; made friends with the girls at church; came straight home after school; said "Yes, ma'am" and "No, sir" at the appropriate times and places; recited Psalm Twenty-Three at the Sunday school convention; helped with dinner; sang in the choir. The worst thing she did was break her mama's teacup.

She was also the good sister, staying up late to unlock the door for Davis; telling his teachers he was sick instead of hungover; acting as the mediator and moderator, making excuses for and extracting promises from him that he'd never keep; hiding his alcohol from him and for him. Secretly envying his rebelliousness and his freedom while begging him to sober up. Though she chafed at the strict rules Davis thumbed his nose at, she implored him, "Straighten up and fly right, like Daddy told you!"

But being good exhausted Glory, and that last fight between him and their parents depleted her faith. Where was their good God?

Delia Gibson wasn't one to shout, but that day, the neighbors could surely hear her raised voice all the way down the street. "Pastor told us that nothing should come before our service to the church—not our jobs, our children, and definitely not your drinkin', Davis Gibson!"

Her brother was lounging in the armchair, his heels propped on the coffee table and his eyes rolling heavenward at what he called her "histrionics." They had this fight once a week.

"I'm serious this time, Davis. I won't have you embarrassin' me anymore. How are we supposed to walk into that church as chairs of the deacon and deaconess boards, and our son stays out carousin' half the night? Comin' in stumblin' three, four times a week. You have to go."

"But Mama, he's only sixteen! You can't kick him out. He's your son, and he needs us." She touched her mama's arm, thinking of her words, *You can't do wrong and get by*. A promise and a threat.

Delia shook off the weary teenaged advocate. "What Davis needs is Jesus! I can't put up with him any longer. It's not my job. God wouldn't have me acceptin' sin."

"But the Bible says this is how we inherit the Kingdom, by helping those in need, starting with home and giving them food and drink. He could be angels . . . or Jesus!" In her youthful ignorance, Glory intertwined Scriptures, homilies, and lessons from VBS, anything to help her mama see reason. *Lord, won't You help him!* she'd implored.

"Davis, do you see how you're corruptin' your sister? I won't have it. Glory, go to your room, and Davis, get out. Don't bother to get your things. Get. Out." Delia had yanked her son up by his collar.

Gentle as always, even in his inebriated state, and probably disbelieving, Davis had allowed their mama to drag him out the front door while Glory hid in the hallway. And before she knew what was really happening, her brother was gone. Ejected from his home, gone into the night.

Mama had stalked by her. "Don't say a word. Not one. We're not supposed to love nobody or nothin' more than we love God. Love Him first, and He'll take care of everything and everybody else, includin' you and Davis. Always remember that. You hear me? Now, clean up in here. I've got a headache and I'm layin' down."

When her mama escaped to her room, Glory fled to Davis's. Her respite, her original happy place. She knew where her brother kept his precious journal, his cigarettes and book of matches, and his flask of vodka. Sipping, smoking, and reading over the next few hours helped her drown her misery and her questions. What type of God asks parents to reject their own child? Why was loving Him above all else tantamount to loving Him instead of anything else?

It was near his bed, surrounded by smoke and flames, where her brother found and rescued her. He scooped up her and his journal and led her mother to safety, leaving his family on the sidewalk to watch the house burn to the ground. They never heard from him again.

The choir at Ebenezer began its last song, "Glorious, marvelous, grace that rescued me . . ." and Glory covered her mouth. For the second time that morning, she sobbed her heart out. It was through her swollen eyes and tear-streaked glasses that she barely saw the form of a man turn up the pathway to By the Book and trod up its steps to the porch. Her heart beat faster, and she wondered, *Could it be?* She called out, "Davis?"

"Davis? No, no. It's me."

Eli. She now realized it was her husband wearing a dark blue suit and a blue pin-striped button-down shirt. "You're . . . you're alive. You're home."

"Of course I am. Are you disappointed to find me on this side of the dirt?" He stuffed his hands in his pants pockets.

"Of course not!" She removed her glasses and dropped them in her seat. "It's only . . ."

"Only what?" He took a step toward her.

Glory knew it was time to confess. "When I sit out here on Sunday mornings, part of me hopes my brother will show up. Somehow, this feels like the right time. If he ever found me, it would be this day of the week. I could barely see you . . ."

Eli closed the gap and gathered her into his sweet-smelling arms. "So, that's why the tears?"

She pressed her wet face into his collar. "These tears are because I'm so happy you're home. I looked for you everywhere. Where have you been?"

"To church, woman. To church."

Eli tightened the strings on his pajama bottoms, then picked up the copy of *My Former Days* from their bedside table. The wounded paper seemed to cry out as he leafed through it. It had taken him and Glory much of the evening and lots of tape to sort and piece together the torn pages as best they could.

"I still can't believe you wrote this, and that I never knew. Anybody else would've been crowing about writing a long-standing bestseller, yet you're so focused on posting about the festival and avoiding publicity altogether. A volume of poetry used in schools and colleges around the country . . . for decades? Come on! But not my Glory, a bookseller yourself. You write under an assumed name, move away from home, and never say another mumbling word about it. You quietly use the money to help other writers and readers."

His head turned this way and that, following the lines of the ceiling down the wall, the floor, and the rest of the room. "We're living in the house that Davis built."

"If you only knew," Glory muttered, listening from her seat in a deep-green, brocade parson's chair. She studied her face from different angles in the cheval mirror near her closet. Rubbing her hands together, she smoothed the lotion over each arm, starting with her wrists. Then she squirted more cream and arced her back to reach it.

Her husband approached her. "Need some help with that?"

She answered by squeezing a glob into his hand.

Eli massaged the lotion into the skin on the back of her bent neck and moved toward the curve of her shoulders, the motion a caress that Glory sensed bespoke of his devotion rather than any sexual overture. His love for her had endured decades of separation, his first marriage, her own initial fears of a romantic relationship. She prayed—*Is that what I'm doing*—that now, it would sustain them through her lies and confession, as the truth about her past unfolded.

"What made you write it, Glory, since you didn't want to gain fame and fortune? You could have chosen to put your brother's name on it, but you didn't. Why not?"

How do I answer? Glory searched her heart.

"You don't have to rush to answer."

"I know, and I appreciate your patient way. But after what I've put you through the past twenty-four hours . . ."

He shook his head. "I've waited more than once in our relationship for a response to one of my 'posers,' and I'm sure this won't be the last time. I'm too old and too slow to run away, so I might as well show some grace."

That wasn't her way—waiting—but their personalities melded together like opposite sides of a penny. *That's about all my thoughts are worth these days.* The most important thing he hadn't had to wait for was her answer to his proposal.

Eli clasped her shoulders with hands now softened and warmed.

Glory smiled affectionately at the reflection of his thinning curls and wrapped her fingers around his. "Maybe you should consider a career change. You're pretty good at that massage thing."

He gave her arms another squeeze before walking toward their en suite. "You make it easy, love. Easy and difficult. These hands wouldn't work on anybody else; my heart wouldn't beat for anyone else. Not again."

Her own heart clung to the words trailing behind him, and they pulled her in his direction. She found herself leaning against the doorjamb as he riffled through a drawer. "You're right, I wasn't running hard after success and riches when I penned that book of poetry. If I had, I wouldn't have used a pseudonym and spent the better years of my life hiding out in this backwater."

"You were only waiting for me." He winked at her.

Glory watched him search through the morass of medicinal items, wondering at his ability to move past her deception and focus on the day-to-day. How she wanted to come clean with him! She'd buried her past, heaping lie upon lie to cover it, like soil thrown on the dead. But here stood the truth, alive and well, *on this side of the dirt*, just as Eli had said earlier.

He glanced over his shoulder. "So, you had something to say, and you needed to share it with the world?"

Such questions had plagued her for years. Glory squared her shoulders. "No. Davis did. If he'd wanted to keep it to himself, he would've taken his journal with him. But he left it with me when he pulled me from the fire. And I promise, I didn't plagiarize his words." Glory shook her head, denying an accusation she'd lodged against herself over the years, not one Eli had spoken.

"I wrote verses that captured what he was thinking at the time. *He* deserved to be heard, not me, despite what my parents thought and told him most of his life. But I wanted to preserve his privacy without taking the credit. To honor him and thank him for saving my life, for saving my mama's life. Because I . . ." Glory choked up.

Eli twisted open the cap of a small vial and shook out a tiny pill. He met her gaze head-on. "Because you started the fire. Not your brother. Is that what you were about to say?"

She pressed the back of her hand to her mouth and nodded.

"I figured as much. I thought a lot about it during church, and I've been daring you to admit it with my comments about Davis. You're a stubborn one, Glory Pryor." He reached for her hand. "Was that so hard?"

Glory squeezed his fingers and let the tears flow. "I didn't have the guts to admit that I had started that fire because I was supposed to be the good one, and I was too weak to disappoint them. How could I tell them I destroyed everything they'd worked their whole lives for! I deserved to be thrown out instead of Davis. Admitting the truth was hard at first; then it became impossible. It just seemed easier to let him take the blame without actually pointing the finger—that's the lie I told myself. Yet, the longer he stayed away, the guiltier I became. I lived in hiding, hoping no one ever showed up who knew me then and who knew the truth. I couldn't risk it."

"Then I showed up."

Her eyes filled. "You were worth the risk."

"And the book?"

"It was the least I could do for my brother."

"And he never came forward . . . I wish I could've met him." He shook his head. "And you, as a bookstore owner—as a published author—you know it's no small feat to do what you did, writing a book, getting it published at a time when your voice wasn't as welcome as it is now and at such a young age. Have you ever considered writing another volume?"

Perceptive but practical, her husband. Always thinking about next steps. Glory edged past him to fill a small cup with tap water. She handed it to him, looking for a task to busy herself with. Smoke and mirrors that would distract her husband as well.

"Writing poetry isn't something you 'consider' up here." She tapped her temple with the tip of her index finger. "It takes a move of, of . . ." Glory floundered, hunting for the right word, much as he'd looked for his bottle of hydrochlorothiazide a few moments before.

"Of what? Of God?" Eli sipped and swallowed.

"Now, you know that's not what I was gon' say," she huffed. The accent slipped out, coating her irritated words. Nothing could get under her skin like the mention of an otherworldly leaning. Unlike her parents, Glory professed command of her own mind, body, and spirit, and she believed there was nothing holy about the inspiration for *My Former Days*. Quite the opposite. It was condemnation and contrition.

Glory stomped from the bathroom, her long, vibrant satin gown shimmering in the glow of the lamps. The wood floors reverberated with each angry step.

This time, it was Eli who trailed behind her and stood silently as she uncharacteristically tossed the dozen pillows to the floor instead of orderly piling them against the wall. He said nothing as she flung back the covers, slipped off her shoes, and climbed into bed. It wasn't until she pulled the blanket up to her neck that his question quietly, doggedly pursued his wife.

"What were you going to say then?"

It seemed he wouldn't allow her to hide from him, with the light shining on her, revealing all the lines sure to be creasing her forehead and creating furrows around her mouth. This was so unlike her husband, this determined priming of answers when they weren't readily pouring forth. It was also unlike her to go to bed angry, especially after sleeping separately the night before and their too-recent reconciliation. That was one Sunday school lesson that had stuck, even if most of the others had slipped away like the lotion from her skin.

More like soaked in, like that same lotion.

Glory shook her head at the persistent voice that was starting to sound too much like her own.

"What's wrong, baby girl?" Eli sat on his side of the bed.

His kindness nettled her even more; she didn't deserve it. "I'm not a baby, Eli Pryor. I'm older'n you, in fact," she growled, fighting the urge to roll on her side and turn her back to him.

"But you're mine. Always have been, ever since I saw you in the hall of Presby Elementary."

They'd been six and seven, he an older-than-average, taller kindergartner and she a younger-than-most, petite first grader. His apple had dropped from a hole in his brown paper bag and tumbled down the hallway between the feet of youngsters filing from classrooms toward the cafeteria. Glory had retrieved it, polished it on her gingham dress, and given it back to him.

In the only letter he'd ever written her after moving away four years later, he'd confessed, "The gap in your top row of teeth has forever left a hole in my heart only you can fill." Glory had kept that sheet of wide-ruled paper under her sweaters even though the faded writing was barely legible.

"Oh, Eli . . ." Glory withdrew her hands and hid her face behind them. She felt the bed sink as he slid beneath the covers, stretched out beside her, and pulled her close.

"Baby girl, it's alright. I'm here when you're ready to talk it all out."

His promise was a whisper in her ear, and it did more to undo her heart than all his pesky, thought-provoking questions.

23

THE SUN'S WEAKENING RAYS were strong enough to catch the iridescent colors in Glory's dress, turning the midnight-blue fabric dark green and aquamarine in spots as she stepped into the room the former owners called a library. Her happy place.

"Ready to kick up some dirt?" Eli switched on the floor lamp by the piano and angled the shade. He adjusted the bench seat at the piano and sat.

She sighed. "How did I let you talk me into this?" Glory set the brown-wrapped packages on the coffee table.

"Because you love me?" His fingers danced on the keys.

"Oh, yes, that. How could I forget?" Glory knew she didn't have a leg to stand on, that he'd earned a million yeses with all he'd accepted and forgiven and overlooked. They'd both brought truckloads of baggage into their relatively new marriage, but hers was taking a great deal longer to unpack.

Still, agreeing to take on Adelle Simonette as part-time help asked a lot from her. "This should cut down some of my yeses by a few hundred thousand. At least."

The music stopped. "What was that about a thousand?"

"Nothing, de-ah. Carry on with your practice. Could I request 'Moonlight Sonata'?" That was the first piece he'd played for her during their courtship. He didn't know he'd won her over with the first measure.

"Knock-knock."

Eli paused again.

"Hey there, Ophelia. Come on in."

His cousin poked her head between the pocket doors.

Glory grimaced as she fluffed the sofa pillows. She and Eli had less than an hour left of their weekend since he'd arranged for Adelle to come by before the standing Famous Quotes meeting. *How's it already Monday? Perhaps he's on to something about closing By the Book and spending more time together.*

"Hey. I hate to disturb, but I thought you should know before everybody gets here."

Glory made a circular motion with her hand. "Are you going to share, or should we guess, Ophelia?"

The woman frowned. "Well, I noticed some things missing from the kitchen."

Eli came to stand beside Glory. "What things?"

"My favorite knife for one, the little one that cuts my pastry perfectly. I kept it in the drawer in the island with all my usual tools."

"Are you sure—" Glory started.

"Yes, I'm sure, and if I wasn't, there are a few other things. Like my wallet I stuck behind the counter in the café and my crystal bowl I use for tips. I don't much care about the change inside it, but the bowl itself was special. Probably the only thing I'll ever get from my former husband, and that's includin' back child support."

Eli cut an eye at Glory before giving his full attention to his cousin. "Did you say your wallet?"

She knew what he was thinking: *Dude*.

Ophelia's red hair shook with the intensity of her hand motions to silence them. "Hold up. That wasn't my everyday purse, so no license, credits cards, or anything, save for an extra key I kept in it. That's why I mentioned the knife and the bowl—they're more special to me. I don't put them out every day, but I think they were here last week. It's probably not a big deal to anybody except me, but I thought you should know."

She backed toward the doors and used her hip to nudge them apart. "I'll check for anything else that's missing, but you told me to keep an eye out. Let's hope they turn up. Bye for now!"

When she disappeared, Glory pinched Eli's shoulder. "That's worth another hundred thousand yeses right there!"

He rubbed his arm. "What are you talking about? And that hurt."

"Never mind that. You had Ophelia keep an eye out because you expect there to be more things 'missing.'" Glory's fingers formed air quotes. "You still think Dude is stealing from us, don't you?"

"No. I asked her to look around, hoping she found the book. Of course I had to explain why." He shrugged. "But . . . he *has* been in the store twice, left unsupervised, and things have come up missing."

Glory couldn't help but picture Davis being mistreated somewhere because of how he looked or where he lived—or didn't live. "Do I have to point out to you again how many people are left unsupervised in our store, besides the guests who troop through here daily? I can't believe you!"

"What? You can't believe I'm trying to protect my wife?"

Glory stalked over to the window and stared out at the backyard, hoping to forestall her growing ire. The leaves had started to change, and the long summer days were behind them, which is exactly where she wanted this discussion: behind them. "I told you, Eli—"

"Oh, so I'm supposed to trust this one thing you told me, as opposed to all the other things you didn't. That more than likely, you still haven't."

"There it is. There it is. I knew it was too good to be true, all that *I forgive you, I understand, I love you,* business. Tell me when you're ready, you said. Well, I've carried this burden by myself my whole life. Why should I just hand it over to you after a few years? It's not like you don't have your own mess, Mr. Pryor.

"You don't know where your fantasy daughter is, but I don't hear you blaming your old girlfriend. You blame me for keeping you from her! You accuse me of hiding my past, but you're abandoning us for something that may not exist. If you're so dissatisfied, you should disappear again . . . for longer than a few hours!" Suddenly the need to defend herself supplanted her desire to defend Dude. Glory was used to self-condemnation, but she wouldn't take it from anyone else—particularly not the man she'd pledged to love and cherish.

"Hey . . . I'm sorry to interrupt, but you have company." There was a belated tap on a pocket door, for Ophelia had already pushed it aside and stuck her nose in. She widened the space and ushered in Adelle and Bennett. Ophelia followed them, set down a snack plate, and ducked out again.

The younger woman waved cheerily. "Is this a good time?"

Listening at the door, Adelle didn't know what to think. She'd come to Gilmore to cause the very thing Glory appeared to be doing on her own: losing what she loved and what she didn't deserve. Grace and mercy in reverse. She told herself, *Check One.*

Glory marched toward her and Bennett. "It's a fine time, Ophelia. I'll ready things for the meeting. Eli can get started here with you."

She bent low at the last second and smiled. "Would you like to come with me to the kitchen if Mommy says it's okay?"

"How can I say no?" Adelle responded lightly but honestly. She had to swallow her irritation when her son took the other woman's hand and left without a second look, his backpack swinging from his hand. When she turned toward Eli, she found him at the piano.

"Is everything okay? I know we interrupted something. If I got the time wrong . . ." Knowing she hadn't, Adelle made a show of glancing at her watch.

Eli's laugh was brief and humorless. "Glory and I were just having a discuss—no, a disagreement, obviously. But it's okay."

Adelle waited to see if he would say more. She felt for this kind man but didn't want to pry. Seeing justice done shouldn't mean he had to suffer.

Eli moved away from the piano. "So, you're willing to work for us, despite the occasional marital fireworks?"

She pursed her lips. "Ben and I had our moments, but he said healthy disagreements were like workouts. They broke down the muscles to build up the muscles, or something along those lines." Adelle would've given anything to argue with Ben again—about parenting, his travel, how she was always running late . . . Anything.

"Thank you. Have a seat."

As much as Adelle wanted to celebrate their argument, the Peacemaker within her wouldn't allow it. *Dear Lord,* she prayed and sighed, "Why don't you go after your wife and . . . I don't know . . . try and resolve whatever it is. Weeds grow when left untended. Don't take any moment for granted, from widow to former widower." *What in the world, Adelle?* But she knew it wasn't her doing. It was His.

Eli bowed his head. When he looked up, he grinned genuinely this time. "Thanks. I will. Be back in a sec." He strode through the parted doors.

Adelle moved about the room, picking up one book after another. It was apparent that Glory took the title *happy place* to heart. Not a sad story to be found in this room. And lots of sheet music, art history books, and picture books. She was surprised the joyful atmosphere hadn't snuffed out the Pryors' argument.

What are those brown packages? she wondered, noticing the table. Figuring she'd learn during the meeting, she walked to the window, where Glory was standing when Adelle had interrupted them. She counted the birds along the back fence, partly shielded by the trees leaning over it. Between its branches, Adelle gazed upon distant hills and an industrial tower of some sort. In another month or so, the thinner foliage would provide a clearer view.

"*Hola*, I heard you were in here. Okay to join you?"

Adelle swung toward the lilting voice that belonged to Noemie. "*Hola* yourself. Good to see you again." This time, she felt better prepared to see the stylish woman since she'd taken the time to dig out a white peasant blouse and new loose-fitting, linen pants covered in bright flowers. If Glory could pull off similar bold colors, she could, too.

Sure enough, Noemie wore a knee-length black dress and matching jacket, having come straight from the jewelry store. "Yes, it is good. Have you been baking, canning, and—I don't know—saucing? So many apples! What were we thinking, letting the little ones roam freely at the farm? And to think I packed these strawberries instead." She laughed and placed a fruit tray beside Ophelia's plate.

Adelle checked her watch again. "You're early."

"I saw you parking, and I told Dale to take over closing up. I wanted to talk to you about something." Noemie took a seat on the sofa and patted the cushion beside her.

Adelle joined her. "Uh . . . sure. But Eli will be back any minute.

We're supposed to talk before the meeting. I'm thinking about working here part-time."

"No worries. He's the one who sent me in here and said we had plenty of time to chat. He and Glory were snuggled up in the front room, watching traffic go by." Noemie waved a hand in that direction.

The knots in Adelle's stomach untwisted. "Oh, okay then. What did you want to talk about?"

"Bennett. I'd like to throw him a birthday party. He mentioned it at the apple farm, missing his *papá* and his friends. I figured I can host it sometime this week or at the next—maybe last?—meeting at my house as it's Labor Day, and we're closing early. Or even better, we could do Sunday after church. At least if you can't have family here, you can have friends. What do you think?"

Before Adelle could answer, Glory and Eli returned, hand in hand, Bennett and the others not far behind.

"Woof!" Oscar barked in greeting.

24

GLORY SPREAD HER ARMS in front of the pocket doors. "I'm here to block anyone who makes a run for it." Only half joking, she hoped her idea for tonight's meeting would meet with the group's approval rather than sending them running.

She indicated the five stacked packages on the table, each wrapped in brown paper.

"You know the adage about the danger of judging a book by its cover? Well, I've taken care of that for you."

Eli chimed in. "We can either draw straws, think of a number between one and twenty, or somebody can volunteer. However we decide, one of y'all gets to choose. Then you'll open it, close your eyes, and let your finger do the finding. Who wants to go first?"

They looked at each other until suddenly, Bennett crawled to the table, grabbed a book, and scurried back, pushing the package ahead of him. He hefted it with a grunt into his mother's lap and crowed triumphantly, "I guess you go first, Mommy!"

Her mouth dropped open. "Wha . . . ! Bennett?"

"Obviously, somebody was listening," Charles murmured to Ophelia. "Open it up and let's give a look-see, Adelle."

Frowning, she peeled off the tape and wrapping. Warily, she studied it. "It's *The Stand* by Stephen King."

"Should we really plaster Stephen King quotes all around the town to advertise the festival?" Dale asked. "They might make outsiders scared to come here if they think we've got clowns jumping out of drains or the kind of stores like the one in *Needful Things*. He's talented, don't get me wrong. But I wouldn't exactly consider him family friendly."

But Noemie had leaned in Adelle's direction. "This book has so many spiritual references. The idea of free will. The fight between good and evil . . ."

"The Walkin' Dude as the devil . . . I lost sleep reading this one." Adelle shivered and set the book on the table.

Jealousy stung Glory, witnessing the growing camaraderie between the two women. *That woman is inserting herself in all parts of my life.*

Glory retrieved the book. "Before we move on, I'd like to hear what my Holy Rollers think of this quote." She flipped to a passage and read, *"Every man or woman who loves Him, they hate Him too, because He's a hard God, a jealous God, He Is, what He Is, and in this world He's apt to repay service with pain while those who do evil ride over the roads in Cadillac cars. Even the joy of serving Him is a bitter joy."*

Glory closed the book with a snap and grabbed hold of each pair of eyes one by one, letting go slowly before moving on to the next set. "What do you think? Is He a hard God?"

Noemie cut an eye at Dale.

Charles rested his cheek on his cane.

"Well?" Glory prompted. "No one brave enough to answer the question? Is God hard or not?"

Eli shifted in his seat.

Jason cast a wary eye at his mother, as if gauging the temperature of the water before daring to stick a toe in.

"Does that mean you love God, Glory?" Adelle quietly launched the question into the room like a grenade.

The bookseller whipped toward the younger woman. "What?"

"I would never go so far as to use the word *hate* when it comes to the sovereign over all creation," Adelle continued. "But we could turn that quote around. If you don't *like* God much right now, then you must love Him some, too, or know Him."

Stumped, Glory opened the book again. "I was only reading what Stephen wrote, not professing my faith . . . or lack of it."

"You have to believe to say you don't believe, especially as vehemently as you do." Adelle forged on in her argument. "He does give us the free will to choose—but the ability to not believe comes at a cost. You pay eventually."

Glory closed her eyes. *I've paid the price and am accruing interest.*

"*Y sabemos que a los que aman a Dios, todas las cosas les ayudan a bien, esto es, a los que conforme a su propósito son llamados.*" Noemie inclined her head toward her clasped hands, her eyes closed.

"Romans 8:28," Dale explained. "We know that all things work together for good to those who love God, to those who are the called according to His purpose."

The jeweler nodded vigorously. "And when God says all, He means *all. Todos.* Including the pain and the loss you've experienced from dealing with man. Men who so desperately want to be God and who hurt God's people in the process. *La amargura* . . . the bitterness . . . that Stephen King writes about doesn't come from serving others or from your true faith. That's inside of us. It's a root that's tangled up and embedded in us, growing from our unmet needs and unexpressed emotions. Our misperceptions."

"Losing people is hard, but God isn't." Charles's voice was low, yet firm.

Ophelia raised her hand. "Church folks are hard. I can admit that."

"And families. Families can be hard," Frederick chimed in.

"School is hard!" Jason took off his cap and scratched his head.

"And teenagers can challenge you, too." Ophelia slapped her son on his thigh.

"Forgiveness is hard. Almost impossible." Adelle looked grim.

Glory didn't know what the younger woman had on her mind, but she had to agree. She didn't know how to forgive her parents for their treatment of Davis, as much as she loved them. But even more difficult than that, she struggled to forgive herself for letting him take the blame for what she'd done by remaining silent. She'd tried to atone by erecting this monument to him and doing as much good as she could. But it turned out that grace was as hard to accept as it was to give.

"God isn't hard," Charles asserted, tapping his cane with each word. "He's good, and His way is easy, and His burden is light. That's something we should put on a poster."

"What say we take a bathroom break so the old folks in the room can stretch their legs," Eli suggested. "And we'll meet back here in five."

Surreptitiously, Adelle watched the couple confer by the piano. Glory was standing so close to it, her hip played flat and sharp notes every few seconds. Yet, Adelle barely heard the discordant music because Noemie's words were in the forefront of her mind: *men who so desperately want to be God and who hurt God's people in the process.* She wondered if that was what she was doing—trying to be God—by coming to Gilmore.

"They make a fine pair, don't they?" Coffee laced Mr. Graves's breath.

Adelle trained her eyes elsewhere. She leaned closer to the older man and replied noncommittally, "Mmm-hmm."

"People in town wondered if she'd ever get married. I could hear the gossip when I took my walk down Springs Church. You see, Mabel in that big old house on the corner lets Oscar do his business by her daisies as long as I pick it up. She's probably thinking I'll come by for some tea or conversation one day." He tsked to himself.

Adelle faced him. "Who, Glory?"

Mr. Graves laughed. "I had a sense you weren't paying me any attention. Where's your mind, miss?"

She smiled. "Here and there and everywhere, Mr. Graves. Are you enjoying this so-called Famous Quotes Group? It's definitely more than I bargained for."

"In our experience, my dear, we've seen that's how life is—more than we expect. That's our testimony. More than we want oftentimes, but I'll take the good and the bad from God over the indifferent."

Frederick sighed and dragged his hand down over his nose.

"Not *Little Women*," Jason groaned.

Adelle risked looking Glory's way. "Actually, I love this book. In my opinion, everything is good, so you can't go wrong if you open it up, close your eyes, and point." She gave the book to Ophelia, who passed it along. The book traveled like a hot potato to Glory's silky lap.

"I'll play by the rules even if y'all won't." She closed her eyes and leafed through the book. When her finger landed, she read, "*I don't like to doze by the fire. I like adventures, and I'm going to find some.*"

Eli sighed. "I'm definitely ready for a new adventure. Not merely ones you read about."

Ophelia sniffed. "Maybe y'all should add some nonfiction and start sellin' travel books."

Glory spoke into the quiet that descended heavily on the room, leading their minds away from the subject of the Pryors' move. "When we were coming up, Mama and Daddy took us away for a week every summer, for 'explorin' time' as they called it. That's the only extra that made them dip into our educational savings, but they saved a little something from each paycheck, starting the week we got home from a trip until the next year. We saw the Rockies; the Great Lakes; St. Augustine, Florida; Mount Washington—"

"Where's Mount Washington?" Noemie squinted, like she was studying a map.

"In New Hampshire. It's the tallest peak in the Northeast," Adelle supplied.

"Sure is. It seemed like a one-thousand-degree drop in temperature between the bottom of that mountain and the top of it." Glory smiled, thinking back.

"Me and my cousin might have skipped that trip!" Eli bumped fists with Ophelia.

"My cousin and *I*. And the wind, y'all!" Glory feigned a shiver, her arms crossed over her chest.

"Honeybun, don't you have a picture somewhere of y'all on a rock, looking like you were about to fall off?"

Adelle smiled a little at the natural push-pull dynamic of the Pryors' marriage. Glory corrected her husband's grammar as easily as she took a breath, and he accepted her correction as easily as he expelled one.

"Adelle, have you ever been there?" Glory asked.

She had been leaning against the sofa, but the question led her to sit upright and clear her throat. "I was, as a child. My husband and I had hoped to take Bennett, but . . ." Her shrug put an end to those hopes and dreams. "But you know, my family had adventures, too. One time, we drove across the country, all the way to Crescent City, California, to camp in the Redwood National Forest."

Glory clasped her hands together. "Oh! I always wanted to go there, but we never did. I don't think there was that much saving in the world for my parents, based on my idea of what Mama brought in from the factory and Daddy's job as a mechanic."

Adelle's eyes narrowed. "Really? You, a camper? I'm surprised you'd want to rough it, with all your silks and caftans and polished nails. Not much opportunity for lipstick and jewelry, sleeping on the ground."

It was Glory's turn to shrug off a memory. "Maybe I should say I *wanted* to want to. My brother used to talk about it all the time. He had big plans of living in California, *gettin' out from under*. I think that's how he put it."

"Under . . . ?" Frederick interjected a question into a discussion that had become a tête-à-tête, despite the four other people scattered about the room.

Ophelia readjusted her position on the sofa. "I take it your parents were unyielding."

"That's how all our folks were in those days. They had to be," Charles commented, his voice thoughtful. "Maybe we're not like Marmee and the girls, running a household while the Civil War rages. But life was full of battles and trials. Still is. Maybe my parents weren't as hard on me as the world was, but they had to be tough to make sure we survived. These young people today could use a little of what we had to face."

Glory grappled with her thoughts, struggling to find the words to agree or disagree. Her mama and daddy believed they were answering God's imperative to discipline their children. Every *no*, every lecture, the final rejection . . . *But what about love?*

"*I'd rather take coffee than compliments just now.*" Eli had taken the book without Glory's knowledge. "That was from Amy—and I agree with her wholeheartedly! Who else wants a cup?"

Five hands rose, but none of them belonged to Glory, who propped her elbows on her knees where she was curled up on the sofa. Eli brushed her shoulder on his way to get the carafe, and she pressed her cheek against his hand. Once all their guests had found their way home, she figured she'd relax over a cup of tea.

Ophelia plopped next to Glory on the sofa. "Mallory, why don't you take Bennett to get some of that chocolate milk I bought and help Eli push the tray in here." When they left, she turned her attention to her cousin-in-law. "Why don't you drink coffee?"

"Because it smells like memories I'd rather forget," Glory answered without thinking. Seeing the questions on their faces they'd never dare to ask—*except that Adelle. I bet she's got a few ready to trip off that tongue*—Glory decided to explain as much as she was able.

"Some of y'all know my brother was an alcoholic. When he started drinking, it was only a little here. A little there. Then more with different kinds of friends. Later he couldn't go to sleep without it, couldn't wake up because of it. So, I learned to make coffee."

As she'd spoken, Glory had found herself studying everything in the room but the other people in it.

"Do you miss your coffee?" Adelle locked eyes with her.

Glory's eyes filled, but she refused to let the tears fall. "I miss my brother more."

"Now that I think about it, I've never seen you drink. Not even a glass of wine," Ophelia commented.

Glory shook her head. *And you never will.*

Noemie, who was sitting in the chair nearest the end of the sofa, reached over and squeezed her friend's toes. "Unlike Amy, I wouldn't mind hearing a compliment or two about my peach cobbler. I left work early to bake that monstrous thing. Dale's *abuelita* taught me how so I could make it for her grandson when she went on to heaven. I had to watch her like a hawk because she measured nothing!"

Glory hoped her smile communicated her gratitude for her friend's help turning the spotlight elsewhere.

"It was delicious, Noemie!" Ophelia gushed. "And if I'm saying so, that's saying something."

Frederick rubbed his stomach. "Indeed, it was. I'd love to have the recipe, or at least come watch you and Dale prepare it. Y'all know I'm always looking for something new to add to my repertoire."

Glory winked at him. "Y'all better tell him, or he'll steal it!"

"What'd I miss?" Eli rolled the cart with the coffee service into the room, followed by Bennett with a chocolate moustache.

Frederick prepared his coffee the minute his host parked the cart. "Sad to say, you didn't miss much. Still talking about *Little Women*, which I knew was coming the minute we formed this group."

"Yes, even Glory has to love this one," Adelle agreed.

"Why do you say, 'even Glory'? I mean, I do, but why am I an exception?"

"Because it's Christian fiction, and I don't think it's your favorite," Adelle argued.

Glory opened the book without bothering to hide her irritation. "It's a coming-of-age novel. And actually, it's one of my *all-time* favorites. *Beauty, youth, good fortune, even love itself, cannot keep care and pain, loss and sorrow, from the most blessed—*"

"*—for into each life some rain must fall, some days must be dark and sad and dreary,*" Adelle finished. "True and beautiful."

"Ah, we did it!" Eli cried out and picked up Bennett to give him a high five.

"Did what?" Adelle gawked at the duo.

"We got you to use the word *true* when it comes to talking about a fictional work. Our job is done. Hip hip . . ."

"Hooray!" Bennett cheered, throwing his arms above his head.

Charles played a rhythm with the rubber stopper of his cane. He seemed to peer at far-off people and places, as if making out details. "That last part. Certainly speaks into my life, Mrs. Simonette."

She stroked her son's hair. He'd returned to the floor at her feet to play with Oscar, who'd somehow wheedled himself beyond Glory's sidewalk. "No, I'd have to agree with you, Mr. Graves. It has poured this past year or so in my life. Torrential rains."

"I've heard that quote before, and I didn't know it came from *Little Women*. But I don't know if it sounds like 'Welcome to the festival . . . yay! The crowd goes wild!'" Jason made quiet cheering sounds.

"I'd have to agree. Next!" Frederick advised.

Little Women in hand, Noemie withdrew a pair of sparkly spectacles from her jacket pocket. "These are from my reading partner over there. Thank you, Glory!"

Glory winked. "Only ten dollars in the store!"

Noemie slipped them onto her nose. Settling on a page, she glanced over her half lenses at the group, her hazel eyes dancing. "Yes, here. I remember this passage because it basically describes my life. Let's see . . ." She focused once more on the page and read:

"Have regular hours for work and play; make each day both useful and pleasant, and prove that you understand the worth of time by employing it well. Then youth will be delightful, old age will bring few regrets, and life will become a beautiful success."

Adelle mulled over her life, particularly the last few years with Ben and the last month in Gilmore. Regret, anger, and bitterness were a tightly braided cord threading through every day, every second. Her eyes drifted to her son. *Ahh, my "beautiful success."* A cough drew her attention to Glory, who seemed to be carrying her own burdens.

Eli stroked his wife's shoulder.

Noemie plopped the book onto the table. "I lived by my schedule—"

Her husband laughed. "And woe to anybody who interrupted it. I remember you being called down to the school a time or two for our children, and you didn't like it much."

Glory smothered a laugh behind her hand. "That son of yours had some growing up to do when he was in high school, but he's straightened up nicely and become a fine young man with a family of his own. Maybe his kids will give him a fit, too, and he'll see what he put his mama through."

Red lips pinched, Noemie continued as if she hadn't been interrupted. "—and I devoted 7:30 to 6:30 six days a week, a little shorter on Saturdays, to the store. Then I worked in my garden every evening for about an hour after dinner. At the time, I'd say those years were pleasant and put to good use. Fairly successful." She surveyed the room.

Frederick nodded. "I've always admired your name emblazoned across your glass door. You started that business what . . . twenty, twenty-five—?"

"Twenty-eight," Dale corrected.

"Twenty-eight years ago." Frederick repeated, almost to himself. "Not too much longer after Glory sold her first book and right along the time I started drawing pictures of chairs. Now you're hosting yearly classes for jewelry designers—"

"And considering opening another location, if that son of ours has his way." Dale sounded both tired and proud.

"Yes, my Etta loved that necklace I bought her for our tenth anniversary. I wish I'd bought her more." Frederick's voice was laden with regrets of his own as he spun to gaze out the window. Darkness blanketed the world beyond the glass. Moths fluttered against the pane, drawn to the bright light inside.

"But my point is that it may look like success to the world, but when I look back, I wonder if I put my attention where it was most needed. All those hours at the store, the name on our front door, folks walking around with our jewelry. But my children were raised by other people, and my husband and I didn't spend much time together outside of work."

In a hushed voice, Noemie continued. "Glory, you have an opportunity. You had your time to work and invest in your business. To be on your own. To grow By the Book. But maybe it's time to rest, to play, to heal. Enjoy your husband."

"That's me." Eli smiled at his wife.

"I wonder what time it is for you and your little one." Noemie nodded at Adelle and Bennett, whose head was leaning heavily against his mother's leg.

Adelle's eyes met Glory's for a second before the older woman looked away.

Mallory picked up *Little Women* and admitted sheepishly, "I didn't tell any of my friends how much I liked it when we studied this in English lit. When you were talking, Mrs. Pearline, I remembered something we read. Um . . ." Her finger traced one page after another. "Here it goes. Mrs. March said this: *I'd rather see you poor men's wives, if you were happy, beloved, contented, than queens on thrones, without self-respect and peace.* I didn't get it until now." She returned the book to the table and didn't make eye contact with anyone.

Ophelia whispered something to her daughter and Mallory nodded, flushing a bit.

Mr. Graves rested his cane against the side of his leg and settled back in the chair. "May I suggest, *Make each day both useful and pleasant—dot-dot-dot—at the festival,* from *Little Women.*"

25

"And you're sure Bennett likes this cake—*chocolate y vainilla, con fresas* . . . ? I can decorate it however he likes." Noemie brandished one of the strawberries she was slicing. At Adelle's nod, she angled it beside the rest in the icing.

Adelle tossed her braid over her shoulder. "Noemie, I'm not sure that's going to work out."

The woman's eyebrows furrowed. "Didn't you say he likes both flavors?"

"Oh, no, no. Bennett will love it. But I'm not sure this is a good idea, this party." Adelle had cried herself to sleep the night before and almost called Noemie to cancel upon awakening. Her son's excitement led her to keep the commitment after dragging herself and him to church.

"Of course it is. We can't have Bennett thinking he has no friends in this new place, that he has no home. It's such a precious age, and he's old enough to remember this time. Who wants to look back and recall loneliness and sadness?"

Adelle pushed her fingers against her lids so hard, her eyes hurt.

Not only had she let the past ruin her present life; she was letting it destroy her son's future. "Noemie. I'm not up for a meeting with . . ." She stopped short of saying "Glory."

"This is a party for the five-year-old. That's what we're celebrating. Not some fuddy-duddy festival nobody is thinking about yet. We can't let somebody else's problem become our emergency, even if it's my best friend."

What if I told you that I intend to break your best friend's heart? Would you be so willing to host this party for us?

But Adelle's loneliness cried out even more loudly. *Won't it be wonderful to sit and think about nothing but honoring your baby's five years of life with people who care? To sing and dance and watch him play with children his age?* Last year, the two of them had blown out four candles before crying themselves to sleep in her bed. Adelle had laid on Ben's side because she couldn't bring herself to wake up and see a child-sized version of her husband in his spot.

"Okay, I suppose so." Adelle gazed into the expansive backyard through the large windows behind the kitchen table. Bennett kicked a ball to Noemie's grandchildren.

"Maravilloso!"

Adelle found a giggle somewhere and shared it. "I take it you said *marvelous*?"

"Yes. Now, put on a party hat and blow up the balloons."

Eli poked his head through their bedroom door just as Glory put her diamond stud in her ear. "Excited about going to a five-year-old's birthday party?"

She fluffed her hair and turned away from the mirror. "I can't say I imagined you'd ever ask me that question, but yes, I am. You made it back earlier than I thought." Glory slung the strap of her leather cross-body bag over her shoulder.

"I left as soon as the pastor pronounced the benediction. I hope one day we can hold hands on the same pew and go out to lunch at Sassafras afterwards." He cupped her elbow and led her from the room.

"Eli . . ." The warning died on her lips without more fanfare. No need to light any fireworks before the real celebration with the Pearlines.

He'd invited her to attend church with him that morning, but she'd quickly straightened his tie for him and sent him on his way after a polite, "No thank you." Then Glory had listened to the choir in her tucked-away corner of the porch and returned upstairs to get ready for Noemie's party for Bennett. While she'd had to give up expecting her brother to appear, she sought a miracle of a different kind during her Sunday-morning routine: peace. *I hope God knows where to find me, too, brother.*

Her husband led the way down the wide staircase to the second-floor landing. "I hope to bake cakes for our grandchildren one day. I love our friends, but I can't wait to celebrate family."

My friends are my family, Glory protested silently. Noemie and Dale had adopted her years before she married Eli; she'd witnessed their children maturing and having babies of their own. She'd come to think of herself as more than a friend to Bennett and wished she could see him grow up—that is, if she could figure out what to do with that mother of his.

But when she watched her husband limp down the last few steps to the main floor, Glory acknowledged that living above their bookstore was getting harder day by day. What had Noemie advised at their Quotes Group last Monday? *Enjoy your husband.*

Glory interlaced her fingers with Eli's and kissed his knuckles, conceding, "I've never tried my hand at homemade icing. Better yet, how about I do the party planning, and you handle baking the cake *after* you track down your daughter? How can I help you take the next step in the search?"

Eli sighed and locked the back door behind them. They walked to his car parked in the alleyway between the jewelry store and By the Book. "You can hope for the best. I'm going to reach out to some other friends I know to verify what the detective came up with."

Glory kept her eye on her husband during the long drive. His frown deepened the farther they traveled. She used her thumb to try to smooth away the frustration etching his brow. "You'll always have me, darlin'. And even if you don't find your daughter, perhaps we should consider moving to a smaller, one-story home. There's a cute Craftsman for sale around the corner from By the Book. We could commute to work like most people. Turn the third floor into a writing wonderland and host writing retreats."

"You'd do that for me?"

Glory caressed his shoulder. "For *us*? As long as there's a sidewalk where I can watch people go by. It's getting time for us to stop looking behind us, fearful of the shadows catching up. Mourning what we lost—"

"And wanting what we don't have. You're right." He gripped her hand. "Maybe I'll reach out to the realtor about that Craftsman."

Glory laughed. "One step at a time, Mr. Pryor! Let me focus on braving your Adelle Simonette this afternoon. If you distract her, maybe I can whisk off Bennett and we can open his birthday present."

Eli glanced at the large balloon-covered bag in the backseat. "Presents, plural. Do you think he'll like the book?"

"Does a bear like honey? Of course he will! It's a pop-up. Even his mama can't argue with this version of *The Odyssey*. And we can work together on the puzzle."

"Having it made from that picture of him playing the oboe was brilliant."

"Especially since it was your idea," Glory chuckled. "Bennett favors you, as Mama would say."

"You think so? I don't see a resemblance." He signaled a left turn and eased down the long driveway that curved through the five-acre wooded property to the Pearlines' house.

"It's something about the eyes." Glory straightened in her seat, her heart thudding in her chest. "But you can see for yourself, because there's the Subaru. Looks like the Simonettes are already here."

Adelle took a deep breath and readied herself. She was fairly certain she'd heard a car approach the house. It could be the Pryors, or perhaps Ophelia and the twins with Mr. Graves. She dreaded the former and hoped for the latter. It was sweet of the man to let Oscar visit Bennett for his birthday, but he was hankering for a four-legged friend of his own after a night with the terrier. A blessing and a curse.

"Are you sure you'll be okay out here with Oscar once I go inside, or should I take him with me?"

Bennett's forceful exhale should have ruffled the layers of her peasant skirt.

"Whoa! That's a lot of hot air we could've used in the balloons, little man. You almost knocked Mommy over." She pretended to stumble back a few steps on the brick pavers.

He snickered at her theatrics.

Adelle realized the time was coming when she'd stop referring to herself as Mommy; he'd already turned five years old. Just as she'd transitioned to calling herself Bennett's mother instead of Ben's wife, at some point she'd only think of herself as Adelle. She dreaded the day, but until then she'd count her blessings.

"Okay, just be sure to hold tightly to Oscar's leash." Adelle stretched to loop the last balloon around a tree branch at the edge of the patio. The sun warmed their heads, and she was glad she'd decided to wear short sleeves. After a dip in temperatures the past couple of days, she'd almost donned her orange sweater but changed her mind at the last minute. Adelle squared her shoulders, steadying her last bit of shaky resolve. Eli was sure to bring up the position at By the Book.

Work. Something that hadn't called her name since before Bennett was born. Adelle had gladly hung up her art supplies and walked away from her director position at a local studio the week before she delivered him. She'd thrown herself into being a wife and mother until that half of her life died, leaving the rest of her identity hanging incomplete, aimless. Until two months ago, when she'd read her father's journals and learned why he'd coughed himself to an early grave. Taking Daddy's words were one thing. Taking his life was something else.

Adelle walked to the house but paused at the French door. Every choice she'd made the past few months had led her to Gilmore, yet Eli's offer presented unexpected help from an unlikely source.

What you mean for evil, God means for good.

She jumped. "Oh!"

"What is it, Mommy? Did you hurt yourself?" Bennett hurried over, Oscar's short legs barely keeping pace.

"No, baby. I almost tripped on the end of my skirt. Mommy's alright. I mean, I'm alright. As long as you are."

"I'm fine, Mom. We're going to teach Oscar some tricks." Her son beamed.

And so it begins, she groaned inwardly, mourning the two letters missing from the name he'd called her barely a minute ago. She also dreaded meeting with Glory without Eli as a buffer, but she hid her feelings behind a cheery wave. "Enjoy your friends!"

Once Bennett and Oscar scampered away, Adelle brushed off her skirt and turned the knob, giving herself a good talking-to as she entered the mudroom. "Okay, get yourself together. This is your son's birthday party. Of course, Glory will be here. This is *her* bestie's house and Bennett loves her, too. Now, stop these one-way conversations. Might as well get it over with." She practiced her smile in the large mirror in the hallway and joined Noemie in the foyer. When she arrived, she found the Pearlines and the Pryors marveling over the birthday decorations.

"Adelle! Look who's here. Welcome!" Noemie extended her free arm. The other was wrapped around Glory.

Of course it was. "Hello, Glory. Eli."

The two nodded but Adelle's eyes skidded elsewhere.

Glory asked, "Where's Bennett?"

"Haven't we overcome this stiffness? We've been arguing like family every Monday for over a month now." Dale's deep voice boomed in the large hall with its soaring ceilings.

"We're where we always were, Dale. I talked Eli's head off in the car, and I could use a large glass of your iced tea. Drinks in the kitchen?" Glory took Noemie's hand and led her toward the wall of windows in the back center of the house.

"What my wife meant to say was, *Hello there! It's good to see you.*" Eli embraced Adelle and kissed her on both cheeks. "Where's the birthday boy? I don't hear him."

She swallowed hard. "He's playing out back with his new best friends. How was the drive?"

"Fine until we got behind one of your tractor-driving neighbors," Eli ribbed Dale.

Adelle felt a pang, hearing his comment. She missed Cabot and her in-laws' farm. The peace she had there. *I could drop this and go home.*

To what? And for how long? I need the money to keep the farm going. But what I'm doing doesn't feel right.

All I have to do is tell him. He already cares about me and Bennett. He's on my side.

Then what? Destroy my relationships with these sweet people all to ruin Glory's life?

What would Ben do?

What would Jesus do?

Still arguing with herself, Adelle trailed Eli and Dale to the kitchen.

"What can I do to help?" Glory scanned the room. True to form, Noemie had things well in hand, but keeping busy would preclude making awkward conversation with the mother of the guest of honor. If she had to milk a cow for homemade ice cream, Glory would do it.

Noemie cast a knowing eye at her friend and mercifully pointed to groceries on the back counter. "I was going to wait, but we could get the toppings into bowls for dessert. Who—?"

A bell chimed loudly, and five heads swiveled toward the front door.

Their hostess clapped. "Wonderful! That must be Ophelia with the food she insisted on bringing. But don't tell her how happy that makes me!"

Glory seized the opening. "Okay, I'll go check on her."

"No, thank you. You and Adelle will arrange the paper goods and the desserts. Dale, help me unload their car and set up the patio. Eli, *venga*. Talk to Charles and pretend you're not helping him into the house." Noemie clip-clopped from the kitchen in her high-heeled sandals, obviously sure they'd fall in line the way people tended to do.

Glory's shoulders drooped, watching the others go, but she immediately went to work opening supplies to get out from under Adelle's scrutiny.

". . . in Cabot, Arkansas, which is relatively close to Little Rock. That made it easy for us to live like country mice and city mice, enjoying more access to amenities but able to run home to our small town." Adelle nodded like she was agreeing to a question Glory hadn't asked.

Or did I? She couldn't remember. This was beginning to feel too much like an interview, when really, Glory wanted no parts of this woman. Something about Adelle unsettled her. She couldn't explain why she dreaded learning more about her background or resisted hearing about her hobbies and skills. Why she couldn't muster more compassion for the widow, despite the similarities they shared and Glory's inexplicable love of her son.

Bennett, Eli, their passion for books. There wasn't much more to talk about, so Glory asked finally, half-heartedly, "I suppose we should discuss the needs of the store. Has Eli mentioned at all what he expects?"

"He expects me to be you." Adelle distributed ice-cream toppings into colorful bowls.

"Excuse me?" Glory's fingers stopped shifting and sorting. Her words cut to the quick, which seemed antithetical to Adelle's casual tone and offhand manner as she snapped the lids on containers filled with fruit-flavored gummies, crushed pecans, sprinkles, caramel, and chocolate.

A hint of a grin played around Adelle's lips. "He expects me to be you . . . in the store. Welcoming and assisting guests, stocking-slash-restocking merchandise, checking in with the teens and Ophelia. You know, being—"

"Me. What about Bennett? If you're me, and I'm doing whatever Eli imagines I need to do, who's being Adelle for your son?" To settle her growing unease, Glory flattened empty boxes and stowed them in the recycling bin. Butterflies—no, mosquito hawks—fluttered in her stomach.

Adelle leaned against the counter, arms crossed. "I can handle Bennett. He's not a problem. I take it you're preparing to sell the bookstore?" Her expression seemed expectant, probing.

Glory slipped her feet out of her wedge-heel sandals. She couldn't dispel the urge to flee this room, and it was easier to run in her bare feet, the way she did as a child, with her brother. Holding their shoes because they knew they had to get home before the streetlights came on.

The shadows gave chase at our first step,
as we hurried through the moon's evening light.
Our pulses throbbed and our hearts, they leapt
at the beauty only childhood perceives.

For the first time, Glory relaxed when she recalled her verse, more at the memory it evoked of Davis, not the words themselves. *The matter's end is overtaking its beginning.*

"What are you thinking about, Glory?"

Glory looped the shoe straps around her finger. "You asked me about the bookstore. Lots of beginnings took place there, and endings, too, from the looks of it. Yes, Eli's talked of selling it."

"But not you?"

"We're married, so we have similar goals."

Adelle's eyes narrowed. "Similar, but not the same?"

At last, Glory's eyes locked on Adelle. "More like complementary. And speaking of work . . ." she took a breath. "Why do you want to work for us?"

Adelle turned from Glory and ripped open a box of plastic spoons. "I don't."

Glory recoiled, like she'd been slapped. This was the second time Adelle had shocked her with an answer that was downright rude. She glared at her back. "Then why—?"

"Because your Eli asked me to. Or I should say, because of my father."

26

"Your *father*. What does Eli have to do with your father? I had the impression . . . Isn't he dead?" Glory looked panicked, like she was juggling flaming swords instead of clutching her sandals.

Adelle touched her temple. She hadn't wanted to talk to Glory about anything, leastwise her father. Not here and not now, but it was time to throw the barn doors open wide. "We've all shared about our lives during those drawn-out talks about those dang books . . ."

Glory dropped her shoes.

". . . and you probably heard me say that my father is enjoying paradise with Ben and my in-laws. I came here because of family. Bennett's and mine. My father's. I inherited something once he died, and I came to claim it, to *reclaim* my family's heritage, what my father believed was lost. I'm not interested in helping you and Eli with your bookstore. I want to run *mine*. By the Book."

Adelle heard the joint click in Glory's jawbone when her mouth dropped open. The truth had been clamoring for purchase on her tongue, demanding freedom, and she couldn't restrain herself any longer. "That's right. I want what belongs to my father, and I'm prepared to take you to court, if that's what it takes. I just pray that's not what it takes."

Prayer, Adelle. Really? Now you talk about prayer?

"Why don't you two ladies join us if you're done in there?" The voice bellowed Eli's arrival before either woman saw him.

"Eli!" Glory called out. Her bare feet slapped the floor as she skirted the island and ran past Adelle.

"Hey, hey, now. What's going on?"

Adelle slowly rotated and faced the couple in the kitchen entryway. Glory's arms were draped around Eli's neck, and his eyes questioned Adelle's over his wife's shoulder.

"Why are you trembling, Glory?" He pulled back, and the questions became accusations when he looked at Adelle again. "Are you crying?"

Leave it to Glory to use tears as a weapon of warfare. But no matter. I have Spirit-filled ones on my side, Adelle reasoned to herself before answering for the bookseller. "She's probably feeling her world crashing down around her, the world she stole from my family—from Bennett and from me."

Eli linked hands with Glory and drew her to his side. "Somebody— and I think that means you, Adelle Simonette—had better speak up, fast and in a hurry, or that somebody will find herself and her son on the doorstep. Have I made myself understood? Now, explain why my wife is so upset." He dropped Glory's hand and pressed her closer with an arm around her shoulders.

The once-talkative older woman said nothing. She shook visibly, leaning into him.

But Adelle didn't need reinforcements. "I was explaining why I came to Gilmore. My father's legacy was stolen, and I came to see justice done. To get it back for him and for Bennett."

"She said her father's legacy is my store, Eli. My home. I warned you about this woman the day I met her." Glory seemed to be drawing strength from her husband's presence.

"How can that be?" Eli asked. "Everybody needs to calm down, because we all know that Glory bought the house decades ago from somebody she didn't even know before restoring it. Are you saying *those* owners owe you? If so, we'll have to take it up with the office—"

"No, that's not what I'm saying," Adelle snapped. She covered her face and tried to regain control of herself and the situation. Even to her own ears, she sounded unhinged. "Listen, I hadn't intended to talk about this today; we're supposed to be celebrating Bennett. But being with you week after week, hearing you talk about moving and selling it to somebody else . . . I couldn't take it! What I'm saying is true, as crazy as it sounds. I wouldn't lie to you." Horrified, tears eked from the corners of her eyes.

"Maybe not, but you're wrong. Someone else has lied to you then." Glory stood strong now. Tall, erect, back in control. Along with Eli, she posed a united front.

Even though Adelle was alone, she was on the side of righteousness, justice, and truth. Which meant God was on her side. Good always triumphed over evil. "My father isn't a liar. I read his journals, and I know the truth. He died a slow death, thanks to saving your life. Then you took his words as your own and built a career on them."

"His journals . . ." Glory took a step back, but Eli's arm kept her from making a full retreat.

Adelle could see she'd struck a blow. "Yes! His journals. The ones you didn't steal."

Eli looked at his wife. Then he asked, "What's your father's name?"

She prayed for the strength to say it. "Davis. Davis Gibson."

Glory's knees buckled, and she covered her face. "I told you he'd come back on a Sunday. I told you. I knew it, and I looked for him," she mumbled.

"Baby, it's okay." Somehow, her husband kept her upright.

It was hard for Adelle to accept his support of Glory—emotional and physical. "It's not okay! And I can't believe you're reassuring her for building a life on my father's words. She took his life after he saved hers. Did you know he coughed until he died?"

The hand Glory pressed to her mouth barely contained her sobs.

"Mrs. Simonette!" Mallory burst from the mudroom into the kitchen. "Mrs. Pearline sent me to get you." Worry transformed her happy face. "Are y'all okay?"

Glory spun away from her, hiding her tears in Eli's shoulder.

Adelle dried her cheeks with the end of her shirt. "Um, yes. We were . . . talking. We'll be out in a minute."

The teenager stared at one after another, obviously reluctant to leave.

"Mallory, tell Mrs. Pearline we're coming," Eli ordered, his arms still enfolding his wife. "But don't say anything about this. We don't want to spoil the party for Bennett. We'll explain later."

The teenager backed away and finally disappeared down the hallway. The mudroom door opened and closed.

"Okay, you two. For the next two hours, if you feel like screaming, crying, slapping somebody, or running away, please remember Bennett. Alright? Now, let's get it together and go eat some cake."

We've sung "Happy Birthday." Now, when will we cut that cake? Glory peeked at her watch, guilt and indignation warring within her. It had taken everything in her to finish her burger and play nice for the past hour. She shifted in her chair, its iron feet scraping on the patio's brick floor. The discussion around her didn't help either. And from the pained looks on Eli's and Adelle's faces, they were as miserable as she.

"Until the day when God will deign to reveal the future to man, all human wisdom is contained in these two words—'Wait and hope.'" Frederick stopped reading.

"That would be a good thought for the festival. You should write this down, Mrs. Simonette: *Wait and hope—dot-dot-dot—at the festival,* from *The Count of Monte Cristo,*" Charles ordered from the rocker near the stone fireplace.

Ophelia spun the covered turntable holding the strawberry-bedecked cake. "That sounds much better than *One can only truly enjoy revenge and justice when one knows that their execution is at hand.* I had to memorize that one!"

"Maybe you should write *that* down," Glory murmured.

"Oh!" Adelle knocked over her cup. Lemonade dripped through the holes in the wrought-iron table and soaked her skirt hem.

Ophelia handed her a napkin. "It's only lemonade. You look like you've seen a ghost, 'delle."

Eli's cousin was one of those Southerners who dropped the consonants and syllables from people's names once she knew and loved them well enough, and that was who they became, in perpetuity. Glory would love to know what Ophelia would call Adelle when she took Eli's home and business.

"This doesn't sound like five-year-old-birthday-party talk." Adelle brushed ice cubes from her skirt.

"Noemie pointed out we could kill two birds with one stone while the children are busy. Now we won't have to meet tomorrow," Dale explained.

"We can't meet tomorrow anyway. I've been dealing with a rental situation back in Cabot. The struggles of having one foot there, and one here."

"Then why don't you put both feet there?" Glory suggested.

"That's a thought," Eli agreed.

Dale eyed the couple suspiciously. "Sounds like a few of us are tired."

"It's been a long day, and we should pack up soon." Adelle raised her arm to get Bennett's attention and waved him over.

Noemie paged through the book. "Just a few more before we serve the cake. How about this one? *Virtue is a luxury only a few can afford.* Mmmm . . . that's good." She passed along the novel.

"I don't think that would work on a sign advertising the festival, telling people they can't afford to come. Nix that one," Frederick pronounced around a mouthful of chocolate-covered pretzels.

Charles opened the novel. He chuckled and read, "*Man proposes, but God disposes.* That's fitting."

"I had no idea Dumas wrote that! Let me see that." Dale took the tome from Frederick's hand. "Y'all are going to inspire me to finish what I started in high school by the time we finish this discussion." He flipped to the marked page. "Why, he sure did! *Man proposes, but God disposes.*"

Frederick chuckled. "Now that you've read it for yourself, how about tellin' us what it means."

Glory jumped in before Dale could respond. "That we don't have any control of our own lives. At least that's what you believe, right? We can plan and hope and work and wish, but it's all up to a capricious God—and malicious man who He created. He determines the course of our lives, and all we can do is . . ." She pinched off the rest of her statement; she considered saying more and closed her mouth again.

"Pray and trust." Eli furnished the words he must have thought his wife was searching for.

"And that circles back to the wait and hope, where we started off," Charles commented. "That's what I'm doing when it comes to my wife."

Glory had held out the tiniest hope she'd see her brother again.

All those Sundays sitting on her porch, waiting and looking. Using Dude as a replacement. All the nights she'd cried herself to sleep, the grief she experienced anytime she thought of Davis. And now the fears had come true, in a completely unexpected way. Now she knew that she'd never see her brother again . . . except in the eyes of his daughter and grandson.

Silence wafted over the patio, carried by the late-afternoon breeze. It was broken by the children's laughter, Oscar's occasional yip, and the crinkling of pages as Noemie riffled through them.

Finally, she read, *"The friends we have lost do not repose under the ground. They are buried deep in our hearts. It has been thus ordained that they may always accompany us on our journey through life."*

Glory squinted at the line of trees growing on the yard's periphery, a natural fence God had planted for the Pearlines. Their limbs seemed to touch the sky. *Will I ever be able to lay Davis and my parents down, Lord? Will I ever find repose, or will I always bear the weight of them?* Memories were ephemeral things. Wisps, shadows. Not testimonies, like the scars on her legs were supposed to be.

A survey of the pensive faces around the table revealed that others seemed to carry their own weighty stories. Was Eli thinking of his daughter? Did Ophelia have her own burden to lay down? Glory refused to consider Adelle's pain.

Bennett's feet pounded toward the group. "Can I-I have something to drink?" he panted.

Adelle handed him her bottled water. "After this, we're going, Ben-Ben."

"Let me slice the cake first!" Ophelia ran inside the house.

"We still need quotes for the festival. I'll keep reading until she comes back." Dale opened the book and pointed to the middle of a page. *"A true man is the one who avenges others as much by his virtues as by his talents."*

Glory and Eli both looked at Adelle.

Bennett was leaning against her and staring into space. His eyebrows furrowed. "Virtues . . . like in *The Book of Virtues* you read to me, Mommy?"

Adelle nodded. She settled back into her chair and helped him into her lap.

Bennett lay back, his head on her collarbone. His feet swung back and forth, inches from the floor, and his shoelaces trailed from his untied sneakers. "Virtues are like . . . knowing what's right and doing it even when it's hard or when nobody is looking . . . And true means real, not fake."

He angled his head until his oval-shaped brown eyes held his mom's, and he didn't continue until she nodded. "Then . . . a real man who knows right and wrong won't want revenge. He'll just do good things. He'll use his powers for good, like my dad used to tell me."

Adelle sniffed. "Ben did say that a lot."

Noemie looked at each of them in turn. "What is going on? Glory . . . Adelle . . . Eli? What is it? You're guests in my home, and really, I consider you family. All of you, including that precious child over there."

Eli took Glory's hand. "You're right to call us all family. According to that woman over there, that's exactly what she is. Family. Glory's niece, the daughter of her missing brother, Davis."

"Only, he's no longer missing." Glory's voice was bitter. "He's dead. Not just dead to me, but gone forever."

"Like my daddy," Bennett whispered.

27

"I'm sorry, baby." Glory went to clutch Bennett's hand.

"No, *I'm* sorry. Stop touching my son." Adelle drew him closer. "You're ruining his birthday, with all this back and forth. This pretense."

"We're ruining his birthday! How dare you? You come to town, lying all the while. Acting like you're on some hunt for the truth, carrying around a secret that will destroy everything I've worked for my whole life!" Glory's dress was the color of flame—orange, red, and yellow swirled together. The color of her anger.

"Glory . . ." Noemie reached for her.

"No, Noemie. You asked for the truth. This is the truth. This person—my supposed niece—hatched some crazy plot and used her son to ingratiate himself in our home. The whole time she's plotting to take us to court and sue me, saying I stole something from Davis. Who she claims is her father."

"That's not what I said . . . ugh!" Adelle banged the table with her fist.

"Don't, Frederick. Every man wants to help a crying young woman." Glory seemed unaware her own face was streaked with tears.

Eli pressed a tissue into her hand.

Ophelia reappeared, brandishing a serving knife. "What are y'all talkin' about? You need to calm down. You're upsetting the child." She stretched for him, but he ran off toward the yard.

"I don't want anything from you. Not anymore!" Adelle screamed, rising. "I just want to be left alone, the same way we were when we came to this terrible place." She moved away, but Charles hooked her arm with his cane.

"Sit down, daughter."

She looked at her arm, then at his face.

He nodded at her empty seat.

Mr. Graves waited until everybody had quieted. "Over the past few weeks, I've heard some of the worst words come from the mouths of some of the best people, including myself. I heard that my wife is dead to me. She's not. Just gone for a time, but I'll see her again. And the same for you, Adelle, with your dear Ben. And you, precious Glory, mourning for your brother, Davis. We're clamoring for things—jewelry, businesses, books, houses, people. All of it will pass away. But our love from God and for each other, the memories of life past and hope for life in the future? Those remain.

"It seems like we're erecting mausoleums for the living. That's where my wife is, of a kind. Where you're living, too, Glory. I heard you didn't even want to see the sunrise for fear of leaving that bookstore. Is that where they'll bury you? Or in a food truck, Ophelia? None of that is worth it. Grab your life while you have it. That's a word for the festival. When the root is bitter, the fruit dies. So, dig it up. Cast it into the fire. Use the ashes to fertilize the soil so something else can grow."

He sighed. "Now, can somebody take me home?"

"I'll get Bennett, and you can go home with me, Mr. Graves. Bennett! Let's go now!" Tendrils that had escaped from Adelle's braid flew around her head.

She didn't look any calmer to Glory after Charles's speech. She gathered herself, figuring she and her husband would provide safer transport. "Eli and I can."

Adelle slid her purse strap over her arm. "I'll have to get the cake another time, Ophelia. Noemie, forgive us for the abrupt exit. Ben—!"

Before she finished calling his name, the boy streaked around the house toward them, holding the leash. As he stepped onto the patio, Oscar crossed his path and tripped the child, sending him sailing toward the fire pit.

"Bennett!" Adelle sprinted, but Dale reached him first. Soon everyone gathered round her and her son. Blood soaked his pants.

"Quick, go get some water," Ophelia pushed Jason toward the house. "Mallory, go find the other children and keep an eye on them."

Bennett pushed away every adult.

Glory could tell a wild-eyed Adelle was starting to hyperventilate, so she edged through everyone and knelt beside her nephew. "Bennett, it's Aunt Glory. Now calm down. Calm down." She didn't know what was true, but she knew she loved the child like he was family. Flopping onto the firepit's concrete surround, she pulled him onto her lap. "Shush, shush. Is anybody getting water to clean the wound?"

"Auntie?" The child hiccupped.

At least his confusion seemed to calm him. "What can I do?" She tore at his pants, and the leg gushed more.

Dale poked at a thick piece of iron. "He fell against this."

Adelle crawled over and took her child's hand. "It's okay, baby boy. What should we do? It's still bleeding a lot. Is it an artery?"

"I don't think so," Glory whispered. "Tear my dress. Quick. Start at the hem."

Adelle hesitated only a second, then did as she was told. She ripped a long, wide strip that revealed Glory's leg beneath. She gasped and met Glory's eyes. "The fire," she breathed.

"Look for the source of the blood and tie it off. Tear more if you need it."

Suddenly, Jason ran up with water. They rinsed off Bennett's leg as directed.

As they all worked together, either in the fray, or clearing back and praying, the group got Bennett calmed down and tended to. Dale helped Adelle load him into the car, and Mallory and Ophelia rode with the frantic mother to the hospital to see if he needed stitches.

The rest dragged themselves to their cars and headed home to wait for word.

28

"Mommy, Mrs. Pryor looked upset. What happened?" Bennett pushed around his macaroni and cheese on his plate.

Adelle wished she was five years old. Then she could refuse to eat; cry, yell, and kick; rail at parental control and the world; question everything and everyone, including God. But she was a forty-year-old widowed mother who had to act with some sense and model faithfulness. Screaming inside, she calmly flipped the pan-fried chicken tender and tested it for doneness.

"She was worried about you getting hurt. We all were. You have a pretty bad cut—seven stitches. Now, eat your dinner. You love mac and cheese." Adelle doled out their chicken.

He nipped at a shell and kept talking. "But she was sad before I got hurt. And you were, too. Why did she say she's my Aunt Glory? Are we friends now, so I don't have to call her Mrs. Pryor?"

Adelle rubbed her eyes. "So many questions for my little patient. Aren't you as exhausted as I am, Bennett?"

"I didn't get to say goodbye to Oscar!" He stuck out his lips.

"Bennett, what did Mommy say?"

"I didn't get my birthday cake!" Tears plopped onto his dinner.

Adelle knew he was overwrought from the day—all the attention, the birthday party, the fall, the excitement of the emergency room, hunger, hearing that woman call herself *Aunt Glory*—but she wouldn't acquiesce to his tantrum. She had to throw her own first.

Her son dropped his fork with a clink and crossed his arms.

For a moment, she wished she knew how to whistle like Noemie. "Bennett Simonette, I'm not negotiating with you. You obey because it's what I've taught you to do."

Bennett lifted his fork and took another bite.

"Now, you will clean that plate—and that means all the pasta, all the green beans, and all the chicken. We won't do a bath tonight, as much as you need one, in order to let the wound heal a little. After dinner, you can read and play in your room; no TV."

"I'm sorry, Mommy," he mumbled.

"I forgive you, and I understand, but there are consequences to our actions." She took her salad to the table.

"I should send myself to bed early for not being one-hundred-percent honest a few minutes ago, Bennett." Adelle stabbed red onion and tomato but didn't eat them. "I'm sorry for not telling the truth, and I ask your forgiveness and God's."

Bennett met her gaze over his empty plate.

"The Pryors and I were talking about something really important, and we both got pretty upset. I can't tell you yet what it was about, but we have things to work out that could change our lives, Bennett. It's just hard."

"Hard for Mrs. Pryor, too? She's so nice. Maybe we should call her and see if she's alright, and you can apologize to her, too."

Her mouth fell open. "Apologize?"

"You said if I know someone is hurting, I should say I'm sorry and do what I can to help. *Do all that you can—*"

"*. . . to live in peace with everyone.*" Her voice was so low, she almost thought the verse. "I won't call her tonight, Bennett, but I will soon. Sometimes, people need time to think and pray. And the Pryors and I will do that before we say more hurtful things. Let's finish our dinner if we can. You and I should go to bed early."

"Early" came after two stories and thirty minutes of playtime with his dinosaurs. After Adelle doused his lights, she trudged down his hallway, through the den, and straight to her hiding place—the darkest, furthest corner of her closet. She'd learned it was the safest spot to lay herself out before God without fear of frightening Bennett.

Tonight, she took more than her sorrow. She also bore her shame and regret. Adelle thought she'd feel better once she confronted Glory, that she'd satisfy her cries for justice and righteous anger. But if anything, the burden had grown with that woman's hurt and grief and Eli's shock and disappointment, pain Adelle had caused. That she had planned and celebrated.

If you roll a boulder down on others, it will crush you instead. Oh, the Lord knew what He was talking about!

Adelle had listened to Glory talk about her brother, knowing he was her own father. That woman wasn't some stranger; she was her aunt. Her precious father's sister who he loved and missed. He'd taken full responsibility for the fire—his baby sister wouldn't have passed out if she hadn't drunk his alcohol and smoked his cigarettes—and he'd lived and died with the guilt. Davis had punished himself by refusing to return and thought Glory was owed whatever success she achieved. What would he think if he'd seen how she'd treated Glory earlier, if he knew about Adelle's dishonesty all these weeks that she'd sat in her house and eaten her food? "Her legs . . ." Adelle groaned.

What does God think now, because He sees all and knows all?

She curled into a ball under the blanket she kept in the corner, weeping and moaning, unloading all the memories she'd buried and anger she'd stoked like a smoldering fire, to keep it burning when Glory's kindness and Bennett's love for her threatened to put it out. Adelle's anger on her father's behalf had overshadowed the joy on his behalf, of knowing he'd fought the good fight of faith and lived a sober life from that fateful night of the fire until he died. It was a joy she had until she found that last journal a few months ago.

Then, she learned the extent of his underage drinking and his life as a homeless teen who wended his way to Cabot, Arkansas. He wrote about the fire and saving his family's life, of taking the blame for the loss of their home and Glory's injuries. Of his taking on the name of Dee Gibs, what he called himself until he died. Who he was to her until she read his private papers.

Adelle could understand the misplaced guilt and the sense of responsibility. That was her good, kind, and loving daddy. He loved their quiet, unassuming life, making just enough to keep the lights on and food on the table for him and his daughter. But what Adelle struggled to forgive was losing her daddy at such a young age to a chronic disease that resulted from the smoke inhalation caused by braving those long-ago flames. Should Adelle continue to mourn her husband and soon lose Ben's family farm to mounting bills, while Glory lived a rich, full life funded by her daddy's childhood pain and private thoughts?

But vengeance came at great cost.

Oh, Father, what am I to do with this?

She heard Eli open the door. Knowing him, he breathed a sigh of relief once he'd found her in the backyard, staring at the empty spot under the shedding maple tree. Glory listened to his footsteps approach and stop right behind her but within a hair of her back. Without facing him, she announced, "The chair is gone, along with any other evidence that Dude was ever there."

"Is that what you're thinking about out here?"

She answered without facing him. "I'm thinking about everything. Our Famous Quotes Group, the party today at Noemie's, the last Sunday dinner with my family fifty years ago. Tomorrow's special opening for Labor Day. Next month's meeting with the vendor. The festival in November and whether I'll be here for it. If I want to be."

"Is it okay if I hold you?" His words were soft.

As gentle as his touch will be if I let him. She nodded.

He hugged her from behind, locking his hands together around her middle. "I'm sorry about what happened. If I'd trusted your instincts about Adelle, I could've protected you from the very beginning."

Glory swallowed. "But you weren't at the very beginning. My choices set all this in motion a long time ago."

They stood there in the evening quiet, listening to the night settle upon them. Glory heard the buzz of a streetlamp and the puttering of the neighbor's scooter, returning from the garden in the country.

"You're still taking the fall, even for Adelle's schemes?"

She relaxed against his chest, drawing from his warmth. "The strange thing is, I finally understand her *why*. I couldn't put my finger on it before, but I get it now, and I don't blame her."

"Because you still blame yourself, Glory."

"No, because I accept responsibility, which is different. I'm also starting to accept what I can't change. And what I can."

She turned in his embrace without loosening his arms. "Let's go inside. I have an unexpected hankering for your hazelnut coffee."

29

GLORY ALWAYS HOSTED A SPECIAL SALE to recognize Labor Day, the only Monday By the Book opened its doors. This year, the baker and the twins had come in on their day off to help, and she was grateful. It had taken longer to fall asleep the night before after having coffee with Eli, and by day's end she was worn out. She was thrilled over conducting more business than usual, but she did a happy dance when she heard the bell tower strike quarter past five. Glory hoped this young man was the last of her customers.

He watched as she set his books in the brown bag. "Do you still have those handmade bookmarks, the ones with the red cord?"

Picturing the box on the third floor, Glory almost said, "No." Then the guest-serving part of her smiled. "Actually, yes, I received a shipment Saturday and took them upstairs. Give me one second."

Glory locked the register and called, "Mallory! Could you take over here for a minute?" Seeing her employee, she pressed the key into her hand. Clad in a denim dress belted neatly around her slender waist, Glory spun on her heel toward the hall leading from the foyer area. Her feet made little noise in canvas espadrilles, though the climb to their sitting room seemed to take forever. "That's what I get for breaking the rule and bringing work in here," Glory chided herself.

When she lifted the box, she noticed her mama's teacup on the corner shelf, looking as forlorn as the abandoned plant next to it. A minute later, she'd made a nest to cushion it among the bookmarks. As she made her careful descent, she heard the jangle of the bell, announcing the arrival of another guest. "Good gracious in the morning," she grumbled but didn't dare pick up the pace for fear of cracking the delicate cup. By the time she made it to the foyer, Mallory stood alone among rows of fiction.

The teenager shrugged. "She said she didn't need any help."

Glory peered around the box. "*She* . . . who?"

"The guest who just came in." Mallory straightened a shelf.

"What about the young man who asked me for a bookmark?" She looked around. Her load was becoming cumbersome, and she really wanted some tea. Glory eyed the large clock mounted near the door. *Five thirty-two. Where is Eli?*

"He left, said he had to go but would come back for it. Don't worry, Mrs. P. This guest is a browser, I can tell. Probably killing time before she goes to a Labor Day cookout. She'll be on her way soon enough, so why don't I put those away? Jason, Mama, and I will close up." Mallory angled a thumb behind her. "My brother can keep an eye on her in the back, and I've got the front."

"Why, thank you. I think I'll accept your offer. You can stow this box under there. Ooh, but first . . ." Glory set her load on the counter and gingerly lifted out the cup. It wasn't like her to leave the store completely under another's care, but the weekend had zapped her physically and emotionally. If her husband didn't hurry home from his mysterious errand, he'd have to carry her upstairs, bad knees or no. "Let me know if you have a question. Feel free to nudge this guest along in five minutes and invite her to come again. I'm going to make some tea and take it to the front room."

And she made good on her promise. While Glory had enjoyed the coffee that morning, Earl Grey still claimed her heart. Her nose hovered over her cup as she shuffled to her sofa and curled up in her favorite corner. "Just in time," she whispered, as the windows shuttered in the spa across the street. They always closed early on holidays to give their staff time with their families. She eyed her fingernails and imagined getting a manicure.

Street traffic was lighter that evening thanks to the holiday. Noemie had locked her doors at five; Glory hadn't heard from her, other than a text with a promise to pray. Charles and Oscar were nowhere in sight, and Mr. Johnson had driven his truck to the beach for a few days. "We might be following him there soon," she warned her reflection. With little to see and less to do, Glory yawned, taking longer and longer blinks.

"Glory?" A familiar voice and a warm hand on her shoulder roused her.

Startled, she moved her knee abruptly, jostling the tea balanced on it. When the liquid soaked her leg, she jumped up, sending the cup flying. She gasped at the sound of the crash, and fully awakening, she watched Eli gather the pieces.

"Is this your mother's cup? Oh, babe."

Glory listened to the shards clink against each other in his large hand, a soundtrack to the movie that had played out the past few weeks.

"I'm so sorry. I didn't mean to scare you." He rose. "I think I have all of them. Maybe we can fit them together."

More like a fitting epilogue to a heartbreaking story. She sighed. "What good was it doing anyway, tucked on a shelf, serving as a monument to a tragedy? I'm glad it's broken because now, I can throw it away. Please . . . here." Glory brought a small basket over and nodded at his hand.

Eli's brows furrowed over the questions in his eyes.

"Yes, I'm sure." Glory laughed lightly, surprising herself, and probably him, too. The pieces made satisfactory thumps against the plastic-lined wicker. Feeling strangely at peace—the part that grew up singing hymns and that still hummed to them most Sundays, she suspected—Glory set the basket down and focused on her husband. "There. Done. Now, tell me, where did you go?"

At first, he seemed distracted by the cup. He slowly swiped his hands together, his attention on the trash.

She clasped his fingers. "Eli?"

"I thought I was bringing back good news for you. Peace for me."

There's that word again, Glory thought. She led him to the sofa, and they perched on its edge. "Where were you?"

"I met with the private detective, and he finally confirmed what I was starting to suspect—that the whole story about my old girlfriend's pregnancy . . . Well, it was just that. A story. Rumors and lies. A bunch of talk. I might have been a philanderer, but I'm no father. I don't have a daughter or a granddaughter."

The relief on Eli's face surprised Glory. She rubbed a thumb over the bristles on his cheek. "Are you disappointed?"

"About as disappointed as you are about that teacup. I'm too old for all this uncertainty, and I needed closure one way or another. Either I was or I wasn't. I guess you get to keep your bookstore."

"Oh, honey." Glory moved closer to hug him, and the old chair creaked. "I guess we're in the market for a new house. That Craftsman we talked about, remember?"

Thinking about that discussion reminded her of their drive to Noemie's; it was hard to believe it was only the day before. "We lose a daughter and a granddaughter, but we've gained a niece and a great-nephew. And maybe an early retirement if Adelle has her way." Glory no longer felt comfortable calling her *that Simonette woman.* If anything, she was a Gibson, like Glory herself. "I'm thinking we need to take a vacation."

They put their foreheads together, and Glory took a deep breath.

Mallory burst into the room. "Mr. Pryor . . . Mrs. Pryor, Jason caught the thief!"

Immediately, Glory looked toward the window, then confirmed the time on her watch. *Six thirty.* "What are we still doing open? We should've locked the door thirty minutes ago!"

"That's neither here nor there at this point, wife. What's going on?"

A wide-eyed Mallory tucked her hands into her back pockets, nervously shifting from one foot to another. "I was working up front while Jason was in back with that last customer—*guest,* I mean. The browser I told you about. Then that other . . . um, *guest*—"

"Customer is fine," Glory interrupted, her tone short. She didn't want the girl stumbling over semantics.

"—returned asking about his bookmarks."

"His bookmarks? He said he'd wait!" Glory's head spun.

"I know, Mrs. P. He changed his mind again and came back. At least that's what he said. He asked for two and wanted to study them. When I was helping him, I heard Jason yelling in back, and the next thing I know, Mama comes flyin' up, the dude I was helping runs out, and then Jason . . ." Mallory took a deep breath, obviously flummoxed.

"I bet the two were working together." Eli straightened to his full height and took stock of Glory, his eyes studying hers. "Ready to take care of our store?"

At her nod, he interlaced his fingers with Glory's. "Lead the way to this tag team, Mallory."

Glory followed Eli to the front of the store where Jason, Ophelia, and a police officer were conferring.

"I understand you caught our thief. Thank you, Jason!" Eli grabbed his hand and clasped his shoulder.

Glory was quaking in her boots, but she regarded the teenager with newfound appreciation. If he could stand strong in the face of wrong, so could she. "Well done, Jason! I didn't know you had it in ya, but obviously, you did."

Ophelia beamed beside him, looking like she could sop him up with a biscuit. "I'm proud of you, son!"

"When I saw her, I remembered a picture you'd showed us when she worked here. I was like, what are you doing back here? You quit weeks ago. And then all this stuff fell out." He pointed to the evidence the police had collected.

The officer stuffed it into a bag. "We'll take it in, but you should get it back. Sounds like she knew where Ophelia kept the extra key, and she started with that wallet, then moved on from there. She took the knife because"—He read from his notes—"*That baker thinks she can cook and knows everything.*"

He looked up. "She enlisted her brother to help her tonight. It seems she was angry about the new employees you hired who took her place. Claims of nepotism?"

Ophelia rolled her eyes. "Nepotism! We'll see what she learns about that word when she's in her jail cell, sitting beside her brother."

"They're going to jail?" Glory couldn't help but feel compassion for the young woman who was once a dedicated employee. *The stories we tell ourselves!*

"Probably so. We'll see what happens when she goes before the judge. But the theft of your classic copy of *The Great Gatsby* classifies as more serious than these other items. Plus, it's technically breaking and entering when she came in without your consent."

"And she kicked my son! That's assault," Ophelia huffed.

The officer inclined his head. "But you can talk to the court."

Glory couldn't help but think of her brother. If only her mother had extended mercy, perhaps she wouldn't have faced such an angry young woman today. "Thanks, officer. We'll talk about it."

As Eli walked the police to the door, Glory hugged Jason. "I don't know what to say, Jason. I'll have to give you a raise."

"I thought about those meetings we had. When Mr. Graves was talking about young people and having good success. Hearing all about how hard y'all have worked and your parents, too. We've had a good time here, me and Mallory. I didn't want to see somebody hurt you, Mrs. P."

Fresh tears rushed down her face as she trailed Eli to the porch. All she could think was, *Thank the Lord it wasn't Dude.* Her husband gripped her around the shoulders as he pulled away.

"Oh, the ironic twists and turns of life, Eli." Glory studied the sky and the stars, pretending all was well by keeping her eyes heavenward. She bowed her head. "If I asked you if God was hard, what would you say now?"

Eli tightened his hold. "I'd say, He's good, baby girl. Good *in* the hard. Maybe we should take a few days to talk about it."

30

A SPRIG OF WILDFLOWERS leaned against the inside of her mama's pieced-together teacup that Eli had recovered, brightening up the tray Glory carried. She set it on the small table she'd angled between their chairs and took a seat on the one in the corner. "Mmm . . ." she murmured, accepting the steaming coffee Eli proffered. "Thank you."

"Happy to. I can't believe you're coming over to the dark side." Eli took his seat and crossed his ankles over his outstretched legs.

"As long as it's a dark roast with a hint of hazelnut," she chuckled.

Eli picked a fat pastry from the plate and held it aloft. "Have one of these pimiento cheese scones Ophelia left for us?"

"I'll enjoy the coffee for now. I can't sing if my mouth is full." Glory cupped her heavy copper-colored mug with both hands and peered through the hedges bordering the front porch. They provided a thick, evergreen shield between them and the street below the store.

He took a bite and eyed his wife, balancing his cup on a knee. "Have you decided what you're going to do?"

"Right now, I'm watching all those folks hurrying down the street.

They should've left for church fifteen minutes earlier if they wanted to avoid arriving all sweaty and going on." She tsked at the woman wearing the white pants. Her mama always wore a dress and a hat to church in order to look her "Sunday best." But Glory was offended that the stranger had broken a different fashion rule. *What happened to "no white after Labor Day"?*

Last Tuesday, she'd hung a large handwritten sign on the front door of By the Book, explaining that the Pryors were taking a much-needed vacation and closing the store for a week. Then they'd driven to the beach and spent a few days talking about the future of the store, their future with or without the store. Here it was Sunday morning, and they weren't any closer to determining the *how* of their next steps though they'd figured out the *what* and the *who*.

Glory closed her eyes, enjoying the morning breeze and the warmth of the sun on her feet, the only part of her body its rays could kiss. Perhaps they would hash it out with Noemie and Dale over dinner that evening, one of the many topics they needed to discuss.

Eli nodded at her coffee. "How's yours? I can make you a cup of tea if you'd prefer."

"No, thank you. I might have found a new Sunday tradition." Glory swirled it, loving the eddy she created.

"Maybe one day we'll have a Bible and Brew group." He cocked an eye at her over his mug.

"Don't hold your breath, de-ah."

"Think we'll ever sit together beside those folks in Ebenezer? They have a pretty rousing service. Reminds me of home, when I was coming up. I don't like leaving you here and walking there by myself after praise and worship; I'd rather we walk in together." Eli had decided to attend church regularly, but he would leave after the musical portion of the service and slip in the back during offering time.

"Maybe if you agree we won't share a pew with your cousin.

Now . . ." Glory gently laid a finger against his lips as the choir launched into its first hymn. Though she had stopped looking for Davis to return, this was her time, and she brooked no interruptions. She sang along, using the old hymnal she'd bought.

> *Blessed assurance, Jesus is mine*
> *Oh, what a foretaste of glory divine*
> *Heir of salvation, purchase of God*
> *Born of His Spirit, washed in His blood*
>
> *This is my story, this is my song*
> *Praising my Savior all the day long*
> *This is my story, this is my song*
> *Praising my Savior all the day long*

The choir proceeded to sing another thirty minutes—a mixture of hymns, gospel music, and a contemporary song accompanied by what sounded like an acoustic guitar. By the time they finished, Glory and Eli were clapping their hands and tapping their feet.

As the choir finished the last bars, Eli checked his watch and rose. "Okay, are you sure you won't—"

"Eli . . ." Glory dropped her coffee on the tray and light-brown liquid splashed onto the scones. She pointed to two familiar forms heading up their walkway.

Eli followed the direction of her finger, aimed at Adelle and Bennett.

Glory resisted the urge to hurry to the child slowly limping up each step and waited as they made it to the stone porch. She rested the hymnal in Eli's empty seat. "Hello."

"Hello, Auntie." Bennett was still adjusting to the title, based on his shy expression.

So was she. Glory wasn't sure how she felt about it. "What about Gigi, until we figure it out?"

Adelle's eyebrows furrowed, but Eli, her marketing guru and king of reconfigurations, worked it out first. "Glory Gibson. *G. G.* Gigi."

Bennett lit up. "Yes, I like it! Gigi. Is that respectful, Mom?"

His mother took a minute to stare at the road. A few cars passed by before she answered. "Yes, son. That sounds about right."

Glory probed her heart, unsure of the emotions tumbling about inside upon seeing the woman. Suddenly, she realized she felt relief, not resentment. Gratitude instead of suspicion. She'd grieved at the thought that Davis was forever lost to her, and here stood part of him, a bit battered and bruised, but alive and well. Glory thanked God she could see her brother's kin this side of the dirt.

Adelle released Bennett's hand and let the strap of her backpack slide down her arm. "I have something for you, at least to read and keep for safekeeping while we return to Cabot."

"You're going back home?" Glory's thoughts and feelings continued to battle within her, fighting for the right to express themselves.

"I'm not sure where home is at the moment, but we're going to take a survey of the house and farm and pray over some decisions."

Eli propped a hip on the brick wall surrounding the porch and extended a hand to his empty chair. "Won't you sit down, Adelle?"

"Yes. Please," Glory asked sincerely and moved aside for her. She knew Eli had always felt some kind of way for Adelle, but she'd had to travel a long road to make room for her in her heart.

Adelle's halting steps to the corner seat—*Glory's* chair—showed she, too, had a ways to go, but she smiled a little when Eli scooped up Bennett and plopped him by his side, then hugged and kissed him.

"Can I get you anything? Some coffee or tea? A scone?" Glory removed the hymnal and sat.

"No—" she began.

"Yes, thank you!" Bennett nodded vigorously.

The adults laughed, and Glory gave him the biggest pastry on the plate.

Adelle unzipped the weathered backpack and extracted a thick sheaf of papers bundled together with thick rope, along with a Bible. "I brought you these. They were Daddy's."

My brother's. Glory was glad for Eli's heft in case he'd need to hold her up. The pages were worn, yellowed, and crumpled. Some of the edges were torn and dog-eared, and the writing looked faded. But she recognized the hand as her brother's. Tears flowed freely as she gazed at Adelle, her niece. "Thank you," she managed as she rested the gifts on her lap, eager to dive in. "I'll take good care of them while you're gone."

Adelle nodded, appearing overcome herself.

Another thought hit Glory, and she hoped it wasn't too much to ask. "Will you mind if I have a copy made if I'm careful? I'd love to keep this close, forever if I could." She touched the woman tentatively on the arm. "One more thing. It's important for you to know that I didn't copy his words. His thoughts are woven through those poems. Davis's hurt and hopes. But I wrote the poems. I published them, and for a time, I prayed they would lead him to me."

Adelle nodded. "I know, and when you read it, you'll see how happy it made him that you understood what he was trying to say. Greed spoke for me. And envy. I didn't want anyone else to know him as well. But . . . there's something else. I had to tell you this before we left. It's really important, probably the most important."

Glory's stomach tightened as she clutched the Bible and journal to her chest. She knew she had to let go at some point and hug Bennett goodbye, but she couldn't release the pages yet.

Adelle took a breath. "That day when Bennett had his first accident . . ." She shook her head in a disbelieving manner. "I was bringing you this journal and a Bible. I planned to come to you and prove something to you before I . . ."

She squeezed her eyes closed and took a shuddering breath, then squared her shoulders. "Before I took the store from you. But I chickened out."

"You mean, she wore you out, arguing." Eli nodded toward his wife. "She has a way with those words of hers."

"Yes, she does. But you need to know that those poems you wrote . . . Daddy's journal was prayers, Glory. He was inspired by the words of Isaiah the prophet, the Psalms, Habakkuk, Micah, the book of Luke, Ecclesiastes . . . God's words. He marked the passages in the Bible that correlate to the poems. You'll see."

Glory gasped.

"He was calling on God for help, praising Him and crying out to Him at the same time all those years ago. And all the days of his life. That day, I was going to throw this journal in your face and tell you that every brick of this house was a lie you erected to hide yourself. So, you wrote a book that was based on God's Word, too. You just didn't know it."

Eli studied the stone, brick, and wood edifice. "So, this isn't the house that Davis built . . ."

It's the house that God built. "By the Book," Glory whispered.

Adelle squeezed her aunt's arm. Neither one was ready for more than that as yet. Glory exchanged the journal and Bible for Bennett, and she held him close to her heart, where she used to hide her tears for her brother. Now, she could wear the truth of her feelings for him on her sleeve. "I love you."

"I love you, too, Gigi."

"We'll be waiting for you when you come back home."

"Back home?" Adelle's and Bennett's voices formed a duet.

Eli aimed a thumb at the door.

Adelle turned. Her lips moved as she read the handwritten sign Glory had hung there. "You're closed?"

"Temporarily," Glory smiled. "Eli and I have been working out some things behind those closed doors. This is the house that God built, but we want this to become the place where you live and work, Adelle. It's as much your home and bookstore as mine. More so."

"We've got our eye on a smaller footprint, something without stairs," Eli added.

"And with fewer bookshelves," Glory chuckled.

"And a short commute to work. When you get back from Cabot, we'll put our heads together and figure it out. Maybe our Famous Quotes Group can help you move out of your rental."

Adelle stared at them, her mouth open, obviously at a loss. "I'm not sure . . ."

"Can we keep *Alice in Wonderland*?" The brightness of Bennett's eyes rivaled the sun's.

His mother laughed. "We'll see."

Glory knew there was a lot they needed to see—and talk about and puzzle over—in the days to come. But she planned to hold on to her family this time, not merely the memories of them.

"In the meantime, why don't we go inside and have a real visit? We can show you around upstairs, so you have an idea of what you're coming back to?" Eli stood, wincing as he moved his hips from side to side. He extended a hand to the child. "We need to figure out what you can call me, find a name that's as cute as Gigi."

When Bennett hopped off Glory's lap Eli gave her the heavy bundle Adelle had brought. The boy followed his uncle to the front door.

Adelle rose and took a step toward them before turning back to Glory, her eyes filled with questions.

"Go on, I'm coming. I just need a moment with them, and then I'll bring them in. We'll have to find a special place."

When they walked inside, Glory clutched the journal to her chest. In her heart, she knew it was time to loosen her grip on them, not on Davis and her parents, but on the stories she'd carried most of her life. Stories she'd told and retold herself. But God—*"Yes, God,"* she murmured—had a way of changing things. Of developing characters and rewriting endings. Now she had something more, something *else* to pass on, a living history that would grow with that little boy inside who at that very moment was probably nibbling on more of Ophelia's scones.

Glory's tears soaked the beloved, dog-eared pages in her hands, Davis's precious prayers and all his hurts and the hopes. The truth of the matter was that the Lord had heard her brother's whispers, and He'd used her to write His answer to each one.

Discover more great fiction by Robin W. Pearson

"Pearson's excellent characters and plotting capture the complexity and beauty of family, the difficulty of rectifying mistakes, and the healing that comes from honesty."

PUBLISHERS WEEKLY, starred review of *'Til I Want No More*

JOIN THE CONVERSATION AT crazy4fiction.com

A Note from the Author

"And He looked around in a circle at those who sat about Him, and said, "Here are My mother and My brothers! For whoever does the will of God is My brother and My sister and mother." (Mark 3:34-35)

WHO IS YOUR FAMILY?

My husband and I have experienced the blessings and the challenges of moving more than a few times in our thirty years together, and we've spent a lot of that time living away from the families that birthed us. We have seven children, unlike Glory and Eli, but the truth of the matter is, we've had to form grandmama, cousin, auntie and uncle, and sister and brother relationships within our community, much like my fictional couple. There've been some lonely days when I felt far emotionally and physically from people who really knew me—sometimes under my own roof—but "our peeps" now live everywhere from New England to Florida and across to California. God has certainly drawn us closer to Him, revealing how He loves us as His children, His family. He's been good that way.

Also, like the Pryors, I dreamed of running my own version of By the Book. More than a decade ago, my husband and I considered becoming booksellers. For months, as we discussed it, I built this cozy spot in my mind, imagining readers curled up in comfortable chairs, drinking tea and coffee, perusing shelves. Whiling away the hours with my books the way Fred Baldwin retreats to the Pryors' stacks. In the end, Hubby decided that it wouldn't work for us, and after I dried my tears, I accepted the decision, believing it to be a "not yet" from the Lord. Eventually, we grew in a different way and birthed something more than that book baby—our seventh child. Our Father's thoughts are certainly higher than ours. One day, though . . .

These are only a few of the stories I've carried with me—dreams, hopes, disappointments, plans, unexpected provision, loved ones, tears. Many I've kept to myself. Some flow like the poetry I wrote for this novel, while others have no rhyme or reason. Some are still percolating and developing, so their endings are unknown to anyone but God. He has had to give me the strength and the grace to bear more than a few, the wisdom to see the truth between the lines, and the creativity to share them with you, my dear reading family.

In Him,
Robin

Acknowledgments

I wonder if readers know how they impact us writers—and not only by buying our books and sharing their reviews. Laura W., who has surely encouraged many an author, sent me a note last year that I use as a bookmark in *Streams in the Desert* by L. B. Cowman. Her letter includes a quote from the September 12 entry of the same book that says, "You are not near enough. I would embrace your care; So I might feel My child reclining on My breast. You love Me, I know. So then do not doubt; But loving Me, lean hard." Laura's message greets me every morning as I open the devotional.

And oh, how I've loved on the Lord by leaning hard on Him for this story! His Word is "a lamp unto my feet, and a light unto my path" (Psalm 119:105). It served as the foundation for the poetry I composed as well as the bookstore Glory and Eli run, in addition to my everyday, moment-by-moment needs. God continues to keep my fingers to the keyboard even as our family walks through the shadows that David the psalmist described, when my father suffered a stroke and during my mother-in-law's cancer battle. He gives me words when I have none.

Of course, I lean on the amazing family God gave me. When I pull all-nighters, Hubby dozes on the sofa next to me. When I don't know where the story's going, Nicholas and Katherine listen and direct.

When I wrestle with social media, Faith takes over my phone—and enlists Hallie and August as models and support staff. When I need a cheerleader, a cookie, or background music, Hillary Grace runs for her pompoms, oven mitts, or the piano. When I require a sparring partner and a Scripture, Benjamin steps forward with a ready word. When I'm too weary to stand, they all band together to hold me upright (believe me, it takes all my peeps, plus my sisters, Atondra and Starlyn, for good measure!). And asleep or awake, you know where you'll find Oscar.

But where would this story be without my community? Beth Seufer Buss and Morgan DePerno from Bookmarks in Winston-Salem, North Carolina, gave life and life's work to one of my favorite literary couples, the Pryors, by letting me peek behind their shelves. Cynthia Ruchti, my friend and Books & Such Literary agent, wields iron-sharpening wit and wisdom like nobody's business. Barb Roose and Jen Babakhan, also Books & Such agents, provide a strong shoulder and a laugh (sometimes wry, often hilarious) and a precious "word spoken in due season" (Proverbs 15:23). Speaking of words, only my editor Kathy Olson could help me jettison nearly ten thousand of them—and scenes I thought I couldn't live without—in a matter of weeks. I wouldn't be surprised if she relied on the indefatigable team at Tyndale: Jan Stob (now retired) who opened the door for me, and Elizabeth Jackson, Karen Watson, Wendie Connors, Andrea Garcia, Shelley Bacote, and Amy Voss. Beth K. Vogt and Belinda Bullard . . . our sisterhood gets me through, up, and over though we don't hear from or see each other nearly enough.

But back to you, dear readers . . . and fellow authors . . . who've provided such love. You make my writing world go round. You're a blessing.

Discussion Questions

1. Adelle is good at hearing God's voice, but not necessarily at listening to it. Is there something you are doing today that is trying to force your will on God instead of listening to what He is trying to tell you? How can we be sure to know that we are hearing His voice and listening to it?

2. Do you understand Glory's fear that others wouldn't understand or accept her if they knew her whole story?

3. Noemie asks Glory, "Who are some of your favorite friends in books?" How would you answer this question?

4. Glory wears long dresses to hide her scars, both physical and emotional. In what ways do we all feel tempted to hide our scars?

5. If you were part of the Famous Quotes Group, what would you write down as your inspiring or memorable book, story, or quote? Was there a particular quote the group talked about that speaks to you?

6. Glory is overcome with emotion at the sight of the sunrise. When have you been awestruck by something in nature?

7. Glory struggles with sacrificing her dreams for Eli's, and with knowing what is important to cling to and what is okay to compromise on. Have you ever struggled like this? How did you come to a decision?

8. How would you answer Glory's question, "Is He a hard God?"

9. Glory observes that grace is as hard to accept as it is to give. Do you find it harder to receive forgiveness or to give it to others?

10. God was able to take Adelle's misplaced vengeance and use it for His plan. What do you think of God's ability to take our mistakes and use them for good?

About the Author

ROBIN W. PEARSON'S writing sprouts from her Southern roots. While sitting in her grandmothers' kitchens, she learned what happens if you sweep someone's feet, how to make corn bread taste like pound cake, and the all-purpose uses of Vaseline. Her family's faith, life lessons, and life's longings inspired her to write about God's love for us and how this love affects all our relationships.

Robin has corrected grammar up and down the East Coast as an editor, writer, and homeschooling mama. She is the author of five novels, including the Christy Award–winner *A Long Time Comin'*, *'Til I Want No More*, *Walking in Tall Weeds*, *Dysfunction Junction*, and her latest, *The Stories We Carry*. Her work has been described as "enjoyable and uncomfortable, but also funny and persistent in the way that only family can be" by *Publishers Weekly*.

At the heart of it all abides her love of God and her husband, seven children, and her dog, Oscar. They're the source and subject of her novels, in the new characters living and breathing in her laptop, and in the stories about her experiences at her own kitchen sink. She writes about them on her blog where she shares her adventures in faith, family, and fiction.

Visit Robin on robinwpearson.com or follow her @robinwpearson on Instagram, BookBub, Goodreads, and Facebook.

TYNDALE HOUSE PUBLISHERS IS CRAZY4FICTION!

Become part of the Crazy4Fiction community and find fiction that entertains and inspires. Get exclusive content, free resources, and more!

JOIN IN ON THE FUN!

- crazy4fiction.com
- Crazy4Fiction
- crazy4fiction
- tyndale_crazy4fiction
- Sign up for our newsletter

FOR GREAT DEALS ON TYNDALE PRODUCTS, GO TO TYNDALE.COM/FICTION